Death Knell

A John Keegan Mystery

JOHN MISAK

To My Good
Friend Randy—
Hope you find this as
well crafted as

Death Knell: A John Keegan Novel
An Empire Strikes Book / March 2007
All rights reserved.
Copyright © 2007 by John Misak

No part of this book may be reproduced or transmitted in any form or by any means, electronic or mechanical, including photocopying, recording, or by any information storage and retrieval system, without permission in writing from the publisher. For information address: Empire Strikes Press.

This novel is a work of fiction. The characters, names, places, incidents, dialogue and plot are the products of the author's imagination or are used fictitiously. Any resemblance to actual persons, living or dead, or events is purely coincidental.

Printed and bound in the United States of America.

ISBN: 0-974-9926-9-0

10 9 8 7 6 5 4 3 2 1

This one is for you, Sharon. I wish everyone
could experience what I feel when I see you smiling.
Thank you for understanding me,
and more importantly, for loving me.

Prologue

I can still see it. The image replays in my mind uncontrol lably, overcoming me at any part of the day. People say it will go away, that time will heal the wound and ease the pain. I know this isn't true. They don't know because it didn't happen to them. I was one of them, one of most of the population who never had his or her life changed in an instant. Unfortunately, I lived too close to it, dangerously too close, and I guess you could say it was only a matter of time.

His face is still there, in my head, in my dreams, in my thoughts forever. Worst part about it was killing him wasn't really my fault. I've concluded that he wanted to die, that he made me his vehicle in an elaborate suicide plot. Maybe I've done this to make the whole thing easier for me to live with. I don't know. I just know that I'll never be the same, forever changed by becoming a killer. I'm sure countless men have gone through the same thing, and I am not implying that my situation is different, or even in any way special. I just know that it is my situation, and only someone who has been through it can understand. I haven't really found anyone that fits that bill, at least anyone who I can talk to. Plenty of guys on the job have killed in the line of duty, and I know a few of them personally, but they don't seem to want to talk about it, instead either shutting themselves off completely or doing their talking behind the psychologist's closed door.

I don't want to go either way. I don't want to close myself off or sit in some office listening to a guy who earned his PhD and now thinks he can solve my problem via a variety of pre-determined techniques and mood-altering drugs. I have to deal with this my own way, though I must admit I haven't succeeded just yet. People who know me will probably say I have closed myself off, but then again, they've said that ever since I became a cop. I just don't like to chatter, and I find most conversations meaningless trips through someone's life and achievements, most of which hold no importance to me. Hearing about how a guy made VP or some other empty title promotion is about as pertinent to me as listening to a lecture on Medieval Drama. Neither has a chance at holding my attention. I'm not always high on the invite list for most parties.

Solace is a hard thing to find when you don't know where to look for it. I could tell you dozens of places it doesn't hang out, most notably the local bar or at the bottom of a bottle. I've looked in both places several times to no avail. That doesn't mean I'll stop looking, only because it's become obvious I need some sort of chemical help, and I prefer the sort that comes in a clear bottle that's easy to open, instead of a little brown one that takes effort.

None of this would really matter if I'd had any ability whatsoever to take advice. I like to think that I listen when someone throws a kernel of information my way, but the truth is I listen with one ear and retain nothing. I prefer to go my own route. I like when I come to something that works through my own efforts instead of asking for directions. Yeah, I'm hell to drive with in this game of life. That's probably why my passenger seat has stayed relatively empty all these years.

So, I killed someone. In the line of duty. I did my job. No charges were pressed, no internal investigations were launched. I had to deal with the same IA bastards that tried to ruin my life a couple of years back, but they are easy to deal with when they have no ulterior motives. I even got pats on the back for my work, along with a certificate from our glorious mayor commending me on a job well done. The damn thing is still in the box they gave it to me in, and it'll stay that way. I keep trying to find a way to justify this in my own moral outlook. I might be all over the board with my views and ideas, and I might give a rat's ass about religion and a God who stares down on me with a smirk. Yes, I know I capitalized the 'G'. I really have no idea what's on his reading list, and I am not about to take a chance. What I'm trying to say is, though I could be accused of being a moral outcast, I have strong feelings on what is right and what is wrong. Murder's wrong. And I can't even find a way to allow it in my moral scope, under any circumstance. I'd never really thought about it until it happened. I don't think anyone really does. Worst part was I didn't even go for a kill shot.

I've seen some strange cases, dealt with corruption, deception, and just about anything else you'd expect a homicide detective in New York City to experience. They told us about the risks in the academy, and they repeated them each step of the way, each promotion and new assignment. Funny, the risks were supposed to be ours, how we had to put our lives on the line every time we put on that uniform or flashed the badge. You learn to put off those risks, remove them from your mind so you can operate. No one ever warned me about taking someone's life while on the job.

1

I like to read the paper. Of all the activities available in this entertainment-based world, reading the paper is the only one that allows me to relax. Even though I find myself at odds with the thinly veiled intentions of most reporters, I enjoy sitting at my makeshift dinner table after work, perusing through the previous day's events. I've made the paper a few times myself, and though this isn't half as exciting as most people think, I secretly look for my name each time I go through whatever paper I am reading.

As a homicide detective, I of course pay particular attention to murder anywhere in the country. It's quite amazing when you realize how many people are murdered over the course of a week. That's not even including the people who are never listed as a murder, which is a number quite higher than most people imagine. Murder, it seems, is a matter of political angling, like just about everything else these days.

On this particular day, I found a mention of a murder in Central Park. Though not my jurisdiction, Central Park holds a bit of an allure to me, mainly because, while growing up, the park had been used by all sorts of lurkers, rapists, drug dealers, and of course, run-of-the-mill murderers. They did some cleaning up in the 90's, and Central Park became a glowing example of what can be done when politicians, citizens, and the police force all work together toward the same goal. To see that a body had been found there caught my eye instantly.

The paper, the *New York Post* on this day, showed a photo of a body bag being carted into the back of an ambulance,

Medical Examiner Bryan Coltrain standing next to the open door, the same empty look on his face that seemed to grace it perpetually. I could feel the scene myself; I could smell the distinct odor of the plastic bag. Instantly, I wanted to be there. I wanted to see the body, search it for clues. I wanted to dig around the area, question family members and friends of the victim in the hopes of leading to the culprit. Yes, the mention of murder excited me. I couldn't help that. Death was part of my job, and I enjoyed my job possibly more than I should have. The same way a restaurateur perks up when hungry people walk into his establishment, I got a tinge of excitement when I read about someone passing on, especially when it seemed that someone else helped them pass on.

I put the paper down and lit a cigarette, a habit that, looking back, seemed all to perfect for a man who deals with death. I ran through my mind the detectives who worked in the Central Park precinct, the homicide detectives that I met in court, at those stupid fund raisers they make us go to, and at the bars we all seemed to find ourselves in at some point in the week. Instantly, I knew who had the case. Marcus Lay, a middle-aged man who I'd actually worked with for a short time when I had a beat. He was a nice guy, and he was black. I'm not saying that there is any relation between the two. I just have to say Marcus is black because that's important to him. I never really found out why, though I suspect it has something to do with the fact that he made it to detective when most of the other guys in his neighborhood made it to jail. Like I said, I liked Marcus, even if he sometimes had a heavy hand in dishing out opinions and advice.

I thought about the last time I spoke to Marcus, and realized it was at one of those fundraisers. At the time, he'd been with his woman of the month, but from what I'd heard, that one had actually won the Lay Lottery and wore an engagement ring from him. I couldn't remember if he'd actually gotten married, mainly because such news just wasn't that important to me. I'd recently decided that marriage was what I wanted, but I didn't think about that on a daily basis, and I could have cared less about hearing the sordid tale of someone else taking the plunge that awaits most of us.

Marcus lived in the city, not far from where I called home. He owned an apartment somewhere in the fifties, in a fairly affluent area, a bit too rich for my taste. To be honest, it was too rich for my poorly planned budget. Marcus was clean. He just kept his head when it came to finances. In the mess I called my kitchen, I found the phone book I rarely used and got Marcus' number. I don't know why I felt compelled to call. Something about that body caught me, and I had to have some details.

Marcus answered the phone on the second ring. It was only eight at night, so I knew I wasn't disturbing him. "Yeah," he said.

"Hey Marcus, John Keegan here."

"Keegan," Marcus said, "what could you possibly want?" He knew. I didn't doubt that for a second.

"Wanted to hear about how the other half lives," I said.

"We live fine."

"You've got the Central Park case, don't you?"

"I might. Is this a business call, or do you just want to hear all the steamy details?" Marcus asked.

"Steamy details. You know I am a sucker for them."

"Not much to tell right now," he said.

"Keeping a tight lid?" I asked.

"Lot of outside influences on this one. Gonna be the sort of thing that we have to carry out carefully." That meant either someone prominent was tied to the victim or just that the media had an interest. I figured the latter. Finding a body in Central Park caught the attention of the media just as it did mine.

"Well, I'd like to hear what you can tell. Busy?"

"Not really," Marcus said.

"Meet me at Donovan's," I said, naming a place that was as low profile as I could think of. I figured Marcus didn't want to meet at a cop hangout. Too many questions to answer there.

"Fine. See you there in a half-hour. Just understand that I'm only going for a free drink, not because I have so much I can tell you."

"I'm sure you'll find a way to entertain me."

I must admit I was excited. It had been a few months since I was involved in any way with a case of substance. I'd worked a few stiffs since my last real case, and that last case had been a doozy, to say the least. Maybe premonition had something to do with why I wanted information on this case as bad as I did. Of course, I can't explain that. If I did, I'd be giving up way too much too soon, and there is absolutely no fun in that.

I found Marcus sitting at a small table toward the back of Donovan's. As its name implies, it was an Irish joint, complete with Guinness on tap and the same wood bar that seemed to be in all Irish-influenced watering holes. The place was busy for a Thursday night, with what seemed like a bunch of regulars seated at the bar watching a soccer game on the three televisions behind it. I walked past them and over to where Marcus was sitting. I noticed he wasn't drinking anything.

As if he'd read my mind, he said, "Person getting the information gets the drinks."

I had no problems with that, even though I have been accused of receiving far more drinks than I bought. "Still drinking that single-malt sissy crap?" I asked.

Marcus smiled. "Good taste never changes. Glenlivet," he instructed.

"On the way."

I walked over to the bartender, a surly man who stood somewhere in the mid-sixes, with a protruding beer gut and bright white hair. He noticed me—actually, he noticed the twenty I held in my hand—and walked over.

"What do you need?" he asked in a heavy Irish accent.

"Dewar's and soda and a Glenlivet, neat."

He gave me a sideways look; this probably stemmed from my 'neat' statement, and then went to get the drinks. I could smell Southern Comfort around me somewhere, a scent that almost immediately gives me the gag reflex. I met Southern Comfort at a bachelor party in my twenties and we certainly didn't hit it off. To tell it right, Southern Comfort kicked my ass.

Thankfully, the bartender was quick with the drinks and brought them over. He took my twenty, trading it for a five and two singles. Thirteen bucks for two drinks in a run down Irish bar. I left him a single and walked back to Marcus.

I handed Marcus his drink and he took a sniff first, then a small sip.

"Nothing tastes better than a free drink," he said, smiling.

"I can think of a few things," I said.

"Yeah, but some of us have never had to pay for such things."

"Not from what I hear. Rumor has it a woman is walking around with a rock that put a dent in your checking account."

"She's got the gold band to match it now," Marcus said.

I raised my glass. "Congratulations, as odd as that sounds."

We clinked glasses. "Thanks," Marcus said. I caught his eyes. There was something there I hadn't noticed right away. Marcus was one of those guys who let just about everything slide off him. He'd seen his share of problems, that I knew, but he never let it get into him. Something had penetrated that defense, and I hoped he'd tell me what it was.

"Alright, I paid the price of admission. Spill it," I said.

Marcus looked around the room, an automatic reaction when you're about to discuss a case. "Like I said, not a lot to spill."

"Well, you've got to give me some value for my dollar. Make that seven dollars."

"Price you gotta pay," Marcus said. "You know they found the body yesterday?"

I nodded.

"Girl. Woman. Thirties."

"Rape?" I asked.

"Looks that way. Dirty job, too. Couple of scratches here and there. Knife wound. What did the final job seems to be a heavy, blunt object. This was an angry kill, if you ask me."

I could tell there was more behind what Marcus told me. We homicide boys have strong stomachs or we wouldn't be doing what we do, so when something gets us acting strange, it sure can't be pretty.

"Go on," I said.

Marcus took another sip of his drink. "They caved the whole left side of her head in. Guys at the ME office don't think the first few shots did her in, and they think the last few were for posterity. Some of the rape might be the same way."

"Nice to know we have such upstanding people in the neighborhood."

"They weren't smart, and if you ask me, they wanted to send some sort of message. Leaving the body in Central Park's gotta mean something too, but I just can't figure it out."

"Little early to be worrying yourself about that," I said. "Now, why the tight lid?"

"She's the daughter of someone with some clout," Marcus said.

"What sort of clout?"

"Dollar-sort. Her father does some pretty good numbers."

"Someone I know?" I asked.

Marcus shook his head. "Doubtful. Doesn't make the papers or the celebrity list, but he's made a name for himself in his own sector."

"What sector is that?"

"Science. Works with some sort of physics. Engineer sort who turned an idea into a windfall. Keeps a low profile, though."

"You meet him yet?"

"No. He's out of town, out of reach. Supposed to be back tomorrow. I don't even know if anyone's told him yet. Gonna be a tough one to take," Marcus said.

Marcus still looked preoccupied. I knew better than to press. He was the sort that would tell me in due time if he wanted to. We were the same in this respect. I think it is why we got along. Marcus was one of those people you tell yourself you should hang out with more but never do. At least, that's how I felt about it. He might have thought I was a complete moron.

"Worst part, being the one who has to tell him."

"I won't be doing that," Marcus said, "That's the wife's job."

"How'd she take it?"

"Initially, in stride. Think it was shock. Couple of hours later, I hear she's at the ME office, demanding to see the body again. They let her in, then had to haul her out. Probably got her on something to kill the pain."

Drugs. For some reason doctors give them away like candy during such times. Guess they figure it is better than letting someone grieve in their own fashion. Can't let people do things for themselves. There's no money in that.

Marcus finished his drink. "Need another?" I asked.

"No. You know what they say about cops hitting the hard stuff."

"Yeah, it gets them drunk."

Marcus laughed. He had a deep voice and a deeper laugh. If you don't know him, the laugh can actually be frightening. Coming from a guy who stands about six-two with a face that looks like it is carved from stone a laugh like his can go right through you. I thought it was funny.

"How're things going for you, Keegan?" Marcus asked.

"They haven't killed me and they still let me carry a gun."

Two of the atrocities of life. Any action by you?"

I assumed Marcus knew about what I'd been through a while back, so I didn't recount the story for him. "Dead."

Marcus laughed again. "I'd be turning down cases if I were you. You seem to always get the bad ones."

"The others just aren't enough fun," I said, finishing my drink. If Marcus would have gone for a second, I would have done the same. I really wasn't in the mood for drinking, so the fact that he didn't was welcome.

"You'd fight for this case if it was in your juri, wouldn't you?" he asked.

I shook my head. "Nah. I don't believe in tipping the scales."

"Bullshit. You called me as soon as you found out, didn't you?"

Nailed. "Only because the park interests me. I think if I worked in your spot, it would have lost its allure a while ago."

"Maybe," Marcus said.

"You request this one, or have it stuffed in your hands?"

"Little of both. I was next on call, but Witherspoon told me he knew I wanted it, so he lobbed it my way to avoid any conflict."

"You flying solo?" I asked.

"No. Cooper's with me. Know him?"

Paul Cooper went to the academy with me. He was a vanilla type, so middle-of-the-road that I had absolutely no opinion about him, which was a rarity.

I nodded.

"Not a bad guy," Marcus said.

"About all I can say about him."

"I've worked a few with him. Good paperwork, decent ideas, and he never fights his position strong enough to piss you off. Sort of like not having a partner."

"Wish I had someone like that in South," I said.

"Calhill back?" That'd be Rick Calhill, my sometime partner and friend.

"Sort of."

Marcus shook his head. "Amazing he came this far."

"He's doing it for the kids," I said. Calhill had to go through a tragedy unlike any I could have ever imagined. He lost his wife, almost lost his job, and got a suspension to boot. I was one of the few that gave him even the slightest chance to make it back to the job.

"Gotta hand it to him. They pair you guys up again?"

"Not yet. Think it's coming soon. He's different. I think I'll even like working with him this time around," I said.

"Calhill's a good man," Marcus said, "and a good detective. I'd work with him any day."

"A year ago, I'd have told you to take him. Now I just hope I can help."

"That's big of you," Marcus said sarcastically.

"I'm not all asshole. Just part of me."

"More than one part."

"What else is going on with this case?" I asked.

"Not much else. Got nothing in the way of motive. Despite the dirty job, the scene was empty. They knew what they were doing, if you ask me. They might have been stupid, but yet they seemed to have a handle on this sort of thing."

"Father involved you think?"

"Doubtful. He's a scientist."

"What does the mother do?"

"Runs a small bookshop on the east side. Nothing there either."

"What do you know of the girl?"

"Out of work. Took some time off to write. Was an editor for a magazine for six years. Think she might have burned out."

"Yeah, magazine writing's gotta be tough."

"Just a hunch on that one. She ran a feminist magazine. Well, they didn't call it exactly, but that's what was implied," Marcus said.

"They never have any good pictures in those rags."

"I guess they do if you are a feminist."

"What do they like to look at, men with needles sticking out of their dicks?"

Marcus laughed again, and this caught the attention of a few people at the bar. This made me laugh, something I never do, so you know.

"Been reading them lately?" Marcus asked.

"Your wife left one at my apartment the other night."

"You could never satisfy my wife."

"Hey, I do have some Italian in me," I said in my defense.

Marcus chuckled. "I didn't mean it that way. She needs someone to talk to. You probably just roll over and go to sleep."

"Sometimes I fall asleep right on top of them. Keeps their upper body in shape when they have to push me off."

"Your sickness knows no boundaries."

"Some, but not many."

I could tell by Marcus' mood that he didn't want to talk about the case anymore. I'd gotten what I came for, some details to go along with the pictures in my mind. I needed them. I really don't know why. I guess it really doesn't make a difference. Something drove me to meet Marcus.

We talked about nothing for a little while, and then he said he had to get back to his wife. I walked out with him and decided against taking a cab back to my apartment. Judging from the extra layer around my stomach, I needed a little exercise. The walk home cleared my mind.

2

I woke the next morning from a dream about someone I'd lost. Throughout my 35 years, I hadn't really met too many women that made an impact on my heart or my life, but there had been one who sparked an interest in me I couldn't shake. Unfortunately, she was murdered, taken from me before I really got to know her well. We had that connection, the connection I had been looking for in a woman all my life. I initially took her death as an indication the powers that be didn't want me married. Then, after thinking about it, I realized her entry into my life was destined to open my mind, and my heart. This might have worked except that Emily Brackens lived on in my dreams, and no woman I met in real life could compare to the fantasy my mind carried out way too often.

I hated driving to work after getting spoiled by having Rick Calhill drive me in for years. I disliked it even more when I had something nagging at me. I pulled into the Midtown South precinct parking lot in a bad mood, something many of my colleagues would say was not at all unusual.

By the time I made it into the precinct I thought I had done a good job of clearing my mind. I'd been through some rough times recently. It seemed each day brought some remembrance of those times. Either the loss, or how it came to be overtook my mind at least once a day. I was growing tired of it.

My boss, Inspector Geiger, met me in the hallway on the way to my desk. Geiger was an okay guy, the sort you don't mind being your boss. He looked a lot older than he should have, most of that aging a direct result of the job-related stress he had been through. I might have been the cause of some of it; at least, that is what Geiger implied from time to time. Judging by his facial expression I assumed I hadn't done anything wrong. He just looked like he needed to talk about something.

"Keegan," Geiger said, "I need to talk to you about something." See? I'm good.

"Sure boss," I said.

Geiger exhaled. "I need a favor, actually."

I don't like to ask for favors and I certainly don't like to do them. Unfortunately, it isn't wise to turn down your boss. Unless, of course, you want to work the worst beat in the precinct.

"What do you need?"

"First, an opinion."

"Got plenty of those," I said.

"What do you think of Calhill?"

"Well," I said, "he worries too much about what he eats, works out too often, and generally drives the people around him nuts." Geiger glared at me mockingly. "What do you really mean?" I asked.

"What do you think of his mental state?"

"Tough to tell. I mean, he appears okay on the surface. He doesn't talk much anymore, but I can hardly blame him for that."

"You think he's ready to move forward?"

"I think he might be. It is a waste of his talent having him file papers. Must be killing him inside."

"I agree. I was thinking about putting him back in the field," Geiger said. I figured this was coming, eventually.

"And you want to partner him with me," I said.

"I thought about it. How do you feel?"

"I wouldn't have a problem with it. Might be a good idea;

get him back in where he is comfortable. I don't know if he would feel the same way with the other guys."

"Everything is good between you two?"

"From my perspective, yes. Then again, I was the one that hit him," I said. I hit him good too. Beat him up for something he didn't even do. Maybe it was the buildup of working with his anal-retentiveness for years that just came through.

"You think he can deal with it?"

"Have you asked him?" I asked.

Geiger shook his head. "Wanted to see what you thought first. If you didn't want him with you, it wouldn't make sense to make that pairing. This is a very delicate situation and I want to make sure I do everything right."

This is why I liked Geiger. Sure, he could be a hardass when he felt like it, but he really took the time to consider things. He was always looking out for his men. I'd worked for a few other guys, but Geiger was the only one who had compassion. He never asked us to do anything he wouldn't do himself, and he tried to take care of us when he could. Couldn't ask for any more than that.

"Sometimes you just have to take a chance. I know he wants to get back into the field, and I am certainly not going to be the one to stop that. I mean, what's the worst that can happen?" I asked.

Geiger shook his head. "Don't say that."

"Well—"

Geiger put his hand up. "Just don't say it. If anyone I know was born under a bad sign, it's you. Last thing I need is for you to throw the kibosh on this. I've had a hard enough time mulling this over. I don't want to have to deal with any of your curses."

I chuckled. Funny thing was, Geiger spoke the truth. "Got you. Just make sure this is okay with him." I thought for a second. "You got anything for us to work on?"

Geiger hesitated. "Yes."

"You don't like it," I said.

"Nope. Don't think you will either."

"What, this going to be something Calhill can get his feet re-wet on? I don't think he needs that."

"Neither do I. It's nothing simple."

"Another all-star case?"

"Don't know that yet, but my instincts tell me so."

"Can't these high-profile fuckers die in another precincts jurisdiction?"

"That would be all too easy," Geiger said. "Besides, you don't like easy."

"You've got a point there, boss."

I sat at my desk looking over the photographs and report Geiger handed me. He had told me the case struck him as something hot, though I have to admit I didn't see any evidence of this myself. The dead guy—as I like to call the stiff—was one Kostya Volkyv, aka K-Drugs, as his friends liked to call him. Russian guy, who obviously had some dealings in drugs. He had a rap sheet—more like a rap book—with several listings of drug and minor violent crime convictions. The biggest one was a rape, and he got four years for that, released in three because K-Drugs demonstrated good behavior. Obviously, that good behavior didn't last on the outside. He was dead. Maybe this was a good thing, but homicide detectives aren't supposed to make such assumptions. People think this might cloud our vision.

K-Drugs was a tall man, standing at six-four, and tipped the scales at 240 pounds. Old K-Drugs' cause of death was a bullet wound in the back of the head. He was lying in the kitchen of his apartment face down, with a pool of blood surrounding his head. My guess was that K didn't see the shooter. Someone was waiting for him. They probably didn't wait too long to do him in.

From the pictures I could see the refrigerator door open,

a container of milk—not opened—lying on the floor in front of it. K-Drugs felt he needed a shot of calcium. Someone else decided he needed more lead in his diet. Normally I felt pity for victims. Most of them were innocent people caught in some violent idiot's path. This here seemed like two of the same type crossing paths. Now there was one less of that type running around.

K-Drugs had been dead for six hours from what the initial report said. Stiffness in the jaw, body temp of around 90 degrees. That meant K-Drugs bit the bullet sometime around 2AM. I was asleep and old K-Drugs was about to have a glass of milk to wash down whatever he imbibed the night before. Only I got to do as I planned and he didn't. Someone had something else in mind for him, the poor bastard.

I looked up and saw that Calhill was still in Geiger's office. He wasn't talking, just listening, an odd occurrence for him. I wondered what it would be like working with him again, after what had happened between us and what had happened to his life. I figured it would never be the same. I realized that was probably a good thing, a very good thing. Rick and I worked well together but we drove each other nuts. Figure *The Odd Couple*, only I am much classier than Oscar Madison. So what if I don't keep my apartment sparkling clean. I sure know how to get it together in a hurry, like when a female is coming over.

I realized I hadn't rush-cleaned my apartment in way too long.

In my twenties and early thirties, it was all about bedding women. No, I was no all-star lover. None of my friends or family would allow me to say that. Well, I was one time, with Alana Gonzalez, but it could be argued that she brought me up to that level. I just enjoyed my time with women and I made sure that time didn't last too long. I engaged women only out of sexual need. Then I met someone who changed all of that, someone who I wanted to spend time with, out of the sack. I thought I had gone nuts, then I realized I'd fallen in love. Then she was killed. Not your typical romance story.

After meeting Emily, my attitude toward women changed, even if only slightly. I know a psychologist would tell me I was using Emily as an excuse to not meet other women. Perhaps he would say I had fear of abandonment. Then again, what the Hell would he know? Unless you've had someone taken from you so quickly there's no way to know what I was going through, no matter what the textbooks and professors said.

Calhill walked over to my desk. He looked empty. He used to be chipper—annoyingly so—and to see him so quiet was unnerving. Calhill was a good-looking guy with sandy hair and a build that made me envy him every time I looked in the mirror and saw the spare tire around my waist. It wasn't a full-size spare, just one of those tiny, foreign jobs that could easily be purchased at a donut shop.

"Hey," I said, looking up from the report.

"John," Calhill said, in a quiet voice. I couldn't tell if this was the new Rick Calhill or if he was just uncomfortable talking to me. We said hello to each other when our paths crossed. We even had a decent conversation about the new mayor when he was elected, but we never spoke. "What've you got there?"

I closed the report and pushed it away. "The report on the dead guy we'll be working on," I said.

Rick nodded. "Anything interesting?"

I chuckled. "Is there ever?" The tension of the moment was getting to me. Rick and I knew each other for years. There was no reason for us to be going through something like this.

"I see."

"Listen, Rick, I just want you to know that I am happy we are working together again. You might think I am just saying that but I mean it. It'll be good. I'm not so sure how you feel about it."

Rick exhaled, a habit I noticed he kept through his tough times. "I have no problem with it. I'm probably as happy as you are about it, just a little uncomfortable. I feel like the department idiot, the one everyone has to be careful around. Everyone knows what happened, there's no way to take that back, but I'm still capable," he said.

"I know that. That's why when Geiger came to me with this I told him it was a good idea."

"He said that. Shocked me a little."

"Why?"

Rick sat down in the chair across from me. "It just did. I thought you might have refused."

"For what reason?" I asked.

"John, even before everything happened you told Geiger you preferred to work without me. I heard about that. Plus, there's still the issue of you thinking I sold you out on the Mullins case."

Rick had sold me out on the Mullins case. He was my partner, and when the trouble was about to strike, he faked an illness. He admitted this to me, and told me he did it for a promotion he never got. When he told me, it seemed so important, a reason to be angry with him. Now, it seemed inconsequential.

"That's over," I said. "You did what you did. Important thing is that you admitted it and that it's in the past."

"You're sure," Rick said.

"I am. And no, I won't go stabbing you in the back to get even. I'll get you from the front."

Rick laughed. "You've already done that."

I stood up and reached out my hand. "Partners," I said.

Rick too my hand. "Partners."

"Good. Now let's get to this case."

I told Rick what I had gathered about our new dead friend, K-Drugs. I showed him the pictures and let him run over the report. He read it a bit and then put it down. He seemed to be thinking about something.

"What?" I asked.

"Anyone interview the neighbors?" he asked.

"It was in the report, I think."

"And no one heard anything?"

"Seems that way."

"Something isn't right. This looks like an anger kill. Revenge, maybe. I doubt that the shooter used a silencer. Something's going on."

I hadn't thought about that. Geiger used to say that he paired Rick and I because we were so different. He figured with two totally different perspectives we'd come up with things that no like-minded pair ever could. There were many times when his theory proved correct.

"Okay, so either he used another device, or the neighbors aren't saying enough."

"I think we should find out."

"Rick, as scary as this is to say, I wholeheartedly agree with you."

Drugs must be good business. Kostya Volkyv lived in a nice area of the city, much nicer than the area I lived in, but not that far away. Of course, the guys who break the rules usually end up better off than the guys that enforce them. If you really want to make it big, however, you have to be one of the guys that *make* the rules, be it on Capitol Hill, or on the streets. Those guys make the bucks.

I pulled up in front of the building, which really looked like a converted brownstone. I stopped the car and looked over at Rick, who had been mostly silent during the ride, unless you count his whistling along with the radio.

"Feel good to be back on the street?" I asked.

"Better than you can imagine."

"Ah, I thought you made a real nice administrative assistant."

"I was doing work. They had me dealing with the dead files."

"Aren't all the homicide cases dead files?"

"You know what I mean," Rick said.

"Of course. They had me do that when I first came to the department. That's how I solved my first case."

"Coleman?" Rick asked.

"Yeah. I had seen something in the dead files. There was a link no one else would have seen."

"Doubt that will happen for me. All I saw were bullshit cases."

"You never know," I said.

We got out of the car and walked up to the front door of the building. There were three buzzers. One said "Dmitriev", another said "Federov", and the last, which I assumed was K-Drugs', was blank.

"Pick one," I said.

Rick looked at the names. "They sound like brands of Vodka."

"Let's try and keep the ethnic humor out of this," I said.

"They do," Rick said. He looked at the names again, then pressed Federov's buzzer.

"You went with the hockey player," I said.

"Aren't they all hockey players?"

"I don't think our pal K-Drugs played hockey. He was into different sorts of entertainment."

"True."

I heard some footsteps, then the deadbolt disengaging. The door opened, and a short, fat woman dressed in all black open the door.

"Da?" she said. I think that meant 'yes' in Russian.

I took out my badge and showed it to her.

"NYPD. Are you Mrs. Federov?" I asked.

"Yes."

"Can we come in?"

"I spoke to police yesterday. Why again?" she asked sternly. Russian women have balls, that much I know.

"We just need to ask you a few more questions."

She huffed, a loud huff at that, then opened the outside door and let us in. She led us to the apartment in the far left corner. We walked in, and I immediately smelled the scent of food I would never dare eat. The apartment was sparsely furnished, with just a couch and a coffee table to the right, and a wooden sitting chair to the left. There was no television, no radio.

"Sit," she said, and we did, on the couch. Next to each other. It wasn't a comfortable arrangement. "Coffee?"

"No thanks," I said. Rick didn't say anything.

Mrs. Federov sat down in the sitting chair and just glared at us for a moment, as if we were intruding. "Yes? You have questions?"

I looked at Rick. I figured this was as good a time as any for him to get back into action. The look he returned was priceless. Instead of saying anything, I just looked around the apartment, at the ancient pictures of families from another country, and the odd-looking brown water stain on the ceiling.

Rick cleared his throat. "For the record, your full name?"

"I gave that already."

"Again, please?"

Mrs. Federov rolled her eyes. "Mariola Federov."

"That's Polish, the first name?" Rick asked.

"Yes." If Rick was trying to engage her with that Polish comment, it certainly wasn't working out as planned.

"Okay, Mrs. Federov. I know that the people you saw earlier today already went through this drill, so I will try and make this as brief as possible."

"That is not possible," Mrs. Federov replied, "it has already taken too long."

What a sweetheart.

Rick tried to deflect that, and said, "This is a murder investigation."

"I didn't kill anyone."

"We don't know that yet," Rick said. Atta boy.

"Don't be funny. It doesn't suit you." Atta girl, Mrs. Federov.

"Anyway. I understand that you are the one who called the police."

"I did, yes."

"And how did you come to see the body?"

"With my eyes. It was there, on the floor."

"What were you doing in Mr. Volkyv's apartment?" Rick asked.

Mrs. Federov corrected Rick's pronunciation of K-Drug's last name, then said, "I cleaned for him. I do house cleaning. He was one of my clients." I looked around the apartment, noticing dust and other dirt and wondered how good of a house cleaner she was. Well, at least she was better than I was. I didn't see any pizza boxes.

"At what time did you find him?"

"6:15. That's the time I usually go in there to clean," Mrs. Federov said.

"That early?"

"Yes."

"Was he usually home when you cleaned?"

"Sometimes. Sometimes he stayed out all night. Most times he did that."

"Okay," Rick said.

"That all?"

"No, it is not all. Please, just bear with me."

"That's what I have been doing."

"Did you hear anything last night?" Rick asked.

"No."

"Nothing?"

"I heard birds chirping."

"Nothing else?" Rick asked.

"No."

I couldn't take it anymore. This woman's condescending attitude went right through me. I looked at her, and said, "Listen. I don't know why you show hostility toward police, but it doesn't matter. What does matter is that you answer our questions. You were the first person to find the body, therefore you are the first suspect. I would assume you'd act accordingly."

Mrs. Federov shook her head with an arrogant air. "I have done nothing. You cannot prove that I have done something."

"I don't have to."

"This is not Russia. You do not take people away in the middle of the night because you feel like it."

"Right, this is America. We do it because we feel there is a reason to."

"You will not threaten me," Mrs. Federov demanded.

"And you will not dodge my partner's questions, or give him some attitude as if he was interrupting your day. A man was shot across the hall from you, shot with a high-caliber gun, and you are sitting here talking about how you heard birds chirping? Either you're nuts, or perhaps you are forgetting something. Which one is it?"

Mrs. Federov looked at me, then Rick, then turned her head toward the window. "Perhaps I hear something," she said.

"Perhaps, huh?"

"Perhaps."

"What, may I ask, did you perhaps hear?" I asked.

"A noise. A loud noise."

"And you thought nothing of it?"

Mrs. Federov looked back at me. "Detective, Kostya was not what you call a nice man. Always he had people there, partying, dealing, doing something they shouldn't be doing. When he hired me, he told me never to look in certain places, and never worry myself about any noises I might hear from his apartment. I only assumed this time was the same."

This, I could understand. If I lived next door to a lowlife like K-Drugs, I too would probably overlook any sort of loud sounds coming from his apartment. I figured the old broad was telling the truth.

"So, you didn't report the noise because it wasn't uncommon," I said.

"Yes. It wasn't the first time I hear that sort of noise."

"Can you specifically remember any others?" Rick asked.

"No."

"What did you think when you saw his body?" I asked.

"I thought he finally gets what he deserves," Mrs. Federov said.

"Why did you work for him?"

"Look around, Detective. You think this place is cheap? This building has been in my family for fifty years, and now, I can barely afford to pay the taxes. The only people that want to live here are ones who want to pay cash, and don't want their names printed outside. I know what sort of people they are, but they always pay. I have no other choice. I do cleaning to make extra money. He paid me well for that too."

I was sure he did. He paid her to clean, and he paid her to look the other way when unsavory things went down. Nothing better than having the landlord allow your illegal practices. I toyed with the notion that Mrs. Federov took a cut of the action, then figured she had more class than that. Of course, she probably didn't, but this wasn't a narc investigation. I only cared about what she saw and heard that night.

"Did you hear anything else?" I asked.

"When?"

"That night. You said you heard a loud noise, which we will assume was the gun going off. Did you hear anything else? Footsteps, anything?"

Mrs. Federov shook her head. "I covered my head with the pillow. I didn't want to hear anything else. I worried for my life. Every time something happened with Kostya, I always worried like this."

"Had you seen anyone around recently that you didn't recognize?" Rick asked.

Mrs. Federov glared at him. "Detective, I am sure you know what sort of business Kostya was involved in. Always strange people came around. I would not recognize any of them. I would not want to."

"Did you ever hear any arguing? I mean recently," I asked.

Mrs. Federov thought about that for a moment. "Two days ago. Someone was yelling at him, demanding money."

"Did it sound like one of his associates? You know, someone who worked with him?"

"No. Customer," Mrs. Federov said.

"You're sure?"

"Yes."

"How do you know?" Rick asked.

"Because the person was yelling about drugs, about bad drugs."

"Had this happened before?" Rick asked.

"All the time. Kostya was not a good businessman. Many times people come and yell at him."

"Did anything ever come of that?"

Mrs. Federov shook her head. "He knew how to deal with them. He told me one time not to ever worry, that no one would dare try and hurt him or anyone in the building. He said he had connections, and that people feared him."

I figured this was true, and the people that came to complain were just strung-out junkies who wouldn't be satisfied with pure stuff because it is just never enough. That's one of the reasons I turned down the opportunity in Vice a few years back. I didn't want to deal with this sort of person. Not that murderers were any better, but at least, at times, they made sense. Junkies made no sense whatsoever.

"And this argument, it was the same?" I asked. I noticed I was adopting a little of the way she spoke. I made a mental note to stop it.

"I think so. The man was angry, but I think Kostya made him happy. Maybe he gave him some free drugs."

"He probably did," I said. I didn't see much there in the way of a motive. Sure, drug dealers always ran the risk of a deal gone bad, but I didn't see that with this one. I wasn't sure if Rick did either.

"Kostya was good with people when he wanted to be. I wouldn't say this if he was still alive, but he was always afraid. I don't see Kostya letting something go bad, go where he gets shot. He made this person happy."

Mrs. Federov made sense. Though she had that stuck-up attitude, she wasn't really a bad person. Still, I knew better than to take everything she said as pure truth. She didn't want us there, didn't want to talk about the fact that someone was killed in her building, and all of a sudden she started chirping. I might just have been overreacting, or I might have been on to something. I figured I'd talk to Rick about it when we were alone.

"We finished now?" Mrs. Federov asked, as if she picked up on my mental cue.

I looked at Rick. "I guess so," he said. He gave her his card. "Please feel free to contact me if you remember anything else about last night."

Mrs. Federov took the card and placed it on her coffee table. "That is all I remember, but I will keep your card, just in case."

We got up to leave, and Mrs. Federov walked to the door.

"Even though I now have apartment empty, the man that killed Kostya, he did a good thing," she said.

"Killing someone is never a good thing, Mrs. Federov," I said, "but I think I know what you mean."

We got into the car and just sat there for a moment. I knew it had been a while since Rick had worked on a case, and I wanted the interview to set in for a moment. I needed some time to do the same. We sat in silence, the only sounds coming from passing cars and the two of us breathing. I couldn't remember ever sitting in the same place with Rick in silence, and it took a little getting used to.

"She's lying," Rick spurted out.

"What makes you say that?" I asked.

"I just know it. You do too."

"I had that feeling, but I just can't put my finger on what bothers me about her. She might just be an obnoxious woman who just rubbed us the wrong way."

"It's more than that. She's happy he's dead."

"Can you blame her?" I asked.

"Of course not. Still, she's not telling us everything. She saw something. She heard something. And she's not telling us."

Maybe Rick was so eager to get back into the swing of things that he was already jumping to conclusions. I might have believed that if I didn't agree with him. But I did. I knew Mrs. Federov had something to hide. I didn't think she had anything to do with the demise of K-Drugs. She did, however, have some information for us. And I needed to figure out a way to get it out of her.

"Well, if she's not telling, we might not ever find out what it is. If she doesn't want to tell us, there's no way for us to make her."

"The John Keegan I remember would have found at least a dozen illegal ways to do it," Rick said.

"I resent that comment."

"But you don't deny it."

"Of course not. I'm not a liar."

I started the car and drove back toward the precinct.

"Go to Coltrain's office," Rick said, "I want to get a look at K-Drugs, postmortem."

"Not a bad idea."

"I have a few others," Rick said.

"Easy cowboy. Let's take this one step at a time."

"I never thought I'd ever hear you say that."

"Neither did I, Rick. Neither did I."

3

I never liked going to the Medical Examiner's office. Sure, I worked with death. I saw death more often than most. I just didn't particularly like being around that many dead bodies. Morticians frighten me. Funeral directors frighten me. And, most Medical Examiners frightened me, though Bryan Coltrain, the ME I dealt with most, didn't. His life might have frightened me, but as a person, he was okay. I just didn't like to see him on his turf. Being around those bodies didn't bother him. *That* bothered me.

I didn't know how Rick felt about going to the ME office. Rick certainly displayed the characteristics of a strange person, the sort that could be a mortician, so it was plausible he didn't mind going to the ME office. Something else that bothered me.

"There a particular reason why we are going to see Coltrain?" I asked.

"I want to get a look at the body," Rick replied, staring out the window. I didn't want to know what was on his mind. I remembered that the last time he went to the ME's office was to get one last look at his wife, who had found her way there through her own hand. It was either the morgue, or Riker's. She chose the morgue. Personally, I think she did him a favor. Instead of dealing with a wife doing hard time, he didn't have to deal with her at all. I don't know what he told his kids about it, whether he ever would tell them the truth about their mother. I wouldn't have told them a thing. It was kept from the papers. If they got smart and tried to research things when they got older, then, well, that would be their problem.

"I'm sure he is just going to look dead," I said.

"He might."

"Bullet in the back of the skull. Perfect ending to a perfect scumbag."

"Perhaps. Still, I gotta see it."

I figured he wanted to get his hands dirty, get the feeling of being back in action. I couldn't blame him for this. The only thing I was happy about was the fact that I hadn't eaten yet. The morgue was perfect for food extraction.

"Well, you'll get to see it. Along with Coltrain and his asexual partner. What's her name again?" I asked.

"Allison. I think she is sweet on you."

"She's only sweet on dead people. I don't even want to know what she does with those bodies when she is alone with them."

"You have way too vivid an imagination," Rick said.

"Can't do anything about that. I know she uses those fluids for lubrication."

"Jesus," Rick said, looking at me, "can you stop that?"

"Why, am I turning your stomach? She slaps some oil on some guy who died with his prick standing, hops on top and goes to town. There are people who do worse things than that," I said.

"Where do you come up with this stuff?"

I tapped my temple. "It just pops in there. Can't help it."

"You should see someone about that."

"Nah. I get it out through people like you. Haven't you missed working with me?" I asked.

"Oh, yeah. All those months I sat with the dead files, I kept thinking that I really needed to be in the field with you, listening to this sick bullshit you come up with out of nowhere."

"I knew it. It's nice to be missed."

"Right," Rick said.

I pulled up in front of where Coltrain's office was, stopped the car, and lit a cigarette. Rick coughed before I even exhaled.

"Christ, I secretly hoped you would have quit that habit already."

"And disappoint you? Never." I said, blowing the smoke in his direction. I'm real considerate when I want to be.

"One day, you're going to regret ever starting that."

"I'll probably be dead, in heaven, realizing that they don't allow smoking. Then, I'll be going through some serious nicotine withdrawal."

"Where you're going, I am sure there'll be plenty of smoke."

"Hell is cold, man. Everyone knows that."

Coltrain was going through the motions with another dead guy when we walked in. From what I could see, this guy was old, the skin was wrinkled and the hair gray. The body just lay there on the metal slab, poked and prodded by a man who must have gotten some sick pleasure from it all. If you live in New York City, and you have the unfortunate luck of dying in Coltrain's jurisdiction, you will get the same opportunity to have him go through your bowels like he was sifting for gold. I planned to die somewhere far away. Like Jersey.

Coltrain was about 45, with thin, light hair and a wiry build. He'd started to get a bit of a gut, probably from the crap he always ate. He ate it while he was working sometimes. He didn't slob over the bodies, like the way they depicted it in the movies sometimes, but he did eat in the same room. I couldn't eat in the same building.

Coltrain turned around and saw us. Without a word, he turned back to the old dead guy lying in front of him.

"Volkyv is in the back. Ask Allison to bring him out for you," Coltrain said.

"Do we have to?" I asked. Rick elbowed me.

"Just go to the back, Keegan. Come talk to me after you've given him the once-over."

We walked to the back, where there were even more slabs. Bodies lay there in bags. I counted three of them. That's four people who had died on the same day, counting old K-Drugs. Four lives ended. Four families forever affected. Four dead, stinking, rotting bodies taking up space in one of the most horrible places in the city. Next to some of those seedier, underground clubs, of course. Yeah, I was having fun.

Allison came from an office to the left of us. She was wearing the requisite white smock I always saw her in. She was rail-thin, with stringy hair that often looked unwashed. Honestly, if not for the long hair, it would be tough to peg her as a male or a female. Add the acne that covered three-quarters of her face, and you have quite an attractive, sexual beast. Well, a beast at least.

"Here to see the former Mr. Volkyv?" Allison asked in a low voice.

"No, we actually came to see Vanna White," I said.

"Ha," Allison said. It almost sounded like a real laugh. In reality, it was more of a cough.

Allison led us to the far table. Under the gray cloth was a mountain of a man. Volkyv looked large in the pictures I saw, but in person, his body was tremendous. Allison took off the cloth, and K-Drugs' naked body was before our eyes, something I could have done without. Allison moved to the back of the table, by Volkyv's head. His forehead had a huge hole in it.

"The bullet entered here," Allison said.

Rick walked around, his rubber-soled shoes squeaking on the floor. "Any sign of struggle? Any other marks beside the GSW?" he asked.

"Interestingly, yes. There is what appears to be some swelling not to far from the actual wound." Allison showed Rick what she was talking about. I decided my life would in no way be improved by looking inside the head of K-Drugs. Call me queasy, call me a bad detective, call me whatever you want.

Rick examined the wound. "What, you think he was hit with something first?"

"I don't know, Detective. He could have been hit with something afterward. Very tough to tell. There is something else."

"What?" I asked. I didn't want to make it appear that I wasn't interested.

"He was kicked in the groin several times. I believe it was postmortem, judging by the lack of bruising. I'd think it was meant as a message of some sort, but such guessing is not my job."

"The assailant kicked him in the groin after he shot him?" Rick asked.

"That's my assumption. Of course, you'd have to speak to Bryan for a detailed analysis. He's the one that performed the examination."

"Anything else we should know?"

"Well, when he came in here, he was wearing khaki pants. They were soiled at the knees."

"And what do you think that means?" I asked.

"That his pants were soiled at the knees," Allison said, "I really don't know what it means. He could have been working and got dirty, or it could mean something else. I had a sample of the dirt sent to the lab for analysis. That should give some indication of where it came from."

"I appreciate that," I said.

"Just doing my job, Detective Keegan." I think that was the first time she ever mentioned my name. Normally, I like women saying my name. There is even some sexuality to being referred to professionally. Coming from Allison, however, there was absolutely no stimulation whatsoever.

Realizing Allison had nothing else to add, we walked out

of the back room and over to Coltrain, who was taking off the gloves he used to inspect the old dead guy. He threw them into a white trash basket, signed the form on his clipboard, and sat down in a chair next to the body. Unfortunately, he didn't feel the need to cover old dead guy. How nice.

"Get a good look at Mr. Volkyv?" he asked.

"Rick did," I said.

"Still queasy, Keegan?"

"I just prefer to look at live people. It's a personal thing."

"Of course."

"Allison mentioned trauma to Volkyv's head that might have been ante mortem," Rick said.

"I noticed that. It was definitely before death. There was enough swelling to indicate that. My assumption is the assailant hit the victim over the head with the gun to stun him."

"Makes sense," Rick said, "Volkyv was a big guy."

"From everything I've seen, I'd guess there was about twenty minutes between the hit and the gunshot."

So, I thought, the shooter had something to say to K-Drugs before he killed him. Revenge kill, no doubt in my mind. It wouldn't be too much of a stretch to figure that K-Drugs had done something to piss someone off.

"Twenty minutes?" Rick asked. "Sure about that?"

"As sure as I can be. It's all in the report." Coltrain reached in front of him, grabbed a folder, and tossed it to Rick.

"What about the trauma to the groin?" I asked.

"Postmortem, no question about it."

"Interesting," I said.

"Might just have been to add insult to injury. Guy must have kicked him a dozen times. Both testicles were crushed."

Ouch. I cringed a little, just thinking about that.

"So, we have a man who was hit over the head, possibly

tormented for a time, shot in the back of the head, then kicked in the groin for good measure," Rick said.

"That's about right."

"Someone must have been pissed at this guy," I said.

"That's for you guys to decide. Want to know about the toxicology report?"

"Why not?"

"Blood alcohol level of .12. Probably was out drinking before. Also, there was a decent amount of heroin in the blood. Bad heroin, too. Was injected through the shoulder. Most of the stuff never entered the bloodstream because of the delivery method."

"So, the assailant shot him up with heroin before shooting him with the gun?" I asked.

"The heroin was certainly enough to kill him. Considering the composition of it, Volkyv would have been dead inside an hour. I think the assailant wanted to make him suffer first, then shot him."

I looked at Rick, and I could tell we came to the same conclusion: Revenge kill.

"So, Volkyv died a painful death. Forgive me if I don't shed a tear," I said.

"It was a rough death. He probably knew he was going to die, if you ask me. He had to have been held at gunpoint."

"Makes sense to me," Rick said.

"Go over the report. If you have any questions, please hesitate to call me," Coltrain said, offering a rare dose of humor.

"Sure thing," Rick said, seemingly missing Coltrain's sarcasm. I never miss sarcasm.

In the car, Rick said, "I want a look at the crime scene."

"So do I," I said. "After hearing all that, I want to see how everything went down. There was nothing in the preliminary report that indicated any of this."

"I noticed the same thing. You know those guys never get into any real detail. God forbid they ever do us a favor."

"When does anyone ever do us a favor?" I asked.

"Exactly."

I drove back toward Volkyv's apartment. Neither one of us talked. Again, Rick didn't say anything. He just looked out the window. I wanted to know what was running through his mind. Okay, maybe I didn't, but I wondered.

I knew Mrs. Federov would be happy to see us. I wasn't disappointed when she rolled her eyes at us after opening the door.

"Did you not get enough information?" she asked.

"Now, Mrs. Federov, I know we are exactly the two people you were hoping to see again today, but you don't have to make that so obvious," I said.

"What do you want?"

"We need to see Mr. Volkyv's apartment," Rick said.

"Of course." She went into her apartment and came out with the key. "I believe everything you want to see is in the kitchen."

Rick took the key and opened the door to Volkyv's apartment. I caught a peek at Mrs. Federov's rear end as she walked back into her apartment. Well, okay, I am kidding. There are some female rear ends I have no interest in seeing. Not many, but some.

Volkyv's apartment stunk of death. This is a very hard smell to describe. If you've never smelled death, the rank, sulfurous odor that accompanies most dead bodies, then anything I can tell you about it will do no good. Dead smell resembles no other odor I can think of.

The first room in the small apartment was the living room, which was clean, almost as if no one lived there. I wondered if Mrs. Federov was responsible, or if K-Drugs was an anal-retentive drug dealer. The thought crept into my head that Federov might have cleaned the apartment after finding the body. There was no way to know this, and I could find no reason why should would do any work that wasn't required of her. I couldn't imagine her doing that.

"Clean," I said to Rick.

"Anything compared to your apartment would be considered clean."

"You really know how to make a guy feel good," I said.

"I learned from the best."

Was he directing that last comment at me? I decided it was best not to ask. I didn't want to get pissed of at Rick already. It should take at least a few more hours for that.

"Let's just get to what we have to do," I said.

"Of course."

Volkyv's living room was lavishly furnished. He had modern, black leather furniture, a huge entertainment center, and a black lacquer coffee table that looked expensive. He also had some random paintings on the walls. Nothing I recognized, but certainly pricey.

The carpet was plush. It felt like walking on air. It didn't make me feel any better when I mentally compared it to the beaten hardwood floor in my living room. Like I said, the people who break the law live better than the ones who enforce it. Sure, we cops can put our head on the pillow at night at ease, compared to how guilty these guys felt. Of course.

Rick walked right into the kitchen, right past the dining set that looked like it belonged somewhere in Beverly Hills, past the fancy sculpture of a naked woman that was both tasteful and erotic. Rick didn't seem interested in these items. The only reason I was stemmed from pure jealousy, disdain at the world and the way it ran itself. Justice lied somewhere. Of course, K-Drugs was dead, but that didn't satisfy me. I wanted him to live in near poverty, struggle to make a rent payment, look at an item in the window of a shop and lust after it, knowing that neither his bank account nor his credit card limit allowed such a purchase. Maybe he had experienced that when he was younger, maybe that explained his turn to the drug world. I didn't know that for sure, so it was no consolation at all.

Though everything looked clean and orderly in the pictures, the kitchen was a mess. I had thought the initial investigating officers had done a good job of securing the scene, but looking at it right then, I realized they botched the whole thing. Footprints were all over the place, blood footprints, and there was no real way of discerning which ones were from the officers, which ones were Federov's, and which ones belonged to the assailant and victim. Well, that's what they were officially called. Mentally, I referred to them as live scumbag and dead scumbag, the latter of which being the preferred sort of scumbag.

"Christ," I said.

"Some mess."

"What, they decide to hold a dance recital in here?"

"Footprints, footprints, and more footprints," Rick said, crouching down to get a look. The container of milk was still on the floor. I wondered if it was spoiled. Children all over the world were dying of hunger, and K-Drugs lets a perfectly good half-gallon of milk go bad. The nerve.

I crouched down myself, analyzing the footprints as best I could. I recognized a Rockport logo, and assumed those footprints came from one of the officers. Most guys on the beat wore Rockports. I did. They were comfortable. Go buy a pair. Maybe Rockport will give me some sort of endorsement deal. I have a killer smile.

The outline of K-Drugs' body matched the photos perfectly. What had interested me in the beginning was the fact that he didn't appear to have fallen far. Instead, it looked like he had slumped over. K-Drugs' head normally was pretty far from the ground, so this meant to me that he might not have been standing when he was shot. This coincided perfectly with what Coltrain told us earlier. The killer had taken his time killing K-Drugs. Somehow, I saw justice in that. Kill me for making such a judgment. Before you do, however, meet a guy like K-Drugs. Introduce him to your family. Then decide if you want to kill me.

Behind the outline of what was once K-Drugs, I noticed two footprints. They were actually in the range of the refrigerator door. The assailant had stood there when he shot our dead drug dealer. This, I was certain of.

I pointed at the footprints and said, "Assailant."

Rick moved closer, careful not to smudge any of the other footprints. "I agree. He stood there when he shot Volkyv. "

"Better get a photo of that."

Rick took out a small camera he always carried during an investigation. Had to hand it to Rick. He always had all the bases covered. He snapped three shots of the footprints, then took out his cell phone. He called Geiger and told him he wanted lab guys down at the scene to get an imprint of the marks, so they could get a make and size of the shoe. This sort of evidence rarely led to a suspect, but it helped nail a suspect at trial. Sure, thousands of guys could be wearing size 9 Ballys, but if you were a guy who had dealings with the deceased, didn't have a good alibi, and bloody clothes were found at your apartment, well, then, those shoes are going to help do you in. You'd be surprised how many suspects don't throw away their shoes after committing murder. Lose your attachment to your footwear and clothing if you intend to kill someone. Or—call me crazy for this—lose your attachment to whatever it is that makes you want to kill someone. If it is your twisted head that is causing the problem, blow it off.

Rick hung up his phone. He looked at me for a second, then looked away.

"What?" I asked.

"Nothing."

"It wasn't nothing. If it was nothing, you wouldn't have looked at me. You'd have looked at this blood caked floor, or maybe the ceiling, or maybe the open refrigerator."

"It's nothing," Rick said.

"It wasn't nothing. Say it was something and you don't want to talk about it, but don't lie and say it was nothing."

"Alright, Christ, I forgot how much of a pain in the ass you can be. It's just good to be working with you again. Man, I never thought I'd ever say that, let alone think it. But I mean it."

"Yeah, don't get all soft on me. I get the feeling we are in another frickin' mess here. We do seem to have all the luck, don't we?" I asked.

"Hey, this was going to be your case either way. I was just added to the roster. Any bad karma floating around is yours, not mine," Rick said.

Did everyone feel this way?

"Thanks."

"Don't mention it."

Not wanting to mess around with anything else in the kitchen before the lab guys got there, Rick and I spent time going through the rest of the apartment. We didn't find much, everything was neat, but I did score a bank statement out of K-Drugs' nightstand drawer. I'd found a half-empty box of condoms and four porno tapes in there too, but the condoms were too small and the tapes weren't my taste. The bank statement was the only thing of use we found in the whole apartment. Interestingly, we didn't find any junk. I don't mean clutter, I mean the junk that gets you high. K-Drugs had none. Anywhere. I'd found a false floor in the closet, but there was only an empty strong box in there, not even locked. This I found strange.

Also, there had been no shell casing in the kitchen. Maybe it had fallen underneath the refrigerator, I thought, and I wasn't about to try and move that thing before the lab guys got there. Something told me there was no shell casing. We waited by in the entranceway to the apartment building for the lab guys for another ten minutes.

Dan Schmidt, a guy I'd worked with before, showed up with some tall, stringy-looking guy I had never seen. Dan recognized me and smiled.

"In waist deep again, Keegan?" he asked, shaking my hand.

"Probably higher than that. I am working with Calhill."

"Chest deep," Rick said.

Schmidt looked at Rick for a second, then I saw a glimmer of recognition, and Schmidt looked away for a second. Everyone involved with the NYPD knew what happened to Rick, and most people had no idea how to deal with it. Guess I couldn't blame them. I couldn't tell if Rick saw the same thing I did, but I figured if he had. He'd gotten used to it already.

Schmidt and his blonde string bean partner walked into the apartment and we led them toward the kitchen. Seeing that I could be of no real immediate help, I went outside to smoke a cigarette. Sure, everyone hated the fact that I smoked, but no one realized that smoking let me think, and I came up with some of my best brainstorms while smoking. The only better place I thought was in the bathroom. I'd tried to join the two, but let's just say that I almost became Johanna Keegan after that debacle.

And no, that cigarette I had outside K-Drugs' apartment did not yield any genius-like thoughts. It just tasted good, and it relaxed me. What more could I ask for?

"They're done," Rick said, opening the screen door.

I flicked the cigarette out onto the sidewalk. "Then, so am I."

"Thank God," Rick muttered, as I walked past him and into the apartment.

I entered the kitchen and saw Schmidt and String Bean packing up.

"Okay if I move that refrigerator now?" I asked.

"Dance the jig if you want, we've got everything we need in here."

"Why didn't you guys come down earlier?" Rick asked.

"Higher ups wanted Homicide to have a look first."

"That makes sense," Rick said, but something told me he didn't believe that. I certainly didn't.

"You guys catch the blood and brain matter on the wall there?" String Bean asked. His voice cracked a little bit, and I would have bet he was going through puberty if he didn't work for the lab.

"No," Rick said, walking over to the wall near the light switch. "Bullet entered here too," he said.

Schmidt held up a plastic bag. "Got it right here. Looks like a .357 Magnum. Someone wanted this guy dead."

Looking at the wall, I realized my theory about K-Drugs being on his knees was dead on. The angle of trajectory dictated that, if old K had been standing up, the bullet would have entered the wall almost at the ceiling. I was no expert mathematician, but this made way too much sense to me.

"He was kneeling," I said to Rick.

"Yep," he said, almost as if he didn't hear me. He seemed real interested in the hole in the wall.

"Got something there?" I asked.

"No. Just getting a good look."

"Well, as soon as you have had enough of a look, do me a favor and help me move this refrigerator."

"Looking for scraps of food? Forget to go shopping again?" Rick asked. He wasn't the one for humor, but I did appreciate his attempts.

"I am looking for a shell casing. If you haven't already noticed, there wasn't one found yet."

"I had noticed, thanks. What makes you think it is under the fridge?"

"I don't think it is," I said, "but this is the only place I haven't gotten a look at yet."

"Right," Rick said, walking over to me. "Let's go."

With a few more strains than I would have liked, we were able to swing the refrigerator out far enough to see what was behind it and underneath it. I needed to start going to the gym. It made me feel a little better to hear Rick breathing heavy. He went to the gym more often than he went to the bathroom. Then again, with all the fiber in his diet, that was a tough call.

"Nothing but dust and crumbs," Rick said. It looked like old Mrs. Federov just swept everything from the kitchen underneath the fridge. Not a shocking revelation.

I bent down to take a closer look at the floor, and noticed Rick was right. No shell casing. The killer had taken it with him. At least, that was my assumption. I'd have to make sure one of the original investigating officers didn't pick it up as evidence. Yes, they sometimes forgot to type that in their initial reports. Incompetence knows no bounds in this world. Trust me on that.

Having gone through the apartment as best we could, we were done with the crime scene. We had to wait for the lab report on the blood, the footprints, and anything else Schmidt and String Bean came up with. I've read that the first 48 hours of a murder investigation are crucial, that if a suspect isn't found in this time, the chances of solving the case go down drastically. Don't believe everything you read. I'd solved plenty of cases where I didn't find a suspect until the 49th hour. Still, there is some validity in that statement. More importantly, it is easy to tell in the first 12 hours of an investigation what your chances are of finding the killer. Judging from what we had so far, I didn't think Rick and I had a shot at finding the killer of K-Drugs. Maybe the guy deserved to get away with it. Maybe his son had gotten cranked up on some of K-Drugs' bad dope, and he came calling. That made me think. It would be a good idea to check any OD deaths in the city within the last few days. It might not have led anywhere, but at least it was something to do. And, I needed to visit a friend of mine, a guy in Vice who would most likely know K-Drugs, and have a line on who would want him dead.

4

Back at the precinct, Rick went off to check K-Drugs' finances through the bank statement. That was a one-man job, so I told him I had a few things to check out. We hugged each other tightly, patted each other on the back, and went out separate ways. Then, I walked into the bathroom, and puked my brains out. I assume you get the picture.

Karl Lavin was an imbecile. Understand I mean this in the best of ways, but even he would never dispute it. Most guys get assigned to Vice against their will, and the ones who choose that beat are usually crankheads themselves, looking for easy scores. Lavin had gotten assigned, and after doing a few years, he was offered several times an opportunity to get out. He refused every time. That's why I said he was an imbecile. At least, that's what all the other guys said. I knew better. I knew why he stayed, what drove him. He hated pedophiles and drug dealers. With a passion. I respected that, because I did too. Nothing worse than some sick bastard who preys on children. They should all be burned. Better yet, Karl Lavin should catch them all. He'd make them wish they were burned.

"Avon calling," I said, after rapping on his doorjamb. Karl was busy pouring over some paperwork. This was the reason why I turned down Vice nearly eleven years before. Believe it or not, Vice paperwork made Homicide paperwork look like a breeze.

"Figures you'd be selling powder puffs," Karl said, still looking down at his paperwork.

"It cuts down on my forehead shine," I said, taking a seat in the chair opposite Karl.

"Guinea like you has to worry about such things."

"Yeah, you Semites are oil free."

Karl pushed his paperwork aside. He looked at me, then smiled. "Last time you came into my office like this, we both almost got fired."

"Well, at least we had fun."

"What do you need? Don't even try to tell me you came here just to see me."

"Of course I did. I just wanted to see how much hair you had left."

Karl defensively ran his fingers through his thinning black hair. "At least it doesn't stop me from getting laid."

"Only when you run out of money will you go without sex," I said.

"What do you want?"

"Need to run a name by you."

"Shoot."

"Kostya Volkyv."

Karl thought for a moment, then shook his head. "Doesn't ring a bell."

"K-Drugs?"

"Ah, now that name I know. And it is *Konstantin* Volkyv. Get your names right."

"All his good friends called him Kostya."

"No, his friends called him K-Drugs. What is your dealing with him?" Karl asked.

"I needed some good shit," I said.

"He wouldn't be the guy to go to for that."

"He's dead. And I have the case."

"How sweet. Just what you needed, a dope dealer biting the bullet when you had no active case."

"Exactly what I thought."

"What do you need to know about K-Drugs?" Karl looked around his office. "I have a file on him around here somewhere. Busted him twice, but he walked. Heard he did some time for rape, though."

"He did. I just need to know if you know of anyone who might want him dead."

"Just about anyone that bought a significant amount of drugs from him. He sold bad shit and sold it like it was gold. I'm surprised he lived as long as he did."

"Someone made this a revenge kill, at least that's what I think."

"Why?" Karl asked.

"The way the whole thing was carried out. Knocked over the head, tormented for about half an hour, then shot in the back of the head after being cranked up on his own shit. Then, for good measure, the killer kicked him in the nuts half a dozen times. Busted both of his balls."

Karl coughed out a chuckle. "If anyone had it coming," he said, "it was our friend K-Drugs."

"Who did he run with?" I asked.

"Mainly Russkies. They have some good representation in Brooklyn. They basically run most of the area. He did most of his business there. He busted some legs, did some other heavy work on the side. I could put you in touch with Chris Galbadon over there. He knows a lot about the Russian mob in that area."

"Great."

Karl wrote down a phone number and handed it to me. Before I took it, he said, "Be careful asking questions down there. Those guys really don't care about killing anyone, including cops. Tone down your usual friendly attitude if you are going to ask about K-Drugs, okay?"

"Yeah, sure," I said.

"I mean it."

"I know you do. Rick will be with me, so he'll keep me in check."

Karl was taken aback by this. "He's back in the field?"

"Yep," I said.

"And partnered with *you*?"

"For this case," I said.

"How do you feel about that? I mean, after all that's happened." Karl had been there when I beat Rick to a mess. He was the one that pulled me off him.

"I think it's great. We've moved past it, and working with me will help Rick get back into the swing of things."

"Or send him off the deep end."

"I don't think so," I said, though I have to admit, before Karl said that, I had never thought of such a thing. Perhaps working with me could make Rick worse. I had to keep an eye on that.

"Your choice. Just be careful."

I stood up and shook Karl's hand. "Yeah, no problem. Thanks for the help."

"Any time. I just hope this is all the help you are going to need."

"So do I," I said, and walked out of his office.

My next step was to check on that idea I had. I wanted to do a quick check of heroin OD deaths within the last ten days or so, just to see if possibly there was a link between one of those deaths and K-Drugs' demise. This could only be called a stretch, but I liked to be thorough whenever I could. Also, I had time to kill. K-Drugs' death certainly appeared to be a revenge kill; all the evidence pointed toward that. Maybe someone lost a child, a husband, a wife, someone important to them. K-Drugs sold bad heroin. Perhaps there was something there.

I went to the computer lab and logged on to the database. Not so long before, the Homicide Department computer lab was constantly filled with detectives playing computer golf for money. One of the biggest culprits, Sergeant Peters, a guy who lost thousands at this game, had left the precinct against his will. I hated the guy, both for personal and professional reasons, and was all too happy to see him go. With him went the computer game gambling. Maybe I mentioned the gambling to Geiger. Maybe I pointed fingers. I might even have had something to do with Peters getting his walking papers. I'll never tell.

I know my way around a computer. I'm not as good as some people, like Rick for instance, but I can do what I have to do. Rick was another guy that spent a lot of time in the department computer lab, but his vice was more along the lines of chat rooms and instant messages, and this vice is what led to the tragedy he endured. Just sitting in that computer lab started to get creepy.

I found the list of OD deaths, then sorted them by the drug. There were twelve heroin OD deaths in the five boroughs over the last ten days. That's a lot of people. I always understood the allure of drugs, the desire to get involved in something that can transport you to a new reality. Still, the horrors and the realization of what sort of transportation you get from heroin baffled me. Well, the attraction is what baffled me. The moment you look in the mirror and see that you've lost three teeth, or the instant you are injecting the shit into your penis because all of your other veins are wasted, some bell should go off. Unfortunately for these twelve people, the bell must have been broken.

Instantly, I was able to cross a half a dozen people off the list. I discounted anyone who had a previous arrest history, along with anyone who was labeled as homeless. I might have been making a mistake there, a quick judgment perhaps, but it was highly doubtful that either type of person would have a family member or friend wanting revenge when they couldn't get them off the street. I was looking for a new user, someone with no criminal past, someone who experimented with the stuff and died from the experiment.

I saw something of interest. One person, a male, 25 years old with no criminal history whatsoever, died in Brooklyn. According to Karl, that was K-Drugs' stomping ground. Kid's name was Steven Troiano. I checked further, getting the father's name and record. He'd been arrested for assault twice. Once for a bar brawl, second time for an altercation after a car accident. Seemed to be a hothead. Guy had a gun license, too. I'd have to check deeper, but it seemed I might have had something there.

I printed the record, and walked through the precinct, toward where hardcopy records were held, to see what sort of gun Mr. Troiano had registered. Before I got there, Geiger stopped me in the hallway.

"Keegan," he said. This was his standard greeting to me. He called most guys by their first name, but chose my last name. Interesting.

"Yes," I said.

"How is everything going?"

"Crime scene was a fucking mess," I said, "footprints everywhere."

"I heard. Sorry about that. I would have gotten you guys on the scene right away, but I had that other issue to think about."

"It's alright. I think we made heads or tails out of it all. Got some good prints, along with a general idea of what happened and when."

"Tell me," Geiger said.

"Well, it's early, but I think this was some sort of revenge kill." I told Geiger about the head wound, the tormenting, and the kicks in the groin. I also told him that I believed K-Drugs was kneeling when he was shot.

"Good work. That all makes sense to me. What else?"

"Well, the victim was a drug dealer, so I spoke to Lavin and found out where he ran his business. Brooklyn. He gave me a contact at the precinct down there, and I am going to follow up on that."

"Where's Calhill?" Geiger asked.

"Checking the victim's bank records. We found a statement in his night stand."

"How is he?"

"Quieter than normal, which is a blessing. Other than that, he seems fine. Still as good as he was."

"You're sure? You'd tell me if there was a problem?"

I smiled. "When have I ever not told you when there was a problem with Calhill?"

"Good point. What are you doing now?"

"Following up on an idea. You see, I think this was a revenge kill, and I have the feeling it involves drugs. Maybe some kid gets juiced up on this guy's bad shit, dies, and then Daddy decides it's time to take the law into his own hands."

Geiger thought about that for a moment. "A stretch."

"I know, but it could lead to something. You never now."

"Got anything solid?"

I told Geiger about Troiano. "Be careful. I don't want you pointing fingers at innocent people because you have a hunch."

"I'll run everything by you. I'll check out Volkyv's stomping grounds first. If it turns out that this Troiano kid bought his drugs from him, and Troiano's father owns a weapon similar to the one that killed Volkyv, then I'll take it a step further. Fair?"

"Sounds good to me. And keep an eye on Calhill. I am still worried about him," Geiger said.

"Sure thing."

I got to the records department, where Pauline McCrory worked. She had gotten assigned to the position only a few months before. Pauline should never have been a cop, she was just too attractive. She had long, curly brown hair, green eyes, and a body that just screamed to be held. And I was the sort of guy that would hold it for her. I made veiled passes at her that she just kicked aside like an agile goalie, but I think I penetrated her mind at one point. Of course, I knew for sure this would go nowhere. I just liked to look at her.

Pauline came to the counter, saw me, and said, "Looking for a record that doesn't exist again, Keegan?"

"No, this one is legit."

"Of course it is." Pauline wasn't wearing any makeup, though it looked like she was. I really liked the sort of woman that didn't need to pretty herself up to be pretty.

I handed Pauline the printout. "I want to see what sort of guns this man has registered."

"Do you need this right now?" she asked.

"Not really. I could sit here and talk to you for a while, if you prefer."

"I'll get right on it," Pauline said.

"Yeah, thanks." If I had any pride, it might have been wounded right there.

Pauline walked to the back. I refrained from looking at her rear end. Sure, hers was one I liked to see, but I'd seen it before and didn't want to risk getting caught. I have some scruples, though it takes some time to locate them.

After about five minutes, Pauline came back. She handed me a sheet of paper, along with the one I had given her.

"Got a few guns there," she said.

Steven Troiano, Sr. had seven guns, to be exact. They ranged from a .22 Ruger to a .45 Smith and Wesson automatic, to, you guessed it, a .357 Magnum. No, it didn't mean anything yet, but I still got a little excited.

Pauline must have noticed this because she asked, "See what you were looking for?"

"Think so," I said.

"Glad I could be of help."

"Pauline, you are always of some sort of help."

"Watch it, Keegan. You still don't know if I like you or not."

"I just assume you don't. That's how most people feel."

This got a chuckle from her. See, I am a master when it comes to the ladies.

I caught Rick at his desk. He had a bunch of papers he was going through. I almost didn't want to interrupt him, but he heard me coming and put the papers down.

"How'd you do?" he asked.

"Got some information. Not sure if any of it means anything, but I guess we'll have to wait and see."

"Well, I've got something too." He reached for one of the pieces of paper. "Volkyv regularly made deposits—cash deposits—but he always kept them below a certain number. He was pretty smart that way. But, he made four consecutive deposits of ten grand a few days before he died."

Drug dealers rarely banked their cash. We'd find out later that K-Drugs had a way of funneling that cash to legitimacy. This was yet another unfair advantage the dirtbags had over the average working man.

Rick handed me the paper, and I saw the deposits. "Maybe business was good that week," I said.

"Maybe, but I don't think so. This screams of some sort of payoff, or something like that. He came into a good amount of money real fast, and it made him change his way of handling his money. He got sloppy. Gotta be a reason for that."

What K-Drugs got paid for, I had no idea. I told Rick what I had found out about Volkyv, and about Troiano.

"That's an interesting slant," Rick said about Troiano, "I don't know if it means anything, but we have to check that out."

"Exactly what I figured."

"Speak to Geiger?" Rick asked.

"Yes."

"He's handling me with kid gloves. I don't like it."

"Well, you can't blame him. He's worried about you, and I think he only has your best interests in mind. Plus, if you do have a problem, don't think you can't talk to me about it."

Rick made a funny expression, almost a wince, then said,

"John, every day is a problem. I think about my wife every day, every night when I put my head on the pillow. Each time I see my kids, I think about the fact that they don't have a mother, and that, even though I know it wasn't my fault, I might have something to do with it." I started to say something, but Rick held up a hand. "Don't say anything. I know it wasn't me that did all that. I know I did something wrong, but I also know it was Andrea's reaction to it all that caused all of this. I am fully aware of that. Still, it's hard."

I didn't know what to say, so I said, "I know."

"Working is the only thing keeping my mind from it. When Geiger had me working with the old files, I had too much time to think about everything. Now, I am in the middle of something. I am working toward something. Sure, Volkyv was just some dirtbag who probably earned the bullet he got in the back of the head. Still, finding his killer will make me feel like I have done something again. It will make me feel valuable again."

"Rick, you were always valuable to this department, and you always will be. Don't put too much pressure on yourself to solve this case. The odds are against us on this one."

"I know," Rick said, exhaling. "Even if I do everything I can, if I come up with ideas that could lead in the right direction, that would be enough. I'll know I still have it, that I can still do it, that I can still support my kids doing something I enjoy."

"Hey, I can't argue with that. I'll do everything I can," I said.

"You've already done your share, John. Most guys would never work with me after all we have been through."

I didn't want to get into that conversation again. Like I said before, I'd put that in the past. I wanted Rick to do the same. "Let's just focus our efforts on doing what we can here. So far, if you ask me, we've done a pretty good job."

"I think so. I particularly like the direction you went in,"

Rick said. "Two years ago, I would never have expected something like that from you. You've come a long way from the guy who used to be pissed off about everything."

"I still am. Just don't get me started down that road."

"Of course. And don't ask you to go to a healthy restaurant for lunch."

"Exactly. We'll be fine, then."

"What do you want to do first?" Rick asked.

"I'd like to take a trip to Brooklyn, see what Lavin's guy down at the precinct has on Volkyv. Maybe we can get some idea of who his customers were and who his enemies were."

"I get the feeling the two may be one and the same."

"Can't argue that."

"Let's go. But I am driving. Your driving makes me sick to my stomach."

"Careful, Rick. Keep that up and I might think you are completely back to normal."

"Some things will never change."

5

I decided to be nice and let Rick drive. I really didn't like driving all that much in the first place. I preferred to be driven, but I couldn't let Rick know that. He drove like an old woman without her glasses; only the old woman would probably be a little heavier on the gas pedal. It took us forty-five minutes to get to Brooklyn. I could have gotten there in twenty, no exaggeration.

I'd been to the Brooklyn precinct we were going to before. I worked a beat there for three months straight out of the academy, and I hated it. Irish people generally had a hard time in that area. Italians, and more recently, Russians dominated it. Even though I had Italian in my blood, the name Keegan, not ending in a vowel, didn't make Italian people warm to me. I got called 'Mick' more times than I ever had in my life. Of course, I've been called worse than that.

Going back to an old precinct usually meant seeing people I worked with, chatting about nothing important, and basically wasting time. Fortunately for me, the guys I worked with at the Brooklyn precinct had all moved on, and no one recognized me when I walked in the door. Nice.

The desk sergeant was busy writing something when Rick and I approached the desk. It was more like a judge's bench, with the sergeant looking down on us like two perps awaiting sentence.

I coughed to get his attention. He looked at us, and made us for cops right away. We all have that intuitive ability. And no, it is not in any way related to the scent of donuts, thank you.

"What do you need?" the guy asked. He seemed real happy to have desk duty.

"Came here to see Sergeant Galbadon," I said. The sergeant peered over his half-glasses at me. He was bald, with gray hair at the temples, and a thick, red nose supporting the glasses.

"Let me see if he is in." He picked up the phone and rang Galbadon. "Two Manhattan boys to see you," he said, loud enough for us to hear him. I wasn't aware of any borough conflicts going on, but then again, I never paid attention to such things.

"You Keegan?"

"So I'm told," I said.

The sergeant hit a buzzer, unlocking the half-door to my left. "He's in the back, last desk by the window."

Rick and I walked through the door, through another door, and into the main part of the precinct. It was much different than our precinct, a lot older. The ceilings in the main room were high, with ancient fans over almost every desk. The place was quiet, probably because it was time for the shift change. I did notice one guy handcuffed to a desk in the center of the room, no one around him. He looked homeless, and he saluted us with his free hand as we walked by.

Chris Galbadon was a huge man. He stood at about 6'3", and was a mountain of muscle, or at least it seemed so underneath his shirt and tie. He had light brown hair, and carved features. He looked like a bodybuilder I had seen in a magazine years before. Not so much like Arnold Schwarzenegger, but pretty close as far as build was concerned. I decided Chris would be a good guy to keep on my side.

"John Keegan?" Chris asked, when he saw Rick and I approach. He stood up, and stuck out his hand. I shook it, losing my hand in his big mitt.

"That's me. This is my partner, Rick Calhill." Chris shook

his hand, and I saw a flicker of recognition in his eyes. Like I said, everyone knew about what happened to Rick.

"Lavin told me you'd be coming down. Got some questions about the Russians?"

"Yeah, why is it the only thing they make well is vodka?"

Chris laughed, and then gestured for us to sit down. "Anyone in particular you need to know about?"

I sat in the highly uncomfortable wooden chair to Chris' right. "Konstantin Volkyv, more famously known as K-Drugs."

Chris raised an eyebrow. I hate people who can do that, raise one brow but not the other. As a kid, I spent hours in front of the mirror trying to do that. Never had any luck. And I couldn't wiggle my ears either. I could, however, make that farting sound with my armpit better than anyone.

"K-Drugs," Chris said, "What a good citizen."

"A good, dead citizen," I said.

"I heard. Can't say I didn't see that one coming."

"What do you know about him?" Rick asked.

"A lot. He was a big part of the local Russian Mafia around here. Not a full-fledged member, but he certainly did favors. The name is well known."

"What sort of favors?" I asked.

"Well, I never could prove any of it, but rumor has it he was an accomplished leg-breaker. Not a tough guy, but he followed orders, from what I know."

"What do you mean, not a tough guy?" Rick asked.

"I think K-Drugs was real worried about getting in good with the boys around here. They run a tight ship, so breaking in isn't that easy. We have had a hard time getting someone on the inside. They know what they are doing, and K-Drugs needed their support, I think. He ran a lot of smack from what I understand, and to be under their umbrella would have benefited him."

"Makes sense," I said, "Lessens the problem of irate customers."

"Exactly. Plus, it helps with distribution."

"Do you know of anyone who might have wanted him dead?" Rick asked.

Chris chuckled. "You want a partial, or complete list?"

"How about anyone that would know what he was up to? You got a birdie on the streets?"

"I've got a few," Chris said. "Not many guys have a finger on the pulse of the Russians, but I know a few guys that might have some information on Volkyv."

"Anyone we can talk to?" Rick asked.

"Not directly. I'd have to take the ride with you."

"Do you mind?" I asked.

"Not at all. Been looking for a reason to get out of here today." Chris stood up and put on his blazer, which made his shoulders look even wider. "Let's go. I'll drive."

I made Rick sit in the back of the car by calling shotgun as we walked into the parking lot. Really, I did that. Let him look like the perp. He thought this was childish, I'm sure. It was.

"First guy we're going to see is some local punk that likes the brown lady. He doesn't really do much wrong, he's just hooked. He runs with some of the bigger guys around here, and somehow, he always seems to have heard something. Most times, he's on the money. Oh, and he just loves to see me," Chris said, while taking a left turn into an industrial area.

"What, he lives down here?" I asked.

"No, he runs his own auto parts store. You know, supes up VWs, that sort of thing."

"You would think that would be a reason to stay straight, having your own business."

Chris gave me a sideways glance.

"I was just making a general statement."

"A generally idiotic statement," Rick said from the back seat.

"Don't make me cuff you back there," I said.

"This kid, Jason's his name, he's just weak. I don't know why the big guys keep him around. If he ever gets hauled off into court to testify, he'll tell everything. He has a very low threshold."

"My sort of guy," I said.

Chris pulled the cruiser in front of a small building, where a sign announced 'VW Speed.' Idiots and their cars. I never could understand why guys would tinker for hours on end with their cars. They say a car is an extension of a man's penis. Fine. I use my penis, wash it when it needs it, and generally leave it alone. I don't tinker with it, at least not too much. I am the same way with cars.

"Does he do well?" Rick asked, as we got out of the car.

"I think so. Every time I stop by, he has several cars in the garage."

"Local mafia cars?"

Chris chuckled. "I don't think they are too big on VWs. They like more expensive German cars. Though, I have seen Jason working on a few BMWs."

"That could be his link."

"Probably. Still doesn't explain why they keep him around."

Chris had to ring a buzzer because the door was locked. "He installed this after I started coming around. It's useless, because he always answers the door when I ring."

"Maybe he needs to put things away before you come in."

"I wouldn't be surprised, but I'd never bust him. I'd lose a valuable information resource if he was sent away."

As shocking as that sounds, it's the truth. Some criminals serve a better purpose to society by staying on the streets, and a smart cop will take notice of this. Jason probably didn't do much wrong besides shoot up, so he wasn't hurting anyone staying on the street. And, as Chris said, he was a valuable information resource. There aren't enough of those.

Jason came to the door. He was a gangly kid, tall, skinny, with red hair and freckles. Certainly not the sort of guy who scored a lot of women. You could see the ravages of heroin in his eyes. His complexion was pallid, and his teeth looked in bad repair.

Jason hesitated, then opened the door. "Sergeant Galbadon, paying me a visit? I haven't seen you in a while." I think, because we were there and Jason didn't know who we were, he tried to be a bit of a wiseass, but his statement came off weak. It was obvious he was scared shitless of Chris. I couldn't blame him. If Chris told me he was going to hit me, I'd probably cry.

"Jason. Just checking up to see how you are doing. Are you going to let us in?" Chris didn't wait for an answer, he just moved past Jason and into the shop, which stunk of oil. We followed. Jason locked the door behind us.

There were seven Volkswagens about the shop, all in some form of disrepair. One, a Beetle, had been stripped of all its sheet metal. It looked like Jason had been working on that one when we buzzed.

"What can I do for you guys?" Jason asked from behind us. Chris had walked over to a Corrado sitting in the middle of the shop.

"Shame they don't make these anymore. I loved the one I had," Chris said. The car was tiny, and I couldn't picture Chris even fitting into it.

"One of the best VWs ever made," Jason said, "but I don't think you came here to talk cars."

"You are always so clever, Jason. Actually, these two friends of mine would like to talk to you for a minute."

"Friends? You mean cops?"

"We don't like civilians using that word," I said, "you can refer to us as detectives."

"Whatever."

"No, not whatever."

Jason shrugged. "What do you need?"

"What do you know about Konstantin Volkyv?" Rick asked. So much for easing in to the conversation. Rick isn't one for small talk.

"Don't know the name," Jason said.

"K-Drugs," I said.

"Oh." Jason moved to a workbench and wiped his hands with an oil-soaked rag. "What about him?"

"That's what we were asking you," I said.

"I've heard of him."

"Did you know he was dead?" Rick asked.

"No." Jason looked at Chris. "You guys don't think I had anything to do with that, do you?"

"Did you?" I asked.

"Of course not. I barely knew him."

"Barely?"

"Well, I'd seen him around a few times. Loud guy. Thick accent." Jason looked at us for some sign that he had the right guy. Not like we knew. Neither one of us said anything. "Yeah, I'd seen him. What do you want to know?"

"Ever buy from him?" Rick asked.

"Buy what?"

"It's okay," Chris said, "They know all about you."

"Great, more cops who know about me."

"Detectives."

"Right. Well, yeah, once I bought from him. Some of the other guys were trying to get everyone to buy from him. Bad idea if you ask me."

"Why?" I asked.

"He sold cheap shit at sky high prices."

"Don't all drug dealers do that?"

"Well, a lot do, but he cut his shit more than most. I think the guys were getting a piece from him, or wanted to. I bought from him once, then started going outside Brooklyn so they wouldn't see me buying from everyone else. They were trying to run the rest of the guys out of the area."

"Know anyone who would want him dead?" Rick asked.

"Sure."

"Who?"

"Anyone who ever bought from him."

"So, you wanted him dead?" I asked.

"Well, not me. That's not my way," Jason said, holding up his hands.

"When was the last time you saw him around?"

Jason thought for a moment. "About a week ago."

"Doing?"

"I saw him at a party. He was loud as usual. Talking about some job he had to do."

"What sort of job?" Rick asked.

"Big job. Said it was going to be his breakout role, that's how he put it."

"Do you know what he was supposed to do?"

Jason shook his head. "I never ask questions. I just know it was something big. He'd beaten up a few guys on contract, guys who owed money and shit like that. This was different. This job meant a lot to him. Maybe he was supposed to kill someone and got killed instead."

Though that was plausible, it didn't explain the evidence I saw. "Maybe. Do you know anyone else who might have had something to do with this job?"

Again, Jason looked at Chris, who nodded. "All of K's work came through Jaro."

"Jaro?"

"Yeah, Spanish guy who's tight with the Russians. Everyone thinks all these mafias are strictly one nationality or another. The Russians work with all types, and Jaro's tight with them. He introduced K to them, and he got K all his jobs."

"Got a last name?"

"I know who he is," Chris said. "Slippery son of a bitch."

"Anything else, Jason?" I asked.

"Well, like I said, that job was big. Jaro kept telling him to shut up about it. I overheard him tell K he was going to have to disappear afterward. I doubt K would ever do that."

"Why?" Rick asked.

"Because that's the way he was. He liked to seem important. Even if he killed someone, he would have to stay around and soak in the attention. Maybe his parents didn't love him enough or something."

"Yeah, maybe. Well, if you find out anything else, or remember anything else, I expect you'll let Sergeant Galbadon know," I said. I didn't want to give this guy my card. I didn't want him to know who we were. Rick picked up on this and didn't offer his card, either.

"Ok," Jason said.

Our next step was to find out what our new friend Jaro was up to.

Chris gave us a brief rundown of the life of Jaro Medina while we drove across town. It seemed Jaro had been in the country for seven years, and in that time, he found a way to make a ton of money, along with getting collared a few times. Each time he got arrested, he posted bail, and walked because of some inconsistency with the law. This was the most frustrating part of being a cop. You work hard, you follow the law, and some slippery piece of shit gets off because the law is full of holes. This happened to me a few times, and I sat in court, usually after staying up all night waiting for the arraignment, only to have some slick lawyer quote a loophole that lets the criminal go. I've seen good men go to prison for one stupid mistake and I have seen lifetime criminals avoid jail because they know how to work the system. And people wonder why I don't want to get out of bed sometimes.

So, Jaro was just another criminal that had gotten away

clean. That bothered me, but I knew I had to keep that in check. We needed something from him. It would be impossible to explain how degrading that was. Unfortunately, I'd done things the hard way many times, stood on principle when the principle wasn't strong enough to hold me up, and realized sometimes it was better to serve the end and stop obsessing over the means. Some cops wouldn't even think twice about looking the other way when the Jaro Medinas of the world walked by. Instead, I looked right at his type, let them know I was aware of what they were, and got what I wanted out of them.

Medina lived in a gated community, with a golf course, for Christ's sake. Chris told us that the legitimate shipping business Medina was a part of helped pay for it all. Everything on record about Medina was above board, and his criminal record had been wiped clean of two of the three arrests. Medina, if you looked at him on paper, was a model citizen who screwed up once, so who the Hell are we to point a finger and say he is bad? Yeah, I really wanted to speak to this guy.

"Have you had any dealings with him in the past?" Rick asked Chris.

"Yes. He's not untouchable, and he is extremely concerned about keeping his record clean. He'll talk to me, though I know most times he doesn't tell me half of what he knows. He's threatened to file a complaint for harassment when I've pushed him, so the best thing to do is make it known he has more to risk by staying quiet than he does by talking."

"You really think he's going to tell us about Volkyv?" I asked.

"Well, considering Volkyv is dead, and we can tie Medina to Volkyv, he might want to talk, to clear himself of suspicion."

"There might be a chance that Medina killed him," Rick said.

"I doubt that. Evidence doesn't point that way, far as I see," I said.

"You never know."

"Medina wouldn't do it himself. He keeps his hands clean, from what I know," Chris answered, "he might have ordered it, but that doesn't make sense either. He had an investment in Volkyv."

We pulled up to a gate and the security guard came out of his little shack. He was a squat man, with a gut protruding over his belt. He strode over to the car as if he were Wyatt Earp. Chris' badge stopped him cold.

"Something wrong?" he asked.

"No, we just need to visit one of your tenants," Chris said.

The security guard got his clipboard and flipped through the papers. "Which one?"

Chris waved him off. "We know how to get there."

"But I need to record—"

"No, you don't," Chris said, sternly, "just open the gate and we will be on our way."

The security guard stood there for a moment, as if he needed to think about what to do. Then, he opened the gate and let us through.

"Put a guy in a uniform and he thinks he is God," Chris said.

"I always thought I was God, even before they gave me a uniform," I said.

After doing a bit of investigating, we found that Jaro was in the middle of a round of golf. The starter, a man who looked older than he could have possibly been, told us we should be able to find the good Mr. Medina at the 11th hole. He gave us a golf cart, and we drove out there, Rick standing in the back where the golf bags go as if he were some Secret Serviceman watching out for snipers. It looked rather comical. If I was driving, I might have took a few sharp turns to see how well Rick could hold on.

There was a foursome on the 11th tee, and Chris sped over there, instantly recognizing Medina. Medina looked nothing like what I expected. Instead of a short, dark man with a thin moustache, Medina was tall, thin, and resembled an actor. He had a commanding presence, even from a distance.

We pulled up to the tee, and Medina, who was about to shoot, held up his hand to quiet us. I watched him go into a smooth backswing, then, as he was coming to hit the ball, I coughed. Loud. I couldn't help it. His shot dribbled into the bushes about twenty yards away.

"Dammit," Medina yelled. He looked at us, but he didn't know who coughed so he couldn't do anything about it.

"Jaro, the language," Chris said.

Medina looked at Chris, then rolled his eyes. He then looked at the three other men in his foursome, all Japanese, and gestured for them to tee off. Medina walked toward us, and I could tell it didn't make him happy to see us.

"Sergeant Galbadon, you are interrupting a business meeting," he said, with a tinge of annoyance.

"I apologize, but these men here need to speak to you about a very important matter."

Medina eyed us, as if he were trying to assess how dangerous we were to him. He had no idea.

"Make it quick. These men will not want to wait."

"K-Drugs," I said.

"I don't know what you are talking about."

"Konstantin Volkyv, aka K-Drugs. We know you know who he is, and we also know a good deal about your relationship with him."

Medina looked at Chris. "Is it a crime to have associates?"

"If you had committed any crime, you'd be talking to me

with your hands behind your back. Now, I'd appreciate a little cooperation."

Medina rolled his eyes, as if this were too much for him, that he was above this. "What do you want to know?"

"I want to know why he is dead."

"Dead?"

"Yes, Mr. Medina. Your *associate* was found early this morning, with a large hole in the back of his head. I thought maybe you might know something about that."

"Kostya was a wild man, with wild habits, as I am sure you know. How he found himself dead is beyond me."

"Not too far beyond," I said, meeting eyes with Medina. "He worked for you. He had a special job to do for you. Now he's dead. Something tells me the two might be related."

"Again, I don't know what you are talking about."

Chris stepped in. "Jaro, we can talk about this here, inconvenience your business associates over there for a few minutes, or we can take you down to the station and go over it, possibly ruining whatever business you have with them."

"That's not fair," Medina said.

"Fair has nothing to do with it. I want to do this the easy way, the way that involves no paperwork for me and no embarrassment for you. I leave the decision up to you."

Medina looked back at the men on the tee. One of them ducked the ball left, into the woods. He ran his hand down his expensive tan pants, then looked back at me. He glared at me, actually, as if he were angry because I found something out about him he wanted no one to know. I had no idea what that could be.

"Okay, but like I said, make it quick."

"The better your answers, the quicker it will be," Rick said.

"Ask your questions."

"What was Volkyv up to before his death?" I asked.

"Many things. I am sure you know about him, what he did."

I nodded, but didn't say anything.

"I told you, he was a wild man."

Still, neither Rick or I said anything.

"This was bound to happen to him sooner or later."

"Why is that?' Rick asked.

"He wasn't careful."

"Explain," I said.

Medina again looked at the rest of his foursome, then he looked back at Chris. "I tell you anything, it never came from me, right?"

Chris nodded.

"He'd been hired. That's all I am going to say. You can figure out what he got hired for. It was supposed to be anonymous, a way of sending a message to someone who wasn't cooperating. Four guys were hired. All Russian, though I only knew about Kostya. This job was supposed to be the final step in their initiation. I didn't like it, didn't like the smell of it."

"Did they pull it off?"

Medina looked away. "Yes."

"How do you know?" I asked.

"I just do. I am not going to say any more than that."

"You think this job got him killed?"

"I wouldn't know. But if I had to guess—"

"You would say yes," Rick said.

Medina gave him a look like he was an idiot. I would have done the same, but that would have made me look like I was siding with the slime bag. Medina, I mean.

"Who set up the job?" Rick asked.

"I don't know what you are talking about." Medina again looked at Chris, then said, "I believe I have cooperated. I told you all I know, at least all I am going to tell. They hired

Kostya to do something vicious. He paid the price in the end, if you ask me."

Of course, that last bit was a hint of sorts, but I didn't know what Medina meant, and I knew better than to push. If need be, we could always haul Medina in for questioning. Right then, all we were looking for was a lead, a finger pointing in the right direction.

We got back into the golf cart, and I decided to stand where the bags were. It looked like Rick had a good time back there. Truth be told, it was fun. More fun that it should have been. I needed excitement in my life.

Back at the precinct, Chris told us that getting any information about who ordered the job would be near impossible. This meant to me that our little excursion with Chris had ended.

"I'll keep shaking the trees to see what falls out," he said. I had this image of him hugging a big maple, nearly ripping it from the ground.

"Appreciate it," I said. "I think we learned a few things today. Hopefully some of it will help."

"Good luck."

I didn't know how much we were going to need it.

6

I drove back to the precinct, only because I couldn't imagine dealing with Rick's moronic driving. Traffic was heavy; the courts had just let out, and we were stuck on FDR, barely moving. I thought about flicking on the flashers and weaving through, but I didn't like to abuse the privilege. Plus, traffic was so dense, we wouldn't have gotten anywhere.

"What do you think?" Rick asked.

"I think we are getting closer."

"Amazing that we even have to waste our time investigating this, if you ask me. Dirtbag got killed by another dirtbag."

"True, but it beats going through the cold files, doesn't it?"

"Of course. What's your take on what Medina told us?"

"He tried to give us something without saying much. Our job is to find out what that is."

"Yeah, he said Volkyv got hired to do something vicious. Any idea what that might be?"

"Murder's the first thing that comes to my mind."

"Same here. Doubt we'll find out anything about that, though."

"Unless it was something big. I wish I knew when the job took place. That would make things a bit easier," I said, turning off FDR Drive.

"He said four guys were hired. You think they'd hire four guys for one murder?"

"I don't know. I have no idea how the Russian mob works. Could be it wasn't murder, that they were supposed to just rough someone up, scare them into cooperating."

"Could be. I still think he killed somebody, then his own people offed him," Rick said, emphasizing the word 'offed' like he knew the mob lingo. It didn't sound right.

"Then we should have three more dead Russians somewhere."

"We'll have to look into that. Unless, of course, they didn't get to them yet."

"I wish we knew someone on the inside, someone who could tell us a bit more about the Russians."

"Galbadon didn't seem to think we had much of a chance with that," Rick said.

"I know."

"You trust him?"

"Galbadon?" I asked.

"Yeah."

"I don't see why we shouldn't. Lavin said he was straight. That's all I need to hear."

"Something just isn't sitting right with me about this. Like something's right in front of us, but we just can't see it."

"Isn't that the way it always goes?"

"Unfortunately."

I pulled into the precinct parking lot. We got out of the car, and just stood in the lot for a moment. There were a dozen things we could do next, but I couldn't figure out which one was best. I still had Troiano to investigate. Maybe K-Drugs' death had nothing to do with the job he carried out for the mob. Maybe it was just a vengeance kill, like I originally thought.

"What do you know about mob kills?" Rick asked.

"What do you mean?"

"Well, I saw somewhere, that when the Russians execute someone, they usually shoot them just above the eye." Rick pointed to his eyebrow. "Sort of like a final insult. Volkyv wasn't done that way."

I'd heard about that. I just couldn't remember if I had seen it in a movie, or if it came from some sort of reliable source.

"He wasn't."

"I'd say, the way he was done, it was amateur."

"You don't think it was the mob," I said.

"I think it was, but the evidence doesn't show that."

"Evidence is rarely clear."

"True. Still, something's not sitting right."

"What if the mob did it this way so as to make it not look like a contract kill?" I asked.

"Good point. That would make sense to me."

"Well, it doesn't for me."

"Why am I not surprised?"

"Because I am not full of surprises."

"Of course not."

Geiger didn't have much to tell us. We updated him on what we found in Brooklyn, and he thought that this was good information, but he couldn't decide what it all meant either. He just said that we needed something to break. Of course we did. We had to wait for the lab analysis, and hope that something came from that. I told him I wanted to talk to Troiano, but he told me it would be best to wait on that, for us to digest what we had already found out, and see if Galbadon shook something from the trees.

Thus, my shift was over. Most times, when working on a case, I didn't have a shift. I just worked until I couldn't work anymore. Being that this wasn't a priority case, Geiger pretty much told us we should go home and think. He didn't say that exactly, but that's how I took it. I was already after five when we got out of his office, so I went to my desk, gathered my things, and got ready to leave.

"Leaving?" Rick asked.

"Yeah. Nothing else we can do until we get that lab analysis."

"We could investigate other deaths, see if any Russians turn up."

"I think it is a bit early for that."

"Well, you go home. I'll stay here and check it out."

"It can wait until tomorrow." I knew Rick didn't want to go home.

"I'll do it. I'll call you if I come up with something."

"Got it. And thanks," I said.

"No problem."

I picked up some Chinese takeout on the way home, Beef Chow Fun if you need to know. After eating, and sifting through the paper—there was a small mention of Volkyv's death—I felt the urge to unwind. This isn't something I was ever good at, unwinding, so I just flicked on the TV and let my mind turn to goo. I had checked my messages when I got home, but only had one, from my mother. She called every other day or so. I figured she just wanted to shoot the breeze. I wasn't in the mood. I didn't want to talk to anyone.

I must have been sitting there for about twenty minutes, watching a rerun of *Seinfeld*, when the phone rang. I had caller ID on my cordless phone, and noticed the call came from a hospital. I didn't want to answer the phone, but I knew I'd feel guilty if I didn't. God only knew who was in the hospital.

"Yeah," I said, mentally flinching, waiting to hear the voice at the other end of the line.

"Johnny," my mother said, "I called you twice at work, left a message at home, and you didn't call back."

"I never got the messages at work. I was out all day."

"Well, you should have called."

"What's the problem?" I asked.

"Your nephew is in the hospital. He had a seizure." I could tell my mother had been crying.

"God," I said, "Is he okay now?"

"They have him stabilized, but he is still in ICU. They don't know whether or not he'll have another one."

This might sound selfish. I really had been looking forward to spending my night doing nothing. The fact that I now had to get up, get dressed, and haul myself out to Long Island. Hey, I loved my nephew, but this is how I felt. People might think I am insensitive, but if you really think about it, a lot of people have such thoughts run through their minds. I am just honest enough to admit it.

I thought about telling my mother I couldn't make it. She hadn't asked me to come down yet. She was waiting for me to offer. I hated hospitals. Well, I can't think of anyone who really likes them. For me, hospitals are a step away from death, and I've already expressed my feelings about dead bodies. Funny I turned out to be a homicide cop.

"Are there still visiting hours?" I asked, holding out a shred of hope that she'd say I wouldn't be able to go there.

"No, but everyone is here. Your sister could really use you right now." I doubted that. I never thought that anyone in my family could actually use me. I was the last one invited to any sort of function or event, and I really couldn't remember a time when I was called just to talk, or that a relative pulled me aside because they enjoyed talking to me. Of course, I could have just been transferring my own feelings on to the situation. Kill me for it.

"Alright. I'll be there as soon as possible."

"Thank you. You'll find us in the ICU."

"Got it."

I got myself off the couch, which required more effort than it should have, dressed in a white shirt and jeans, and headed out of the house. I did my best to clear my mind, so as not to walk in to the hospital with a negative attitude. I already was considered miserable, and though I wouldn't have minded cultivating that reputation even further, I didn't think this was the place to do it.

It took me forty minutes to get to Oceanside, where South Nassau Community Hospital was. The lot was jammed, so I pulled into the Emergency Room lot. A guard walked toward me.

"That's fifteen-minute parking," the tall black man said.

I flashed him my badge. "Keep an eye on it for me?" I asked.

"Sure thing," the guard said. It was nice to get some professional courtesy every once in a while.

I entered through the Emergency Room and followed the signs to the ICU. Navigating through a hospital isn't unlike a labyrinth. I think they did this on purpose, so that you might accidentally get yourself holed up in one of the rooms, paying the high rent hospitals charge.

I found the ICU and went through the double doors. A nurse sat at the station right in front. She spotted me and held up a hand.

"Sorry," she said in a voice that was much deeper than I expected, "no visitors."

I pulled out my badge again. "I'm here to see Christian Steiner," I said.

The nurse, a fortyish blonde who wasn't all that bad looking, eyed me. She rolled her eyes. "Go ahead. He's in the back, left corner."

"Thank you," I said.

The ICU was a vivid mixture of sight, sound, and smell. Most of the people here weren't going to make it out. You could smell decay in the air, subtly lying underneath the smell of disinfectant. Various blips, beeps, and wheezing sounds emitted from all about the room, making it sound almost rhythmic. I tried not to look at any of the people lying there, but I couldn't help it. I caught a glimpse of a guy who couldn't have been five years older than my father. He lay there, half a dozen tubes going in and out of him. He was losing the battle. I could see that from the look on his wife's face. I thought about that. How, though my father didn't seem to age from the time I was a kid—in my mind, at least—but yet, time moves forward. It could have been my father lying there. Hell, in the blink of an eye, it could be me.

I didn't want to think about that anymore.

I found Christian's bed where the nurse said I would. My sister, my brother-in-law, and my mother were there. Christian was lying on the bed, asleep, his own tubes going in and out of him. He was sweaty, and to be honest, he didn't look good. Six years old and he's already had the hand of Death on his shoulder. I smoked, I ate garbage, and I didn't take care of myself, yet Death stayed away from me. Maybe it was my breath.

"John," my brother-in-law, Donny, said to me.

I put my hand on his shoulder. "Donny. How is he?" I looked over at my sister. She looked like she had been crying, and would be crying again real soon. I wanted to walk over and give her a hug, but I figured that could wait a moment.

"Doctor says there is no damage," Donny said, fighting tears, "but he doesn't know if this is an isolated incident, or a chronic problem. He could have been having small seizures for years, and we just never knew."

"God," I said.

"Thanks for coming," Donny, said, patting me on the back.

I walked over to my mother, and kissed her hello. She hugged me tightly. Man, I really felt guilty about the thought of not coming to see my family. "Thanks," was all my mother said.

I kissed my sister hello, and hugged her too, but I didn't say anything, and neither did she. I think if she tried to say something, she would have burst into tears. I just held the embrace for a moment, and moved back toward Donny. I looked at Christian, the innocent little kid who was suffering for no apparent reason. During times like this, I always wondered where the justice in the world was. I knew several criminals who lived the good life, and here was my nephew, a good kid who just wanted to be loved, suffering. There was no sense to be made of it.

"You okay?" I asked Donny, quietly.

"I think so. I'm trying."

"Need anything?"

He shook his head. Donny, though I didn't think much of him in the beginning, turned out to be an excellent father. He treated his kids and my sister right, and that was all a brother could ask.

"Where's Dad?" I asked.

"In the waiting room. He needed some air," he said.

I could understand that. The ICU stunk, and the lingering feeling I had gotten from everyone, though unspoken, was that Christian wouldn't survive another seizure. That would be the only reason why they had him in the ICU. I decided to go see my father.

"I'll go see how he is doing," I said.

"Okay," Donny said. I looked at my mother, and she nodded toward me, as if giving her approval of my decision.

I walked out of the ICU, and toward the waiting room. I couldn't imagine a room where more tears were shed than the waiting room of an ICU. Not much good news is heard in such a room.

My father was sitting in the corner. He didn't look good. He looked stressed. I guess seeing a grandchild go through something so horrible must wear on you. I don't have grandkids, so I really can't comment on that.

"John," my father said, when he noticed me. He stood up. I walked over and hugged him.

"Hi Dad," I said.

He took a step back, looked at me, and said, "You should have called as soon as you got the messages."

Here we go, I thought. "I didn't get the messages at work," I replied.

"Of course you didn't."

"Are you saying I didn't?"

"Come on, you always used to like to tell your little white lies to get yourself out of trouble," my father said.

"Don't start that," I said, "not here. Not now."

"It's true."

"It *was* true."

"You always told your little lies," my father said again. I really didn't know what he was up to. My father was a straightforward guy. This made no sense to me.

"Enough," I said.

"Don't talk to me that way," he said.

"How about you don't talk to me that way?"

"I am your father."

"Right. You're also a man. So am I. Maybe one day you'll realize that and show me the respect that comes with it."

This didn't sit well with my father. He glared at me. "Respect?"

"That's right. Now, let's just drop this. Like I said, this isn't the time or the place."

"I'll decide what the right time and place are."

"Oh, you will?"

"Yes. I know you like to think you are in control when you are with your friends and all that, but I'm not going to stand for it. Your mother called with a family emergency, and you just decided it wasn't important enough to warrant a return phone call."

"What are you talking about? I already told you I never got those messages."

"And the one at home?"

"Mom just said to call her back. She always says that."

"And you never call back. Look where that got you this time."

I tried to control my anger. Like I said, I didn't know where this was coming from. I did understand that, no matter how old I got, my father always saw me as a child. Maybe some parents can make the transition, but I think most can't. What the parents don't understand is, when their children are adults, they think like adults, and make the stupid assumption that they should be treated as such. There were times when I just grew tired of the fact that my father forever thought of me as fourteen. I tried to remove all of this frustration right then, but I must admit, I failed miserably.

"Just drop it. I don't want to argue right now."

"Of course you don't. You know it all, I know nothing. Isn't that right?" my father asked.

"What? I didn't say that. Come on, everyone's inside. This is a tough moment. Let's let it go."

But for some reason, my father didn't want to. "I want to know why you didn't call back."

"I don't care about the family. I only care about myself. Is that what you want to hear?"

"That sounds more like the truth than anything else you've said so far."

"I'm not going to listen to this. I don't deserve it. You've got something stuck up your ass, so you deal with it."

I turned to walk back into the ICU. My father walked right up to me.

"You always have some fucking excuse for why you can't come around, why you can't show up for family functions. Everyone else sacrifices but you. You're the special one."

My father really was never like this. I told myself this all came from the stress he was under because of Christian. Still, it got to me. "Well, with this sort of treatment, do I really have to explain why?"

"Oh, now you're the one that's always treated poorly. Poor Johnny. Never gets treated right."

That was it. I couldn't take it anymore. The anger built up, and I had to let it out. I said four words that, for the rest of my life, I would never forget. "Go to Hell, Dad," I said, and walked back into the ICU.

7

I walked back into the ICU, and told everyone that I had to go. There really was no sense in sticking around, and I certainly didn't want to make a scene with my father in front of everyone. I think it was obvious, by the look on my face, that my little meeting with my father didn't go well, but no one said anything and no one made a comment about the fact that I was leaving. It pissed me off that I went all the way out there just to get shit thrown in my face. I was angry at my father, incensed that he was able to get to me the way he did. I couldn't understand it. We had gotten along fine for years. Something was on his mind, but I was in no position to ask what it was. Life really sucks sometimes.

I couldn't go home. I had way too much anger built up. It was stewing in my gut, tearing out my already beaten insides. The only thing to do was drown this problem with alcohol, so I went to a local bar I found myself in more times than I should have. I guess a lot of us find ourselves in bars more often than we should. That's why there are so many bars in the world.

Kasey's was quiet, thankfully. A new guy was tending bar, some young kid who always wore rolled up short sleeves to show off his muscles. These guys bothered me. It was as if they thought that a large bicep validated them somehow, set them above guys who didn't have bulging muscles. To me it meant the kid had too much free time on his hands, and spent it either at the gym or in front of a mirror. Plus, it doesn't matter if you can curl 100 pounds, especially if you can't take a good right hand on the chin.

I took a seat at the bar, something I rarely did. Actually, I shouldn't have that night. It turned out that the seat I took was the one I sat in when I had first gone out with Emily Brackens. Bringing her memory back right then was possibly the worst thing I could have done, but it was too late. I could see her sitting next to me, giving me that look she always gave, the one that insinuated I was out of my mind. For someone I knew for only a short time, she had this uncanny ability to see right through me, right through the face I show to the world. She knew 90 percent of what I said was bullshit, statements to draw a reaction out of people. Most people took me seriously, which meant most people thought I was insane. Emily knew better, and I instantly loved her and hated her for it.

The overly buff bartender came over. He was too good-looking a guy, and at that moment, I wanted to rap him across the teeth to fix that problem.

"What do you need, buddy?" the guy asked.

I need you to not call me buddy, I thought. I need you to shut up and pour me a drink, and then go back to posing in front of the mirror. I need to finally be understood by the people close to me, ones that aren't dead or not talking to me. Well, I guess what I really needed was a drink.

"Dewars on the rocks, splash of water," I said.

The bartender looked at me for a moment. "You a cop?"

"I'm a customer. One that needs a drink."

"You look familiar."

"Maybe you saw my picture hanging up in the post office," I said.

The bartender chuckled, then went to make my drink. I missed the usual bartender, who rarely said more than three words to me. Things were changing. I wasn't. This was the start of a problem.

The bartender came back with the drink. He actually held it so that he could flex his arm at the same time. I'm not making that up. It's what he did. I put a twenty on the bar and took a pull on the drink, draining half of it. The scotch burned a little, but it was a good burn. Made me feel alive.

The bartender came back with my change, just as I finished the drink.

"Thirsty, eh?" he asked.

"Make the next one a double, please," I said.

"You got it, buddy."

Emily's face was still clear in my mind. I remembered the contour of her skin, the shape of her nose, the odd blue color of her eyes. She had eyes I could just stare into. Those eyes, along with the rest of Emily Brackens, were rotting in some cemetery in Queens, all because someone had a severe chemical imbalance and killed Emily for something she didn't do. I'd say she was taken from me, but she wasn't mine yet. I was just denied the chance. I wondered if I'd ever get over it. I wondered what would help. Would time just cover the wound and make it bearable, or was there someone else out there, someone who could take the place I thought she was to hold? I realized years before that asking questions to yourself doesn't make answers come, but that didn't stop me from doing it.

The bartender came back with the drink, in a glass nearly as big as a water glass.

"This one's on me. Looks like you're having a rough go at it, plus I recognize you now. Cheers."

I didn't want a putz like this bartender to be nice to me. I wanted to hate him, along with everyone else. I wanted to feel the burning sensation that only true anger and disdain can bring, and this guy had to douse those flames with a free drink, a nice gesture. I didn't even have luck at hate, let alone love.

"Yeah, thanks. Just don't fucking tell anyone else who I am," I said, not like I was some celebrity. Unfortunately, a few of my cases turned out to be of the highest interest to the city media, and my mug made it to the small screen a few times. All I needed was an agent, and I'd be a true asshole.

I took a tug from the new drink. No, it didn't make me feel better. It didn't make me feel anything, and I was happy with that. It didn't make me wonder about its motivation, its intentions. It didn't make me have to say something in return, question some ideal. It just was, something I wanted to be but in no way could. Envy of a drink is probably the start of some serious psychosis. I could deal with that, I figured.

I looked around the bar, noticing the couple making out at the end. Why they felt the need to slobber each other in public was beyond me. It seemed like they had just met, and were going to head home and sleep with each other. Classless people carrying out a classless act. No problem with that. At least they were doing as expected.

I lit a cigarette, taking a long inhale, then letting it out slowly. I wasn't the sort to sit around thinking about the meaning of it all, but the events of that day forced such thought. K-Drugs dies, a slime like Jaro Medina gets to live in luxury, and my nephew, who couldn't even have the thought of hurting someone, lies in a hospital bed, the specter of death hovering over him like a storm cloud ready to douse the flame of life. I moved from day to day with the same stream of consciousness, the same meaningless meaning, not thinking about the fact that every day in this life is nothing but a tick on a clock that is set to stop at a predetermined time. I lived my life with some unconscious purpose, desires that leaned me one way or the other, but I had no real grasp of what they were. When was I going to find out? When would I know what I wanted, and have the nerve to actually go and get it?

Thinking about death did this to me, thinking about how, if we retain any sort of consciousness in death, I'd be totally disappointed with myself if I were to die any time soon. Realizing that my nephew might have his chances taken from him before he even got to use them made me see that I had to take some of my chips and cash them in. Sitting at the crap table of life indeterminately, in the hopes that I could walk away a big winner, just didn't make sense. I hadn't won anything, and though I felt I had lost a little, sitting there, trying to win it all back, was senseless. I needed to spend my life, not try and recoup my losses.

Yeah, I came to all of these conclusions while sucking down straight scotch. None of it would really set in, and I doubted that any of it would affect my life one way or the other. Yet, this is how I passed the time when I drank alone, especially if I had something big on my mind.

My father's actions didn't help matters any. Whenever he angered me, I rededicated my efforts to ensure I ended up different. I used such opportunities to mentally point out his shortcomings, and realize I suffered from different ones. It wasn't a matter of being better than him—saying one man is better than another is one of the more subjective things you can do—it was just about being different. I wanted no one to be able to say I was just like my father, no matter how big of a compliment that was.

Part of being a police officer had to do with this. Growing up, I had always envisioned some validation ceremony, some moment when my father would acknowledge my manhood, accept me into the circle. This never happened, though I suspect my father thought it had, that some passing statement he'd made to me had satisfied this need. Perhaps this stemmed from my grandfather dying young, in his fifties, when my father was barely a man himself. Regardless, I became a police officer for many reasons, but one of them certainly was in search of recognition. Not a pat on the back, not a statement of how proud my father was of me. Maybe this is something that never comes. Maybe no father ever did this for a son. It didn't matter. That's what I expected, and it is real hard to let go of so high and so important an expectation.

I loved my father, respected him. After adolescent battles, we rarely fought. We got along very well, actually, so my father's actions that night did nothing but baffle me. I thought maybe I really had done something wrong, that some of the things he said were true. I should have known they weren't. My father had something else on his mind, and I was his vehicle for releasing it. Unfortunately, letting go of pent up anger from such a situation is difficult, and I spent a good part of that night thinking about how angry I was at him, how wrong he was, and how I was a better man than he.

I downed four double scotches that night, a healthy dose of alcohol, even for a pro like me. Luckily, Kasey's was close to my apartment, and I was able to stumble back home without much incident.

The emptiness of my apartment only soured my mood even further. I thought about how I had plodded through most of my life alone, rejecting the company of others more often than not. People like me need their space. This is what I'd tell people. Part of it was true, but another part was just a defense mechanism, a way to not let people get to know me too well. Once people get to know you, they are able to penetrate your defenses. I liked my defenses impenetrable. Another bit of evidence for a psychologist to prescribe some magic drug for me, the sort you see advertised on television. The kind that makes you happy, with the only side effects being that you shit your pants and had dry mouth. Why is it that all medications caused dry mouth? What the fuck is dry mouth?

If I'd had scotch in the apartment, I would have drank more. Luckily, I had insisted I only keep beer in the apartment, and I was all out of that. So, I went to the refrigerator and got a can of Diet Coke, because I was thirsty. I sat on the couch and watched the television I had left on, which was now showing some stupid sitcom.

In an effort to clear my mind of the night's events and the plight of the stereotypical queer, I turned my thoughts to K-Drugs and the situation surrounding his death. Like I said earlier, I figured his death was addition by subtraction, but I loved figuring things out. That was my validation; my ability to figure things out most people couldn't made me feel like I had earned my right to live. Scary, I know.

Konstantin Volkyv dealt drugs, bad drugs. He buddied around with low-life Russian mafia guys. He had a slippery son of a bitch like Jaro Medina in his corner. For a bad guy, he had it pretty good. I couldn't see either the mafia or Medina putting a bullet in Volkyv's head. Both had an investment in him. If this last job was the final stage of his initiation, then K-Drugs had some value, and killing him would be a waste of resources.

Rick had been on to something when he said everything was before us, but we just couldn't see it. I felt the same way, and I kept going back to Troiano. A father could definitely carry out a murder like that of K-Drugs'. Vengeance would explain the twenty minutes between the hit on the head and the bullet in the brain. A father's revenge could definitely act as justification for the shots to the nuts. Mob guys wouldn't do K-Drugs like that. Even if he had done something horribly wrong, their job would have been cleaner.

Troiano sure sounded good, but there were problems with him doing it as well. Not so much in the ideology of it all, but instead, with evidence. All I had was the fact that Troiano's son died of a heroin overdose, and that he owned a gun similar to the one that killed Volkyv. Linking Troiano to Volkyv would be near impossible, and landing any evidence at the scene would rely solely on what the Crime Scene Investigators found. The lab had that evidence, and at that point, it was an unknown. I needed to find something to lead me in the right direction, but like Rick said, though it might have been right in front of me, I couldn't see it.

I fell asleep on the couch, thoughts of the meaning of life and the death of K-Drugs clear in my mind, taken over only by the same image of Emily Brackens that haunted me every night. I woke up with a back that felt like a pretzel and a hangover that rivaled one of my worst. The next day was going to be beautiful, I figured.

8

Getting ready for work that morning took more effort than usual. I wasn't a morning person to begin with, and having a hangover and a general bad feeling certainly enhanced this. I cursed the shower, the cold floor, the can of Diet Coke that served of breakfast, and the freaking sun that decided to shine brightly that day, as if it were some glorious achievement that it could shine.

Though we were back working together, Rick hadn't seen fit to reinstate the chauffeuring he used to provide before the Hell storm came to town. This meant I had to drive myself or take a cab, and I chose the latter. Since I'd nearly wrecked my car not so long before, I used it less and less, afraid that it would fall apart on the road. I have a wickedly vivid imagination.

Hailing a cab took some time, and I had to sit there with the sun beating down on me. The bright sun made me sneeze, a phenomenon I carried from childhood and still couldn't understand. Rays of sun actually tickled my nose, causing me to sneeze. My mother had told me years before it was because I was part vampire, which would certainly explain the fact that I was much nicer at night than I was during the day. That is, of course, if you are willing to accept the blatant lie that I can be nice at any time during the day.

The cabbie that picked me up had a less than commanding knowledge of the English language. Actually, he knew the word 'Okay' and little else. I had to direct him to the precinct. Some people think love makes the world go around. Others tend to believe money is the fuel of the earth.

Me, I've figured it out. Incompetence makes the world move. How can a man who speaks no English and has no knowledge of the city he is working in get hired as a cabbie? Shouldn't there be a cabbie test? You know, something where these guys are asked to find a certain major attraction on the map. Of course, as usual, I am asking too much of the world. I should be happy that, when I breathe in, oxygen gets into my system.

"Criminal?" the cabbie asked. I'd tell you his name, but it was just a string of consonants that made no sense to me. Plus, I didn't know which one was the first name and which one was the last. And I could swear I saw the circle with the slash through it somewhere in there.

"What?"

"Pick up criminal? Lawyer?"

This insipid twit thought I was a lawyer. As if the insults could get any worse. I didn't think I looked like a soulless individual, but I guess that's arguable. Still calling a cop a lawyer is like calling an Arab a Jew. Very touchy.

"No."

"You bail someone out?"

I didn't want to talk to this guy. I just wanted him to find the precinct and get me out of his foul-smelling cab as quickly as possible. Again, I was asking for way too much.

"No. I am going to find criminals," I said.

"You find them there?"

"I put them there."

"Police?" the driver asked, this time looking at me through his rear-view mirror.

Instead of replying, I just held up my badge, which turned out to be a bad idea. The driver saw it, then I felt the car slow down to a near crawl. Instantly, this guy became concerned with the road and the laws that applied to it. I wanted to tell him to speed up, but I didn't think his peanut-sized mind could comprehend that.

It took an extra ten minutes to get to the precinct, so again, I walked into work in a bad mood. Like I've said before, this is something that most people who knew me had gotten used to, but I wanted just one day when things would even go marginally well, a day when I could think about smiling, despite the fact that I never would anyway.

Rick was at his desk. He looked tired. His eyes were dark, and for what had to be the first time, his attire was disheveled. He had on different clothes, otherwise I would have thought he spent the night at the precinct.

"How's everything going?" I asked.

"I didn't find much. Couple of people with Russian last names kicked in over the last two days, but all of them were either too old or too young to be the people we are looking for."

"Could just mean what we said yesterday, that they didn't get to them yet." I walked over to the counter behind Rick's desk, where the coffee was. I wasn't a big coffee drinker, but I needed it that morning.

"Yeah, but I would have liked to have found something, anything that would point us in the right direction, make me think that we are doing something right."

"We're looking for a killer, of course we are doing something right," I said, pouring a ton of sugar into my cup.

"You know what I mean."

"Of course I do, but relax there, Ricky-boy. This isn't something that's gonna happen overnight, especially considering the circumstances and the victim. There's still a chance this was a professional hit, and if that's the case, then we are going to be taking some serious twists and turns before we solve the damn thing."

"You don't believe that," Rick said.

"Of course not, but the possibility is still there. I think pretty much along the same lines you do, as frightening as that sounds. Proving what we suspect is going to take some time, some patience, and a fucking Hell of a lot of luck." I sat down at my desk and took a sip of the coffee, which tasted like sweetened, coffee-flavored non-dairy creamer. "Any word on when the lab report will be ready?"

"Geiger told me before noon. That's all he said."

"So, we have to wait until then before we can do anything?" I asked.

Rick shook his head. "We can still check out that Troiano guy."

"Geiger told us to sit on that until we had the lab report."

"Since when do you listen to what Geiger has to say?" Rick asked, smiling.

"A little time off, and you turn into a good cop. How great is that?"

"Come on," Rick said, standing up, "I've already got the route to his office mapped out. Maybe Mr. Troiano has some information for us."

Rick had done plenty of work since I'd left him. When finding dead Russians didn't pan out, he investigated the death of Troiano's son. Turned out that the kid got his juice from K-Drugs' neck of the woods. Coupled with the fact that Jason had told us K-Drugs was becoming the only guy in town to buy from, it wasn't too hard to figure out that the kid bought his drugs from K. This was yet another little piece of the puzzle, and if Troiano was K-Drugs' killer, then the piece was in the right place.

Troiano worked in Westchester, in a small town called Mamaroneck. In the center of the town was a strip of stores that looked like Main Street, USA, from the fifties. It was like being in a time warp. The place felt comfortable and homey. It also felt a little weird, like these people got lost somewhere along the timeline.

Troiano's building was one of the largest in the town. Fleet Bank owned the building itself, and it towered over the rest of the town like a lighthouse on a small island. We pulled in the parking lot, which was behind the building if you need to know, and got out of the car.

"God it feels great to be born again," Rick said.

"Yeah, easy there. Let's make sure we ease into this guy, instead of hitting him with both barrels. After all, his son died recently, and we are going to be dredging up that memory just by coming here."

"I know what I am doing," Rick said, as I opened the door and walked in.

"I know you do. I'm just telling you how I think this should go. Considering I have the lead on this case, I expect you'll follow."

"You've gotten bossy."

"You always were."

Rick laughed. This caught the attention of the snoozing security guard behind the small desk near the elevators.

"Help you?" he asked. He was ridiculously fat. If someone tried to rob the place and ran, this guy would never catch him. Unless, of course, the perpetrator was carrying a roast beef sandwich. That changed the odds dramatically.

"We need to speak to Steven Troiano," I said.

"I don't have any visitors listed for him," the guard said.

"That's because he didn't know we were coming," I said, holding out my badge. The guard eyed it as if he'd never seen one before.

"Oh, okay. He works for DeLuca and Selig, law firm on the top floor."

"Got it. Thanks."

The receptionist at the law firm certainly didn't look happy to see us. She was tapping at her keyboard, and barely paid attention to us, even after I introduced myself. Some people are just plain rude.

"Who did you say you wanted to see?" she asked, not taking her eyes off the computer screen. I thought she might have been working—which would have almost been excusable—until I heard the rings of an instant messenger service. I'd learned to hate those blasted things.

"Steven Troiano," I said, loud.

She looked up at me. Her face indicated she didn't like the way I spoke to her. She looked back at her computer screen, and said, "He's in a meeting."

I leaned on her desk. "I don't care. Tell him two detectives are here to see him, and we'd prefer not to have to barge into his meeting."

Again she looked at me with disdain. "One minute."

"Thank you."

She picked up the phone, punched a few buttons, and said, "Mr. Troiano, two *detectives* are here to see you. Yes, I told them that. They said they need to speak to you now. Okay." She hung up the phone, and without looking at us, said, "Third door on the left."

"Thank you so much," I said, and Rick and I walked to Troiano's office.

The office door was open, but no one was inside. The sign on the door said, "Steven Troiano" but it gave no indication of what position he held with the firm. Rick and I walked into the office, and sat down in the two leather chairs in front of Troiano's desk. After about two minutes, Troiano walked in.

He was a short man, but stocky, probably about 5'7" 175 pounds. He had close-cropped gray hair, and a general presence of pissed-off. I guess he wasn't too happy to see us. I tried to give him the old John Keegan once-over, where I try and decide right there if someone is innocent or guilty, but he was unreadable. I didn't like that.

"Detectives," Troiano said as he walked behind his desk, "my receptionist said it was important that you speak to me."

"I apologize for the interruption, but your receptionist was a bit less than helpful."

Troiano laughed. "Katie's generally useless. If she wasn't Selig's niece, I doubt she'd have the job."

"I hear you. I'm Detective John Keegan, and this is my partner, Detective Richard Calhill, NYPD."

Troiano sat down. "I didn't figure you two to be locals. What can I do for you?"

"Well, I am not sure. You could start by telling me where you were last night, say between 12 and 4am."

Troiano looked at me as though I was nuts. I was used to this look. "Home. Asleep. Why?"

"Do you own a .357 Magnum pistol?"

"I do. What is this about? Do I need a lawyer?"

"I am sure there are plenty of them around," I said.

"What do you want?"

"Mr. Troiano, are you aware that your son, prior to his death, was buying heroin in Brooklyn?"

"I knew he was taking heroin, but I never knew where he was getting it from."

I looked at Rick, who shrugged.

"Do you still have the Magnum in your possession?"

"Yes, it is locked up in my basement. I'd really appreciate it if you could tell me why you are asking these questions. If I didn't know any better, I'd think I was being considered a suspect in something."

Not too far off the mark, I thought. This was a tricky situation, because like I said, we really didn't have anything but light evidence pointing to Troiano. I didn't want to accuse him of anything. Rattle his cage a little, perhaps, but not much more.

"We're investigating the murder of a Brooklyn heroin dealer, who was shot with a .357 Magnum. We're fairly certain he is the one your son bought from."

Troiano leaned back in his chair. "Well, as happy as I am to hear the man is dead, I can assure you I had nothing to do with it. You're welcome to have a look at the gun and see that it hasn't been fired any time recently."

"There's no need for that just yet. Understand, Mr. Troiano, we came here mainly as a standard procedure. I am sure you realize how we could make the assumption."

"Of course. I was on the job. Jersey Trooper."

There was no mention of this in his record. Then again, I didn't look at it that closely. "I didn't know that."

"How many years?" Rick asked. I think we both felt a bit uncomfortable.

"Twenty. I am doing P.I. work now, for the firm."

"I see," Rick said.

"Can I help you with anything else?" Troiano asked.

"Not that I can think of. I apologize for the intrusion," I said.

"Don't worry about it. You're doing your job. I'm almost happy you came, so that now I know the guy who helped kill my son is dead."

I stood up and shook Troiano's hand. "Guess he had it coming."

"Well, I wouldn't go on record as saying that," Troiano said, "no need to point more suspicion my way."

"As long as your alibi is solid, I don't think you have anything to worry about."

"Of course it is."

"Sorry again," I said, and Rick and I walked out.

In the car, Rick said, "Well, that turned out to be a waste of time."

"We had to check it out, and you know damn well we are going to make sure everything he says adds up."

"You going to have a look at his gun?"

"Not unless the lab report points something else in his direction."

"I want Volkyv's apartment searched more thoroughly," Rick said.

“What for?”

“There has to be something there. If he was hired to do some sort of job, there might be some evidence there, something to help us out.”

“I can’t argue with that.”

“That’s surprising. You can argue anything.”

“Only when I am in the mood, Rick. Only when I am in the mood.”

9

When we got back to the precinct, I checked my messages. There were two from my mother the previous day, which reminded me of the argument the night before, something I really didn't want to think about. I felt guilty about that, which pissed me off because I really didn't do anything wrong. There was also a message from Marcus Lay, and I figured he was just doing me a favor by updating me on his case. That case really wasn't important to me right then. I decided to call him later, when I got home.

Geiger gestured for Rick and I to come into his office. We walked in, and sat down.

"What have you got so far?" Geiger asked.

"Troiano seems clean," I said. "He even offered to let us have a look at his gun."

"Lab report?"

"They said it should be ready any minute," Rick said.

"So, basically, we have nothing."

"Basically," I said.

"Something's bothering me about this one."

"I think something is bothering all of us. Personally, I usually tend to think that most of these cases are a lot simpler than they appear. This one is probably the same."

"We've got a drug dealer dead, apparently because of some revenge, but we don't have any idea who did it."

"Maybe it just isn't that important."

I expected Geiger to snap at me for that, but he didn't. Instead, he just exhaled loudly. "I don't need all of this now."

"What?"

Geiger stood up, and closed his office door. "What I am about to tell you guys stays in this office, got it?"

"Of course," I said.

"No problem," Rick said.

"Got a visit from the Commissioner earlier today. I'm one of the candidates for Captain."

This was something that was a long time coming. Geiger was a hard worker, but had been overlooked several times when such an opening came up. He deserved it more than anyone I knew.

"That's great," I said.

"Of course it is, but I don't need some dead drug dealer to screw things up."

"Why would it?" Rick asked.

"Because that would be my luck. I keep feeling that this case is important, even though I know it isn't."

"You're just worried, overly concerned."

"Maybe. But I want you two to make sure all bases are covered on this one. I know the other guy up for the position, and he's in tight politically. You guys know I'm not, so any mistakes from my department, and they can use it against me, understand?"

"As much as I don't like it, I do," I said.

"Then I can count on you two to make sure we close this case as soon as possible."

"You can."

"Good. Get the lab report. Get Galbadon to find something for you, anything. If you need to operate out of the Brooklyn precinct, I can arrange that. Just get me something on this guy. Solve what seems to be an impossible case, and I think I just might have a shot."

"We'll get it done," I said, even though I was about as certain of that as I was that I would win the lottery.

"I appreciate it," Geiger said.

Now we had something else hanging over our heads. On top

of Rick's quiet troubles, my family problems, and the seeming impossibility of solving the Volkyv case, we had Geiger's promotion to worry about. And that was the thing, we were both worried about it. It concerned me on two levels. First, I didn't want to be responsible for Geiger not getting the promotion, and I would feel that way if we didn't solve the case and he got passed over no matter what the circumstance. Second—and this one bothered me more—I couldn't even imagine working for someone other than Geiger. I had no idea who would replace him. No one in the department came to mind. Rick had more seniority than anyone next to me, and I didn't think they'd put him in that position. He would do a good job, but he had a few hurdles to clear before they even thought about it. Plus, they would get a shit storm because promoting him would cause a deeper investigation into what happened to him a few months before. This meant they would probably bring someone in from outside the precinct. Judging from how well I got along with people, I figured I'd hate my new boss within a week.

Rick went to his desk. I remembered when I used to watch him on the phone with his wife, a woman who did not seem pleased unless she was breaking his balls. It used to seem entertaining to me. Right then, I felt bad for him. Sure, I had no one to break my balls either, but he had grown used to it, probably missed it. Actually, I couldn't even fathom what he might be thinking. I didn't want to.

Rick picked up the phone. I just stared around the department, noticing how drab it was, how it lacked character. I think I might have been burning out a bit, getting tired of working at the same place, seeing the same people, noticing the same, boring surroundings. I liked stimulation, but unfortunately, I found it nowhere in my life. This was a cause of endless frustration. Most things were.

Rick hung up the phone and came over to my desk. Certainly not the sort of stimulation I was looking for.

"Lab report's ready," he announced.

"When will we have it?"

"It's downstairs right now."

"Go get it," I said. I somehow got myself into a sour mood.

"Okay," Rick said, probably wondering what was wrong with me. A lot of people did that—including myself—but no one could come up with any answers. He turned around, and went downstairs to get the report.

It wasn't that I didn't want to see the report. I had just gotten myself into a funk, and I didn't want to do a damn thing. The mere fact that people inhaled oxygen bothered me right then. Great way to feel, let me tell you.

Rick came back after about five minutes, holding a manila folder in his hands. He was leafing through it when he sat down in the chair in front of my desk. He sat there quiet for a moment, just looking through the papers.

"Gonna tell me what's in it?"

"Oh, now you're interested in the lab report?" Rick asked.

"Cut the shit."

"Hey, I'm the one who hauled my ass downstairs to get it, therefore I get the first peek."

"Whatever," I said, and began tapping a pencil on my desk, loudly.

"Nothing," Rick said.

"What?"

"There's really nothing in here. We have a shoe size and make on those footprints. Kenneth Cole. Size 10. Nothing out of the ordinary there. They found some fibers, from clothing that didn't belong to Volkyv from what it says here. Some blood other than Volkyv's, but it is AB, so again, that'll lead to a dead end."

"Great."

"They did find a few long hairs. Could be the assailant's. They've been sent for testing. The results of that will be in tomorrow."

"Anything else?"

Rick shook his head. "Not really."

"Just what we needed. What sort of bullet?"

"Oh, .40, most likely a Glock."

"Odd gun."

"Yep. Not a Magnum."

"And Troiano didn't have one of those, that I remember."

"So that clears him."

"I didn't really have much suspicion of him after our meeting today," I said.

"Me neither." Rick put the report on my desk. "So, what do you want to do now?"

"I like your idea of turning Volkyv's apartment. Maybe we can find something there, something that might help."

"Beats the crap out of sitting here and looking at each other," Rick said.

"Absolutely."

Being that Volkyv was killed, we didn't need a search warrant to go through his house. We weren't looking for anything to incriminate him—at least not officially—we were looking for clues as to how he died. His apartment was a crime scene, therefore we had free access to it whenever we wanted. If I had decided that sleeping at his apartment would give me a better feel for how the murder took place, I could have probably done that, though I never tried, so don't quote me on it.

Mrs. Federov didn't say much to us this time, mainly because she was relieved we weren't there to ask any more questions. She just unlocked the door and tucked away into her apartment. Rick and I walked in, looked in the kitchen again to see the actual murder scene, then split up. Rick took the living and dining rooms, I took the bathroom and bedroom.

Looking for clues, that was the best part about the job. Puzzle pieces, little pieces of seemingly insignificant evidence that gain greater importance when looked at through the right eyes. This is what I got paid for, what I worked for, and, unfortunately, what I lived for. I think most of us detectives got into it for the same reason. We liked to tear things apart and put them back together. Maybe we all would have been better off as car mechanics.

Volkyv's bathroom was clean, cleaner than a guy's bathroom should have been. There were no brown rings in the toilet, no water stains in the sink, and even the tile floor was nearly spotless. I did say nearly, didn't I? I'll get to that in a second.

First thing I did was what 60% of people do in a strange bathroom; open the medicine cabinet. Inside, I found two more boxes of condoms, toothpaste, nasal spray, and various prescription medications written out to several different names, none of them Konstantin Volkyv. This didn't surprise me, but I did write down the other names in my little notebook, just in case they might have been aliases of the dearly departed K-Drugs.

I then opened up the cabinet underneath the sink, and I found something interesting. Among the two rolls of toilet paper, a box of tissues, a plunger, a bottle of Mr. Clean, and Epsom salt, I found a container of industrial strength cleaner. This was the high-grade stuff, the type of cleaner you couldn't buy in a supermarket or hardware store. This was specialized stuff, and it didn't take much effort to realize what K-Drugs needed it for.

I picked up the bottle and opened it. It had been used. The container was almost half-empty, or half-full if you are an optimist, though I don't know if that really applies to cleaner as it does to a glass of water. The odor from the cleaner was strong. The bottle said it was safe for hard surfaces, but nothing porous. What that meant for K-Drugs, I had no idea.

Now, if K-Drugs needed a super-cleaner, he obviously

was cleaning things up that needed special attention. He kept the cleaner in the bathroom, which might not have meant anything, but then again, could have meant everything. I decided to get a good look at his tub and tile floor.

The tub looked clean. I couldn't see anything glaring. The floor was another matter. It was one of those tile floors that had very small tiles, with grout in the middle of them. The tiles themselves seemed clean, but the grout was another story. Right by the tub, I noticed the grout was discolored. Red-discolored, which meant one thing to me—blood. Maybe it was his blood. Maybe it was someone else's. Either way, this was a find.

"Come in here," I said to Rick.

I heard him shuffle his feet toward the bathroom. "What?" he asked, from the doorway.

"Look at this," I said, pointing to the spot I had seen.

Rick came over and knelt beside me. He got his face close to the tile, and stared at it for a moment. "Blood?" he asked.

"Could be."

"We need ultra-violet in here," he said.

"Exactly what I was thinking. Get on the horn and have the CSI back in here. We need to sweep this whole place. My feeling is, if this is blood, it might be related to the job old Konstantin had to do."

"Only if we are lucky."

"Don't even say the word luck. Just get on the phone and get them down here."

Rick took his cell phone from his belt, and walked out into the living room to make the call. I looked elsewhere on the floor, and found three other similar spots. I decided the best thing to do was leave the bathroom, so I didn't foul up anything.

The next step was to go through Volkyv's bedroom. I'd been through it before and didn't find anything, but now I had something in mind, something in particular to look for.

If Volkyv had been careless at all, I was going to find some evidence of blood in his room. Maybe something on his sheets, maybe something stowed away in his closet. Something, somewhere. I wanted a blood sample. Getting that from what we found in the bathroom was impossible.

I rummaged through the closet, not finding anything. Frustrated, I took off the comforter on the bed and looked at the sheets. They were black, so, without the light, again we had nothing. I looked under the bed, and then moved to the dresser. Nothing there either.

Rick came into the room. "What are you looking for?"

"Bloody clothes. Bloody something."

"You sound British now."

"Thanks."

I had gone through everything in the dresser, and most of it was on the floor.

"Try underneath the mattress?"

I hadn't even thought of that.

I walked over to the bed, and Rick helped me move the mattress. There was nothing underneath. Then I came up with an idea.

"Give me your keys."

"Why?"

"Just give them to me. I left mine in my desk."

Rick reached into his pocket and handed me his keys. "Good place for them."

"Can't lose them that way."

I took the biggest key on his ring and drove it into the thin cloth covering the box spring. I tore through it, ripping most of it completely off.

"Got a flashlight?"

"What, I look like a hardware store?"

"Never mind," I said.

I poked my head inside. In the far left corner, was a rolled up t-shirt. It was almost unnoticeable. I pulled it out.

"Well, what do we have there?" Rick asked.

I opened up the t-shirt, and found a stiletto knife inside. "Major clue number one." I took a good look at the knife. There seemed to be some blood at the fold.

"Wow," Rick said.

"Yes, Rick, wow. I think we found the weapon used for Volkyv's job."

"Now, if we could only find out what that job was."

The CSI team arrived five minutes later. Nice response time. Generally, it was unusual to call them back a second or third time, but we found new evidence, and this evidence obviously pertained to another crime on top of the initial homicide. They hadn't swept through the entire apartment on the initial run. This was not entirely out of the ordinary because it seemed all of the action took place in the kitchen. The blood stains in the bathroom could have been written off as from Volkyv's killer, who might have had the sense to clean himself up at the scene of the crime instead of home. It shocked me that more murderers didn't do this. Why get blood all over your bathroom when you can just do it in the victim's?

The blood in Volkyv's bathroom could have been from the assailant, except for the fact that we found the knife under Volkyv's bed. Volkyv's body had no knife wounds, so it was safe to assume the blood in the bathroom and the knife under the bed were related, and pertained to another crime. This is where homicide investigation got exciting. A whole new world of possibilities opened up, and it was up to Rick and I to find the correct path, and follow it to the end. I really, at that moment, believed we would. And I am ever the pessimist.

Under the ultraviolet light, dozens of specks of blood showed up. They were in the tub, on the floor, and in the sink. This meant he scrubbed the place, and there had to be rags or paper towels somewhere. The CSI team would get the honor of going through garbage and such. These guys work hard. And, they rarely get credit for the work they do.

"What do you think?" I asked Schmidt, the same guy who had come down earlier.

"Definitely a good cleaning job. My guess, this stuff is over a day old. Don't think it was from Volkyv's murder."

"Well, the knife we gave you proves that."

"Maybe." Schmidt got closer to the floor. "This wasn't a murder that took place here. He came here to clean himself up."

"My guess as well."

Schmidt took the light and we followed a trail right to the door to Volkyv's apartment. "Messy job, whatever it is he did. Has to be murder, with this much blood. Violent."

That made sense.

"We need to check his car," Schmidt said.

I shook my head. "He doesn't have one."

"Check for a rental, then. He had to get around somehow, and I doubt he used a cab."

Rick came over to us, by the front door.

"Blood stains in the kitchen sink," he said.

"Could be the assailant with that."

"Might not be."

"Can you take a sample from the knife?" I asked Schmidt.

"You'd be surprised what we can do. I found two spots in the bathroom that we might be able to lift a sample from, believe it or not. Technology's gotten out of control, if you ask me."

"I don't understand any of it."

"We'll take all the samples we can. Your boss told me this case was a priority, so I might have something for you before the day is done." I knew this meant that Schmidt wanted to get to work without having two flatfoots following him around.

"Alright. Just call either one of us if you find anything else of interest."

"Will do," Schmidt said, already drifting off into his work.

"Let's go," I said to Rick.

It was time to eat. I never followed any set schedules, but when my stomach alarm went off, I stopped what I was doing and filled it. Call it weakness, call it nature, call it what you want. I just felt that, if you don't eat, you might not live very long.

Rick and I generally never agreed on what to eat, when to eat, and where to eat. Being that we hadn't worked together in a while, I figured I would be nice and see what he wanted.

"I'm hungry," I said.

"Me too. All this thinking about blood and death has really fired up my appetite."

"You serious, or being a fucking wiseass again?"

"Little of both."

"What do you want to eat?" I asked.

"Doesn't matter."

"Excuse me?"

"That's right, it doesn't matter. Arguing over where to eat really doesn't seem all that important to me anymore. You just go wherever you want, and I'll find something."

"No, we'll go where you want. Lord knows I have broken your balls enough over the years about that."

"It really doesn't matter to me," Rick said.

"Well, make it matter. I am hungry, and I really don't feel like sitting here trying to figure out where we are going."

"Burger King," Rick said. I wanted to pinch myself, see if I was really awake. Either that, or speak to someone who could validate the fact that I was on Planet Earth, and that everything was okay, that I wasn't caught in some *Twilight Zone* episode. Rick, of course, couldn't do that.

"Burger King?"

Rick chuckled. "Don't worry, I haven't totally lost my mind. They have a new veggie burger that's low in fat. Supposed to be real good."

This threw me. Why go to Burger King to eat a veggie burger? "You order chicken in a steak house, don't you?" I asked.

"No. Sometimes I get the fish."

"Unbelievable."

"Let's go," Rick said "Talking about food is making me starved now."

I drove to Burger King, and lo and behold, they did have a veggie burger, which Rick ordered. He got a side salad too, with fat-free dressing. Then, he went in the back and gave the manager a blow job. Well, in my mind, he might as well have.

Somebody messed with the menu at Burger King, one of the last bastions of unhealthy food. Among the veggie burger and fat-free dressings were a Chicken Whopper (yes, that's right) and low-fat muffins. I'd been taken to Hell, that's what it was. Hell is not terrible, so you know. It's just frustrating. Hell is all about reversing your expectations. And I was there. My mother warned me about eating meat on Good Friday. I think I was paying for the time when I ordered a pizza on Good Friday, with meatballs and sausage.

I ordered a Whopper Combo, King-sized, with a cheeseburger to wash it all down. I walked over to the table where Rick was, and he gave me a look of pure disgust. He didn't say anything, thank God, but he certainly couldn't hold off that look.

"How's the veggie burger? Taste like broccoli trying to masquerade as beef?"

"It's not bad, actually. Want a bite?"

"No thanks. I'll stick to the real thing."

Usually Rick would take this opportunity to lecture me on how red meat stays in your colon for seventeen years, or how my arteries were more clogged than the Midtown tunnel during rush hour. He didn't do that, and I almost missed it. I did say almost.

"How are the kids?" I asked, decided to move the topic from nutrition, which I knew little about, to kids, which I knew even less about.

"Doing well. Chrissie has really taken to school. It's surprising to see how enthusiastic she is about it," Rick said, crunching on his salad.

I chomped into my Whopper, plopping ketchup and mayo onto the wrapper. The burger nearly fell apart. You'd think, that after going through the extensive training fast food employees must endure, that they'd figure out a way to make everything stay nicely. Rick's burger seemed neat. But, then again, it really wasn't a burger.

"That's great," I said, my mouth full of fat-laden food. I think I might have spit a piece of pickle onto Rick's lip, but he didn't notice, and I wasn't going to say anything about it.

"I think they are both starting to move past it all. I made it more difficult for them in the beginning, mainly because I was a mess." I didn't expect Rick to get into the whole topic, and I regretted even mentioning the kids. "Now that I have settled down about it, they seem to be taking everything in stride."

"Good for them. Good for you."

Rick took a bite, then looked out the window. He looked back at me. "You see the way every cop looks at me when they find out who I am?" he asked.

I couldn't deny it. I wanted to, but couldn't. "Yeah."

"Everyone knows."

"Of course they do. Cops are worse than washwomen, you know that. It took a while for me to shake the time I got locked up, even though I was wronged."

"I wish I could say it doesn't bother me, that it doesn't mean anything, but it does. This is my life. I chose this profession, chose it over my wife, you could say. I paid the price for that, and I don't even have the men who are supposed to support me showing me any sort of respect. I don't deserve that, no matter what people think I did, or what they think really happened."

"You can't look at it that way. I think people are just surprised to see you, shocked that the person they heard so much about is standing right in front of them. Don't sweat it. I think a lot of guys respect you. You came back from it all, rose above it. I respect you, and that's more than I would have said two years ago," I said, hoping Rick would change the subject soon. I was running out of smart things to say.

"Do you respect me, or do you just feel bad for me?"

"I don't understand what you mean."

"It's a simple question. Do you really think I did something worthy of respect, or do you just feel bad because of all I went through?" Rick asked.

"I respect you."

"You're sure?"

"Didn't I just say that?"

"I don't want anyone's pity. I don't want people to think about how rough it must be for me, how bad they feel for what happened. That's all bullshit, and no one will ever take me seriously if that's how they think of me. I'll just be some pity case."

"I don't think it will be that way. Hey, don't get me wrong, I do feel bad for you. It's hard not to. But that isn't the essence. That's just a reality."

Rick took another bite of his 'burger'. I understood how he felt. I would have felt the same way. Screw pity. It doesn't do anyone any good. I don't feel pity for anyone, really. Even someone who's crippled. I don't feel pity because I don't want people to feel pity for me. A little sympathy is okay, but when you pity someone, you are generally assuming that you are better than the person you are pitying. You can't pity someone who you think is in a better position in life than you are. You look down on someone when you pity them. You rob them of their self-worth.

"You thought the same thing I did when Geiger said he was up for promotion, didn't you?" Rick asked.

"What's that?"

"That, even though I now have seniority in the department, they would never consider me for his position if he gets promoted."

"I can't say that I thought of it exactly that way, but it did make me think you are the first in line," I said, skewing what I had originally thought just a little bit.

"You really think they would even think about giving me Geiger's job?"

"Honestly?"

"No, lie to me."

"No. Two reasons. One, because you were recently suspended. There's no getting around that. They put you up for Geiger's job, and there'll be a call for a deeper investigation of what happened. Two, even if you never were suspended, and the whole situation never happened, they still wouldn't give you the job. These guys are famous for bringing someone in from another precinct. You get a major promotion, you get a new precinct to call home. Happens all the time."

Rick considered this for a moment. "Geiger came from Midtown South."

"Geiger was a special case, if you ask me, and that was a long time ago. They do things differently now. They don't want a guy like Geiger holding that position anymore. They don't want someone who is liked by their subordinates. Divide and conquer, that's their scheme."

"I never knew you were such a cynic," Rick said.

"Cynicism has nothing to do with it. It's a fact. The two guys who had seniority over you were transferred when they made Lieutenant. Just the way it goes. My prediction is, within a few days, we'll get some used-to-be-Sergeant turned Lieutenant transferred here, and then he'll get Geiger's position. That's how I see it."

"Well, you might be right, but I still think I deserve a shot at that job, regardless of what happened. I've got a great track record, and they know it."

"Your record is okay. Don't let it get to your head," I said.

"I just believe in what I've done."

"As you should. As we all should. Personally, I just want to investigate cases and go home after the work is done. You've always wanted more than that. Even though I don't agree with it, I understand it. Just don't get upset if you are looked over for Geiger's job."

"I won't."

"Not that it matters. They won't promote Geiger," I said.

"Why?"

"I don't know. Just a feeling. They always pass him over. They get his hopes up, then send him back to reality. I'm not saying he doesn't deserve it, I'm just saying he won't get it. If it happens that way, at least my faith in the failure of the system will still be intact."

"Gotta keep that going," Rick said.

"You betcha. It's one of the cornerstones of my belief system."

"I didn't know you had a belief system. You always struck me as someone who never took the time to think about what life is all about."

"I do. I've realized we'll never figure that out, so why bother questioning it anymore? There's no need to have that mental confrontation all the time. It's a waste, and I won't do it."

"If you had kids, you'd see things differently."

"Everyone always says that. What if I never have kids? Does that mean that I will never 'get' what life is all about, that I will never be a man?" I asked.

"If you don't, then it will be something else that will make you confront yourself. That's one confrontation I'd prefer to be on the sidelines for."

"You and me both," I said, finishing off the last of the Whopper and moving to the cheeseburger.

"The way you eat, you should be 400 pounds."

"I am. I just wear a really tight girdle."

10

There was a message from Chris Galbadon on my machine when I got back to the precinct. Maybe his tree-shaking had produced some fruit, or, hopefully, some fallen monkeys.

"Galbadon," he said when I called.

"It's Keegan."

"I'm happy you called. I have some information for you."

"I didn't think you called to ask me to dinner."

"You're not my type."

"Hope not. I think I would have a tough time holding you off."

Chris chuckled. "I found out the name of another one of the guys hired for the job K-Drugs carried out."

"That's great. Any idea what the job was?"

"All I know is that someone needed to be shown what the cost of not cooperating was. Got a pen?"

"Yes," I said.

"Alex Antanov. Got a rap sheet, but nothing major. Runs around in your neck of the woods, in a small bar called 'The Score', on 52nd. He's a number runner, among other things. I don't know a lot about him, but I heard from a reliable source that he was involved. From what I know, he's still alive."

"That's good news. When can I find him over at that bar?" I asked.

"Pretty much all the time. Not a pleasant guy, from what I understand, but he shouldn't give you too much trouble."

"He was hired for a murder, from what I can see. He's

going to cause some trouble if he hears cops are looking for him."

"I'd assume this was an in-organization job, the sort that people don't report to the police. I'm sure Antanov thinks he got away clean. Just approach him carefully, and you should be okay."

"You know nothing about the luck I have," I said.

"I've heard enough. Maybe you want to talk to Lavin before going to see him," Galbadon said.

"Not a bad idea."

"Alex Antanov," Lavin said, leaning back in his chair, "You come to see me about the most upstanding citizens."

"You know him?"

"I know of him. Runs numbers. Got pinched about three years ago. Bitch of a situation, too. Guys who were following him took a tip from the Italians, who were only ratting out Antanov to improve their own business. They take in Antanov, then strike a deal with him to turn over some Italians. Antanov did six months, some Italian guy, Conte I think his name was, did a year. That caused bad blood all around. One of the cops who handled the cases got roughed up outside his apartment, and the word is either the Russians or the Italians did it."

"You have the best stories," I said, "we don't get any of that in Homicide."

"That's because most of the people I deal with are still alive."

"Good point."

"What else do you know about Antanov?"

"Not a lot. I can tell you this, though, no one touched him while he was in prison. Part of that is because he is a tough guy, the other part is because he is well-connected."

"I have reason to believe he isn't that well-connected," I said.

"What do you mean?"

I told Karl about how Antanov was hired to do a job that would have counted as the final stage of his initiation.

"Okay, that makes sense. Still, he's always had friends. You know how it goes. Some guys need to be made before they have any clout, and some guys, because they are valuable, have clout almost from the outset. I would say Antanov is one of the latter, and I would be careful around him. What do you need him for?"

"K-Drugs was hired for the same job, and there is a good chance he got killed for it."

"That would mean that Antanov is somewhere on that line. Either that, or one of the guys who did the job is doing the killing. Wipe out the others, and there are no witnesses."

"I didn't even think of that," I said.

"That's what you have me for."

"I knew you served some sort of purpose."

"If you want my opinion, if any of the guys hired for the job could carry something like that out, it would be Antanov. Even though he mainly runs numbers, I find it quite interesting that he has little problems when it comes to getting paid."

It amazed me that guys like Lavin knew all of this about criminals, that these criminals were carrying out their business and though the details were known, they were still able to do it. I knew that most times it was just a matter of getting the right evidence. I mean, there was no sense in busting a guy like Antanov for one count of number running when he could be nailed for something more serious. Still, it bothered me.

"Okay. What you're basically saying is, Antanov is a dangerous man," I said.

"That's exactly what I am saying. And it is starting to sound more and more like you are headed for disaster again."

"Again?"

"Just watch your ass, will you?"

"I'll let you do that. You like my ass, and you derive a sick pleasure from watching it."

"How's Calhill doing?" Karl asked, deftly changing the subject.

"He's still mentally in one piece."

"Remember what I said."

"Same thing you keep telling me, be careful," I said.

"Yep, that's right."

Rick was going through some papers on his desk when I went to see him. He had the initial report, the first lab report, and Volkyv's ME report in front of him. He had spread the papers out in front of him, as if by doing so, something he couldn't originally see would come clear.

"It doesn't work," I said.

"What?"

"Willing something to jump off those papers. Doesn't happen that way."

"I've had success doing this."

"Is that how you can explain your exemplary track record?"

"What do you want?"

"Galbadon called. He got us a name of one of the other guys involved in that job," I said.

Rick looked up at me. "Really?"

"Really. Alex Antanov. Galbadon told me to speak to Lavin about him, and I did. Turns out he isn't such a nice guy."

"That's a shock."

"Come on. I've got a place we can find him in, and I'll fill you in on all the gory details on the way."

Rick got up. "Beats sitting around here praying for information."

"Is that what you call it?"

In the car, I told Rick about what both Lavin and Galbadon said about Alex Antanov. I also told him about what Lavin said, the part about how perhaps one of the guys hired to do the job was planning on killing the others.

"That's an interesting twist, something that makes sense," Rick said.

"Same thing I thought. Lavin seems to think that, if there was a guy who would do such a thing, Antanov's the one."

"Nice. And we get to meet him?"

"Only if we are really lucky."

"Any strategy?"

"I hadn't thought of one yet."

"Think he'll talk?"

"No."

"That's optimistic."

"I try to be, whenever I can."

"I think we should just play the angle of K-Drugs' death. I don't think we should point any fingers at Antanov."

"He doesn't sound like the sort of guy I want to point anything at but a nine-millimeter."

"Well, you've got one of those, but I am sure he has at least that, if not more."

"I'm probably a better shot than he is," I said.

"I've seen you shoot. I wouldn't necessarily agree with that statement."

"Fuck off."

"You sure get testy when someone levels criticism at you," Rick said.

"That wasn't criticism, it was a direct attack upon my manhood. Shall we stop by the firing range and see who the better shot is?"

Rick laughed. "You know as well as I do that Homicide cops are the worst shots on the force. If you're bad, I'm worse. At least I can accept it."

"Whatever."

I drove to where I was told we could meet Antanov. I'd decided it was best if we treated this punk not as a murder suspect, but instead as someone who was in danger. There were risks with this plan, most notably the part about us knowing why Antanov would be in danger. Mention of the 'job' he was contracted for would not draw a happy response from him. Instead, it would probably irritate and worry him, and the worst sort of punk is a scared, irritated one. I tried to keep most punks calm, because, in this world of political correctness and frivolous lawsuits, it was frowned upon for a cop to defend himself.

"So, what are we going to do?" Rick asked, as I stopped the car.

"We come to him like people who are on his side. We just say that his name came up, and that he is probably in danger. We ask if he knows anything about Volkyv's death almost as if it were an afterthought. That should fry his brain a bit, and keep him guessing."

"You think we'll get anything valuable that way?"

"I don't know," I said, lighting a cigarette as I got out of the car. "We might. Even though Antanov is supposed to be a tough guy, he might get a little scared when he hears he's next on the list."

"What if he is the one who has the list?"

"Well, I am hoping that will be evident."

"How will it?" Rick asked.

"If he runs, or shoots at us, that is probably a good sign."

Rick sighed. "Let's hope he isn't the one with the list. Considering how bad both of us are at shooting."

"Shut up."

The outside of The Score looked like anything but a score. The sign was faded, the windows were nearly opaque with grime, and the door itself was battered. If you are looking for the perfect shithole in New York City, drop by The Score on 52nd. I promise you won't be disappointed.

"Nice place," Rick muttered, as I opened the door. Smoke and the faint smell of body odor greeted us. The body odor was of European origin. How do I know that? Well, it's a fact. I've met several Europeans—on vacation and in the city—and for some reason, a good percentage of them have body odor. I attribute this to the general lack of deodorant out there. Of course, the Europeans I refer to are your lower-class ones, but remember, there are more lower-class people in the world than upper class. That means a lot of stink.

There were four people sitting at the bar, huddling over their drinks as if they were their last. The bartender, a short, stocky Russian, glared at us over his glasses. I put him at about 65, but he seemed tough, and probably didn't take any crap. I didn't plan on giving him any.

I took a drag of my cigarette—a deliberate attempt to seem tough—and walked up to the bar.

"Yes," the bartender said. I noticed he was eyeing Rick a bit more closely than me. Maybe he thought we were looking for a different sort of bar, if you know what I mean.

Careful so that only the bartender could see it, I flashed my badge. As tough as these guys appeared, I didn't think they'd rough up a couple of cops, unprovoked. Then again, Rick's very appearance could count as provocation.

"I need to speak to someone," I said.

"Who?"

"Alex," I said.

"Alex who? There are several that come here," the man said, a bit louder than I would have liked him to.

"Antanov," I said, which drew raised eyebrows from the bartender.

"Why?"

"Official business," I said.

The bartender didn't say anything.

"I am not here to arrest him. He is in no trouble from the law. We just need to talk to him," I said, sensing that the bartender didn't want to be the one to get a guy like Antanov pinched.

"Last one, at the end there," the man said, gesturing with

his head. I looked up, and saw Antanov, a tall, lanky guy, standing at the end of the bar. From what I could tell, he'd been watching us the whole time. When my eyes caught his, he smiled. This was not a smile of fear, but one of confidence. Almost as if he'd expected to see us.

Rick and I walked over to Antanov, who was sipping vodka from a small glass. No ice, no mixer. I couldn't imagine the taste of warm vodka, let alone at two in the afternoon. I've been accused of imbibing a bit more than I should, but I do have my limits. I like my alcohol mixed, and cold. Anything else goes.

"Mr. Antanov?" I asked.

Alex nodded. "NYPD," he said.

"How'd you know?"

"No one else comes in here and talks to the bartender without ordering a drink."

"Well, we weren't incognito." I gestured to the two seats to the left of Antanov. "Mind if we sit?"

"Do what you choose," Antanov said, in perfect English. He had a long scar across his forehead, which I hadn't noticed right away. He attempted to cover it with his hair, but the hair wasn't long enough. His teeth were stained, and his overall complexion was pallid, at best. Alex Antanov looked like someone who had been through the war known as street life. So far, it seemed street life was kicking his ass.

Rick and I sat down. "My name is—" Rick started to say. I put a hand up to quiet him. I didn't want this guy knowing our names. Just a precaution.

"Our names aren't important," I said. "I don't think Mr. Antanov here really cares."

"I don't," Antanov said. "Names are inconsequential."

"Sometimes," I said, "but I have one name that is rather important right about now."

"What name is that?" Antanov asked.

"Kostya Volkyv."

Antanov's expression changed, if only slightly. "What about him?"

"He's dead, did you know that?"

"I did. Heard earlier today. No big deal," Antanov said, adding a smile at the end of the comment, in an apparent attempt to seem flippant.

"I would figure this would trouble you," I said.

"Why?"

"Well, if my partner here were to be killed after we worked on a case, I would be a bit worried. I wouldn't be able to help it."

"What are you saying?" Antanov asked.

"Volkyv worked a job with you recently. Very recently. An ugly job, from what I know. Perhaps whoever hired you ordered Volkyv dead. Or, maybe one of the victim's relatives did it. Even more likely, one of the guys who was on the job with you did it. Regardless, I would think you might be in danger."

"I am in no danger. No one ordered Kostya killed. He got himself that way. He took chances, opened his mouth. He probably pissed off one of his customers. That's my guess."

"You're certain about this?" Rick asked.

"No, I am not certain. This sort of life involves risks. We all know that." Antanov pointed a finger at us. "Your life involves risks too. Sometimes you are aware of all of them, sometimes not. Kostya obviously was not aware of a risk. That risk killed him. It doesn't matter who pulled the trigger. What matters is that he wasn't careful."

"How dangerous was your job?" I asked. By the look on his face, I could tell Antanov didn't believe I asked that question.

"Like I am going to tell you," he said.

"Hey, if we wanted you for that job, we wouldn't be talking to you like this right now. We just need to know what risk it was that Volkyv missed."

Antanov took a sip of his drink. "It was dangerous. Very dangerous. But only the job itself, not anything after."

"What do you mean?"

Antanov looked left and right before answering. "What we had to do, how we had to carry it out, that was dangerous. Getting caught? Well, that would be dangerous, but unlikely. Getting killed for doing the job? Highly unlikely."

"I think I understand," I said.

"I think you do."

"And the others?"

"What others?"

I laughed. "Alex, your comment about getting caught might be a bit off base. The streets talk, and we know there were four of you."

"The streets are like a whore. They might talk, but you had better know why they feel it is necessary to. Sometimes the streets lie on purpose, just to throw people off."

"There were four of you, Alex. Don't ask me how I know. Just understand it came from a reliable source," I said.

"Reliable source? Is there such a thing?"

"Well, that's for you to decide. I made my decision already. There were four of you. I am not asking for names. I just want to know if you know of the whereabouts of the other two."

Antanov exhaled. "They are alive."

"Okay. Now, was that so hard?"

"Don't patronize me."

"Of course not. Hey, I don't like people like you. But, the way I see it, without people like you, people like me wouldn't have a job. So, though your existence sickens me at times, I understand there is a need for people like you. I came here for two reasons. One, to find out what you know about Volkyv, and two, to warn you. Evidence points to some sort of revenge. Perhaps revenge for what you were contracted to do. If that's the case, you might want to watch your back."

I turned, and walked away. Rick followed, seemingly reluctantly.

"K-Drugs died because he was stupid," Antanov yelled after us.

Without turning around, I said, "Well, then a smart guy like you has nothing to worry about."

11

"You sure you handled that correctly?" Rick asked me when we got back into the car.

"Of course."

"Telling him what we knew, I thought that wasn't the plan."

"The plan was not to accuse him of killing Volkyv."

"And why didn't you want him to know who we are?"

"I'll let you answer that yourself," I said.

Rick thought about that as I pulled away from the curb. "You think he has connections?"

"He was expecting us, which just could have been because he knew Volkyv was dead. Still, I didn't see the need to take the risk."

"But, if he has connections, he'll know who we are," Rick said.

"Right, and then we'll know for sure that there's someone we can't trust."

"Galbadon?"

"Could be. Doubt it, but I thought it was a good idea to cover our asses."

"So, what do you think?" Rick asked.

"Well, I think Antanov had nothing to do with Volkyv's death. But I think he's scared. I think he agrees with us, that someone tied to their job killed Volkyv, and could be coming for him next. I'm not certain, but I think I rattled him a bit."

"You got all that from him?"

"Yep. He raised the intonation of his voice more than

once. That either indicates lying or nervousness. I vote nervousness, since the only things he lied about were obvious."

"He lied about the number of guys hired for the job," Rick said.

"And then confirmed that number for us. That, by itself, made the meeting worthwhile."

"True," Rick said, "but we're still no closer to finding out who killed Volkyv."

"But the pieces are starting to come together. Antanov gave us some pretty significant information when he explained the danger of the job he was hired for. My guess is that it was brutal, and because they needed to send some sort of message, I figure, it was dangerous when they carried it out, but not afterward. If you accept that it really is dangerous afterward, then we can safely assume this was a major crime."

"Murder?" Rick asked.

"Or rape."

"What makes you think rape?"

"I don't think rape, but that is another crime that is dangerous when you carry it out because of the time element. Killing someone can be quick. Raping them, multiple times, takes time."

"I am shocked at how much sense you are making," Rick said.

"I have temporary flashes of brilliance."

"Temporary is certainly the word," Rick said.

"Thanks."

"Don't mention it. Considering you are experiencing one of these flashes, you mind telling me what you think exactly happened?"

"Job gone wrong," I said.

"What?"

"Something left at the scene, perhaps," I said. I was doing this on the fly. Just spurting out ideas as they came to me. Sort of like detective brainstorming. "Even better, rape/murder that didn't end in murder."

"You think the victim survived?"

"I don't know. Makes sense, though. Something along those lines. Either that, or someone got wind of this, someone found out who did the job, and they killed Volkyv as revenge. That would make Antanov or one of the others next."

"But we don't know the others, so when they die, we might never see the link."

"True," I said. "Maybe we should have someone keep an eye on Antanov."

"For what?"

"To make sure he doesn't up and die on us. And to make sure he doesn't help anyone else die."

"What about Medina?" Rick asked.

"What about him?"

"Well, he knows what they were hired to do. Why can't we press him and find out?"

"Because he wouldn't tell us," I said.

"Maybe, maybe not. But why can't we just try?"

"It's an idea. I'm not sure I like the idea. But it's an idea."

We got back to the precinct, just in time to see Geiger in the hallway. He was heading out somewhere.

"Don't forget about tonight," he said to us as he passed by.

"Tonight?"

"PBA benefit," Geiger said, "and I want to make a good showing, so I expect both of you there. The only thing that will suffice as an excuse will be a death certificate. Your own."

"Got it boss," I said.

"Shit," Rick said.

"What?"

"I hate those things."

"So do I."

"What do you think he'd do if we didn't show?" Rick asked.

"Kill us."

"That wouldn't be so bad, compared to mingling with other cops."

"I hear that," I said.

I took the opportunity, being back at the precinct, to head over to the records department. I wanted two things: to see what sort of record I could get on Antanov, and to see Pauline McCrory again. Such secret crushes are dangerous, I know. Still, I'd read somewhere that the average person has a better than 50 percent chance of hooking up with someone at work. Far be it from me to claim to be better than the average guy.

"What do you want now, Keegan?" Pauline asked. "You want a record of what sort of underwear I prefer?" Okay, so I had been outward with my affection on more than one occasion. Of course, it was all in good fun.

"Shockingly, I am here on official business again."

The look on Pauline's face almost resembled disappointment. Was it possible she enjoyed my antics? Okay, that was doubtful.

"What've you got?"

I handed her the piece of paper with Antanov's name on it. "Could you dig up whatever you can on this piece of crap?"

"Talking about the name here, or the person handing it to me?"

"Ouch. Is there really a need for you to be so cruel?" I said, mocking offense.

"That's for me to decide, Keegan. Any rush on this?"

"Oh, you know, the usual. He's only murdered a couple of people."

"You going to the benefit?" Pauline asked.

"Do I have a choice?"

"If I get it done in time, I'll give it to you then, okay?"

"Fine."

"And Keegan?"

"Yes?"

"Please don't embarrass the precinct like you normally do at such functions."

That was shot number two. "I promise not to be seen with you," I said, "That ought to do it."

I walked away, nearly bumping into Karl Lavin, who was busy making himself a cup of coffee.

"I thought you Vice guys drank tea," I said.

"Only when we need to impress someone."

"So, you never drink tea."

"You need to bang her," Lavin said.

"Who?"

"What do you mean, who? McCrory. If she isn't all over you like those suits you wear, I'm gay."

"I have noticed that you take more peeks than necessary at my ass."

"That's because I can't believe how big it has gotten."

"Thanks."

"Just bang her."

"She's not that way."

"Of course she is. She is a woman. She has a round hole, you have the round peg that fits."

I didn't see this the same way. I don't know why. Something just told me McCrory had no interest in me. "Yeah, right."

"Do it, or I'll start worrying about you."

Lavin walked away, leaving me to feel self-conscious about my perception abilities with women, my sexual orientation, and, worse, the size of my ass. It couldn't be that big. And yes, men worry about that sort of thing. Don't believe any guy who tries to tell you otherwise. Just don't say you heard that from me.

I went back to my desk, clearing the unimportant thoughts from my mind, and trying to concentrate on the case. Rick was nowhere to be found, so I was on my own for a bit. Unfortunately, whenever I try to clear my mind, it becomes cluttered, with thoughts that usually have nothing to do with the task at hand. This time, my father came to my mind, and again I felt guilty for an unknown reason. I ran the argument through again and still came to the conclusion I had done nothing wrong. Well, telling him to go to Hell might have been a bit over the edge, but he had provoked me into that. His fault, I figured, not mine.

I thought about Rick, about what must go through his mind on a daily basis. I'd never really known tragedy, at least not on the scale he experienced. I enjoyed my streaks of bad luck from time to time, but I'd never even come close to having my entire world crumble before me. There were times when I would think losing Emily was a tragedy, but I really never got to know her too well, and the loss I felt was something I had fabricated in my mind, not something that I ever experienced for real.

This is my biggest fault. I don't enjoy life all that much, mainly because what real life turns out to be is never even close to what I imagine. For instance, I thought making detective would be one of the most glorious moments I could ever experience. I built this achievement up in my mind. Then, when it actually happened, I felt good, but also empty, because the moment was not as exciting as I expected. Most times, I go through life feeling disjointed, as if I am not all there, that I am only experiencing half of what's going on. What happens to the other half, I have no idea. Maybe the plug of my life isn't in the socket all the way, and some of the juice of existence is leaking out. Or, perhaps, I am out of my frickin mind.

After mentally jumping back and forth between topics, I found myself centered on the case. I pictured K-Drugs and Antanov together. I'd never met Volkyv before, but I had a good line on what type of person he was. He was hyper to

Antanov's calm, which would make them a good pair. I could see Antanov becoming frustrated with Volkyv's antics after a bit, but I was certain Antanov didn't kill him. Though there might have been an unknown motive, Antanov didn't strike me as someone who would have murdered Volkyv. There was another element, another person behind this. My instincts told me I was close, my intelligence said I was far away. Both, in my judgment, were right.

Of course, all the theories and thinking in the world can't solve the unsolvable case. That's what this was becoming. Each time we found a new aspect of the situation, we realized there was more to the whole thing than we originally thought. Instead of a dead drug dealer—apparently killed by an angry junkie or relative of one—we had a mob ladder-climber, killed after the mission that would have brought him to the top step. We had an unknown victim of an unknown vicious crime. We had suspects of this crime we couldn't arrest. On top of that, I had this feeling we were being laughed at behind our backs. The cops who think they know something but really know nothing at all. That bothered me.

I could have sat there all afternoon, thinking about the case, wondering which direction was the correct one. Unfortunately, I had a benefit to attend, in order to appease my boss. Geiger generally didn't ask for much, so I had to oblige him on this one. Plus, considering that the benefit started at five, I could leave early in order to get dressed. If the Volkyv case was hot, if we had a lead we had to follow, then we would be able to get out of going. Geiger didn't care about a dead drug dealer. Seems no one really does. If you deal drugs and you die, don't expect a big turnout at your funeral. And don't expect the cops to break their backs solving the case if it turns out you were murdered. Sort of goes with the territory, I guess.

Rick came over to my desk, taking me out of my thoughts.

"What's up?" I asked.

"You leaving for the benefit soon?"

I looked at my watch. It was nearly four. "Yeah. Have to go home and change real fast."

"Want me to pick you up?" Rick asked.

"No."

"Why not? Thought we could go together."

"Not a good idea."

"It isn't?"

Rick generally doesn't get this sort of thing. "Going *together* is not a good idea, if you know what I mean."

"Oh. I forgot you worry about that sort of thing."

I was about to tell him that, as a married guy, he didn't have to worry about appearances as much. Then I realized how bad of an idea it would be to bring up the word marriage.

"Yeah, I do. No offense."

"None taken," Rick said.

"It's at the Marquis, right?"

"It is."

"See you there," I said.

"Yeah."

I raced home and got changed, surprised at how happy I was to get out of work. There's something about being home when you are normally not supposed to that is euphoric, and I felt it in droves that day. This could be considered a direct result of my job's effect on me, how it invaded my life, and how getting away from it even for a moment released all the tensions I had built up. Though possibly true and certainly relevant, to admit that would not tell a full truth. You see, I was aware of how the job affected me. I don't mean 'The Job' like you hear on television, I just mean my place of employment, in many ways a place no different than Joe Average's. People try to elevate the importance of a police officer's job—something I understand and mostly agree with—but to do so in an all-encompassing way is senseless. I can compare it to owning an expensive car. Sure, in the beginning, when you get that fancy car, it's the best thing in the world, a super extension of your manhood, your reason for being. Then, after a while, it becomes nothing more than something that gets you from 'A to 'B'. I had a sports car that I loved. After three months, I didn't even realize I was driving such a nice car.

Being a cop is pretty much the same thing. With every promotion and precinct change, things are fresh and exciting, but after a while, it just becomes another job. My only argument is that I earn my money, whereas some people don't. Some of us are noble workers, and others are no different than the snake oil salesman selling water to the drowning. That's an entirely different story, of course, and has nothing to do with what I am trying to say.

Like I said, I was aware of how the job affected me, and it certainly did take over my life. Watching how even the seemingly normal can hack a body of a loved one to bits changes your perception of the world and the people that populate it. I had a hard time separating work and social life, mainly because the people I met either reminded me of a killer, or I was certain they were no different than the groups I put behind bars. It's difficult to trust people when you've wiped away the false shine and see them for what they really are. Understand that the person you trust most would kill you in a second for the weakest of reasons, and you understand human nature. And all that tree-hugger crap about the goodness of man is recycled establishment-generated bullshit to trick us into going along. Trust me on that.

For those who believe I have just gone over the edge, that I've taken the bad I've seen and applied it to the rest of the world, I'll offer an example. I was called to a domestic dispute about two years after I got out of the academy. Back then, I thought it was all about Justice, Truth, and the American

Way. My partner and I arrived at the scene, and the wife was lying on the floor, blood oozing out of her head. The husband was standing over her, the phone receiver in his hand. He cracked her over the head with it. Know why? Because she overcooked his dinner. He had no past history, no mental problems, no violent behavior. She just overcooked his meal one time too many. She would never be the same. He almost killed her. Over a fucking dinner. Think about it.

Anyway, I enjoyed the few minutes away from work. I briefly toyed with the idea of staying home, skipping the benefit. The only thing that stopped me was loyalty. I owed Geiger for putting up with me, and getting me out of some ugly situations. Twice, when things were looking bad for me, Geiger was one of the few still there. That's something I don't forget. Even when watching cartoons seems like a better idea than going to a police benefit.

I dressed in a navy blue suit, the only real suit I owned that still fit, and a white shirt. I thought about a tie, and decided against it. The beauty of being a Homicide detective was the dress code. All the other guys would have to go in full uniform. We didn't. I guess this was the compensation for having to see all the dead people. Eyeball the corpses, but hey, skip the formal attire. How nice.

Because I left work early, 'fashionably late' would not do. I had to get there right at the start, and, unfortunately, probably stay to the end. I had to talk to people too, I thought, be a social jackass in a weak effort to promote the department. Man, I hated all the political bullshit. If I were Geiger, I'd walk up to one of the guys in charge of the promotion, and say, "Alright, I know what needs to be done to get this promotion. You want me to get on my knees here, in front of everyone, or can I save some pride and get you off in private?" Maybe this was why promotions didn't come my way too often.

I made it to the benefit at five minutes to seven, just before the doors opened. There were several cops waiting to get in, all desperately waiting to get to the bar and start numbing their brains for this mindless bullshit. The benefit was for leukemia—a noble cause—but it wasn't as if our being there had any effect on anything. It was obligation. The fat cats who would be donating the money wanted to see us there. It made no sense to me. Then again, little does.

Unfortunately, I didn't see anyone I knew other than by face. There were a couple of guys that I recognized, but no one I would have a drink with, or even say something to, for that matter. I like people as much as I like root canals. And, so you know, my father is my dentist, and he thinks his son should be able to handle more pain than the rest of his patients. I wanted a cigarette right then, but didn't think it appropriate. I did have some manners.

The benefit was on the eighth floor of the Marriott Marquis hotel, one of the classier places in the city, thought normally a tourist hangout. The eighth floor contained a ritzy bar and a conference room, where our benefit was being held. Instead of standing by the door, waiting, I could have easily walked over to the bar and gotten a drink, but this would have been foolish. Why pay ten bucks for a drink that would be free in five minutes. Sometimes, I am smart with my money. It all has to do with priorities.

Not good at waiting, I ducked into the bathroom to kill time. Urinating can kill quality time, and it certainly is a good idea to get all those toxins out of your system on a regular basis, especially if you intend to bombard your body with more of them. The bathroom had an attendant, one of those annoying people who feel they are earning their money by turning the tap handle for you and handing you one friggin' paper towel. Try and get another one, and it throws him so far off base that he needs to think about it for a moment. I do this regularly, because my hands are rather large, and I prefer them to be dry when I leave the bathroom.

Not a total schmuck, I did toss him a buck for his troubles, but that dollar cost him a piece of gum, a book of matches, and a spray of a cologne I would never buy myself. I walked out of the bathroom prepared for just about any situation, and I felt that I smelled sexy. I am sure a skunk thinks the same thing. Regardless, I had to smell better than I normally did.

When I exited the bathroom, I noticed everyone had gone inside, and there were more people coming by the minute. I strolled into the room, which had a huge chandelier in the middle, a wood dance floor, and, most importantly, a bar in the right corner. It wasn't one of those low-class porta-bars. This was a black lacquer bar with stools. There was one stool open, so I grabbed it. Sitting down, I figured these fund-raising people would be a lot more efficient if they held these bashes at less-costly hotels. Not that I was complaining.

The bartender, a woman about forty years old with golden hair, came up to me. She was too attractive for her age. Her body seemed perfect, hair was nice, eyes were crystal. But the age showed on the skin. No good. Still, I'd have tossed her around the back room if she wanted.

"Dewars, on the rocks," I said.

"Sure," the woman said, in a voice that had just a hint of a British accent. Sometimes the world just isn't fair.

"John Keegan," the man to the right of me said. I looked at him, a middle-aged guy with middle age gray hair, middle age gray mustache, and a middle-age gut. I recognized him, but his name I couldn't remember.

"Hey," I said.

"How's the head?" he asked, leaving me wondering if he meant in a physical or mental sense. I decided to lie, on both counts.

"Fine."

"Some case, the murder of Mullins. Guys down by us wonder what would have happened if the guy would have made it one more block and the thing ended up with us."

"You guys might have fucked it up just as good as I did," I said, recognizing the voice. It was Ralph Pilson, Homicide detective that I had worked with for about three weeks before they transferred me. He was a good guy, a little stuck up, but a good guy.

"No one does that better than you, Keegan."

"Thanks. Can I buy you a drink?" Pilson was about to accept, and then must have realized all the drinks were free.

"Funny. You take care of yourself."

"With guys like you looking out for me, sometimes I don't think I even have to bother."

Ralph laughed at this, then walked away, thank God. Maybe now it is more understandable that I don't like people. Part of it is because people don't like me.

The bartender returned with my drink, and I silently tried to convince myself that she wasn't 40, that the light in the room made her older. I tried to make the argument that British women just didn't age the same way, and, though this might have been true, it didn't make me look at the lass in a more positive light.

I took a five-dollar bill out of my pocket and put it in her tip jar, but she had turned and didn't see it. I hated that. I took a sip of my drink, letting the scotch slide down my throat. I wanted a cigarette, and almost did a happy dance when I saw one of the guys at the end of the bar smoking. Most functions were smoke-free. God forbid one of those whiny non-smokers get a whiff of smoke. They eat shit that causes cancer, live near power lines that cause cancer, breathe in exhaust, but cigarette smoke? It was pure evil. The politicians used this attitude to balance their budget by jacking up the cigarette tax, causing me to pay nearly eight bucks for a pack. It was a 'Sin Tax'. Booze and cigarettes. Sins, they said. Funny, I've read the Bible. I combed the whole thing, and I never saw a derogatory statement about tobacco or alcohol. Lots in there about killing, stealing, and banging people you shouldn't be banging, but nothing about the so-called 'Sin' items that politicians based their budget on. I'll have my day. I just don't know when.

I turned around to look at the door and saw Geiger walk in, with Rick trailing right behind him. This was good. I made it there before the both of them, thus elevating my status as a good employee and all around great guy. Such status requires plenty of maintenance, let me tell you. Geiger saw me and nodded, then when about pressing the appropriate flesh. Rick also saw me, and came over.

"Want a drink?" I asked.

"Aren't you afraid someone might think I am your boyfriend if you get me a drink?" he asked.

"You aren't my boyfriend, you're my bitch, and I have no problems displaying that in public."

"You don't have to tell me that. Get me a vodka and seven."

"You drink while it is still light out?" I asked.

"Only on special occasions," Rick said.

"Even you need alcohol to get through these things."

"Exactly."

I ordered the drink, and the bartender, who was becoming increasingly attractive, got it. I think she might have been giving me the eye. I've noticed that women can't help but do this, and though it is a burden at times, I have learned to deal with it. We all have our cross to bear.

"Stop flirting with the bartender," Rick said, she's too old for you. You're still going to proms, right?"

"Never know when a pretty one is going to get upset with her date," I said. "And I am not flirting with the bartender. She's coming on to me."

"Right," Rick said, rolling his eyes and taking a sip of his drink. He sure knew how to rob a man of his pride. "Someone called for you right after you left, by the way."

"Who?"

"Marcus? Marcus Lay?"

Marcus must have really wanted to talk to me. "Did he say anything?"

"When he found out you weren't in, he asked if you were coming here. I told him you were, so he said he would talk to you then."

"Okay. You'd be a great gal Friday."

"It's Thursday."

"Don't be such a wiseass."

"I find it makes you more tolerable," Rick said.

"Nothing makes me more tolerable."

"True."

I glanced at the door again. I didn't realize it then, but I was waiting for Pauline. I felt antsy. She was behind the spray of cologne, my choice of suit, the fact that I brushed my teeth for the second time in the day. It's funny how, looking back, I see all of this, but then, I really had no idea. A woman can consume you without you even realizing it, thus making them the most dangerous species on the planet. The pissed-off, scorned woman takes the top seat, of course.

Pauline hadn't walked in yet—or at least I hadn't noticed—but Karl Lavin did. He walked in alone, which I figured was his preferred method. He certainly was not above picking up women at these functions. A couple of years before, Karl scored with some rich socialite. He told me he got oral service in the boiler room from a woman who routinely made the gossip pages in the newspapers. Luckily for him, that incident didn't make those pages. Karl told me he scored with such women because he had the ability to 'trial close'. This is a sales term, and it generally involves asking the customer if they are ready to buy the item before you even pitch it. I've seen him in action. He went up to two women, talked to them for about a minute, then asked, "What do you guys think about a threesome?" That's the trial close. It didn't work that time, but they didn't pour a drink on his head, either. Somehow, it just magically works.

Karl walked over to Rick and I. "Well, I see I found the loser section immediately."

"You just completed the section, thanks. Now that's out of the way," I said.

"Get me a Citron, flatfoot." Karl looked at Rick. "How's it hanging, Calhill?"

"Low, near ground level," Rick said.

"We can all dream." The bartender came over. "Nice rack."

"Citron for the rack connoisseur," I said.

"Right," the bartender said. I was certain she had no idea what I was talking about.

"Damn shame God paired that pair with that face," Karl said.

"I don't think she's that bad," Rick said. "John seems to be fond of her."

"That's because Johnny thinks she wants him."

"Fuck the both of you, how about that?"

"That'd be the best sexual endeavor you ever experienced," Karl said. The bartender returned with the drink.

"You want another?" she asked me, just a hint of interest in her eyes. Either she found me attractive, or that five-spot I threw in the jar meant the world to her.

"How much are they again?" I asked, finishing the drink.

"Coming right up," the bartender said, in that luscious accent that made me melt.

"Johnny Boy's got wood," Karl said.

"Only for you Lavin, only for you."

"Both of you are sick," Rick said.

"Hey, don't get jealous. I'd poke you too. About as close to a woman as a man can get."

Karl was sipping his drink when I said this and nearly gagged on it. In an apparent attempt to change the topic, he asked, "How are things going with the Russian bastards?"

"They aren't, really," I said.

Soft music began to play. A three-piece band in the far corner of the room decided it was the appropriate time to butcher a Billy Joel tune. Not that Billy Joel's music can really be worsened.

"The Ruskies are sneaky bastards. Be careful with them. They know how to operate and manipulate. Sort of the opposite of Johnny over here. If a Russkie was getting the signals Johnny is from that bartender, she'd be pregnant already."

"Maybe I just have morals."

"And maybe I am Richard the Lionheart." The bartender brought my drink over. "Hey," Karl said to her, "how much longer will you wait before you lock on to another target?"

"Excuse me?"

"You know what I mean. How much longer before you forget about Johnny over here and go for someone who responds?"

"I think he's responded just fine," the bartender said. This caught me by surprise.

"Don't mind my friend," I said, "They just upped his Viagra prescription and he is a bit charged."

The bartender laughed.

"What's your name?" I asked.

"Linda."

"Hello Linda," I said, extending my hand. She shook it. She had very soft hands. "I am—"

"John Keegan. I know who you are. I've seen you on television."

"I keep forgetting those appearances," I said.

"I can see why. You are much more flattering in person."

"Thank you."

Linda turned and walked toward another cop thirsty for a drink.

"You're welcome," Karl said.

"What did you do?"

"If I wouldn't have started in that direction, you'd be going home holding yourself."

"I only hold myself when I need it," I said.

"Then that's pretty often. You have a constant need for consolation."

"Thanks."

We stood there for a moment, a rare, temporary period devoid of wisecracks. Neither of us meant the other harm, though I think it is human nature to chop away at those closest to you in an attempt to keep them from getting ahead. A defense mechanism, perhaps, but everyone has it. And I don't want to hear about these socially well-adjusted people who claim they only want to bring out the best in everyone. No one is that well adjusted. From what I have seen about the human species is that we are a maladjusted group. I get scared when I think about it sometimes.

"What the hell are you thinking about?" Karl asked.

"How you've survived for this long without couth," I said.

"Pot calling the kettle black," Rick chimed in, breaking his silence.

"Whatever. When's this party gonna get going?" Karl asked.

"You're just waiting for another socialite to bang," I said.

"I'm waiting for anyone to bang," Rick said.

"Whoa, Calhill does have some balls. Good for you, Ricky boy. Tap some ass, instead of beating around the bush like Keegan does here. Guy turns down more than most people ever get. Makes me wonder sometimes."

The conversation had degraded past my point of caring. I enjoyed Karl's company, but he operated on a level I didn't relate to. I found this problem amongst most people I knew, and that I didn't. I used to attribute it to being a cop, that seeing the ills of society on a near-daily basis made me unable to carry on a normal conversation, or what would count as a conversation to 'normal' people. Then, I came to the conclusion that I just do not relate to people well. I can't just sit and talk about meaningless bullshit all afternoon without walking away with a bad headache.

Like I said before, I am not high on invite lists.

I wanted Pauline to show up. I felt a tinge of discomfort as I realized this was what I wanted, but I knew for sure that I did. I live my life by what I feel, and I felt strongly about this. This was the good part of relationships for me, the part before anything happens, when anything can happen, and I could play it out in my mind any way I wanted. The problem came when real life didn't compare to the fantasies I had already lived.

As if she were psychically linked to me, Pauline walked in the door, dressed in a simple black gown, her hair tied up. Immediately, nothing else existed in the room but her. I never really got to experience such sensory tunnel vision, so I enjoyed the rare moment. I think some people go through an entire lifetime without ever being consumed by someone. It's a liberating experience, one of the magical things about life that makes it worth living. I don't mean to get all mushy, but Pauline had this effect on me right then. I thought maybe she just filled a void, or perhaps I was making more out of what I felt for her than there was. I decided right then to, for a change, not worry about it.

Pauline noticed me but didn't come over right away. A few higher-ups intercepted her. She never really dressed in a way that showed off what now appeared to be a flawless body, so I couldn't blame the other guys for flocking to her. She really did draw attention. I got jealous. I always claimed that I couldn't get jealous but I was right then. I envied the attention she was giving to other men instead of me. I wanted to be the center of her attention. Hell, I really wasn't even sure if she liked me. I felt like a teenager, and loved the hell out of it, to be honest.

"Looky here," Karl said, "looks like you're stacked for the

night, Johnny-boy. Who will it be, McCrory, or the bartender?"

I didn't answer, preferring instead to live in my own world than be brought back to the real one.

"Hey, go easy there."

"I'm fine," I said, hoping that a quick answer would shut him up.

"She looks good," Rick said, "I never realized how pretty she is."

At least Rick showed some sort of class. Karl had class too, but didn't always display it. I liked him for this reason, thought at times, it wore thin. It was anorexic right then.

Pauline finally made it through the crowd of admirers, and was standing before me. I really don't know what took me over, what changed her from a girl I knew to a girl I wanted to know better. Everything about her right then was perfect, as if she were matched to me. I believe that certain people can be a perfect match at specific points in our lives. I think we change over time. That's why the high school sweetheart you would have chopped a leg off for becomes someone you can't even imagine liking years later. Pauline was perfect for me right then. Enough said.

"Hi," I managed, feebly.

"You're working it, McCrory," Karl said.

"And you're pushing it, Lavin."

Karl laughed, then started talking to the bartender, figuring I had made my choice. He was right.

"Hello, Keegan," Pauline said. She smiled at me.

"Nice dress."

"Don't bust my chops. I have to wear this thing. You guys get to dress the way you always do, like shit."

"Actually, it was a compliment. But thanks for not returning it."

Pauline laughed. "I am not used to that from you. Thank

you. And you don't look so bad. A little heavy on the cologne, if you ask me. But other than that, you look presentable."

"Thanks. Can I buy you a drink?" I asked.

"About the only time you'll make such an offer, so yes. I'll have a gin and tonic."

I walked over to Karl and told him to get me a gin and tonic. It seemed he had already made headway with the bartender. She shifted from me to him rather quickly, I thought. Then again, she didn't seem like an amateur. She knew what she was doing. So did Karl, so they were a good match.

I came back to Pauline with the drink.

"Thanks," she said. We experienced that uncomfortable moment of silence, just looking at each other, then looking away. I hated this, but didn't know what to say. I figured I should have talked about something. I felt like an idiot, afraid anything that would come out of my mouth would sound idiotic. My senses told me I had her, that she was just as interested in me as I was in her. Maybe this was the problem. Again, the fantasy/reality thing. Plus, I loved a good conquest. If she laid down too easy, I would be disappointed. I wanted her to play with me a little, make it hard for me. I just didn't expect that she would.

"Keegan?" Pauline asked.

"Yes?"

"Shut up."

"Thanks."

"You're not yourself. What's wrong?"

"Nothing."

"Could have fooled me. You look like a virgin on prom night. Afraid to open your mouth because it will adversely affect your chances of getting laid."

I opened my mouth wide to show my lack of fear.

"Well, you're not getting laid anyway. Not with that cologne on, at least. You buy that stuff at the zoo?"

I shook my head. "Free spray from the restroom here."

"They should be paying you."

"About this not getting laid thing," I said.

"Yes, you're not. Simple."

"What made you think I'd want to?"

Pauline nearly choked on her drink. "Ha. You'd stick anything that stood still long enough. Trust me, I am not flattering myself. It's a known fact."

I tried to think of a good quip to come back at her, and the mind went completely blank. This doesn't happen to me often, I usually have a vast array of one-liners and off-the-wall statements at my fingertips for such occasions. With Pauline, I lost connection with this resource. I stood there, saying nothing. It wasn't going good.

Then, Marcus Lay saved me.

"Keegan," he said, coming toward me. He stopped and admired Pauline. Not in a dirty way, but an appreciative one. He was dressed in a dark blue suit, ever the consummate professional. "Do you return messages?"

"Sorry, been busy."

"What the hell you been busy with?"

"Want a drink, Marcus?" I asked.

"I want to talk to you."

"Shoot."

"Not here. This is about business. It's about the Central Park case."

"I've got my own things to handle right now," I said, thinking Marcus thought I was still interested in his case. It amazed me how bored I got sometimes.

"Yes, I know, the Volkyv case. I think we should talk. Stop by my precinct tomorrow. It's important."

"Alright," I said.

Marcus walked away. He didn't really seem angry, he seemed eager, as if what he knew would do one of us some good. I figured he would be the one to benefit. I never benefit from anything.

"You always that bad with returning phone calls?" Pauline asked.

I seized the opportunity to save my future self. "Yes. I just forget. It's been a problem for a while. Part of it is my not feeling comfortable talking on the phone."

"And the other part is that you are a lazy, forgetful piece of shit?"

"Something like that. I really can't win with you, can I?"

"Depends on what you are trying to play," Pauline said.

"I don't want to play anything."

"Don't get all serious on me, Keegan. I might not recognize you."

I wanted to be serious. More than that, I wanted her to be serious. I wanted to have a real conversation. Sure, I had laid the groundwork for this relationship by constantly making obvious plays at Pauline, and for busting her chops at every opportunity. It bothered me that she felt that, in order to even the playing field, she had to do what I did. There's nothing wrong with being a wiseass if that's what you are, but if you're trying to be one to match someone else, or to make someone happy, then it's just weak.

The only thing Pauline had going for her was that she was good at it. Very good.

"Me, serious? Give me a break," I said. I looked her up and down. "What, you had to go to a funeral earlier this week?"

"Funny. I do wear things other than a uniform."

"I'd never know it."

"That would require you to pay attention, Keegan."

"I am a detective. It's my job to pay attention."

Pauline giggled. It almost came out like a squeak, but it was cute, nonetheless. "There are so many things I could say about that."

"But nothing you could actually come up with. You're slipping."

Pauline looked me in the eyes. "So, why did you brush off that other cop? It sounded like he had something important to say to you."

I decided to try a new approach, honesty. "I preferred to talk to you," I said, holding her stare.

For the first time, it appeared that Pauline didn't know what to say. I hoped she wouldn't come back with a wisecrack, ruining the moment and making things even more uncomfortable. "That was nice," she said, flatly.

"I can be nice every once in a while."

"I am sure you can," Pauline said.

I noticed out of the corner of my eye that Geiger was coming toward me. I figured he was walking in my direction to talk to Rick. I felt like I was doing something wrong, flirting with a coworker. Geiger would certainly be against it, and I wouldn't put it past him to say something right there.

Geiger was dressed in a nice black suit and a blue tie. He looked professional, someone who had an air of superiority. He didn't prance around the office like that. It seemed strange for him to be that way, but I knew why. He was campaigning, angling to get a higher position. Geiger wasn't the prototypical ladder climber. He did deserve the promotion. I hoped he got it.

"Keegan, McCrory," he said with a nod.

"What's up, boss?" I asked.

"Just stopping by to thank you for showing up on time, Keegan. I appreciate it."

"Would you expect anything less?"

Geiger rolled his eyes. "Don't make me say anything in front of McCrory here," he said.

"Oh, nothing you could say about him would surprise me," Pauline said.

"Thanks, both of you," I added.

Rick walked over. "Hello," he said.

"Calhill. I don't really want to get into business here and now, but be sure the two of you stop by my office first thing tomorrow morning. A few things have come to my attention that might help with the investigation."

"Sure thing," Rick said. I just nodded.

"Have a good time and thanks again for coming." Geiger walked away.

"You'd think he was running for mayor," I said.

"He's just playing the role," Rick answered.

"He's not a role player. It must be uncomfortable for him."

"Geiger is a smart man," Pauline said, "He knows what he needs to do."

I didn't know if Pauline was aware of Geiger's opportunity, but I decided not to talk about it in detail. If he wanted the whole precinct to know, he'd tell them. Lunchroom whispers belonged in the lunchroom. I wasn't going to contribute any more information.

"He is smart," Rick said. "I hope he gets the job." Of course Rick hoped Geiger got the job. He thought he had a chance at Geiger's position. I tried not to imagine what it would be like working for Calhill. Yeah, he was a good guy and was certainly capable. It would change our relationship, though. I didn't even want to think of the particulars of that.

Rick stayed by us, despite my glances to hint he walk back to where Karl was. "Lavin's gonna score," he said.

"He's smooth enough," Pauline said. I wondered what she meant by that. Was she attracted to him? I couldn't imagine Karl was her sort of man, but that was based mainly on what I knew about him that others didn't. Maybe a guy like Karl was exactly what some women wanted. I just hoped Pauline wasn't one of them.

"He likes to talk a good game," I said.

"He plays a good game," Rick said. "The guy could charm the pants off of a nun."

"That's a nice thing to say," I said, looking at Pauline, then back at Rick to indicate he shouldn't talk like that in front of a woman.

"Are you getting gentlemanlike, Keegan?" Pauline asked.

"No. There is just a time and a place to talk like that."

"I can't think of a better time or a better place."

"John's a little shy," Rick said, "don't mind him. He's such an angel all the time, so such talk rattles him."

Pauline laughed. "I'm sure."

I wanted to take Pauline out of there. I think that being around coworkers kept her in work mode, which for her was a relentless slew of wisecracks. I wanted to see her act naturally. I wanted to see her more intimately, she the look of want in her eyes. What I mean is that I wanted her to look at me with the look of desire. Not sexual desire, but instead I wanted to see a look of wanting to be with me. This is how I felt toward her. I had a desire to just be with her, to lie on the couch with her, her head on my chest, watching television. I know, this sounds corny. The average person who knew me would never expect me to be this way. The average person didn't know a damn thing about me.

I didn't expect such a thing would happen any time soon. Pauline seemed to keep herself well guarded. I did too. This wasn't exactly a recipe for success. One of us had to open up and take a chance. Normally, I waited for women to do this with me. There is nothing more uncomfortable than throwing yourself out there to the wrong person. Okay, I feared rejection.

Rick turned out to be more perceptive than I figured. "I'm going back over by Karl. Anyone want a drink?"

"I'll take another," I said.

"Dewars, right?"

"Yes."

"And you?" Rick asked Pauline.

"Gin and tonic. And tell that floozy over there to put some gin in it this time."

Rick laughed and walked over to the bar.

"He's a nice guy," Pauline said.

"Yes, he is. It took me a while to get past his quirks."

"We all have our quirks. It's a shame the way people talk about him behind his back."

I'd never heard most of that because I was his partner. I figured most of the people that talked about Rick talked about me as well. I was, after all, just as much a part of that situation as he was.

"People are idiots. Especially cops with nothing else better to do than talk."

"It's human nature," Pauline said.

"It's an ugly part of it."

"You did the right thing by allowing him to work with you again, by the way."

"I didn't even have to think about it."

"You know what you're problem is, Keegan?"

"I have a lot of problems."

"You're a nice guy who is afraid of being thought of as one."

"That's pretty psychological."

"It's also true."

"I don't think so."

"Of course you don't. I get the feeling that, when it comes to things that matter to you, you don't speak your mind."

"I do."

Pauline smiled. "No you don't. You only speak your mind when it is safe."

She was right. I hated it. "I always say what I think."

"You've been careful with what you say since you started talking to me tonight."

I didn't think she'd play such a strong hand right there.

Was she trying to get me to talk about her? I wasn't going to fall victim to that. "Not true."

"Oh, stop it. Why don't you just tell me what you are thinking?"

"I have."

"You haven't."

"What do you want me to say?"

"How about telling me what is behind that look you've had in your eyes since I walked over to you?"

I wasn't used to a woman who was so blunt. It scared me a bit, but it also excited me. "The look behind my eyes?"

"I can see right through you, Keegan. Why do you rely on my interpretation of you? What if I get it wrong?"

"What do you see?"

"That's cheating. You want me to start the conversation."

"You won't let me get away with anything, will you?" I said.

"No."

"Alright. I'm interested. That what you want to hear?"

"You make it sound like it's an obligation."

"It's not."

"Then don't make it sound so bad," Pauline said. I could tell she was enjoying this. I don't think in a bad way. I think she just liked to aggravate me.

"It could be torture, for all I know. I see how you are down at the precinct. You could be the original pain in the ass," I said.

"There you go again, making jokes."

"It's what I do."

"I see."

Pauline looked around the room for a moment. She had such keen eyes. She always seemed to be analyzing things, always keeping an eye on what was going on around her. She could carry a conversation and scan the room at the same time. She reminded me of myself.

"See anything else you like?" I asked.

"There's that hotshot rookie, Williams, over there," she said, inclining her head toward the blonde haired guy to my left. Garrett Williams was the newest detective in vice. Karl had told me the kid was sharp. He seemed to have a lot going for him, not counting the shiny gray suit he was wearing. It was clear he didn't play dress up too much. I'd thought he was a pretty boy the first time I met him, sort of a Rick Calhill in training. This, of course, was not a good thing.

"Too young for you," I said. This drew the appropriate glare from Pauline. "You don't want to babysit, do you?"

"I'd probably have to do that with any of you guys. Lord knows none of you could possibly take care of yourselves."

"I might surprise you."

Pauline rolled her eyes. I liked when she did that. "Please, Keegan. You just learned how to tie your shoes."

"But I am very good at it."

Pauline glanced down at my feet, which were covered in brown loafers. "I see that."

"So, you'd be willing to take a chance on one of us?"

Pauline smiled, something I liked even more. "Maybe."

"How about taking a chance Saturday night?" I asked.

She pretended to think about it. I couldn't believe I'd asked, taken a chance so boldly. I wasn't afraid of women, not by a long shot, but I wasn't exactly one to go out on a limb and risk rejection in such a public arena. Karl surely knew what I was up to and there was a good chance Rick could figure it out. They'd want to know how I did. Normally, I would avoid taking the chance so that I wouldn't have to admit defeat.

"You don't really expect me to go out with you, do you? I mean, a detective, someone from work. It seems a bit too risky."

I couldn't tell if she was busting chops or not. I figured she was. Still, normally I would have busted them right back.

Instead, I surprised myself. "Risks are what life is all about. I think this is a risk worth taking."

She looked me over, not saying a word for what seemed like a month. In all, it probably took about six seconds. "You're persistent, I like that. At work it means you will bust my chops until you get what you want. I assume that applies to the outside world as well."

"I am all about consistency."

"I see. Where are you taking me?"

"Wherever you want to go."

"Why? Why are you so determined? Two minutes ago you couldn't even tell me how you felt."

"I just have a feeling, Pauline. I think you do too."

A nervous smile, this time. I hadn't seen that from her before. "I might. I just might." She opened up the small black purse that hung from her shoulder and wrote down her number on a small piece of paper. I wanted to make a joke about how prepared she was, how she must have done this all the time. It seemed like it might ruin the moment. I decided to just wait.

"I expect a call by tomorrow. None of that 'wait three days' crap. If you want to make plans with me for a Saturday, you had better call, and come up with something interesting."

"Nothing but the best for you," I said. Again, I refrained from the wisecrack. It just didn't seem appropriate. Or, more likely, I knew that her reply would be far wittier than anything I had to say.

"You're going to keep this between us," Pauline said. Then, she looked in Karl's direction. "Okay, I am sure that the Idiot Crew will detect something, so I suggest you tell them to keep a lid on it. This isn't really a precedent I'd like to set."

"I understand. I'll let them know to clam up."

"Good boy," she said.

"Always."

Pauline snorted. "I am going to mingle a little bit. If I

stay here making girly eyes at you any longer, everyone is going to know what we are up to."

"Makes sense," I said. "I am sure I will see you around."

"Not if I see you first, Keegan. And, I'll have my eye on you. Watch the scotch."

Pauline smiled one more time. There was something about that smile that went right through me. I wanted to take a picture of it but I knew I wouldn't have to. It would replay in my mind until the next time I saw her. I found myself already looking forward to seeing her again. This was either going to be a fantastic relationship, or another disaster in a long line.

I didn't even want to think about that.

12

I stayed at the function for as long as it seemed required to. I made sure I wasn't the first one to leave or the last. Karl had managed to score with the bartender but I'd figured she would tear right through him. A guy like Karl doesn't see a man-eater like her coming. I hoped it would turn out that way. He needed some straightening out. Maybe we all did.

Walking home, I did my best to keep my thoughts from Pauline. It wasn't going to do me any good. A psychologist would tell me I had commitment anxiety or some other disorder and they might have been right. There was no question I had some sort of problem, but at least I had an excuse. Not many people could say that a prospective love of their live was murdered not six months before. Sure, I'd never gotten the chance to develop a relationship with that woman. That didn't stop me from idealizing her and making her everything I thought I'd needed. Pauline was the first after that. And, I hadn't even tried to like Pauline. It just happened, the way my parents and others had always told me it would.

Not wanting to dwell on the subject and frighten myself out of something that could be good, I shifted my thoughts to the K-Drugs case. Rick and I had covered a lot of ground. I'd gotten a better understanding of how the Russian underworld operated. I couldn't say that I had much experience with the criminal underworld, the various mobs and their counterpart underlings. Sure, I arrested plenty of connected men. This was different, isolated incidents not threaded together with organized crime. K-Drugs wanted to move upward in that world. He'd found himself on the wrong side of a bullet. That, in and of itself, was a beautiful thing.

Medina hadn't really offered enough information, nor had anyone else. Really, the way I figured, we had to wait for something to happen to Alex Antanov. Death seemed to be the most likely result. If someone killed Antanov, then we might have had another link. Someone else was involved, no doubt, and we needed to wait for that someone to move. I hated waiting for someone to act.

My better instincts told me to look closer into the case, find something that would put it all together. Maybe it was the three drinks I had, or the night air. Something had sharpened my thoughts enough for me to realize I needed to analyze the murder again, find some piece of evidence which would shed light on who was responsible. K-Drugs had left clues somewhere. It was my job to find them.

My cell phone buzzed in my pocket. I thought for a moment about letting my voice mail get it, then changed my mind and allowed the interruption. The Caller ID flashed a number I didn't recognize.

"Yeah," I answered, expecting someone whose sole intention was to annoy me.

"Keegan," the deep voice at the other end replied. It was Marcus.

"Mr. Lay. How can I be of service?"

"I don't like the way you brushed me off tonight."

"Most people don't. Don't take it personally. I wasn't in the mood for business."

"I want to talk to you in private. I don't want to do this in the office."

Considering that Marcus was straight-laced, this must have been important.

"Okay. What do you have in mind?"

"Same place as last time. I'll get the drinks."

"You sure know how to make me smile."

"This might be the only time tonight I do that."

"Don't kill the moment, Marcus."

"Be there in a half an hour."

The bar was two blocks away. Talk about convenience.

"I'll be there in five, even prime myself up with a drink out of my own pocket."

"See you soon," Marcus said, and hung up.

I should have known that things were going to come together. Something had told me from the outset that this case would be unusual. The problem was, I'd gotten so used to the unusual that I couldn't even notice it anymore. I took it for granted. That was a mistake.

It seemed no one was in Donovan's when I walked in. Only two people sat at the bar, a middle-aged couple that, by the looks of them, spent a lot of time in bars. His thick red nose and her ridiculously thick makeup gave that away. A new bartender stood behind the bar, a tall, lanky kid that couldn't have been over 25. Yes, it bothered me that I considered someone 25 a kid. Life goes on.

At first I thought about getting a table. That seemed a bit conspicuous considering the amount of people in the place. I could at least sit at the bar until Marcus got there. Then, I could let him decide what he wanted to do. It was his privilege for buying the drinks.

I sat in one of the thick wooden stools. I tried to swivel, which it seemed the chair was designed to do, but couldn't. I must have looked like an idiot. No real stretch there, I know.

The bartender walked over and I resisted the urge to mention how slow it was. I always hated people who stated the obvious because they had nothing else to say.

"What can I get you?" the kid asked. He had thick, curly black hair that seemed to be too much for his head. It appeared to weigh him down, almost.

I wanted a Dewar's, that was my drink. For some reason,

I didn't feel like getting drunk. I didn't want that tired feeling that always seemed to come over me when I stopped drinking and started again. It was like a haze that came over me, clouding all my thoughts except for those about going to sleep.

"What do you have on tap?" I asked.

"A lot. What do you like?"

"Something amber. Got anything like that?" I don't know why I wanted something like that. I couldn't remember the last time I had an amber beer, if I had one ever. I just didn't want a Budweiser and I didn't like light beer all that much. Amber just seemed right.

"I've got Killian's and John Courage," the bartender answered.

"What's John Courage?"

"British beer. Not bad."

"You sold me."

The bartender turned around and poured the beer. I looked over at the couple, who were at the opposite end of the bar. Both of them stared straight ahead. They hadn't even looked at each other since I walked in. I couldn't imagine being in a relationship like that.

The bartender returned. I reached into my jacket pocket for my money. Nothing there. I fished through my pants pockets and still came up empty. I could feel the blood rush to my face. I hated stuff like that. I hated looking like an idiot, something I should have gotten used to years before. I knew I had money on me. Instantly, I thought I lost it, dropped somewhere when I had gone into my pocket for something else. I didn't carry a wallet because I hated them and always figured that pickpockets grabbed a wallet first.

At the party, I had tipped the bartender, this much I remembered. There was more money with the five I gave her. I checked all my pockets again and still came up empty. The bartender stared at me for a moment, then smiled.

"Forget your money?" he asked.

"No, I have it. I just had it a few hours ago."

The bartender didn't say anything but the look on his face didn't exactly display belief. Certainly he had dealt with many drunks who'd either forgotten or spent all their money without realizing it. Now, I was one of them. The heat on my face intensified.

"It's got to be here somewhere," I said, trying my best to speak clearly so he wouldn't think I was drunk.

The bartender nodded. "Take your time. I am sure it will turn up." I guessed he didn't think it was worth the effort for one beer.

After checking my pockets a third time, I finally remembered where I put my money. There was a pocket on the front of my suit jacket that I rarely used. For some reason, after I tipped the bartender at the cop function, I put my money there. Luckily, I remembered that in time. I took a twenty out and put it on the bar. The bartender watched me do it but he didn't come over right away to take it.

I couldn't wait for Marcus to get there.

I took a sip of the beer and was surprised how good it tasted. I'd expected it to be bitter, which it wasn't. Also surprising was the fact that it wasn't as carbonated as normal beer, which made it go down easier. The last thing I needed was something that went down easy. I didn't have a problem with being able to drink. I think I've already made that clear.

I didn't know what to do with myself. I'd seen many people, when alone, tapping away at their cell phones, sending text messages, playing games. I took my cell phone out of my pocket and looked at it. It didn't have all the bells and whistles other phones had. It wasn't color, it couldn't take pictures, and, as far as a I knew, it didn't double as a teleportation device. From what I can tell, this was a good thing. I think there were a few games on the thing—the snake game probably—but I had never played them. Games were for computers and consoles. What was the sense in playing something on a phone?

Actually, I had seen a commercial for a cell phone that played MP3s. The idea behind it, it seemed, was that life was too boring without your own playlist running through your head at all times. And, don't fret, listening to music won't get in the way of getting the unimportant phone call. The music automatically paused for that. This is what people had become; consumers so programmed to consume that they didn't even think twice about the ridiculousness of it all. Personal audio players seemed so advanced when the Walkman came out. Now, they had these devices incorporated into everything. They had DVD entertainment centers in cars because kids can't be expected to look out the damn window. There were personal video players, for people who absolutely need to watch a movie any time, anywhere.

Okay, maybe I was jealous. I don't know.

Before I came to a conclusion about that, Marcus tapped me on the shoulder. He was dressed in the same suit he wore to the function. It was a navy suit with a very subtle light blue pinstripe. He wore a silver tie with a white shirt. On his sleeves were small silver cufflinks. He always dressed sharp. I hated him for that. He looked at my beer, back at me, and said, "John Keegan?"

"Shh, I don't want my public to know I am out and about," I said.

"Drinking beer?"

"Wasn't in the mood for scotch."

"That seems wrong."

"Wrong?" I asked. I noticed Marcus didn't seem to want to sit down, so I knew the best thing to do was get a table. He had something important to discuss.

"Beer just doesn't seem your speed."

I gestured toward the bartender, who just so happened to be talking on his cell phone. I think I was the only one that found this practice offensive. Talk on your own time, not when you are at work. This seemed obvious to only me.

The bartender looked at me, then continued to talk. I gestured again. Still, the same response.

"Hey," I said, probably louder than I should have.

The bartender glared at me, then, from what I could tell, told the person on the other end of the line that he'd call back. He walked over, the look of aggravation evident on his face.

"Yes?" he asked.

"My friend here would like a drink, and we'll take it at the table over there," I said, gesturing to the table all the way in the far corner of the room. If he hadn't have been so rude, I would have walked the drinks over there myself.

"Right," the bartender said. "What can I get you?" he asked Marcus.

"Glenlivet. Neat."

"Neat?"

"Yes, neat. It means straight up," Marcus said, politely.

"Then why not just say straight up?"

"Because the proper term is neat."

The bartender shrugged. "That makes no sense."

"Of course it doesn't," Marcus said, his tone implying that it only made sense to people who knew what they were talking about. A bartender should have known.

"Glenlivet," the bartender said, "*neat.* I got it."

I stood up. "And bring another John Courage as well."

"Gotcha."

We walked over to the table without saying a word. I knew something was about to change right then. Marcus would steer the case in a new direction. I am not adding emphasis to my premonition after the fact, that's really how I felt. I didn't get such instincts too often and I don't want to talk about how many times I was wrong. This time the feeling came too forcefully to be anything but right. I wish

I could say won't gloat about it for the rest of my life. Really, I do.

I sat in one of the wicker chairs facing the door. Marcus took the one directly across from me. He just sat there for a moment, as if he needed the drink to get things going. That wasn't Marcus. If he had something on his mind, he let it out, though he was far more diplomatic about it than I was. I think this was just an awkward moment. I spent the time staring at his face, noticing how deep his eyes were set, how thick his skin seemed on his nose.

The waiter came over with the drinks. It seemed to take a lot out of him because he huffed when he turned away from us. He was also on his phone. My grandfather would have beaten him to death with that phone. There was a man who had believed in the work ethic, in the idea that a job well done reflected on the person who did it. No one cared about that anymore. I wondered for a moment which side I represented. I didn't want to know.

Marcus took a long sip of his drink. "I'm probably making a bigger deal out of this than I should," he said.

"I doubt that."

"Seriously. Something has come up with the Central Park case that I think pertains to you."

"Me personally?" I asked, realizing that the pitch of my voice went higher than it normally did. I took a tug of my beer to soothe the throat a bit.

Marcus shook his head. "Your case, the dead drug dealer. I think our cases might be related."

I couldn't imagine how this was possible. "What makes you think that?" I asked.

"The girl we found, her name was Ilana Yigevny, the daughter of Boris Yigevny, the physicist."

Marcus looked at me for a signal of recognition. I had no idea who the guy was, so I shrugged.

"You should get out more."

"I get out too much."

"Anyway, it appears that Ilana paid the price for her father. We've done some investigating and found out that the Russian mob has been very interested in Boris but he hasn't been cooperative. We don't know what the link is but there is definitely something there."

"The Russian mob. You're sure?"

"Sure as I can be right now," Marcus said. "Theory I am working on right now is that they went after the daughter to get the father's attention."

"I'd say they have it."

"Boris is a meek man. I don't understand why they needed to go this far. He strikes me as the sort who would do whatever you wanted if you just glared at him the right way."

"Maybe this is something big. Something they needed to make a big statement about."

"Or, this could have been rookies, guys trying to impress the boss and went too far. I don't think they were supposed to kill her."

Now it made sense. If K-Drugs and the rest of his newly formed crew were only supposed to rape her and things got out of hand, there would be a price to pay. I'd originally thought K-Drug's death was a revenge kill. After hearing what Marcus had to say, I started to believe it might have just been the mob making him pay a price for his screw-up. Little did they know how bad he screwed up.

"That's very possible," I said. "I don't take it that the Russian mob likes it when their boys make such a big mistake."

"Especially one that makes the front page of every newspaper in the city," Marcus said between sips of scotch.

"So, you are saying that you think K-Drugs might have been ordered to get the daughter?"

"It's something that ran through my mind. That's why I am here talking to you."

"I don't know."

"Come on, I have a dead girl of Russian heritage with a father who has been approached by the mob. You have a dead Russian mobster. It's not a huge segue."

"True. Still, K-Drug's death really doesn't fit the description of a mob hit. Don't they always shoot the guy in the eye socket?"

"You watch too much TV. I am sure that's the way some Russian mob hits happened, but not all. Maybe they were trying to mask the fact that this was a mob hit."

"Whoever killed him kicked him in the nuts postmortem. Think the mob would actually do that?"

Marcus grimaced. "You never know with those guys. I certainly wouldn't put anything past them."

"So, Yigevny had ties to the mob?" I asked.

"I wouldn't say ties. I think they were interested in him, maybe interested in what he was working on. I don't know for sure."

"There definitely could be a link, if we accept the fact that K-Drugs was even hired for this job, which is a stretch in the first place. There are plenty of other mobsters in the city, and your murder/rape could be just a random gang incident."

"Of course it could. It very well might be. Still, we can't ignore the possibility."

"No, we can't," I said, finishing my beer. This was how cases were solved. It's a slow gathering process, the kicking around of ideas and theories. You accept some, you reject others. Those of us that really know what we are doing rarely reject an idea out of hand. The last thing you want is to find out that a theory you were presented with but rejected turned out to be the right one. That never happened to me. Not ever.

"What do you think we should do?"

"I'd like to talk to Rick, see what he thinks."

"How's he doing?"

"Well. He's really involved with the case." I gestured over to the bartender to tell him to get us another round. I didn't want to miss out on another free drink just because Marcus had gotten to his point fast. The bartender first appeared to ignore me, then went about his job of making drinks.

"What do you mean?"

"He's focused."

"Or burying himself so he can't think about any of it."

I felt the urge to defend Rick, then remembered his words about being pitied. I did pity him. I can't really think of anyone who wouldn't. Pity does lessen a person, makes them insignificant. So, I decided to let Marcus think whatever he wanted. I doubted his opinion would change based on anything I had to say.

"He's doing a good job. I don't care why," I said.

"You think there's a chance he might blow?"

I shook my head. "I doubt it."

"Maybe he is just working so hard because he thinks he has a shot at Geiger's job if it becomes available."

I didn't know how Marcus knew. I was aware of the fact that nothing stays a secret long in a precinct, let alone the entire NYPD if the story is juicy enough. I would have never thought anyone cared about whether or not Geiger got the promotion. I decided not to deny or validate what Marcus said.

"I think he just wants to get back to doing what he does. If working so hard takes his mind off his problems, then so be it. If he has other motives, fine. None of that crap has anything to do with me."

"Unless you end up working for him," Marcus said.

"I've always figured that one day, I would be. He's as upwardly mobile as they come. It's inevitable."

The bartender brought the drinks over. "This round's on me," he said.

Damn. Whenever someone else buys drinks, they get freebies. It was rare I did. Sure, bartenders bought me a drink from time to time, but whenever I was footing a large bill, it always seemed that they added drinks instead of helping me out.

Marcus leaned back in his chair. "How's life treating you, Keegan?"

"Treating me? It's doing anything but."

"It can't be that bad. You're living the single life, no one to answer to, no one to nag you."

"The single life only looks good when you are no longer single," I said.

Marcus laughed. "Maybe. How does married life look from your side?"

"Like a nightmare. I know plenty of married people. I see married people at the mall, dragging the kids. They don't seem too happy."

"Maybe they are and you just don't see it."

"I doubt that. What's the divorce rate these days. 60%? That's ridiculous. Even if I decided to settle down, find the right girl for me, I have a 40% chance that she won't divorce me."

"You can't look at statistics. You just have to know."

"Know? How can you know? How well can you get to understand someone before you get married?"

"As well as you want to," Marcus said. "That divorce rate you're talking about includes all of the lesser minded people who got married because it just seemed like the right thing to do, or they got someone pregnant, or any number of things."

"Okay. I can handle the married thing. It's the kids I don't think I can handle. If I had gotten married in my twenties, I'd be dealing with dirty diapers, or, actually, a kid who does nothing but suck money out of my pocket. Think about it. Parents, good ones at least, invest a lot of time, emotion, and money into their kids. I know my parents did. I've done the math, I don't think I've offered a very good return on that investment."

"Kids aren't an investment, you idiot. They are a creation. They are an extension of you." Marcus stopped for a second and chuckled.

"What?"

"I realize that might not be such an attractive way for you to look at it. I doubt an extension of yourself really entices you."

"You're right, it doesn't," I said. I started to get bored with this conversation, though I was amazed that during it, Pauline came into my mind. I actually thought about what it would be like to marry her. Yes, it was way too soon to start thinking about that. I did it all the time, though, and it's why I always ended up single.

"Other than women, what else is going on with you?"

"Nothing. I am bored out of my skull outside of work."

"Who isn't? You need a hobby, man. Something to incite some creativity."

"Like what?"

"I fish. Love to fish. Monday through Friday, all I can think about is the fact that I can get on my boat on Saturday and fish."

"Fish? Just sitting there, putting a pole in the water? If I am bored now, fishing would make me suicidal."

"You have to give it a shot. It's relaxing."

"Relaxing things put me to sleep."

"Then find something else. Trust me, you'll thank me later."

I couldn't even imagine any sort of hobby that would keep me interested. I used to love videogames, though I didn't think they qualified as a hobby. Plus, as the games became more advanced, I lost my interest. I also realized that I sucked at them. What was I going to do, play chess?

"I am not a hobby person."

"Do you exercise?"

"No."

"Obviously," Marcus said, "I don't even know why I asked."

"Why is everyone so concerned about working out? What the hell is the benefit of lifting weights? I don't lift heavy things throughout my normal day, so why should I practice doing so in the gym?"

"You carry around that truck tire you've got there," Marcus said, pointing to my belly.

"That's temporary."

"They usually start out that way. Then, you end up inflating it more and more until you don't even realize you've gained 50 pounds."

"Can't we talk about something else?"

"Like what?"

"How about your wife? Tell me about her," I said.

"Crystal is a dream. She's tough when she needs to be tough, and sweeter than anyone I know every other time. I knew I was going to marry her on the second date."

"The second date? How'd you know?"

Marcus smiled. I don't think I have ever seen such a genuine smile. "The way she looked into my eyes. Something sparked, ignited. I don't know, insert any Hallmark card cliché in there. I just knew."

I thought about Pauline. I'd liked the way she looked at me, too. Had Marcus found one of the true tests of love or had he just convinced himself? I'd always thought of love not as an emotion, but a state of mind. You convince yourself that you love someone because they have certain qualities you think fit your needs. Children love their parents out of necessity. That's what it all is, we all just want our needs met and, like the dog who respects the master that fills his bowl, we fall in love when we perceive someone has done just that.

This was the thought that entered my head. As if on cue, the memory of Emily Brackens followed right behind it.

"You okay?" Marcus asked.

"Fine." I didn't realize that I'd made some sort of face. I always thought I kept my thoughts to myself.

"You seemed out there for a minute."

"Just a lot on my mind, Marcus. You know how it is."

"Sure. I'd say you've got a full plate. Suspicious case, borderline partner. God knows what else you have going on in your life, but that would be enough for me."

"I don't worry about Rick, even though everyone thinks I should."

"You know I like the guy, respect him. Still, he's been through Hell. We don't know if he's gotten out of it yet."

"I think he'll be fine."

Marcus and I stayed at the bar for another hour. The conversation skipped around a bit but generally stayed on superficial things. We both tired of the serious talk. Marcus even told me a joke, a racial one. I won't say what it was, but I'll tell you that I laughed harder than I ever had. When I asked him why he would tell a joke that would appear to be offensive to him he told me that jokes are just jokes, and anyone who got upset about them needed their head examined.

Unfortunately, the joke hadn't cleared my mind as much as I wanted. I went home that night with Pauline and Emily battling for space in my head. I've heard that grieving is a process, that letting someone go takes time.

I didn't know I'd get a comprehensive course in that so soon.

13

The next day was supposed to be my day off. I never understood why they even bothered to put it that way. When on a case, a detective doesn't take time off, especially when the case is as important to his boss as this one was to Geiger. I didn't have to go in. I had the right to stay home. I figured I would catch some sleep and go in a little later than normal.

I woke with a jolt. Something had woken me up but I didn't know what. I hadn't set my alarm. I rarely did, only because I thought it best for the mind to wake me up. My father had taught me a way to make my mind wake me up. I just had to repeat a few times before going to bed 'I will wake up at 7am' and more often than not, I woke up right at seven. It sounds crazy, but it worked. And, when I set my alarm, I found that I always woke up a minute or so before it went off. That was a pain.

So, it wasn't my alarm that got me out of that vivid dream of Pamela Anderson I'd so enjoyed. We were on a cruise ship, and for some reason, people thought there was a bomb on it. I started investigating and found that Pam was doing the same, being a celebrity and all. She told me we should work together, and, we did. She's a great kisser, by the way.

Whatever yanked my lips from hers was going to pay a huge price. After a minute or so, I realized what it was because I heard it again. It was my door buzzer. Someone was outside and wanted to come in. I looked at my watch, it was 8"M. Someone was going to die.

I dragged myself out of bed, thinking about baseball and

old women in bikinis. Luckily, this trick worked and the effects of Pam wore off. I tossed on a t-shirt, looked in the mirror, and walked over to the door.

I hit the button for the intercom. "Whoever you are, you had better be bringing me money," I said.

"No money," Rick answered.

"What in God's name do you want? Ever hear of a phone?"

"I tried calling you. The phone goes right to voice mail. You turn it off?"

I thought about that for a moment. I couldn't remember what I had done with my phone. "No."

"Let me come up. I found something out last night."

"I don't want you to come up. I want to go back to bed."

"Trust me, it's important."

I debated for a moment about letting him in. He knew me fairly well, and I had to assume he knew better than to bother me in the morning for something trivial. I'd chewed his head off many times in the car on the way to work for such things, so it seemed the right thing to do was let him in. That didn't make my decision absolute, of course, but I finally decided to hit the buzzer so he could enter the building.

I looked in my jacket for my phone and realized it wasn't there. I didn't have a house phone, so my cell phone was the only way I could be contacted. I'd lost so many cell phones I was the company's favorite client. At three hundred bucks a pop, they were making good money off me. They were about to hear from me again, it seemed.

Rick knocked at the door. I didn't want to let him in, regardless of the fact I had promised to. I didn't want to see anyone that morning. I just wanted to be left alone, something that seemed cosmically impossible. I walked over to the door and said, "Go away."

Rick didn't say anything, which was the correct response. I opened the door.

"Still cheery in the morning, I see," he said, walking into the apartment. "And still a slob."

"I'm just not anal retentive."

"That's obvious. Got anything to drink?"

"Scotch?"

"I was thinking more along the lines of water."

"There's a tap in the kitchen," I said.

"You're kidding."

I didn't say anything. I just looked at Rick. He walked into the kitchen and got himself some water, which I knew was difficult for him. He must have worried about the germs, the debris from the pipes, any number of things that could be wrong with tap water. I figured tap water was fine. I'd never heard of anyone dying from it. It just got a bad name because the people who somehow convinced the general moronic public they needed bottled water wanted it that way.

"You came here for a reason," I said.

"I would have thought you dealt with that whole morning problem by now."

"Well, I haven't. What've you got?" I walked over to my beaten recliner and sat down. Rick sat on the couch across from me. I saw a bag of Doritos half-submerged behind the seat cushion next to him. I only hoped he didn't notice so I could escape another neatness lecture. He was good at those.

"Got the lab report back from the second sweep at K-Drugs' place," Rick said, taking another measured sip from what had to be a dirty glass. If he only knew.

"What'd you get?"

"It's pretty interesting, actually."

"I am sure you think it is."

"The blood we found on that knife matches a murder victim," Rick said, leaning back on the couch. I expected to hear a crunch from the chips but didn't.

"That would make sense. I didn't think he used it to gut a deer."

"The Central Park victim."

This seemed way too coincidental. I'd just spoken to Marcus about this. "Yigevny?"

"How'd you know?"

"I was talking with Marcus Lay last night. He was telling me that he thought our cases were related. He seemed to think that K-Drugs had been hired to rough up this Yigevny girl because the Russian mob is interested in her father."

"The physicist?" Rick asked, making me feel even more uninformed. It seemed everyone knew more than me. Maybe that was a good thing.

"Yes."

"Why would the Russian mob go after the daughter of a physicist?"

"Beats me."

"That's certainly a different perspective."

"Yes, but now we have a problem," I said, as my thoughts cleared and the obvious hit me square.

"What's that?"

"K-Drugs' apartment now becomes part of Marcus' investigation. Our cases are cross-linked. They are going to want jurisdiction, don't you think?"

Rick shook his head. "Doesn't make sense to me. The way I see it, their case is all but closed right now."

"Not if they find out we're looking for the other guys involved with the Central Park case. They're gonna want to know about Antanov, Medina, and anyone else we talk to."

"They can't just shut us down."

"No, but they can hamper us. You know how this precinct bullshit goes," I said. "Plus, we're investigating the death of a drug dealer and now probable murderer. Their case has a high profile victim. We're done."

Rick seemed to think for a moment. It looked like a strain for him. "Not if we do things on the sly," he said.

"You don't do things on the sly."

"I never did. This time, it might be necessary."

"Is that the right thing to do?" I asked, not believing the words actually came out.

"No."

"I like it."

"Look," Rick said, "This case is important, for a lot of reasons. It's important to Geiger, and it is important to me. I don't want my first case since I'm back to be thrown aside because of perceived priority. We're working on this case, and we will stay on this case. I don't give a God damn what anyone else has to say about it."

"I have no problem, you know that. I think that we should speak to Geiger, though. It's sort of his ass on the line."

"Agreed. Get dressed."

"That would mean I'd have to leave you here alone."

"Yeah?"

"Don't go nosing around."

"Like I would want to risk my health."

I showered, my mind running through all of this new information. Just twelve hours before, Rick and I had nothing to go on, no real direction to take our investigation. We had suspicions and instincts. Both of us knew fairly well K-Drugs had done something big, something horrible to earn his stripes with the mob. We suspected it had gone wrong. Now, our thoughts had crystallized. K-Drugs had been a part of the murder of Yigevny's daughter; it seemed impossible to think otherwise.

We lived for this stuff, the excitement, the mental wrangling with facts and evidence. Detectives are like investigative computers. We take information, process it, and come up with a conclusion. We don't always get it right, but we exist for this purpose and most of us do a good job with it.

Standing in the shower, letting the hot water hit my back and steam surround me, I realized the core of my life was staring me in the face. People spend years, some even spend a lifetime, trying to figure out who they were and what they should do. I had been blessed with the ability to find out, and I saw that I liked it. I enjoyed what I did. That time in the shower, right then, when I felt so relaxed, so at ease with myself, was a defining moment. It's one thing to know what you want to do with your life. It's another to try and do it. To realize that, to see that you actually succeeded in such a venture, that was rare.

I got dressed, a sort of uplifting air about everything I did. I felt at ease, a sense of purpose guiding my actions. I took more time thinking about what I wore, what my hair looked like. I wanted my outward appearance to reflect the inside, the newfound happiness I'd just achieved. The eternal night I'd seemingly endured for years yielded to a new sunrise. I knew it right then, my life would be different from that moment on, and I was prepared.

Geiger's face strained when we gave him the news. It looked like he actually experienced physical pain at learning about the crossing of our case with the Central Park murder, the biggest story to hit the city in some time. I felt bad for him right then. I wanted to make things easier for him, help him out somehow. I wondered if perhaps someone had put something in my drink the night before. I never felt this nice, so at ease.

"I was hoping for some good news," he said, not looking directly at either one of us. "This isn't good news."

"Sorry," Rick said, "but I figured you should know right away."

"Of course, of course," Geiger said, drifting off. I could sense he was watching his promotion slip away from him.

"It doesn't necessarily have to be bad news," I said.

Geiger snapped back. "What do you mean?"

"I mean we can still go about our business. There's no reason why we should be impeded in investigating a murder in our jurisdiction. If the guys working on the Central Park case want to know what we know about Volkyv's involvement to the Yigevny girl's murder, that's fine. We don't know shit, actually. We just have what could be the murder weapon and some street talk. Not much of it is documented right now, and none of it is solid enough."

Geiger took this in. "The attention will be off our case. They will get priority for everything."

"Which is exactly how I like it. Let the pressure stay on them. No one is going to care about our investigation, which will allow us to operate under the radar."

"We can pretty much do what we want," Rick added. I was very impressed with how Rick stayed quiet.

"True. But, it also means our investigation won't have the same effect I'd hoped it would have."

"No, it won't. But it can still show how effective this department can be when left alone. I think, in the long run, that will serve you far more than a high profile case that already seems headed for disaster," I said.

"Headed for disaster?"

"They entered my territory. They've gotten my karma involved. You know nothing good can come of that."

"Good point, Keegan. You two keep going. Try and stay out of here for as long as you can. I can't pull you off a case if I can't get a hold of you," Geiger said, "and report everything directly to me before you type up any reports."

"We can do that," Rick said.

"Maybe we can make something positive out of this. Find Volkyv's killer, and you might solve the Central Park case by accident. That, my friends, would be sweet."

I'd find out later that no more than five minutes after we left Geiger's office, he received a call from Marcus's boss. The guy actually had the balls to try and close down our investigation, saying that it was a conflict of interest with a case that had bigger implications. These were his exact words according to Geiger, who never exaggerated or embellished.

The guy had a point, but murder cases should not be controlled by how important they are. Someone is killed, the cops investigate until they either find the killer or run out of leads. You can't dictate who gets priority. Of course, this isn't the way it works.

Geiger, in no uncertain terms, told the guy to go play with himself. Unless the Chief of Police, or the mayor, said something, we would continue investigating. Geiger probably knew that bought us very little time, because Marcus's boss was very politically connected, something Geiger lacked. To his credit, Geiger never told us this. He let us investigate without the worry such pressure would have added. Maybe he did this for our benefit or maybe he did it because he knew he'd be better served if we operated optimally. It doesn't matter. It was a smart thing to do, regardless of the reason.

Our first priority was to find out what we could about Yigevny without raising any flags. We needed to know what the link was between him and the Russian mob. Then, we'd need to find out what arm of the Russian mob was involved. That would help us discover who was hired for the Yigevny job. None of this would be easy. We needed to be both careful and efficient. I couldn't remember when I was either of those.

Rick decided the best thing to do was start with records. Geiger wanted us out of the precinct as soon as possible. If we needed the precinct's resources, we'd better get them early. No sense in going back when we didn't have to. This made perfect sense to me. And, I was happy because I knew it involved seeing Pauline.

"Keegan and Calhill, the Laurel and Hardy of Midtown South. What can I do for you?" Pauline asked.

"First tell us which one is Laurel and which one is Hardy," I said.

"You don't want me to answer that question."

She was right, I didn't. Rick was tall and thin. It was fairly obvious, anyway. "We need a full background report on someone, but we need it kept as quiet as possible," I said.

"Quiet?"

I nodded, trying my best to put on a serious face so she would know this wasn't a time for wisecracks. To her merit, she picked up on it right away.

"How do you want it delivered?" she asked.

"Can you email it?" Rick asked.

"I don't know if that is a good idea. It can be traced easily."

"We aren't worried about that," Rick said, "by the time someone traces it, it will be no big deal. We just don't want anyone finding out about it now."

"You want me to do this through back channels, then. No using the NYPD main system."

"That would be nice."

"It can be arranged."

I slid a piece of paper to her. "That's the guy. We want everything. Place of birth, criminal history, credit check, how long he's been in this country, how he got here. Everything."

Pauline looked at the piece of paper. "That's easy. Guy like this will be highly visible. Especially now that his daughter has been murdered."

She now knew why we wanted to keep it quiet. Most people who work in the police department long enough learn how things work. I knew Pauline had a keen eye. I trusted her. This was a new experience, me trusting anyone, particularly a woman.

"How long?" Rick asked. Luckily, it didn't come out as a pressing question, just a courteous inquisition, if you know what I mean.

"Three, four hours?"

"Perfect." Rick wrote down an email address and his cell number. I was jealous that he gave her his instead of mine. Then again, I had no clue where my phone was. Being reminded of that made me feel vulnerable, naked. Without the phone, I was out of touch. What the hell did people do before the advent of cell phones? Where did they get their sense of security?

Pauline took the information. "Alright, I'll get right on this." I wanted to think her eagerness to help stemmed from her liking me, not her professionalism. The thought of her bending over backwards because of some affection she harbored for me felt good and I wanted it to be true. I can't say that it was; she gave no indication as to what inspired her to be so helpful.

"That one's got the hots for you," Rick said as we walked away.

"What makes you say that?"

"Common sense. Please tell me that you at least see the way she looks at you."

"I don't."

"Come on, you can't be that blind."

"I'm not blind. I just don't see what you do."

"After seeing you two talking at the party, it was obvious to me. It has to be obvious to you, as well."

Of course I knew Pauline was interested in me. She'd told me that much. Still, I didn't think her affection for me matched mine for her. I wanted to think that, but I couldn't actually believe it. Also, I didn't want to betray Pauline's trust by talking openly about us in any way.

"I don't think it's that obvious. I think you created this idea in your head, and you are now forcing yourself to see what you want to."

"And I think you are full of it. Play pretend if you want, but I have to tell you this; you'll be the biggest idiot I know if you let this one slip through your fingers."

"Point taken, now can we move on?" I asked.

"Where are we going?"

"Galbadon."

"Can we trust him to stay quiet?"

"Who knows?"

"Who's driving?"

"I am. I need to stop by the store first and get another cell phone."

"Sounds like fun."

14

The fact that cell phones had invaded our lives never really was clear to me until that day. I'd had a phone for a long time but I never felt like it was a necessity until that moment, until I sensed the nakedness going without a phone provided. I should have been worried for the future of the human race, I should have paid attention to the fact that we were being led by the nose by mega-conglomerates, but I didn't. I never do, actually. Most of my knowledge comes post-disaster.

I stopped by the Sprint Store, a virtual beacon of the pervasiveness of cell phones itself, and picked out a fancy new model. I was paying through the nose anyway, so I figured I might as well splurge. After all, as every commercial suggests, I deserved it. I earned the right to spend more money than I needed on something that I'd convinced myself was a necessity.

"Do you want one that takes pictures?" the sales guy asked. He was dressed in the standard yellow golf/sales shirt that everyone who was hawking something wore.

"Pictures?"

He looked at Rick, who shrugged. "Yes. You can take digital pictures."

"What, like a video phone? I can see the person I am talking to?" I asked.

He shook his head. "No. You can take snapshots and send them to people you know."

"Snapshots of what?"

He seemed puzzled by this question. "Of anything."

"What would I need to take a picture of?"

Again he looked at Rick. "Whatever you want."

"But I won't be able to use the camera as a video phone? Even if the person I am talking to has a camera phone too?"

"No."

"Then what is the sense in having a camera on the phone?" Of course, I knew the answer. The idea was similar to just about every other electronic device foisted upon the masses. Convince the people that something useless, something absolutely unnecessary, is needed. Years ago, no one needed a cordless telephone, or a TV, or a computer. Try living without one of those now. Camera phones were just another incarnation of a brilliant marketing ploy.

The clerk seemed frustrated now. "It's just for fun."

I looked through the glass counter separating us. "Which one of these is a camera phone?"

If I am not mistaken, the guy held back a laugh. "All of them, actually."

I was about to ask him why he even bothered to pose his original question when I realized to ask that would have been as useless as that original question. "Give me that one," I said, pointing to the bright silver flip phone, two from the left.

"A fine model."

"Which one is the best?" I asked, out of curiosity.

"That depends on what you want it for."

"Phone calls?" Again, I was about to ask a useless question, this one pertaining to the idea that a cell phone had any other purpose besides phone calls.

"This one here," he said, pointing to the wide, flat one on the right, "it does everything."

"You mean it sends *and* receives phone calls?"

The clerk rolled his eyes. "This is a Treo. It is like a phone/computer. It keeps all of your contacts, can browse the web, play games. You can create spreadsheets, access your email, and synchronize with your computer…" He drifted off, realizing that his pitch was falling on the wrong ears.

"How much?"

"If you extend your plan 2 years, $299."

"And how much for the one I selected?"

"$199."

"What sort of bells and whistles am I getting with my phone?"

"It takes pictures."

"Anything else?"

"You can access the wireless web."

"Can I create spreadsheets?" I asked.

"No."

"Can I access my email?"

"Sort of."

"Can I synchronize with my computer?"

"Nope."

"I'll take the...what did you call that thing?"

"The Treo."

"Does it take pictures?"

"It has the capability to."

"What?"

"With a camera attachment, the Treo can take pictures."

I found this interesting. There really was a phone that wasn't just a fancy camera. "So, what you're saying is, the Treo isn't a camera phone."

"No. It is a portable computer with phone capabilities."

"Sold. Does it come with a headset?"

"No."

"Can you throw one in?"

"No."

"What about a car charger. I need a car charger."

"They are $24.99."

I looked at his nametag. "Listen, Ralph, I am spending 300 bucks on a phone that we both know is far more than

I will ever need. The least you can do is make me feel good about the purchase and throw in a car charger."

Ralph thought about this for a moment. "I don't know."

"Sure you do. It's the right thing."

"I'd have to ask—"

"Your manager? Come on now, Ralph. We both know he's not going to throw away a $300 purchase, along with a 2-year extension that is probably going to cost me a couple of hundred to get out of next year."

"Okay," Ralph said, "but don't go telling all of your friends I did this, or I'll go broke."

"Rick here is my only friend, don't worry." Thinking about that, I realized it wasn't too far from the truth.

Ralph processed my new phone purchase, activating the new phone and conveniently putting the charge for the damned thing, along with the $20 headset, on my next bill. The phone was strange. It looked like a Palm Pilot, with an antenna at the end of it. When talking on it, the screen rested against my cheek. It was too big and way too much technology for me. To this day, I don't know what possessed me to buy it.

"What the Hell possessed you to get that thing?" Rick asked.

"Now we can talk to each other with technology, instead of actually having to see each other, isn't that great?"

"You should have gotten the other phone."

"The one that takes pictures? I refuse to own a picture phone."

"So you bought some state of the art computer phone, that makes a lot of sense."

"When did I ever say I make sense?" I said, opening the door to the car.

"Good point."

We got into the car and I fiddled with the phone. The first thing I did was plug it into my free car charger. The car charger had made the whole purchase justifiable. I would not have gotten the free charger if I had bought the cheaper phone. So, technically, the phone I got only cost me 75 dollars more. And, to think of how much extra phone I got for that money. I honestly don't know how much extra phone was involved because such technology was far beyond my grasp.

"How do I make a call with this thing?" I asked Rick. There were no buttons. Everything was on the touch screen.

Rick took the phone from my hands and fiddled with it. "Wow," he said.

"What?"

"You've got AOL Instant Messenger, Internet Explorer, Outlook, Excel, everything."

"Which one of those makes the phone call?"

"None of them."

"So, how do I make a phone call."

"Hold on, I am checking."

I started the car and drove off toward Brooklyn, to Chris Galbadon's precinct. My idea was to throw the latest news at him and see what he thought. We needed to know what Yigevny's link to the mob was. Perhaps Chris had heard things through his contacts, or he knew someone who could find out. This wasn't our territory. I didn't like that.

On the FDR Drive, Rick found something. "Got it," he said.

"You know how to make a phone call?"

"No, I was able to set up your internet access."

"Does that cost anything?"

"I don't know. Do you have wireless web service?"

"How would I know?"

"Then you don't. If you had it, you'd know, I presume."

"So, what good is setting up my internet access?" I asked.

"I don't know."

"Thanks."

"Don't mention it."

FDR Drive was more like FDR parking lot. The courts had just let out, and now the streets were packed with the agents of evil, otherwise known as lawyers, and other court people. Nothing shot my blood pressure up quicker than traffic, and I didn't even have my new phone to divert my attention, Rick was still busy playing with it.

The only thing I could do was think, think about the case, about how, if things went like they always did, we'd be screwed. I didn't fault Marcus for this, Marcus was a good man. This was politics. Politics exist in every facet of human interaction. Police politics, though different on the surface perhaps, are no different than office politics, college departmental politics, mall politics, and just about any other sort you can think of. People who know people get things done for themselves. Those who are not connected, not part of that elusive inner circle, get the shaft. I'd rather get the shaft that have to kiss the butt that the shaft belongs to, personally.

I couldn't get rid of the notion that something was staring me straight in the face. Why would a seemingly important physicist get involved with the mob? I had to put it out of my head that they approached him out of nowhere. One thing I learned from being a detective is that very few things in this world happen for no apparent reason. Sure, things can inadvertently happen, but most times, when murder is involved there is nothing inadvertent about it at all.

So, I thought, what was the reason? Drugs? It was possible that Yigevny used drugs and somehow got himself into a situation with the people he bought them from. I'd like to say that I dismissed this idea because Yigevny was a brilliant scientist and therefore was smart enough to stay away from drugs, but I can't. People have an uncanny ability to surprise, but those surprises, more times than not, are of the disappointing variety. Yet another sad fact of life.

For the moment, I put the drug idea from my mind, only because it complicated things more than I wanted to at the moment. There had to be another link, I figured, but what? One that made a bit of sense to me was gambling. Gambling is the refined man's vice. People from all walks of life can become degenerate gamblers. Politicians gamble, stockbrokers gamble, and janitors gamble. Everyone wants to take what they have and risk it for the chance to make it more. Most people don't seem to realize that Las Vegas is as beautiful as it is because the odds of being able to increase your wealth through gambling are slim, very slim.

So, maybe that was it, that was the link between Yigevny and the Russian mob. It was possible that he owed some sort of gambling debt and welched on it. The mob wanted their money, and in a creative move, they went after the daughter. K-Drugs and his pals maybe went a step too far and raped the girl, then had to kill her because there wasn't any other way out. though a bit flawed, this idea seemed to work for me.

"Okay, I've got your phone set up. This is really a nice piece of equipment," Rick said, pulling me out of my head.

"Great, I am back to being able to make phone calls." No sooner than I finished saying that, the phone rang. Rick handed it to me. The caller ID said it was the precinct. "Keegan," I said.

"Detective Keegan?" the female voice asked at the other end.

"That's what I said."

"I have an urgent message here from your mother."

"I'm sorry?"

"Your mother called. She said it is very important that you call her back. She left a number." I dictated the number so Rick could write it down for me. "Okay, got it," I said.

"What was that?" Rick asked.

"Some number my mother wants me to call her at. As soon as we are done with Galbadon, I'll give her a call."

We reached Galbadon's precinct in Brooklyn. Suffering the

same stares as last time, we made it to his desk. He seemed unhappy about something. I hoped I had nothing to do with that.

"The Midtown South boys are back. What can I do for you?" he asked.

I explained the situation we were in, how we needed to crack the case under the radar. Chris listened, with not even the slightest hint of what he was thinking on his face.

"Is Geiger going to hold the fort for you?" he asked when I was finished.

"I think he's going to try. Tough to know how successful he'll be."

"How can I help?"

"I think our first order of business is identifying the two other men involved with K-Drugs and Antanov. We're fairly certain there's four altogether."

"Knowing who they are will give us a line one the killer's next target, particularly if the killer is one of the four."

"You don't think it is Antanov," Chris said. I could tell by the way he said it that he didn't think so either.

"No," I answered. "My guess would be one of the other two, or someone else in the organization who has been ordered to clear them out of the way."

"The amount of effort we put into investigating dirt-bags," Chris said, thinking out loud.

"I know."

"Well, finding out the names of the other two shouldn't be that hard. We could stop by my friend down at his auto body shop. He might know a name or two that could lead us in the right direction."

"What about Medina?" Rick asked, echoing my thoughts.

Galbadon shook his head. I don't think it is a good idea to incorporate him into our plans at the moment. Medina has too many resources at his fingertips to create disaster for us."

"I really don't give a crap what sort of resources he has.

Medina might have connection, along with knowledge of what happened that night and why."

"I understand," Galbadon said. "Still it would be unwise to involve him right now. Let's focus on the street guys, see what they can bring us before we invite the trouble Medina can bring us."

I wondered if Galbadon had an ulterior motive in staying away from Medina. I knew that cops working a particular beat for a certain amount of time inevitably fall under the web of corruption they are trying to root out in the first place. Being surrounded by these gangsters could make any man see the ease of giving in. Fighting crime every day, seeing the hopelessness of battling a constant flow, tests the will of everyone involved. Maybe this happened to Galbadon, and I instantly thought less of him.

I considered myself a man of integrity. Sure, I did things wrong. I never followed orders; I took shortcuts when it came to investigations and procedures. I am not talking about this, and I am not trying to exonerate my own sins by highlighting worse ones. There is a difference between being a human being, with the imperfections and weaknesses inherent with humanity, and being a human being with integrity, with the knowledge of what is right and what is wrong along with the strength to follow the right path. No, I was no saint. I didn't deserve any accolades for staying the course. I was a rarity, a symbol of the past when what was behind what a man did was more important than the end result. In the present day, a man falling victim to his weaknesses was considered just like everyone else. He who is without sin cast the first stone, and all that shit. I didn't buy it then. I never will.

Maybe Galbadon was dirty and maybe he wasn't. One of the difficulties and beauties of life is the fact that you never really know. Various people enter and exit our lives and most of them we never get to truly understand. Motives, desires, and intent rarely reveal themselves. Sure, if we bother to invest the time necessary for finding out we might discover the truth about people, and, thus, the truth about ourselves. I'd argue that such truths are better left unknown. You are much better off thinking incorrectly that the person you loved all of your life loved you back equally. What is the value of finding out, on your deathbed, that your spouse loved someone else and cheated on you all those years? Self-discovery sucks. Discovery of other people helps little, as well.

"Your phone is ringing," Rick said, handing me the vibrating Treo. Yes, I know that sounded funny.

I took the phone, tapped the area on the screen that said 'Answer' and greeted the person at the other end. "Yes," I said.

"Christ John, I've been trying to get a hold of you for a while now." It was my brother-in-law, Donnie. I couldn't move for a second, fearful that the call involved my nephew. I'd had a feeling of death ever since I'd walked into the hospital that night.

"Donnie," I said, with no other words able to come out of my mouth.

"John, you really need to get down to St. Francis." Donnie was having a hard time speaking as well. I couldn't imagine why.

"Is your son okay?" I asked.

"It's not him. It's your father, John. I am sorry to have to be the one to tell you. Your mother has been trying to reach you since yesterday."

I couldn't think of what to say. I felt the urge to defend myself above everything else. "I lost my cell phone. I just got a message before from the precinct to call. I am in the middle of something right now."

"You have to get here, John, that's all I can say. He had a heart attack last night."

I am certain everyone has a different reaction to hearing this sort of news. I assume this has to do with whether or not the person is an optimist or a pessimist first and foremost. All I could think of was how I'd never considered my father to be mortal. It's not that I thought of him as superhuman, I just always thought he'd be around. Upon hearing he had a heart attack, that something threatened his life, I felt something escape me, some certainty leave my consciousness. I knew I'd never get it back. At the moment, I didn't even know what it was. Now, I do. It was my sense of security, my belief that, even though I had no faith in anything, eventually what was right would take precedent in the world. That was what my father believed, and in turn, I believed it as well. The mere fact that Death had reached out his hand and touched my father made me doubt just about everything.

"Is he okay?" I asked. I knew the answer. It laid right in between Donnie's inability to speak and the words he was able to get out.

"You need to come here."

"Okay."

I hung up the phone. I don't even remember how I did it. I looked at Galbadon, then at Rick. They could tell something was wrong.

"My father had a heart attack," I said, before they had a chance to ask.

"God," Galbadon said.

"I'm sorry," Rick added. "Is he okay?"

"I don't know, he's at St. Francis."

"Good hospital for that," Rick said. I wanted to say something to the effect that no hospital is a good hospital. People always look for little bright spots in such times, it is a reflex, I guess, a desire to make thing seem better than they are. I knew the situation was dim. I knew it in my mind and I knew it in my heart.

I would never see my father alive again.

"I am heading over there now."

"I'll come with you," Rick said. I knew he wanted to be there for support. Still, he didn't belong.

"No, you two continue. We need to get this case solved." I didn't care about the case. I only wanted to be left alone.

"Are you sure?"

"Positive. No sense in holding everything up. We have enough obstacles to begin with. I'll contact you as soon as I can."

"Don't even worry about that," Rick said, "And I will call Geiger, just to let him know."

"Thanks," I said, standing up and putting my hand on Rick's shoulder. "You'll be able to get home?"

"I'll get him home," Galbadon said.

"I appreciate it."

"Our prayers will be with you."

I smiled, acting as if such a gesture made me feel better. Nothing could have made me feel better. I knew the certainty of death. I knew death was lingering about. I just didn't think he would act so soon.

I drove all the way to St. Francis on auto-pilot. I had barely paid attention to my surroundings. I don't even know how I got to the hospital. I just drove, and the car took me where I had to go. I didn't drive very fast. I just drove naturally. It was the only way I could do it.

Of course, I was overcome with a sense of guilt. I felt guilty for not answering my mother's message sooner. I felt guilty for losing my cell phone. My inability to handle even the simplest of responsibilities had once again caused me pain. The worst part about that was I knew I wouldn't learn my lesson and I'd do something similar in the future. The most guilt came from the argument I'd had with my father. I didn't necessarily feel guilty for the argument itself, I had very little to do with that. I felt guilty for the thoughts I'd had afterward. I'd made my father out to be a monster in my mind then, and I felt guilty for thinking such things about a man who was dying.

My father was no saint, no better or worse of a man than I was. I instantly upgraded him in my mind, realizing how good of a father he'd been, how he'd sacrificed for the good of his family, how I didn't appreciate him enough when I had the chance. That sacrifice, what did it get him? He lived a life that seemed full. I wondered if I ever got to really know him, if I ever really understood what he wanted out of life. He acted as though he was happy, but there was no way to know for sure. He had some money, had a good wife, and two kids. He had a grandkid. I guess this was the goal of life and he had achieved it. Thinking that he might die, I almost felt sympathy for a life that, on the surface seemed complete, but might have been just the opposite underneath.

All of this ran through my head during my drive. I felt the responsibility to truly understand my father. Some of that stemmed from a desire to understand myself, I am sure. Still, I felt the need to know, the need to comprehend fully what made my father the man he was. Perhaps I wished for all of this because I knew I'd never get the chance to have it. I don't know that I would have endured the time and tedium of sitting and finding it all out.

I used my police privileges to park in the circle in front of the hospital. A guard walked toward me but stopped in his tracks when I flashed my badge. He didn't ask any questions. Not all security guards are useless or abusers of their limited power.

I walked into the lobby of the hospital, the sanitary scent instantly attacking my nose. There was another scent I sensed, one which I knew existed only for me at that moment. It was the scent of death, the same scent I felt when I'd been to the hospital to see my nephew. I tried to tell myself I'd created it in my mind, that I was the one who convinced myself it was there.

I knew that was a lie.

Nothing I'd ever experienced could have prepared me for what room 1031 had in store for me. I'd been involved with death for years. I worked with death. I'd thought death was a partner, an entity along for my particular ride in life. I guess, every once in a while, even the best partner hurts you, strikes you where you are most vulnerable. Only a close partner can do this, and Death was closer to me than anything else. He hit me hard, taking from me that which was most sacred. He took my belief. I allowed him to do it. I enabled him to strip me of my core, because I had left it unattended for so long.

Seeing my father hooked up to machines that did nothing other than produce the requisite beeps the nurses need to hear took my essence from me, removed my consciousness for long enough that I didn't even notice my mother, my sister, or my brother-in-law. All I saw was my father, the man who had helped mold me, helped make me the man I was. Sometimes he did it directly, sometimes indirectly, making me want to do the exact opposite of what he instructed so that I could emphasize my own character. Rebellion usually helps us define ourselves. Exerting ourselves this way adds to what makes us who we are. My father even helped in this way.

Looking at him, paralyzed while watching his chest rise and fall with the help of machines reminded me of everything he stood for, everything he tried to teach me. I owed him more than I ever gave him. I knew right then that the last words he'd hear from me were the ones I spoke at the end of the argument we'd had. This was the final gift I'd given him.

"John," my sister said. I heard her voice as if it were an echo, there and not there at the same time. I wanted to answer. Nothing came out. She moved toward me and put her arm around me. I could feel her trembling vibrate through me.

It took all I could muster just to touch her arm with my left hand. I found the strength to look at her. She'd been crying, the tears had left their remnants on her cheeks. I wanted to say something, offer strength as my father would in such a situation, like he had more times than I could count. It didn't happen.

Donnie came over next. He didn't say anything. He just patted me on the back. I knew why. They'd known the truth, known he wasn't going to make it. They must have guessed at the guilt which seemed to control my every thought. They were already passed recognition of what was to come. Shockingly, so had I. I knew it the minute I'd spoken to Donnie on the phone.

I couldn't let my mother come to me. I had to go to her. She was sitting at my father's side, holding his left hand in both of hers. On her face I saw that she was already trying to deal with the remainder of a life that would be lived without the man she'd loved for as long as she could remember. No words of mine had the power to intervene with that. So, I just made my way over to her and embraced her, giving in to the pain which came at me. My mother was the only one who could vanquish that, even if only for a moment. The rest was mine to conquer or succumb to.

"It's okay," my mother said, I think for lack of anything better. I didn't want her to say a word. I wanted to just stay there, in the safety of her embrace, even though I knew it wouldn't last.

"I'm sorry," I said, the words coming on their own, with no control whatsoever from me.

"I know, Johnny, I know."

I had questions. I wanted details. I wanted to know how it happened. I wanted to know why. No one knew why, I am sure, but I still wanted to know. Of course, I'd never find out.

15

My father could only hang on for six more hours. I wish I could say that I sat next to him and whispered in his ear all of the things I wanted to tell him. I had wanted to do just that, but I couldn't find a way to do it. The words escaped me. For someone who always had something to say, I was uncharacteristically silent.

We were in the waiting room, sleeping, when he passed. A young nurse had the painful privilege of letting us know. My mother and sister both wept silently. I kept my sorrow within, choosing instead to let it out the next day in my apartment, safe within the only place I felt safe enough to do so. My mother had wanted me to stay at the house, but I couldn't do it, couldn't walk the hallway I'd seen my father in countless times. I couldn't sit at the table he loved to sit and read the paper at. I couldn't face his ghost, not yet.

Sitting in my living room, staring at the blank wall across from me, I tried to come to some sort of conclusion about everything. I'd always thought the answers to the questions I asked myself over and over would eventually come. Right then, I realized the problem was not so much finding the answers. It was more about stopping the questions. When I had questions and doubts it was safe, I was allowed to not make a decision.

Maybe my father's spirit was there, directing me one last time, imparting what he'd learned in his life to his son; a last effort to finally make a complete man out of me. I can't say it worked instantly, but I certainly felt something in me change.

I remembered the conversation I had with Marcus, talking about children and fathers and how a man doesn't become a man until his father dies. I'd never think that again, because it would deprive my father of the credit he deserved for helping me achieve manhood. Maybe the death of a father can help the son realize his manhood, but it didn't help achieve it. That needed to have already been achieved.

I sat there on the couch, the tears stopping and starting but never really coming through freely. Every time I started to cry I stopped myself, intent on not wallowing in pity over my father's death. I didn't deserve to mourn him, I'd shunned him the last opportunity I had to speak to him. I'd squandered my right to mourn. What I needed and wanted to do was remember.

I don't recall how long I sat there, blankly staring. It could have been an hour or three, for all I knew. I hadn't checked my watch. What I did remember was how my father had reacted to his own father's death. It is the role of fathers to die, I'd read somewhere. Every father has lost a father. Every son must deal with the death of his so-called leader. My father had cried openly at the funeral, one of only a handful of times I'd seen him even remotely vulnerable.

That night, after the funeral, my father told me a story of how my grandfather had taken him fishing the weekend after the family dog had died. Grandpa had known how torn up my father was about it, and he took him to an uncle's cabin to discuss the ways of the world. They talked all weekend, not even caring about how many fish they caught. My father told me how Grandpa explained the idea of death. He described it not as inevitable, but actually something that should be desired. He said death was the great releaser, the only way a man can finally become close with God. Grandpa was a very religious man. My father wasn't so much so, and besides this discussion we had at the dinner table after Grandpa was buried, he really never mentioned it to me again. He did try to explain to me what his father had told him, that death was not something to worry about or mourn about.

I remembered asking him why he cried. My father told me that the tears were of selfishness. He didn't cry because he felt bad for his father, he cried because he would miss his father. I told him I didn't understand.

"When you see people crying at a funeral, they are crying for themselves. If they believe that their loved one is now in heaven, shouldn't they be happy?" he asked.

"I guess so."

"Right, they should."

"Do you think Grandpa is in heaven?" I asked, ever the questioning preteen.

"If any man is there, my father is."

"So, why did you cry today?"

My father smoked back then. He took a drag of the True cigarette and exhaled. I remember to this day the smell of cigarettes on my father's clothes, the way he filled a room with smoke, a bluish smoke that only he seemed to produce.

"I think I cried for two reasons, John. First, because I know I will never see him again. I'll never be able to talk to him the way you and I are talking now. Just talking like this with you reminds me of him, of how he used to answer my questions."

I didn't say anything because I didn't fully understand back then.

"The other reason was for my mother and the rest of the family. Their lives will be less full without him in it. Grandma will live the rest of her life thinking about him, thinking about how she loved him, how she misses him. I know my life will be similar. The man who used to wake up early to fight the cold so we didn't have to, the man who made sure the world was even just a marginally better place, is gone forever. He'll only exist in my heart, and in my mind. Do you understand?"

"I think so," I remember saying, trying my best to sound as confident as I could.

My father replied with an answer he gave me all through my life. I never fully understood it until that day in my apartment. "You will, son, when you get older."

I think what he meant was when I experienced it for myself. Maybe not consciously, but he certainly thought it subconsciously. And I did understand. I'd never be able to go to my father for support when things turned on me like they always seemed to. I'd never again be able to ask him for advice. I'd never be able to argue with him, something we didn't do often but did damn well. It would take getting used to, the fact my father was gone.

I didn't want to think about it any more. Though I felt better understanding things, I couldn't bear the pain any more, the emptiness. I felt the desire to have a drink, and would have, if there was anything in the house that resembled alcohol.

Luckily, fate and I have a strange relationship. She always throws something my way when I need it the most, even if it isn't always something I want. This time, she brought me a ring of my door buzzer.

I mechanically got up from the couch and walked over to the intercom.

"Go away," I said.

"John, it's me."

At first, I didn't recognize the female voice. Then, I realized it was Pauline. I couldn't imagine why she'd come. How did she know in the first place that my father had died?

"I'm not in the mood to take visitors," I said.

"Please." That was all she had to say.

I hit the buzzer and let her in. Part of me wanted to talk to someone, and Pauline would have been at the top of the list, if I'd even taken the time to think of such a thing. In the back of my mind, I heard a voice tell me this was dangerous, that letting a budding relationship get its start in such a situation was only a guarantee for disaster. If I let her be a shoulder I could lean on, would this define the relationship? I put the question aside and opened the door to let her in.

She was dressed in a black button down shirt and a pair of jeans. Her hair was pulled back. I'd never seen her like this. She looked stunning to me at that moment. I don't know if anyone else would have seen what I saw in her right then. I don't know why I felt this way, it could have just been because I was open emotionally, or perhaps my feelings for her were developing.

"Hi John," she said, standing in the doorway.

"Hello." I walked over to the couch. "Have a seat."

I sat down and she took the chair across from me.

"Are you okay?" she asked. I could tell she didn't want to ask such a question, it was just a reaction to the situation.

"No."

"I am really sorry."

"So am I."

"I won't sit here and tell you anything like how I know what you feel like. I've never lost a parent. I just wanted to stop by and say hello. I don't know why. Something compelled me to come here."

"I appreciate it."

"Tell me about him," Pauline asked.

"What?"

"Tell me about your father. I want to know."

"I don't know what to say."

"What did he like?"

I thought about that. "He liked a little bit of everything. He liked sports, he liked kids. He loved his job, loved seeing his patients. His patients loved him."

"What else?"

"I don't know. My father liked to talk. He liked to listen to people. I think that's why he was such a good dentist."

"I didn't even know he was a dentist."

"He was. He loved my mother, that much I can tell you. Maybe he didn't tell her all the time. He wasn't the sort that went around talking about things like that. I think he just was confident in the fact that she knew."

Pauline nodded. I didn't understand why she was asking me this, but it did feel good to talk about it this way.

"My father was a man of principle. He always told me it didn't matter what I believed in, so long as I believed in something. To him, that was all that mattered."

"Did it work?"

"What?"

"His advice. Did you ever find something to believe in?"

"I'm not sure. I guess I believe in a few things, but I am not like him, not like the way he was, I mean. Damn, I have to talk about him in the past tense."

"Don't worry about that. What did he believe in?"

"He believed in something I never could. He believed in people, that there is good in everyone."

"You don't believe in that?"

I looked at her for a moment, as if to tell her that she too worked in the police department and saw all the bad things I did. How could she not have seen what I saw almost every day?

"I can't," was all I said.

"Because of what you do, I presume."

"Yes."

"Had you ever talked to your father about that?"

"Yes. He told me not to let the bad people blind me from the good. He said that even those people at one time had some good in them. He really believed that."

"So do I," Pauline said. "Did you ever wonder why your father's beliefs didn't pass down to you?"

"I question too much. Everything that I see, I question. Been doing that since I was a little kid. I understand why my father believed what he did. I can see the reasons and the rationalizations behind it. I just can't incorporate it into my own beliefs because I can also see the other side, why I shouldn't believe it. Those reasons are just as strong. That make sense?"

Pauline giggled. "Surprisingly, yes. I sort of pegged you for an over-thinker. You should try giving yourself a break."

Listening to her made it all the more obvious that I needed someone like her in my life. Having already thought about how my father dealt with my grandfather's death by talking to me had highlighted my desire for having a son of my own. To do that, I needed a woman in my life, something I'd never truly experienced. I'd never let someone in that close. On top of that, Pauline appeared to be a perfect match for me. We were similar in some ways, but we had opposite views in enough areas to compliment each other.

"I never give myself a break. No one else does, either. It just seems to be procedure."

"Seriously, John, you need to give yourself a chance to come up with some sort of decision on life. You seem to me to be someone who does everything but that. You sit on the fence on just about everything, don't you?"

I wanted to deny that, but couldn't.

"I'll take your silence as an agreement on that."

"Perhaps."

"Just give it some thought." She giggled again. "Just not too much thought, okay?"

"I'll try."

"You do that. Do you feel better or worse talking about all of this?"

"A little better," I said.

"You just saying that?"

"No, I mean it."

Now, I don't know why I felt I had to do what I did next. It could have been only because I was upset and vulnerable.

Or, it just might have been that my feelings for her had gotten to the point where I had to express them. It doesn't matter. What does matter is that I went through with expressing them, something I hardly ever did.

"I want to talk to you about something."

"What," Pauline asked.

"We talked at the party about how we have feelings for each other. I know we covered most of it, but there are things you don't know."

From what I could tell, Pauline wasn't even the least bit flustered. "Like?"

"I am a difficult man, Pauline. Very difficult. I am bad tempered, ill-mannered, and generally rude when I feel like it. I say what is on my mind when what is on my mind is offensive. When it comes to matters of the heart, I say nothing."

"You're talking now."

"This is a rarity. I don't even know why I am saying this now. All I can say is that I won't always treat you right. I won't always openly appreciate anything you do for me. I'll get more wrong than I will right. I'll most likely make you unhappy more than happy. But I want you to know that make me want to try. You make me—"

"Shut up, Keegan. You need to learn when to shut up." She walked over to me and kissed me. I'd thought I'd connected with a woman before. That moment taught me I knew nothing about such things. "long with the elation that goes along with a connection like this came a strong fear of the future. Believe it or not, it was a good fear.

She pulled away from me first, further exerting her control over this particular situation, something I have to admit I didn't mind. She looked me in the eyes. "I'm not going away like Emily Brackens," she said.

"How—"

"Don't ask," she said, "I know a lot more about you than you think."

"I'm not sure that is a good thing."

"It's a good thing," Pauline said. "Now don't get all soft on me," she said, obviously catching the look in my eyes.

"I'm never soft."

"Watch it."

Pauline and I sat and chatted for a bit longer before I had to go to the wake. I wanted to be there from start to finish. I wanted to sit by my mother and offer her whatever meager support I could muster. She needed that, no matter how strong she was on the outside. It was my obligation to do so, along with my desire.

The wake drained me even more than I expected. If a man can be judged by the turnout at his wake, my father was a king of a man. Nearly 200 people came to the first session, and half of them had to stand outside in the lobby of the funeral home. They were an assortment of family, friends, and patients, people who knew my father in different ways but respected him just the same. I felt proud to be his son, honored to talk with these people and hear their stories of how my father touched their lives. It made me feel closer to him right then, made the pain soften a bit, if only for a short while.

The experience is one I won't ever forget. For most of my life I thought wakes were morbid affairs. Displaying a dead body just went against all I believed about spirituality and life. Standing there among these people, I realized the value. Sure, part of it is to pay respects to the family, offer condolences and kind words. Also, the wake offers people a chance to come together and discuss the deceased in ways they will never get a chance to otherwise. I found out some things about my father I never would have if we didn't have the wake. One of those things was his constant concern about me, his worry that he wasn't helping me enough in finding what was important to me in life. Several people told me about this, about how he spent a lot of time talking about me, touting me along with expressing worry that I worked too hard and hadn't found someone to love. I could have guessed some of this but it was wonderful to hear it. If my father only knew how much he had done for me.

Pauline showed up on the second night, and I introduced her to my family. She took to my mother and sister as if they were old friends. My mother always stayed at arms length from any woman I was involved with, as did my sister. It didn't happen with Pauline. It amazed me that, after over 35 years of cloudy, weak signals, life was broadcasting loud and clear something which was right for me.

We buried my father two days later, on a Friday, early in the morning at St. John's Cemetery in Queens. It rained that day, as if the earth was softening itself to accept him. This is actually what I thought as I watched the dirt being pulled from the ground by two young, stocky men in hooded sweatshirts.

Death stood next to me throughout this whole process. I could feel its presence. I didn't know exactly why, but I'd be lying if I said I didn't have a clue. The Death Knell had rang. The echo was coming. I knew someone was next.

I swore to the powers that be, if they took Pauline from me, I'd curse them until my dying day, as if this could sway them one way or the other. They didn't take Pauline. They did take someone close to me, though.

16

Most of the department, at least the people I was close to, showed up at one time or another for the wake. Geiger came, Karl Lavin came, and Rick did as well. They stayed quiet, choosing to sit in the back of the room and talk among themselves. Rick had pulled me aside when he saw there was a break in people coming up to talk to me.

"I don't know if you're interested, but I wanted to give you an update of what's happening."

"Sure, come outside while I have a cigarette," I said.

We walked out the back door, where one other person, someone from another wake, was smoking. Rick and I walked further into the parking lot, stopping by a large oak tree.

"What's the latest?" I asked, lighting my cigarette and being mindful to exhale away from Rick. I can be nice when I want to.

"We got the information on Yigevny. He's clean, though there seems to be some sort of arrest not long after he came to this country, in 1985."

"That's probably not a big deal."

"I took it a step further. We looked at his son, Anton. The kid's got a nice list. Drugs, aggravated assault. There's strong suspicion he's worked with the Russian mob, though nothing conclusive."

This was interesting. "You think that's the link between Yigevny and the mob?"

"Has to be."

"What does Galbadon know?"

"Not much about the kid. We went to his informant

again, the car guy, and he said he knows of Anton. Thinks the kid even bought heroin from Volkyv."

"You don't say."

"I do say."

"What's next?"

"The kid is slippery. We can't seem to catch him to question him. I got a tip that we can find him at his father's house tonight. Dad lets him host a small card game very Thursday night."

"You think about talking to Boris himself?"

"I doubt he has any insight into any of this. What do you think?" Rick asked. It actually sounded like he valued my opinion. He might have been doing this considering the fact that we were at my father's wake.

"Sounds to me like the kid is crap. If nothing else, he certainly knows something. We need to find that out."

"I'd ask you if you want to come along tonight, but I doubt you can."

"You're right, I can't. My mother and family need me around. Give me the details tomorrow, okay?"

"No problem."

"Keep me in the loop," I said, actually fearful that I wouldn't be kept in.

"Of course."

After the burial, we went to a local restaurant and did what most people did after a loved one died; ate and drank. It felt good to be surrounded by family at this time. It prevented me from wallowing in the guilt I felt for every time I hurt my father, each instance I hated him for trying to discipline me, every day I said I cursed him for punishing me or telling me no when I desperately wanted to hear a yes. These thoughts came in and out of my head.

I actually was surprised I didn't deal with death better, considering I experienced it on a weekly basis. It was so much easier to watch someone else deal with it. I had always thought the toughest thing in my life was delivering the news of a death to someone. I secretly wished it was someone else's father who died. I envied everyone, even people in the room, who still had their father. I wanted to tell them to cherish the blessing they had. I knew better than to voice this.

After the meal, I took my mother home. She stayed strong on the outside, as expected. In the car, she opened up to me.

"Let it go," she said.

"What?"

"Daddy told me about the argument you had at the hospital the other day."

"I'm not thinking about that," I said.

"I know you. I know you are. He admitted he gave you a hard time. He wanted nothing else than for you to be happy. He seemed to think you aren't. The argument was just his way of trying to show that."

"I don't want to talk about that now."

"You need to. You need to know he understood. He didn't take to heart what you said to him when you left."

"He told you?"

I looked at my mother. She nodded.

"I didn't mean it. I was so mad at him."

"He was mad at himself. He wanted to talk to you about it. He wanted to apologize. He loved you more than anything in this world, Johnny."

I didn't even try to hold back the tears. "I know."

"Do you?"

"Of course I do. If nothing else, I know what sort of man he was. It just used to make me angry, that he was more of a man than I could ever hope to be."

"You're more of a man than you give yourself credit for. He only gave you a hard time because you created such expectations in him. No one was more proud than him when you joined the police department. He never told you, but he made it a point to announce to every one of his clients for the next month when you made detective."

This was something I never knew, never would have expected. It's not that it surprised me. It just felt really good to hear it.

"I'm going to miss him. I am never going to forget how I never got the chance to tell him everything he did for me, that I appreciated him."

"It's not your way. He knew that because it really wasn't his way either."

"He was better at it than I was," I said.

"Maybe. But, he knew. He knew his son. The same way you knew him."

"Why did it have to happen this way?" I asked, my thoughts verbalized without my even thinking about them.

"There are no answers. I'll never stop asking why god took him from me. I know there are never answers to such questions but I'll ask anyway. I just want you to stop thinking about that argument. I could see you battling yourself ever since you came to the hospital."

"I have a lot to feel guilty for."

"Why, because you didn't come right after it happened? Do you think you could have changed anything? Do you think you could have saved him?"

'Of course not, Mom. I just feel like I should have been there sooner."

"Don't. Thinking that way won't do any good. You're better off thinking about the good things. Spend your time remembering him, not regretting."

I've always considered my mother a fantastic woman. I never really got to see how smart she was on top of that.

"I'll try."

"You're life is changing. I see it. I've seen the changes in you for a while. Let the changes come."

"I'll do my best."

I stayed at my mother's for about an hour. We talked about my father. She told me things I never knew, about his dreams when he was a young man, how he wanted to conquer the world the way every young man does. I enjoyed hearing about him. My mother used to tell me things about him before, usually when I hit a hard spot in life. She tried to show me that no man is perfect, that even my father questioned himself the way I did. Hearing about him then, in the kitchen where I always used to talk to him, made me realize how alike we were. I'd spent so many years trying to convince myself and others how different I was from him. It seemed so much better to realize the exact opposite was true.

My mother was tired. She'd been through even more than I had. She had a rough road ahead of her. I wished there was something I could do to ease that. I knew no such thing existed. She'd get through it, this much I knew.

I kissed her goodbye, embracing her more for my own comfort than for hers. If nothing else, I'd make sure that my father's death would make me appreciate my mother more, while I still had her. She went upstairs and I walked out of the house, the essence of my father with me, his very being present in my mind like never before.

I walked over to my car and stood there for a moment, not sure where to go or what to do. I thought about going to the department, to bury myself in work to forget about everything else. I figured Rick hadn't called me yet because he didn't want to bother me. He didn't realize he'd be helping more by doing so.

A car pulled up to my mother's house and stopped right next to me. It was a Ford sedan, a department car. I looked through the window and saw Karl. He opened the window.

"Get in," he said.

"I have my car—"

"Get in the fucking car," he said. He was genuinely angry,

this much I could tell. I opened the door and got in. He drove away, fast.

"What's going on?" I asked.

Karl didn't say anything at first. He just kept driving.

"Are you going to tell me what's happening? I've had a tough enough day as it is."

He pulled the car over right before the parkway.

"Rick is dead."

I was paralyzed. I'd known Death had someone else on his list close to me. I don't know how or why I knew, I just did. I'd never even thought Rick was the one.

"Rick?" was all that came out of my mouth.

"Yes."

"How?"

"He went to Yigevny's last night, I'm sure he told you about that."

"He did."

"They found him and Galbadon off the side of the road about 200 yards away from the house. Rick had been shot and someone had rammed them. Galbadon is in intensive care."

"What happened?"

"No one knows. We're going to find out," Karl said, the conviction in his voice stronger than I'd ever heard it before.

I felt a humming through my entire body, running right through to my fingertips. It was rage, pure rage racing through me.

"Yigevny?"

"No one knows. The kid is AWOL. Father is too."

"You think they killed him?"

"I don't know John. I don't know."

I thought for a moment, doing my best to cull all the training, all the experience I'd gained over the years to find the best approach to this. The anger blocked me but I fought through it. I kept back my feelings of despair, the hopelessness I experienced thinking about what Rick and been through, how life repaid his diligence by killing him.

"We won't get near him."

"Who?"

"Either of them. We need to go somewhere else."

Karl put the car in drive and pulled away. "What have you got in mind?"

"There's a piece of shit we need to see. Two of them actually. I only know where to find one of them."

"You direct, I'll drive. Someone's gotta pay for this."

"Oh, someone will, that much I can tell you."

17

I don't doubt there are people I have met who don't understand me, don't know why it is I do what I do. I understand this, even accept it. Never having taken a stand on anything forcefully enough to warrant any real respect for my opinions or actions, it's acceptable that these people cannot fathom why I act the way I do when I actually decide to act. I've never really taken the time to try to explain myself to others. I don't give a shit if people misinterpret me. I've, for a long time, considered people who do not understand me as people who don't take the time to try and understand.

I remember now the thoughts that ran through my head that day. My father, freshly buried, stayed in the forefront of my thoughts. My partner, my friend, my only true friend, Rick Calhill, apparently killed in the line of duty, sat at my side one last time. They were persistently in my thoughts, in my heart. I believed they controlled my actions at this point, directed me in what was right and what was wrong. I could do no wrong. Justification lied within me, integrity overrode anything else. I needed answers. I knew investigation, the standard forms at least, would offer me nothing. Karl would come along with me. I didn't know if he would risk what I knew I was prepared to. I didn't ask. It was up to him to decide.

There are certain times in a man's life where risk doesn't matter. For most men, this is usually a tradeoff between risk and reward. If the reward is great enough, the risk becomes unimportant. This isn't what I am talking about. I am talking about the times when risk is thrown out the window because the issue matters more than risk. For some people, this never happens. They live their lives afraid of risk, fearful of being labeled or being judged or being considered wrong. For me, this particular day erased risk. I didn't care about my job. I didn't care about procedure. I cared only to know. Rick wanted nothing else than to solve this case. I would solve it for him.

I know that there will never come a time when I will fully understand how I acted that day. I know a lot of it has to do with my feelings. I'd been overcome with guilt and anger, two emotions that often come together and each only highlights the negatives of the other.

"Want to tell me where we are going?" Karl asked. I looked over at him. We weren't young men anymore, the way we were when we met years before. We had cares and concerns, aspects of life that usually don't come until later. I knew he had an idea what I wanted to do was against policy. He knew me well enough to know that.

"Bar in the city."

"Which one?"

"The Score."

"Sounds like a class joint. Who we going to see?" Karl asked, turning onto the Belt Parkway.

"Alex Antanov. Rick and I went to see him the other day and he was generally unhelpful. He knows something, and we are going to get it out of him."

"The guy you asked me about. I remember him .Sounds like my kind of work." Karl paused for a moment. "Geiger knows I am with you."

This took me by surprise. "What about your boss?"

"Today's my day off," he said.

"Working on your day off, huh?"

"I know this is something that has to be done. You tell me what we have to do and that's that."

"This could lead to trouble. I usually perform better when I have someone to keep me in check."

"We don't need that now. We need answers."

"What did Geiger say, exactly?"

"He told me to come get you. He said he had an idea what would happen after that. Didn't say anything else."

"Silence protects him."

"Guess so. I don't give a shit. I know Calhill was a good man and I know this is hitting you harder than you are showing. I'm just around for the ride."

"It's going to be a bumpy one."

"I don't go on the sissy roller coasters. I like the ones with the drops, dips, and flips."

"I've got you covered."

We pulled up in front The Score and sat in the car for a minute. I lit a cigarette, expecting to hear Rick complain about it. Karl used to smoke, and occasionally had one when drinking. He didn't say a word about the smoke. Under any other circumstances, this would have been a pleasant change.

"What do you want to do?" Karl asked.

"I want to have a chat with Alex."

"I know that. How do you want to go about it?"

"I'm just going to take it as it comes. No plans."

"The last time you did that, it ended pretty messy."

"And it probably will this time too," I said, looking out of the window. The whole city seemed only a blur to me. It was out of my area of focus at the moment. All that mattered was what had to do with the case. Every other thought I pushed back further into my mind. And, there were a lot of them.

"I would expect nothing less. Just do your best to keep your head about you. I know there are going to be lines that we'll cross, but only cross the ones we have to, okay?"

"I don't think I will be able to tell the difference," I said.

"That's what I am here for."

"You done with the speech?"

"I am."

"Let's go talk to Alex."

"Let's," Karl said, shutting off the car and getting out. I hesitated for a minute, a deep fear rising within me. Something else was going to happen, soon. I didn't know if it was another death, or something different. I just knew something was going to happen, and it wasn't going to be good.

Alex Antanov was sitting in the same place he was the last time I saw him. He sipped a beer and stared off into apparently nowhere. He didn't appear to be someone concerned about his own well-being. I'd have expected him to lay low and was pleasantly surprised to find him.

"Which one is he?" Karl asked.

"Third one from the left," I said, hearing the door close behind me. My initial anger had passed. I had to focus a little harder, keep myself motivated. I didn't want to go hunting for that anger, because in order to do that, I would have to get in touch his the despair attached to it. I couldn't do that. I had to bury it and focus on dealing with Antanov.

"Ready?"

"I am," I said, not knowing what would come next.

Karl and I walked over to where Antanov was sitting. He didn't acknowledge us at first, and I didn't know if he recognized me or not. From what I could tell, he didn't care.

Karl leaned on the bar to the right of Antanov and looked at him. "Hello Alex." Alex didn't answer. Karl tapped him on the shoulder. "Over here."

Antanov glared at Karl, then turned to look at me. "Police department lackeys coming to bother me again?'

"I'm doing my best to be polite to you," I said, that rage I was holding back coming through a lot quicker than I expected.

"Oh, don't go to the trouble for me, Sergeant Keegan."

"You know my name, impressive."

"You are not as safe as you think you are. You are being watched, being analyzed."

"Are you threatening him?" Karl asked.

"I do not threaten," Antanov said, a hint of a smile coming to his lips. "You want something. What is it?"

"Tell us about Yigevny," I said.

Antanov didn't flinch. "I don't know who you are talking about."

"I think you do. I think it is why K-Drugs was killed. Something went wrong."

"Then, ask him about it. You two pigs will get further with that."

I wanted to slap him, that was the feeling that came over me. I knew better, of course. I knew I shouldn't strike him because, not only was it abusing my position, it also would have opened up my emotions. If I hit him once, I wouldn't be able to stop. Even though I didn't think he had anything to do directly with Rick's death, I had no idea who did, it would have been easy to take it out on Antanov.

Unfortunately, Karl Lavin did not have the self-restraint I did. While Antanov was looking at me, Lavin swept the bar stool out from under him. Antanov fell forward and downward at the same time, his chin bashing against the end of the oak bar with a crack. Lavin caught him by the hair just as his chin hit the bar and lifted him back him, placing him back on the bar stool. It happened so fast I couldn't tell how he was able to do it.

"Looked like you need to be whacked out of that bad mood," Karl said evenly. Surprisingly, no one at the bar moved toward us, even looked at us. Perhaps this happened often.

Antanov shook his head. I thought his jaw might have been broken, which would hamper his ability to speak.

"Got something to say about Yigevny now?" I asked.

He looked at me, a flicker of anger in his eyes. It passed

quickly. "You want to stay away from this," he said slowly, as if to be careful about hurting his jaw further.

"No, I don't want to stay away from this. I am already all in. You guys took my partner. I know it won't stop until I stop it."

"You can't stop it. Move on. Let it fall away."

"Tell me about Yigevny. Tell me what happened with his daughter."

Antanov exhaled. "It was a mess, a fucking mess."

"And you're going to tell us all about it."

"I know this is not your case. I spoke to the other man, the black man. He doesn't know as much as you do."

"That's not important."

"If you push this too far, you're going to ruin your life. Walk away, Sergeant Keegan, while you still can."

I saw the look in Karl's eyes. He was ready to strike again. "You had better start talking. My friend is losing his self-control again."

"Not here. I cannot talk here. My life is in danger as it is."

"That's not all that is in danger," Karl said.

"I will go with you. I don't have any choice. You don't have a choice either, but you haven't realized that yet."

"Save your talking for the station," I said.

We escorted Antanov to our car and drove him to the precinct. We were headed for trouble. Technically, we were interfering with Marcus' case by even talking to Antanov, let alone bringing him down to the station to take an official statement. If Antanov was involved the way I expected, we might get even more than that, thus complicating matters even further.

Driving to the precinct, I had an idea. I figured a way to make this good for all those involved. I'd have to run in past Geiger and hope he saw things the same way I did.

"You drag an informant from Lay's case in here for questioning without my approval, and now you want what?" Geiger asked, not nominally angered.

"I want Marcus here for the taking of Antanov's statement. The guy is directly involved with both our cases, but he wants to talk to us."

"What's the matter with his face?"

"I don't know. He looked that way when we found him."

Geiger looked right through me. "You sure you have your head screwed on straight? I know what you've been through over the past few days. You thinking clearly?"

"As clearly as possible."

"And this guy came willingly?"

"Quite," I said.

"You think he has something to tell?"

"Absolutely."

"Go ahead. I don't know how this is going to work out, but I surely don't have a good feeling about it. Not at all."

I wanted to say something about that, that I felt the same way, but I didn't want to stir Geiger up any more than necessary. Things needed to get done so starting down the wrong path wasn't going to help.

I decided to pay a visit to an old friend who could help me with this interrogation. Jacob had offered his services to me many times when I desperately needed someone to lend a hand, and I knew he'd help right then too.

I walked into his lair, the precincts tech room filled with the latest of his gadgetry. I'd learned long before to not touch anything.

Jacob was at one of the four computers, tapping away at the keyboard and clicking the mouse in a rhythmic fashion not unlike a pianist. He wore his fiery red hair shorter, and the beard was neatly trimmed. Gone were the rebellious clothes he used to wear, replaced by khakis and a denim shirt. The mystical air about him had not dispersed however. He appeared as a guru, a man of intense knowledge and deep thought. The only difference with the new Jacob was that he was getting laid regularly. At some point or another, everything does change.

"Jacob," I said, standing at the doorway. He swiveled around in his drafting chair.

"Hey," he said, and swiveled back, "how've you been?"

"Getting by."

"Sorry about your pop."

"I got the flowers. Thank you."

"You know I would've made it if I could."

"I know."

"What underhanded business brings you to me?"

"Interrogation."

"My favorite sort. Use room three. I just installed a new system in there no one knows about yet. Got infrared sensing, check body temperature and all that. See if a guy is sweating at the pits."

"Nice."

Jacob turned to look at me again. "Who you questioning?"

"Alexei Antanov. He's involved with the Russian mob."

"Confession?" Jacob said. He raised his eyebrows as he said it, a new twitch he'd developed recently. I got paid to notice such things.

"Maybe."

"And you don't think he's going to tell the truth."

"You never can tell with these guys," I said.

"I can."

"That's what I was counting on. Thanks." I turned to leave."

"Hey, what are you doing Saturday?"

"Nothing planned."

Jacob reached for a piece of paper, which looked like some sort of flyer. "Me and the old lady are having a sort of house warming. I'd like you to come down," he said, handing me the paper. It was a fairly fancy looking flyer, but it wasn't surprising considering his technical wizardry.

"Sure," I said.

"Bring a lady friend."

"A lady friend?"

Jacob raised his eyebrows again. He turned back to his computer. "Someone with some class."

"I don't know..."

"Do your best."

I walked out of Jacob's office, still somewhat dazed with how much he had changed over the seven months or so that he started dating his girlfriend. People change, this much I knew. I just hoped that dating Pauline, or anyone else for that matter, wouldn't change me so drastically. Jacob had spent a lot of time away from women, so I figured this explained his change.

I had Alex transferred to Interrogation Room 3. He sat in the chair, the bruise on his chin visible even from the window. He seemed a bit fidgety, constantly moving his hands from his lap to the table and back again. This was completely out of character for him, at least from what I knew about him. From my years of handling people in this situation, I took this as a good sign. I figured he was nervous because he was about to sell out some high level people.

Karl was outside the door, waiting for me.

"I don't know if you should be here," I said, "This really isn't your job."

"I know. I'll just watch from the outside. He's all yours."

"I told Geiger—"

"That he looked that way when we found him. I figured that's what you would say."

"You're good."

"The best."

I opened the door. The smell of fear came at me as I did. If you don't know, fear has a stench not unlike cold sweat, a sort of heavy, salty scent. This must be what dogs smell before they attack. I think women who are about to carve the heart of a man smell the same scent. I know this because it is what I smelled like the one time it happened to me. Okay, two times. Three, tops.

"Why do we have to do this this way?" Antanov asked, his speech slower. Not that I cared. The Antanov's of the world deserved to get their jaws broken often.

"The other options wouldn't be so good."

"I don't want to talk here."

"You don't have to. You can leave."

He looked at me, trying to ascertain whether I was serious or not. His eyes registered something, though I must say I can't be certain what it was.

"I'll talk."

"I know you will," I said, "But you won't only talk, you'll answer. That's far more important."

Antanov nodded. He looked weak, scared. He didn't look this way before. Maybe it was the bright lights in the interrogation room that made this more evident. The Score was dark, smoky, and a poor place to get a good read on someone's face. The interrogation room was brightly painted and lighted by powerful fluorescent lights. It was understandable that I'd see things there that I didn't see in the bar.

I looked around the room, wondering where in the white drop ceiling Jacob had installed his infrared cameras. I thought I saw something, a white plastic disc that blinked every once in a while but I realized that was the sensor that turned on the lights when you walked into the room. I knew Jacob was too good for me to be able to spot his handiwork.

"First question. State your name."

"Alexei Antanov."

"How long have you been in this country?"

"Eleven years."

"Are you a citizen?"

Antanov paused. "You know that."

"Answer."

"Yes."

"Where do you work?"

"LMN Imports, Bayside."

I sat down in a chair. I had a bad habit of pacing around a room and this didn't help when trying to get someone to relax and answer questions. From what I was told, it unnerved people. I did that a lot.

"For how long?" I asked.

"Seven years," Alex said, his eyes indicating he didn't know why he had to answer such mundane questions. It was done mainly to soften the person up a bit, get them to relax and get used to answering questions. Most times, it worked. I knew Alex wanted to talk, but this was also sort of a lie detector technique which I figured would help Jacob with his heat imaging, or whatever the hell it was he did in there.

"Mr. Antanov, has anyone in this department coerced you in any way to speak today?"

"No."

"Has anyone threatened you?"

"No."

"Have you plea bargained on your own behalf in return for this information?"

"No, I have not."

"Are you saying that the information you are about to give will be given of your own free will?"

"Yes."

"Okay. Let's begin, then."

Alex looked at me as if to ask whether or not he should speak. I nodded, but he didn't say anything right away.

"You said you knew something about Kostya Volkyv's death," I said.

"Yes, Kostya. I know why he was murdered."

"Why is that?"

"He knew too much."

"Mr. Antanov, for a murder investigation we don't need

dramatics. He need direct facts. Why is it you believe Kostya was murdered?"

"Because he was part of a plan to shake down a wealthy man. He tried to make his mark and get ahead in the organization. He had one final test. He passed it, but complications arose from it."

"Are you talking about something in particular?" I asked.

"Yes."

"Would you care to explain in more detail?"

Antanov squirmed in his seat. Maybe he was having second thoughts. Though I couldn't blame him, I wasn't about to let him get away with it. I needed answers. I needed a reason why Rick was killed. I needed the truth.

"I'm not sure," Alex said.

"Not sure? You seemed sure an hour ago."

"It is only speculation," he said.

"By all means, speculate."

"You know what I am talking about. You know the sort of people that are involved in this. Your own people are involved in this."

This shocked me. I hadn't expected that. "My own people?"

"Police officers. They turn the other way for the Russian mob. Everyone talks about the Italians, or even the Chinese. No one really knows how serious the Russian mob is. No one wants to know."

"Mr. Antanov, I appreciate the warning but I really just want to know what you came here to tell me. I want to know why Mr. Volkyv is dead."

"They killed him," Antanov said.

"Who, the Russian mob?"

Alex nodded.

"Please state yes or no."

"Yes," Alex said, through a sigh. I could see sweat forming on his forehead. Something had him worried.

"Who did it, and why?"

"You know I cannot tell you that."

"I thought that's what we came here to talk about. I thought you wanted to tell me who was responsible for Volkyv's death. All you've said is the Russian mob. From what I know, you're in the Russian mob, so it could easily be you, couldn't it?"

"That won't work, Detective. I know your tactics. I didn't come here to be threatened."

"And I didn't set this up to be lied to and evaded. Please tell me what you know. It's in your best interest," I said, knowing it most likely wasn't.

"You know most of the facts. They have been staring you in the face. You just haven't found the link to put them together."

"I kind of thought you would do that for me."

"K-Drugs—Kostya, he was given an assignment. It went wrong."

"Central Park?"

"Yes. Yigevny's daughter. They were supposed to frighten her. Kostya, from what I heard, got out of control. People said he was high. He raped her. Then they had to kill her. They were only supposed to scare her."

Normally, I would ask an informant why they didn't go to the police with such information. It was obvious why Alex didn't. He operated outside the police.

"So, who killed him?"

"I don't know who."

"How do you know Kostya raped Yigevny's daughter?" I asked.

"Everyone knows. It's all over the street."

"Who else was involved?"

Alex didn't answer that.

"Who else?"

"I won't answer that question."

"I don't think you have much of a choice."

"Sure, I do."

"Were you one of them? All of the evidence we've found so far points in that direction."

"I was not there," Alex said.

"You seem to know a lot about it."

"So?"

"That would make me believe you were there. I've had other people tell me you were there as well. Seems to make sense to me."

"You don't know what you are talking about," Alex said.

"Of course I do. But, it doesn't matter. Tell me something else. Who killed my partner?"

"I don't know."

"Come on, of course you do," I said, leaning closer to him. "You seem to have your fingertip on the pulse of the Russian mob. Tell me. I want to know."

"If you think about it, you'll figure it out."

"Yigevny's son?"

"I wouldn't be foolish enough to answer you," Alex said.

"You understand that I am working closely with the people investigating the Central Park murder. If it turns out that you were there, I will do whatever possible to ensure you go away for the longest term possible. Now, if you help me, maybe we can work something out."

"I am not charged with anything. I can't make a deal for something I haven't been charged with, can I?"

The bastard was smarter than I thought. "Perhaps. You can look at it that way if you want."

"I will."

"Tell me something else. Give me something to work with."

"I told you everything I am going to tell you. Kostya was killed because he knew too much and because he screwed up a major assignment. He was too crazy. Everyone knew that but they thought they could control him. It turns out they couldn't, so they had to get rid of him."

"What about Medina?"

"Medina?"

"Yes, Jaro Medina."

Alex looked to his left. "What about him?"

"How does he fit into this?"

He looked back at me. "He set it up."

"Kostya's involvement. Really, he set up the whole thing."

"Can you prove that?"

"Everyone knows it."

"But a jury doesn't. My department doesn't."

"Your department should work on its investigation. Everyone on the street knows about Jaro."

"Why won't anyone point a finger at him?" I asked.

Alex gave me a look which seemed to indicate he thought I was stupid. I've seen that look many times.

"Okay, because he is powerful."

"He is handling Yigevny's son, as well. He was the initial contact with the Yigevnys."

"Why was Kostya hired to scare Yigevny's daughter?"

Alex exhaled. He paused for a moment, as if to think whether or not it would be worth it to tell me about this. I then saw a look of resignation in his eyes, something which indicated he realized he didn't have much of a choice.

"Yigevny had a hard time getting out of Russia back in the 80's. This was before our countries were friends. This was when Gorbachev hadn't gained enough power to dismantle our country. Way before Yeltsin drank away our pride. Yigevny had invented something, some physics thing, and he knew it would make him a millionaire if he could only get out of the Soviet Union. He was watched closely. They knew he wanted to run.

He knew that even if he made it out, the KGB would hunt him down until they found him here in America. He had nowhere to turn but the mob, who promised him they would get him out and protect him once he made it here. He made the deal. All he had to do was share in the profits of his invention.

From what I know, he did at first. Then he forgot all about the people who helped him and protected him. I think after he saw that there was no more KGB he realized he didn't need the mob protection any more. He tried to renegotiate, I think. No one does that. Without the mob, he would never be here. He would have rotted in some lab in Chernobyl. He might have even died there."

I thought about how hard it must have been for Yigevny to make that deal in the first place. Most people in this country don't realize what freedom is until we see a genius like Yigevny who isn't even entitled to his own thoughts. The Soviet Union had control over his ideas. Yigevny's only way out was to make a deal that would eventually destroy his life.

"I think I understand. But why scare him?"

"To make him pay. Nothing else worked."

"And Medina had something to do with this?" I asked.

"He helped arrange Yigevny's arrival first at Cuba, then here in the states. From what I was told, the two of them escaped from Cuba together."

"They have a history, then."

"Sure. Medina funded Yigevny's defection."

"But Medina isn't Russian," I said.

"Russian, Cuban. Back then it was all the same. We were allies. We were brothers in oppression, or that's what some thought. I always believed we were better off under Communism than trying to be like America. We are not American."

"So, Medina was counting on the money from Yigevny's invention," I said. I felt the urge for a cigarette but I fought it. I envied the guys who worked decades before when it was okay to have a smoke while interrogating someone. It just helped with the nerves and the thought process.

"Medina built his company on that money. Of course, he is not nearly as rich as Yigevny, and that is what bothers him."

"Let me get this straight. Medina helps Yigevny come to America in exchange for a piece of the action. Yigevny gives him some, but then reneges. Medina then orders his people to scare Yigevny's daughter as a message to her father, is that right?"

"Yes."

"But it went wrong, so now we have a dead girl and a dead drug dealer. This is what happened?"

"Yes," Alex said.

"Where does the son fit in?"

"Yigevny's son has always wanted to be a part of the mob."

"And Medina took him in, just like that?"

"Medina is using Boris Jr. He is trying to get to his father. Using Ilana, his daughter, was only a second idea. The original plan was to get Boris Jr. into so much trouble that his father would have to give in."

"So, Boris Jr. is not really a part of the Russian mob?"

"He *thinks* he is. But he's not. He only runs errands. He's never been one to want to get his hands dirty. He grew up with too much. He can't handle the streets."

"Maybe he is the one who killed Kostya for Medina," I said, throwing that out there.

"I doubt it. I don't think he is capable."

"You're lying," I said.

"You can think that. You're allowed to think anything you want."

"So, it is Medina that ordered Kostya's death. Any idea who might be responsible for that?"

"Does it matter?" Alex asked. I could tell he was getting tired of answering questions. Everyone has their breaking point. I'd reached Alex's.

"Well, it matters to me, considering that I am investigating his murder. Sort of helps to have a suspect, you know?"

"Worry about other things, not the death of a low life. There's nothing you can do to change it, and there is nothing you can do to stop the next one."

"What next one?"

"I was just saying. Medina will order someone else dead. It's what he does. You won't be able to stop that."

"Maybe I should try."

"Maybe you should get your head examined."

"I've been told that before."

18

Alex didn't give me any more information. I couldn't expect much else. He'd put his life on the line telling me what he did and I tried to be thankful, as much as I didn't like the guy. There wasn't much to make sense of, mainly because it made pretty good sense in the first place. Medina had brought Yigevny to freedom and expected to get paid for it. I figured Yigevny was an idiot for turning his back in the deal. From my limited experience, you don't do that with mobsters. They don't like it very much from what I've been told.

I couldn't expect that everything Antanov told me was the truth. No one tells the complete truth. They always hold a little bit back. This is human nature from what I have noticed. We try to keep a little for ourselves. Complete exposure doesn't sit too well with us. I wish I knew why this was. There were a lot of things about human beings—particularly women—that I wanted an explanation on. It wasn't ever going to happen, from what I can tell.

Unlike the mysteries of women or the phenomenon we call popular culture, I could find an explanation about the truth in what Antanov told me. Jacob had certainly analyzed the whole interrogation and I trusted his conclusions completely. I wasn't ever sure how he did it. There was plenty of speculation in the department about that but no one ever came up with anything remotely believable. Some guys called it magic. I wasn't so sure about that. All I knew was that his success rate was incredible.

I could tell by the look on his bearded mug that Jacob

had something to tell me. He always squinted a lot when something was on his mind. He looked funny when he did it but I never bothered to tell him that. I liked the way God arranged my face.

"What've you got?" I asked, standing in his doorway. I could feel a cool breeze coming from his office. That room was always ten degrees cooler than any other in the precinct. He said it was because of the valuable computer equipment in there. I think it had something to do with his propensity to sweat like a bastard.

"Interesting characters you interrogate," Jacob said, swiveling back and forth ever so slightly in his chair.

"Always."

"He likes to lie."

"I figured. What untruths did he lay on me in there?"

"Well, he came across cool in the beginning," Jacob said, turning in his chair and pointing at a monitor on his desk. I could see the image of Antanov. It was orange. "His temp is normal here. Through most of the beginning. The only anomaly is when he got uncomfortable talking. You can see in his armpits and forehead that there is more heat. He didn't want to talk to you."

"No, he didn't."

"But, his voice stayed steady. That was genuine."

"When did he lie?"

Jacob put his hand on something that looked like a small orb and scrolled to another image. Now, both Antanov and my images were there. I started to feel a bit uncomfortable myself, but I'd rather not say why. "This is right when you asked him if he was part of the Central Park thing."

"So, you think he lied about that," I said.

"Absolutely."

"I figured as much. When else did he lie?"

"Few things here and there. When you asked him how he knows things. Also, it seems he might have lied when you asked him if Boris Jr. killed Kostya. It's not as conclusive. There might be a chance that he just doesn't know. He certainly was uncomfortable, though."

"Really."

"Yes." Jacob turned and looked at me. Then, he turned back to the screen and scrolled to another image. "I think I know why." He zoomed in on my body until only my ass was on the screen. There was a red area there. I'd never seen an infrared image of a fart. It was quite enlightening. "Eat something that didn't agree with you last night?"

"No."

"Sure about that?"

"Yes. Can we get back to Antanov?"

"You put him under duress. This could affect your investigation."

"Seriously," I said. I could feel my ears getting warm.

"Are you embarrassed?" Jacob asked.

"No."

"The mighty Detective Keegan brought to his knees by his own flatulence. This is priceless."

I could only imagine Jacob printing that image up and hanging it somewhere in the department with some witty caption. I didn't think he'd do something like that to me. Then again, if I had the opportunity, I'd do it in a second.

"Yeah, priceless. Like I am the only one who does such a thing."

"I told you I had heat imaging going on in that room."

"I didn't think you'd have it on me, for Christ's sake. Anyway, back to Antanov, please?"

Jacob chuckled. "Don't worry, it's not like I was going to show it to Pauline McCrory or anything."

I didn't ask how he knew. I didn't care to know. There were dozens of things Jacob knew. I'd used him for his knowledge of department affairs many times so I couldn't complain.

"Thanks."

"You guys make a good couple. I assume she's the one you're bringing to my place," he said. It wasn't a question. It was his way of telling me he knew more than he was ever willing to admit.

"Antanov?"

"Yes. Well, there isn't much else I can tell you. It seems that long diatribe he gave you about this guy Medina seems true. I did some quick research and found that the guy is pretty slippery. What is interesting is that Medina and Yigevny did come to this country at almost exactly the same time."

Jacob had a wealth of information at his fingertips. Unfortunately, much of it I could never use as evidence considering its less than legitimate acquisition. Still, when I needed to know which angle to go on a case, Jacob many times helped.

"What do you know about Yigevny?" I asked.

"What do you want to know?"

"What did he invent?"

"Well, it wasn't so much of an invention as it was a revolution. It has to do with the physics of movement. Have you seen those Segway People Movers?"

I shook my head.

Jacob held up his hands like he was holding on to motorcycle handlebars. "You know, those things that you can move around on? They look stupid? The Mayor wanted to use them for police officers?"

"Oh, those idiotic things. Sure."

"Yigevny came up with a proprietary way to alter the way machines can interact with the environment. I won't bore you with the technical details, but the Segway is only touching on the technology, and Yigevny gets a cut of everything. If I am not mistaken, seven different companies have licensed the technology from him. He's also invented a few other things since then. Guy's a genius, if you ask me."

"He's obviously got no common sense," I said.

"Maybe he has too much estrogen," Jacob said.

We both laughed. Then my phone rang. I fumbled to get it out of my pocket and tried to answer it but hit the wrong button.

"Damn," I said.

"What've you got there, a Treo?"

"Yeah?"

"That's like giving a ten-year-old a Ducati as their first bike."

"What?"

"Don't worry about it. Let me see that thing."

I gave the phone to Jacob. He took it and plugged a wire into it, then started working on his computer. He amazed me when he typed. His fingers just glided over the keyboard.

"You don't have much set up with this," he said.

"Right."

"It has voice activation, so you don't have to keep fucking up when you answer the phone." Jacob handed me a tiny microphone. "Say 'yes'."

"Yes."

"Now, 'no'."

"No."

"Good," Jacob said, "all you have to do is say yes or no into the phone if you want to answer it. Pretty cool, huh?"

"I guess."

"What a waste of technology," Jacob sighed.

"Of course. It's what everyone else has said."

"I am setting up your voice mail, which you haven't done yet. What's this, you don't have a data package?"

"A what?" I asked.

"Data package. So you can get email. That's one of the major reasons to get a Treo."

"Uh, what the hell am I going to do with that?"

"You can read, right?"

"Yes."

"Then you can figure this out. Trust me, it will make things easier. You'll never have to talk directly to people you don't want to any more."

"That sounds appealing."

"Figured it would."

"But I thought that cost money," I said.

"Who told you that?"

I remembered it was Rick who told me that, one of the last times I saw him. It instantly made me angry. Sure, Rick had been tough to deal with but he was still a friend and someone had killed him. All he wanted was to do his job. I'd say that death was a risk and Rick fell victim to it but wasn't what I believed. I wanted vengeance for him—even more so for his kids.

"Calhill told you," Jacob said in a somber tone.

"Yes."

"Sorry."

"For what?"

"It's just something you say."

"Not me."

"You know what I mean," Jacob said, turning back to the computer. "I'll sync everything up for you and get you the entire package. Most cellular companies don't know that the Treo can be hacked so easily. You'll never pay overage charges again."

"Isn't that—"

"Illegal? Yes. But you'll never get caught. They'll just think it is a malfunction. It will work without a hitch."

I didn't bother to tell Jacob that I never went over my minutes anyway. "Okay," I said, watching him do his work.

"What's your email address?"

I gave that to him along with the service provider I used.

Jacob disconnected the phone and handed it back to me. "It should be a lot easier to understand now, too. Remember, just 'yes' or 'no' to answer or ignore a call."

"But does 'no' really mean 'no'?"

"In this sense, yes. And if you get email a big envelope will appear on the screen. Just tap it and it will open your email. Think you can handle that?"

"Maybe."

"You'll do fine."

"I always do."

"Now, about this Medina guy. I know you're going after him."

"What would make you think that?"

Jacob rolled his eyes. "He's dangerous, from the little bit of information I've gotten. On top of that, you don't have much in the way of evidence. It's not like this Antanov guy said he was going to testify."

"We have his testimony taped. It's admissible."

"Not necessarily. You know how the courts work, or don't for that matter. Just be careful is all I am saying."

"I will Mommy."

"Don't ever call me that again," Jacob said.

I never did.

Though Antanov hadn't really given me much to work on, I did have a few leads I could go with. I wanted to talk to Marcus—just to get his angle on everything—but I knew this was a bad idea. Our cases had crossed and it didn't appear his department cared much for mine. Interprecinct squabbles happened often and I'd been a part of a major one. They just never made any sense to me. We were all cops, for Christ's sake. Hell, it wasn't like I was a Fed or something. Not wanting to share information with me because I was a Fed, now that would be understandable.

I wanted Jaro Medina. I hadn't liked him when I first saw him. He was the slippery sort of son of a bitch that got away with everything, leaving others to suffer. I didn't doubt he ordered K-Drugs and the rest of his crew to go after Ilana Yigevny. I only wondered what they were really supposed to do. Maybe they were just supposed to rough her up a bit. Maybe they were supposed to just scare her. It appeared obvious that K-Drugs had been the one who went too far.

I thought about Rick and what had happened. Someone had shot up the car he and Galbadon were driving. Firing on police officers, though common in movies and on television, didn't occur very often and required an insane amount of balls. The entire NYPD would be investigating Rick's death and, unfortunately, there was no way I could interfere with that. Of course, my case led directly to the guilty party, I figured. I could solve K-Drug's case, close Marcus', and put to rest the man or men responsible for Rick's death.

Just thinking about Rick made me sick to my stomach. It made me realize how I'd treated him, how I'd always complained about him, and how he didn't deserve any of it. Unfortunately there wasn't anything I could do about it. I couldn't change the past. I could only try and make sure not to do something like that again in the present and future. Not an easy thing to do, let me tell you.

"What's on your mind?" Lavin asked. I looked up and saw him leaning on my desk.

"Just thinking about a few things."

He nodded. "What did Grizzly Adams have to say?"

"Jacob thinks Antanov was telling the truth about most of what he said. The only thing he might have lied about was his involvement with Ilana Yigevny's murder."

"We sort of new that though, right?"

"I'd assumed."

"Can't he be arrested for it?"

"No evidence at all."

"None?"

"We don't have anything on Antanov. We just have some loose ties between him and Volkyv."

"Vice is so much easier. The arrests are pretty straightforward."

"And you get to deal with such upstanding people," I said.

"And Homicide is much better? Konstantin Volkyv was up for some civic awards or something?"

"You know what I meant."

"I never know what you mean. But what I was saying is that it's easier to get someone behind bars who deserves it in Vice," Lavin said, sitting down in a chair in front of my desk.

"Yeah, you guys circumvent that thing called the burden of proof."

"Sometimes. Just don't tell anyone."

"I don't know anyone," I said.

"What's up next?"

"Jaro Medina. He's a model citizen. I think he even donates to children's charities."

"I know who he is. You seem to like these slippery sons of bitches. Can't you ever investigate a case when the people involved aren't total scumbags?" Lavin asked.

"How about the Mullins case, or the Dawson case?"

"Okay. Then find a case that doesn't involve scumbags *and* doesn't get you near dead."

I shrugged. "That I can't help you with."

"Didn't think so."

"I am going to pay Mr. Medina a visit, but first I want to speak with Chris Galbadon. I heard he is awake now."

"Think you'll get in?"

"Why wouldn't I?" I asked. "I work for the NYPD. I have a right to see a guy that was helping out with my case."

"Yeah, try that. Let me know how it works."

"I will."

What I didn't realize was that by going to see Galbadon I'd have to go into a hospital. The last time I'd been there was when my father died. I was instantly reminded of the day my father passed away when I pulled up to St. Mark's. I did my best to not think about it but images of my father lying in that bed with tubes stuck in him kept coming to my mind. The guilt of that day came with those images, intertwined and interconnected. It amazed me how easily I could be taken over by such things. I missed my father right then and I realized once again that I would never be able to speak to him. He was lost forever. Forever is a tough concept to comprehend. Try it sometime. Really try it.

Galbadon was held on the fourth floor, heavily guarded by NYPD. I didn't completely agree with this; it wasn't as though he was a witness in a major case or anything like that. He was a victim. I had questions for this victim. I only hoped that I wouldn't get caught in some inter-precinct crap. Like I said, precincts didn't always work well together. There was a chance the guys from Brooklyn would deny my entry into Galbadon's room. There was no real reason for this but I have learned that, much like an argument with a woman, reason rarely applies in reality.

There were two uniforms standing outside Galbadon's door. The nurse at the information desk had told me access to his room was restricted but she relented when I showed her my badge. Most people relented when you showed them a police badge, particularly a gold one. Of course, there are some people who actually react with anger when they see the badge. I've labeled those people as chaotics and decided they only want to destroy the American way of life as we know it. I have no use for such people.

One of the uniforms, a twenty-something with dark brown hair and slight build, stood up when I approached.

"Sorry, there are no visiting hours," he said in a deep voice.

"I am not here to here to bring flowers," I said.

The uniform looked confused. He turned to the other guy, a redheaded tall man who seemed to be about ten years older. He just shrugged.

"Who are you?"

I took out my badge again. I was beginning to think I should just wear it on my shirt, along with a nametag. I could also shoot myself in the temple. "Detective John Keegan, Homicide, Midtown South," I said. Immediately the guy eased up, I could see his shoulders sag from their previously stiff position.

"Oh. What brings you here?"

"Galbadon was working on a case with me."

"Was he?"

"Yes. How is he doing?"

"He's come out of it. I don't know too much, but I've overheard that he is talking now."

"He's still a bit out of it," the redhead said. He seemed to not want me to know anything. Maybe he didn't trust me. I didn't give a shit.

"Well, I just want to see him for a minute."

The brown-haired uniform—I saw his last name was Stein—looked at the other guy and said," I don't see why not."

The redhead—Freeman—didn't seem so crazy about this. "His name isn't on the accepted list."

"No, I didn't get an invitation, but Galbadon knows me and he has information pertinent to my current investigation. If I have to, I can go through all the channels and come back here with a higher up. There's no need for that."

Luckily, Freeman gave in. "Alright, but only for a few minutes."

"Thanks," I said and walked in the door.

Galbadon was lying on his side with his back toward me. There was only one machine hooked up to him—a heart monitor—and it beeped intermittently. Galbadon rolled over when he heard me walk in. I needed quieter shoes.

"I just took my meds," he said weakly.

"But it's time for your sponge bath," I said.

Galbadon rolled completely over and saw me. His eyes lit

up. Before I said anything else to him, I realized there was a chance he wasn't told about Calhill. I decided it best not to say anything unless he mentioned it. His experience was traumatic enough already.

"Keegan, God it's good to see you," he said.

I walked over to his bed and he sat up. I extended my hand and he shook it weakly. It amazed me how such a strong man had been so weakened. His face was drawn. He looked like he lost about twenty pounds.

"How are you feeling?" I asked. I knew nothing of his injuries.

"Better. Still don't have all my strength back and my left side is still a bit numb. Doctor says I am lucky. If the impact had been even slightly worse, I'd be paralyzed."

"Well, thank God for that," I said, for lack of anything better.

Galbadon looked at me, then looked away. "I'll never know why I was lucky and Calhill wasn't." He looked back at me. "There was nothing I could do, John."

"I know," I said.

"It all happened in an instant. I don't remember much."

"What were you guys doing?"

Galbadon sighed. "We were headed toward Yigevny's house. Rick thought his son had something to do with Volkyv's death and we were there because we got a tip that the kid had a poker game that night," Galbadon said.

"I know. He told me before you guys went."

"On our way there, we noticed a tail. Rick was driving. They came up along side us once we were near the house and tried to ram us off the road. Before I knew it, I heard a gunshot. I don't remember anything else."

"Understandable. You've been through Hell. Who do you think was following you?"

"I don't know."

"Who told you about the card game?" I asked.

"I don't remember."

I scanned Galbadon's face. I couldn't get a read on him. I certainly didn't believe him. He had to know. For some reason, he just chose not to tell me. I thought about pressing him but I didn't think it would do any good. The poor guy was lying in a hospital bed, weak. I couldn't take advantage of that.

I could tell by his expression that he realized I didn't believe him.

"I really don't remember," he said.

"Okay."

"I don't remember everything from that day. It's crazy. It's like I lost half a day."

"What do you remember, anything else?" I asked.

"Not much," Galbadon said through an exhale.

I was going to ask him about Medina, but I instantly didn't trust him. Galbadon was being shifty. If I knew better, I'd have thought he was in on this somehow. His lying in the hospital bed sort of deterred me from believing that. It would be far too great a risk for him.

"I want to know who is responsible for Calhill's death," I said.

"I know, John. I don't blame you. I do too."

I didn't believe that. I don't know why. "Of course."

"This whole thing has gotten out of hand. I thought this would just be a normal investigation. I never would have believed it would go this far."

"I don't think anyone did."

"At least you have one case solved," Galbadon said. I didn't know what he meant at first, then it clicked.

"The Yigevny murder."

"Yes."

"What do you think of the son?"

"I don't know. I believed he was involved at first. Now, I am not so sure."

"I heard he is involved with the Russian mob."

"From who?" Galbadon asked. He looked like he was sweating, which I wanted to believe was because of how weak he was. I knew better, though.

"A few sources."

Galbadon gave me a glance which told me he knew I wasn't going to keep him in the loop anymore. He was out and I think he knew he deserved it. "I wouldn't believe everything you hear."

"I never do."

I wasn't going to get anything out of Galbadon. I was starting to formulate my own theories about what happened the night Rick was killed. I figured Galbadon was never supposed to be in the car. It was supposed to be me in that car. This hit me as I stood there, looking at Galbadon. It made sense. The only thing I needed to know was who was responsible. It all pointed to Medina.

"Be careful," Galbadon said.

"I will."

19

So, Galbadon was involved somehow. Driving back toward the precinct, I became more convinced of this. I no longer pitied him for having been injured in that accident. I felt he should have been the one to die. I didn't like wishing such things on people but I figured the powers that be would agree with me on this one. I wouldn't want to be a part of an afterlife controlled by someone who favored betrayers like Galbadon. Of course, I had no evidence to back up my suspicions.

Before I got back to the precinct I decided the evidence I desired lay between the ears of Jaro Medina. There wasn't anything I could do at the precinct. I had to see him directly. Perhaps I should have taken someone along with me. If my beliefs were correct, Medina had ordered someone to kill Calhill and I. Going to see Medina would be walking right into the reaper. Screw the reaper. I can say that because, from what I've been told, he doesn't read very often. No time.

I wasn't sure where I could find Medina. I decided to call Pauline and see if she could get some information for me. I kept the call short—though I tried to sound genuinely interested in talking to her—and she was able to give me his business address. Pauline had detected what I was up to and tried to warn me. I told her, like everyone else, that I would be careful. One day I am going to have to look that word up in the dictionary and see what it means.

Medina worked out of an office building in Astoria, not exactly a nice town and certainly not close to where I was. I should have called Geiger to update him on the investigation but I knew he'd bitch about my going to see Galbadon without asking him. I was in no mood to hear it. I didn't like to make him more concerned than he deserved to be but I didn't see any other way right then. I wanted to speak to Medina. I was focused on that and that only. He was my suspect in everything.

The building Medina operated out of was at the end of a street in an industrial area of Queens. I had to drive through a metal gate to get to the property. The building itself was small, set back on what appeared to be a construction site that wasn't completed. I saw two other cars parked in the small lot, a Chevy Suburban and a Lincoln Navigator. Everyone drove SUVs. Everyone also paid a lot of money for gas.

I parked the Ford sedan I was driving in front of the small white building. I took my gun out of the glove box and checked for the small one I kept at my ankle. I prayed I didn't have to use either of them but knowing they were on me offered a level of comfort incomparable to anything else I know. And I could shoot a guy like Medina. I wouldn't have had a problem with that, or at least I thought.

I got out of the car and saw that it was about to rain. I didn't mind the rain but right then it gave me a sense of foreboding, that something was going to happen, and not something good. Foreboding feelings never brought anything good. Remember that.

Medina's building was only two stories and had no markings on the outside. It was old but it looked out of place at the site. It looked like someone just dropped it there. It was built of red brick, with small white-framed windows. A guy like Medina didn't seem to be the sort of man to work out of such an old building. Of course, I knew whatever he did out of there was extremely short of legitimate.

I walked up to the front door. There didn't seem to be too much activity going on either outside or inside. I tried to peer through the window but all that was visible was the hallway. I didn't see anyone. I can't say I liked the feeling I was getting.

I tried the door and it was locked. With nothing else coming to mind, I knocked, loud. At first, no one responded. Then, I saw someone coming toward the door. I went for my gun in my shoulder holster as a reaction. I tried to calm myself. It didn't work too well.

The guy who came to the door was tall, about 6'3" and dark skinned. He was fairly bulky but not imposing. I noticed the gun bulge at his belt immediately. This wasn't going to end well, the way I saw it.

"We're closed," he said.

At first, I thought to show him my badge. I reconsidered. I didn't think it was a good idea to announce my arrival to the people who wanted me dead.

"I thought so. I just want to speak to someone," I said.

"No one here wants to speak to you."

"How do you know?"

The guy looked me up and down. He had a nasty disposition about him, the sort that made me think he liked to beat people up and was good at it. I didn't want to get into a scrape with him. I'd leave important body parts behind. I was getting to old to recover from such things.

"Who are you?" he asked me, moving a bit closer.

"No one important," I said.

"That's Detective Keegan, Carlos," a voice said from behind me. I remembered the voice. It was Medina. I tensed. "Stop bothering him."

I turned and saw Medina dressed almost exactly the same as the first time I saw him. He must really have liked golf. This didn't make me like him any more.

"Mr. Medina," I said in the strongest voice I could muster. Even I wasn't impressed.

"How can I help you, Detective Keegan?"

"I just wanted to talk to you about a few things."

"I really don't have much to say." Medina moved toward me. He seemed carefree, certainly not worried, excited or moved at all to see me. Needless to say, I was hurt.

"You don't even know what I want to ask."

"You're right. And I'll have to idea what the answers are to whatever it is you want to ask. I don't know anything." He said all of that with a smile.

I looked at Carlos then back at Medina. "Just give me a few minutes of your time, alone," I said. I tried to remain in control. I firmly believed he ordered Rick's death. I wanted to strangle him for that.

"I am a busy man, Detective. Perhaps we can do this another time."

"I don't see a need for that. Plus, why do you want to reschedule if you don't know anything?" I asked.

Medina didn't flinch. He just looked directly at me and said, "I am only trying to cooperate."

"Well, I appreciate that. Still, I'd rather take care of this now, alone."

Medina held up his hands. "Okay, okay. Carlos, go back inside. The detective here means me no harm, I am sure."

Carlos took another look at me, then walked inside.

"What do you want to talk about?" Medina asked. He was about five feet away from me. For a moment, I thought he was trying to intimidate me. It wasn't working.

"I want to know about Chris Galbadon," I said.

"Who?"

"You know who I am talking about."

"Okay, the cop who you were with the other day. I know him."

"How well?"

"I am not sure what you are getting at, Detective."

"How well did you know Chris Galbadon?"

"Not very well. We've met a few times before. That's all."

I looked into his eyes. Medina didn't seem to be hiding

anything, but it was tough to tell. He moved his eyes around a lot when he spoke, which usually indicated someone who was being less than forthright. Medina could have just been a shifty bastard.

"You lied to me about Konstantin Volkyv," I said.

"How so?"

"You were the one who arranged that job he was assigned to do."

"Absolutely not, Detective. I had nothing to do with that."

"But you knew what it was. That's withholding evidence, the way I see it."

"You wouldn't try to pin that on me so don't try to pretend you would. I've walked away from far worse than that. Don't threaten me again or this conversation will end."

I didn't like him threatening me in any way but I had to withstand it to get what I wanted. I only wanted to get a read on him. This wasn't an attempt to get any sort of confession out of him. He wouldn't give in ever, I knew that. I just wanted to get in his face and let him know he didn't scare me and he wasn't going to. I didn't want to press him too much. I just wanted him to know that I was still around. For all I knew, he could have thought I was in the car with Rick.

"I was just letting you know," I said.

"Of course. Anything else?"

"What do you know of Anton Yigevny?"

"Boris' son?"

"Yes. I understand you are close with the family. What do you know of the boy?"

"Not much, Detective. I just know who he is."

"Well, he's probably going to be charged with the murder of a cop. My partner, to be specific."

Again, Medina didn't flinch. "I find that surprising, kid from a family like that. Then again, you never know."

"You're right, you don't. Still, I thought that, with the history between you and Yigevny, you might know more,"

I said, throwing that out there to see if he took the bait. He was too good for that.

"Again I find myself not knowing what you are talking about."

"I'm sure you don't. What's important is that I do." I walked away from Medina. "I'll be keeping an eye on you, only because I don't have much else to do."

"That's a shame, Detective. I am sure there are more productive things you could do than follow a legitimate businessman like myself. I'd hate to see you charged with harassment."

"So now you go to threats. Interesting."

"Not at all Detective. I would just not like to see that."

"You take care, Mr. Medina."

"Stay in your precinct, Detective. You don't belong out this far."

"True, but I like it around here. Much quieter than what I am used to."

I must admit I felt like a coward after leaving Medina. Sure, I tried to be witty and cool but that really didn't work. In reality, I should have beat the crap out of him right there. Sure, I had to worry about procedure along with Carlos and his seeming ability to damage my internal organs. That didn't matter, though. It always seemed easier to act after a confrontation instead of in the heat of the moment. I'd done the smart thing but I hadn't done the manly thing and my ego reminded me of that. John Wayne wouldn't have backed down from Medina. Then again, John Wayne was dead.

I found myself thinking of my father again, wondering what we thought of me, looking down from heaven. Would he have been proud that I didn't let my temper and testosterone get the best of me, or was he up there shaking his head trying to figure out how he raised a man with no balls? I figured he would have leaned toward the former, at least that's what he would have said to me. Still, I had the feeling he would have wanted to me, as a father, to splatter Medina all over the lot.

I had one more idea in my head. The way I saw it, someone was feeding the bad guys information. My initial guess was Galbadon did. Most likely, that was the case, but there was nothing wrong with trying to isolate him as the primary suspect. It was time to enlist the help of Jacob once again. I knew that if there were anyone out there who could assist me in getting the information I wanted, it was him.

While driving back toward the precinct, I felt my thoughts swirling in my head. I couldn't grasp onto anything particular. I thought of my father, Rick, Pauline, and I thought of Galbadon. The minute a thought about one of them came to the forefront, another fought for position. I had all of these loose concepts with no way of tying any one of them down. This happened to me often and I found myself lost in my head more often than can be considered healthy. It's a great characteristic to have as a homicide detective but it got in the way of my regular life far too much.

In an effort to control this, I focused on Anton Yigevny. I didn't know much about his life or his personality so I created as much as I could. Unlike his father, it appeared he lived a comfortable life from the beginning. He didn't know struggle and he probably didn't know sacrifice. He only knew privilege. This sort of person ends up dangerous because they feel they are entitled to everything. What has not been given to them must then be taken. You can see this even with spoiled young children. Enough is never adequate. Too much doesn't even sate them. What they want, whether they realize it or not, is everything. The only way to be happiest is to ensure everyone else has nothing. Anton Yigevny struck me that way. He wanted identity on top of all else, and it seemed to me that he searched for it in the Russian mob, among the likes of Alex Antanov and Kostya Volkyv. When you choose such guides in life you can't really complain about where you end up.

What I needed to tie together was the leap Anton seemingly made from spoiled rich kid to likely cop killer. The only thing that could accomplish this was the discovery of motive. I didn't doubt someone could make that leap I only doubted the likelihood of my finding out what that motive was. It's the toughest part of a murder investigation. They make it seem so easy on TV and in the movies. I've heard so much about motive and the elimination of it in the perfect murder. If you want to get away with murder, remove the motive, they say. I don't think it is so simple. Like much of a murder investigation, discovery of motive is complicated. I had a hunch good old Anton Yigevny had sufficient motive. It was my job to find it, along with concrete evidence to prove it.

This is where the investigation becomes interesting. Many times, motive doesn't come into play in my work because the evidence makes the motive unnecessary. Either the suspect makes their crime known through acts of foolishness or we find the murder weapon and bloody clothes in a suspect's home. A slick, headed-for-the-pits-of-Hell defense attorney might be able to work around some of that, sure. Still, most times evidence trumps motive. It is in a case like Volkyv's, one with a relatively clean crime scene—clean in terms of definitive evidence—where motive becomes incredibly important.

It didn't take long to hit me. I had Anton tied to the Russian mob. I had the Russian mob responsible for his sister's obvious rape/murder. It wasn't much of a stretch to believe that Anton somehow got wind of who was responsible and decided to exact his own form of justice on the men. Considering that it seemed Volkyv and his boys screwed up their job, the heads of the mob probably had no problem with Anton doing their house cleaning. In theory, this seemed solid. Coupled with Anton's seeming involvement with Rick's death, I had a winner. All I had to do was cash in the chips.

I drove with a renewed sense of purpose, happy to be able

to think clearly without the other things that nagged me overtaking my thought process. There would certainly be a time when I would truly mourn the death of my father and the loss of Rick. Along with that, I would deal with my feelings for Pauline—which at that time scared me because of how quickly they moved—at my own pace. I controlled my mind, not vice versa. The funny thing is I actually believed that. I'd forgotten that the mind, when it has something to do, takes control of everything. What I didn't know was how hard all of this would come down on me, at the same time.

Jacob wasn't in his office. This was the first time I'd ever not seen him there. He was a fixture in that office, not unlike the space age desk he sat at or the hi tech audio gear stacked on the far wall. I felt the temptation to really get a look at that stuff but figured he had it so well guarded that I would be vaporized if I touched the wrong dial. Still, I must admit such knowledge didn't completely deter me. I moved toward the audio equipment. All I wanted to do was catch the brand of equipment he used only because I had always been curious about that and he would never tell anyone.

Before I got within ten feet of the rack I heard, "Touch that and die, Keegan," from behind me. My heart ended up somewhere near my tonsils. I'm not exactly sure where. In the midst of trying to calm its beating, I realized the voice was not Jacob's. I turned around, and noticed Geiger standing in the doorway.

"You owe me a pair of underwear," I said.

"You think I am going to let you screw around with this equipment? Without him and his gear this department would be handicapped. We'd be left solely to the abilities of the detectives here."

"Of course, Boss."

"I assume you were looking for something to record some sort of report for me, right?" Geiger asked.

I wanted to walk out of the room only because I felt

uncomfortable standing in someone else's office when they weren't there. "I was going to see you."

"When?"

"Right after I talked with Jacob."

"What did you want him for?"

"I've got a hunch that someone is feeding the Russian mob information and I wanted to know if Jacob had any way of helping me find that out," I said, taking a step closer to Geiger. I really didn't want to be any closer to him but, like I said, I didn't want to get caught in Jacob's office, either.

"What do you think he'd be able to do for you?"

"I don't know." Part of the reason I didn't get specific was because I didn't want Geiger to know everything I was up to. The other part was because I had no clue what Jacob could do to help me. I just knew that he'd bailed me out a few times before.

"That sounds like a solid plan. Come with me," Geiger said as he walked toward his office. I felt relieved.

We walked into his office and I sat in my usual seat, the one to his right. Rick always took the other seat and I felt the lack of his presence. Geiger must have too, but he didn't say anything about it. He wasn't the sort to do something like that.

"Tell me what you are working on."

"Well, I've spoken to Antanov. He gave me some good information about what's going on with Yigevny. He also gave me some ideas about who might be responsible for Volkyv."

Geiger shook his head. "All this effort to find the killer of some piece of garbage. You'd think we'd just quietly thank the guy who did it."

"Unfortunately, it doesn't work that way. We have to investigate this bum's murder. Unless, of course, there is something else you want me to do."

"Don't try and lie to me. You're not investigating Volkyv's

death, you're investigating Calhill's." I started to say something in weak protest but Geiger held up his hand. "Trust me, it's what I want you to do. The whole NYPD is going crazy about his death. This precinct is going to be under the microscope for a while."

Actually, I'd been surprised at the lack of attention Rick's murder had gotten. It made the papers but not the front page. People didn't react to police killings like they used to. Much of this was due to the hatred bred from the special interest groups that tried to paint us police officers as racist, or evil, or both. Sure, there are racist cops. There are evil cops. This is because in all walks of life exist the lower-class people. Still, you'd expect the community to be outraged at the death of a cop like Rick. There wasn't.

"I don't think it is anything to worry about," I said.

'Well, consider it a problem because I said so. Now, what else are you working on?"

I told Geiger what I thought about Anton Yigevny, how I thought he had motive and the ability to commit the murder. I told him how I tied this together with Rick's death. Geiger didn't say anything at first. He just sat there, nodding.

"You really think the kid is capable?" he asked after the uncomfortable pause. He did things like that often.

"I do. I don't see anyone else."

"Well, you should definitely pay him a visit," Geiger said, "Without question. I don't know if I agree with you on this but it pays to check it out."

"You think it could be someone else?"

"I don't know. Kid's got some reasons to do it but he has more to not do it. Maybe you should speak to his father first."

"And tell the father that we think the son is guilty of murder? The poor guy just lost a daughter. Finding out that his son might go to jail certainly won't help things."

I really didn't like being in that office discussing a case

without Rick there. It just seemed so uneventful. Rick and I always argued about cases and even when we weren't working a case together, it always felt right to know he was in the precinct somewhere, mentally disagreeing with me even if he was unaware of it. Sitting there going over a case with Geiger just felt empty.

"I don't think that is something we need to be concerned with. Tell me the truth, do you think Anton Yigevny could have killed Calhill? Is that what you are really thinking?" Geiger asked. I couldn't tell if he was saying this because he agreed with me or not.

"Yes. It's all I have to go on right now so I'm gonna run with it. See where it takes me."

"We've seen where that tactic leads," Geiger said, rolling his eyes. I didn't appreciate that so much. "What about Marcus Lay, have you spoken to him about any of this?"

"They haven't exactly been cooperative."

"That's unfortunate. You should speak to him."

"I don't think that would be a problem. I can pull it off."

Geiger nodded. "What about Galbadon?"

I knew he must have heard I went to see Galbadon. "Spoke to him. He didn't have all that much to say."

"Nothing?"

I shook my head.

"You think he's hiding something?" Geiger asked.

"I don't know, Boss. He says he doesn't remember much. He always came across as an honest guy to me. You never know, though. I've seen what appeared to be better guys go wrong."

"Christ. There's something going on here. We're scratching at it but we just can't seem to get to it. You need to find the connection. You said before that someone in the NYPD is feeding the Russian mob with information. What makes you think that?"

"A few things. First, we have Antanov coming out and

basically saying exactly that. Then, you've got Rick's death. How did they know where he was going? Galbadon did say they noticed a tail on their way to Yigevny's. Someone had to tip them off."

"Unfortunately, you're most likely right. I'm telling you, we don't need this. We don't need the negative attention. We don't need the bullshit that is going to come with this. We need an open and shut case and it doesn't look like we are going to get it."

"We never do."

Geiger ran his hand through his hair and took a deep breath, staring up at the ceiling. I knew he was upset about Calhill's death. I also knew he was concerned about the promotion. I didn't think any less of him because of that. As idealistic as I try to be sometimes, I would probably be thinking the same way Geiger was. He was most likely believing that the fates were in some way conspiring to screw him out of the promotion. If I were up for a promotion, I am sure the fates would have referred to a battle plan drawn up a long time ago.

"Alright, go see Jacob. See if he can offer you some help," Geiger said through an exhale. "Then, I want you to pay Mr. Yigevny a visit. Maybe he knows something we don't. After that, arrange a meeting with Lay."

"Maybe I should speak to Lay first. He might have spoken to Yigevny. It could save the trip."

Geiger looked at me without saying anything. I could see his mind churning. He really didn't know what he wanted to do anymore. It had gotten that bad. "Okay," he said, and it sounded like he was giving in. I wasn't arguing with him. I knew better than to argue with him. It never got me anywhere.

"I'll nose around and see what I come up with," I said.

"Keep Lavin in the loop. I sort of had him reassigned to our department for a bit, considering the levity of this case." He meant Calhill's death, I figured.

"Sort of?"

Geiger leaned back in his chair. "It's not official. He requested it and it was initially turned down. Still, he hasn't been assigned any new cases from Vice and he won't until this is over. If you want, you can treat him like a partner. If you don't want to do that, treat him like an expert on the Russian Underworld. Get it?"

I nodded.

"I know you two are friends, so I figure this is a good thing. He's a great cop, from what his superiors told me. You two should work well together."

I tried to play down my excitement. Normally, I would have preferred to work alone. Not this time. I needed someone there to take the place of Rick. I needed someone to keep me sane. Karl would be able to do that. He knew my personality and the complications that went along with it. Geiger easily could have assigned some other schmuck with me because of the importance of the case. I appreciated that he didn't.

"Thanks," I said.

Geiger smirked. He knew what I was thanking him for. "Get to work." I stood up to leave. He paused. "And Keegan?" he asked as I was just at his door.

"Yeah, Boss?"

"I'm really sorry about your father. I know how difficult this all is for you. I didn't want to say too much about it. Just wanted you to know I understand."

"Thanks," I said, and walked out of the office. I remembered that Geiger's father died about a year after I became a detective. I'd gone to the funeral out of respect but I didn't know Geiger that well. I could remember that Geiger had stayed stoic during the funeral. He didn't flinch. There is something about men and their thinking that holding everything in at such times is respectable. Perhaps it is. Or maybe it would be better if we just all cried every once in a while. I think that might be healthy. And no, I won't be the one to start the trend.

Karl caught me on the way to my desk. He seemed eager. I could tell because he had a serious look on his face—a strained look actually—something you didn't see on Karl Lavin too often. He took life as it came and never seemed to let anything really get to him. I envied him for that.

"What do you think we should do first?" he asked, sitting down in my chair.

"You really think Homicide is a good fit for you, don't you?"

"I'll tell you one thing; it is a Hell of a lot easier than Vice. The threat level is insignificant considering that the crime has already been committed."

"I think in this case the crimes are not finished. We still don't know who the other men were that killed Yigevny's daughter. I would assume they are prime suspects. It also appears that the people responsible have no problems killing off cops, which makes us targets as well," I said, taking a seat across from Karl. The department looked different from there. I saw things on the walls I'd never noticed before, like a 'No Smoking' sign. I thought back to the days when it was okay to smoke at your desk. As a smoker, I initially thought it was great back then. I came to realize how stupid it was to just spew smoke all around an office. It stunk, and it really did subject other people to smoke they didn't deserve. Don't get me wrong, I hate non-smokers with a passion unlike any other I've experienced. I do, however, know how to see both sides of an argument.

"Child's play, this case," Lavin said. "You really think we are at risk? These bumbling idiots won't come near us."

"I am happy you are so confident."

"It goes with the territory. So, what's first?"

"I'm going to chat with Jacob. He might have a way for us to get information on some things."

"Like what?"

My suspicious nature started to get the best of me. Sure,

I'd known Karl all my life. Still, the only person I could be certain wasn't funneling information to the Russian mob was me. Anyone else could be suspect. Karl could be suspect."

"Just a couple of things," I said.

"Like?"

"Nothing important."

"You cutting me out already?" Karl asked. He leaned closer to me. "Maybe you don't like working with me. Maybe this is how you always worked. It isn't how I work. You got something on your mind, you let me know about it," he said in an extremely calm yet angry tone.

"It's not like that."

"Yes, it is."

"Listen, you're not exactly my partner. You've been called in because of your experience with the Russian mob. This is my case and I will handle it as I see necessary."

"Nice speech, but sorry, won't work. I didn't get transferred just to be someone's bitch."

"You'll do as I say or you can go back to busting third rate drug dealers."

"At least I can do that with some degree of competence," Karl said.

"Not from what I've heard." I could feel the anger brewing inside of me. He wasn't going to tell me what to do. It was my decision.

"What case have you really solved with any level of accuracy?"

"I'm not going to sit here and list my cases," I said.

"Because you can't. Calhill did all your work for you."

I stood up.

"You're going to hit me too? Trust me, it won't work out the same way it did with him," Karl said, rising up out of his chair to meet me.

I might have been able to take him, I really don't know. I didn't actually want to hit him. I was just angry. Everything was spiraling out of my control. Events were taking place that I couldn't understand or manipulate. Karl wanting to know more than I wanted to tell only exemplified this. I knew I was being foolish, even right then. This knowledge had absolutely no effect on my behavior, unfortunately.

"I think you overestimate yourself. No shock there."

Karl's face reddened. "Come on, Keegan. Take a shot."

I wouldn't do it. Fear had nothing to do with it. Karl tried to bait me for some reason. He should have known how I was, how my moods shifted. Maybe he did and just didn't want to deal with me right then. Perhaps he deduced what I was thinking, that I couldn't trust him.

"I'm not playing your games. I'm going to talk to Jacob."

"Yeah, go ahead, run away. Doesn't surprise me one bit."

I didn't respond. Instead I just walked away. Believing I was the bigger man, I approached Jacob's office. He was there, sitting at his desk, staring at one of the many computer screens there.

"Hey," I said, sitting down in a chair in the right corner of the room. My body was still tense from my argument with Karl. Already my mind was starting to formulate the belief that I had been wrong. It doesn't take too long for my mind to come to its senses, so to speak.

"Having a rough day?" Jacob asked without turning around.

"Not necessarily," I said.

Jacob swiveled around in his seat and just looked at me. He wasn't the sort to roll his eyes. He usually just glared, which he did right then. "You forget I have this whole place wired?"

"I always suspected but you never told me."

"Oops. Guess I have to kill you now," he said, returning to his computer.

"Would be doing me a favor right now."

"John, you're a conglomerate of angry emotions right

now. I don't think there is a person in the world who would expect otherwise. On top of that, you've got guys pulling you in all different directions. Geiger wants one thing from you, something you can give him; devotion to your job. He wants you to solve this case. Lavin wants something you normally do give him but can't now; trust. You need to give one to be able to give the other. To produce for Geiger you'll have to trust Lavin. You don't have any other choice as I see it."

I didn't want someone to make such simple sense of my feelings the way Jacob did. I wanted to stay angry because anger would keep me away from other emotions. Jacob sliced right through that. He made me feel as though I was being childish. Maybe I was. Certainly wouldn't be the first time. Certainly wouldn't be the last time.

"I take it you overheard the argument."

Jacob nodded. "You were both wrong. Don't think I am taking his side. I get the feeling you guys are going to be working together more often, so it might be a good idea to remember what his personality is and what yours is. You are both stubborn."

"I'm not—"

"Yes you are stubborn, John. I've known it. Most people who have hung around you for more than ten seconds figure this out. It's not big deal."

I looked around, trying to find the psychology textbook. "Anything else?"

"That's about it. Just wanted to offer you a bit of advice."

Truthfully, I did appreciate that. It was damn near impossible to say it, though. "Uh, thanks."

"There you go. Now, what is it you want me to do?"

"I would guess you already overheard."

Jacob smiled. "I have my computers tuned to the mention of my name. If anyone in the precinct mentions it, I get a little popup window alerting me to it. You've been throwing my name around all day. Haven't been able to get a lick of work done."

Jacob moved his considerable mass over to his other computer and brought up a window. "What's that?"

"Just confirming a food order for the house warming. You *are* coming, right?"

"Yes," I said, not so sure if I was or wasn't.

"You're the only one I have invited from the precinct. Well, you and your guest, if you are smart enough to bring her."

"Whatever. To think that you waste department resources on such things," I said.

"I save this department ten times the amount I waste."

"I know."

"So, you want me to find the mole, huh?"

"It would be nice."

"Perhaps I already have."

"What?" I asked. I knew Jacob was good, but not that good.

"Since Calhill was killed I've taken an interest in these cases as well. I ruled out Marcus Lay and his department because I know that you guys have been keeping them in the dark about what you are doing. This would leave the Brooklyn precinct you have been working with."

I expected Jacob to keep talking but he stopped. The first thing I thought was that it was Galbadon. This seemed the logical choice. He knew plenty and he might have had an ulterior motive to skew things in the direction he so pleased. He didn't strike me as the sort of guy who would off another cop but I learned a long time ago not to trust my instincts. People can be deceptive when it serves their purpose. This talent in humans has perplexed me from birth, starting with one of my aunts and continuing with two-faced friends, untrustworthy fellow officers and has culminated in politicians. My aunt was the worst, though. I don't want to talk about it. I'll just say that she led two lives. And she preached to everyone about honesty and morals. Bitch.

"It's not Galbadon," Jacob finally said.

"How did you know—"

"No, I haven't implanted anything into your head, yet. You seemed to be troubled by whatever you were thinking so it was an obvious guess. But it's not him."

"Are you sure?" I asked. I wanted it to not be Galbadon but knew I couldn't be fooled by my own wishes.

"Positive. There's been information transfer while he's been in the hospital."

"Okay, that would explain his innocence."

"I am not saying he didn't know beforehand. I can just say that he seems fairly clean. You never know for sure," Jacob said.

"Damn right about that. So, who is it?"

"Not entirely sure. It is someone in his department."

"How do you know?"

Jacob smiled. "I have my ways."

"Of course. Which particular way did you use this time?"

"I checked outgoing emails from our department, Lay's, and Galbadon's. You'd be amazed at how stupid people are when it comes to email. Just the things flying in and out of this department would scare you."

"I don't doubt it, and I won't ask how you are able to do it."

"It wouldn't be admissible as evidence, that much I can tell you. Anyway, there's someone sending information to a random Internet email account. It seems the information pertains directly to Yigevny and the case you are working on."

Jacob's techno-wizardry never failed to impress. Ditto the average person's idiocy. How someone could send such information over unsecured lines baffled me. Jobs obviously were at stake. Some people just don't care, or they don't have the wherewithal to comprehend the risks.

"So, what did you get?"

"I have a name."

"What sort of name?"

"Another one that worked on the Yigevny murder," Jacob said.

"Another cop on the case?"

Jacob shook his head. "No. Another mobster. Name was Latanoff. I think he changed his name, Americanized it."

"Americanized it?"

"Usually, a Russian name like that would have ended with a 'v'. This guy uses two 'f's."

"Interesting," I said.

"Not really. Happens all the time."

"Any other information about him?

"Just a first name. John."

"Even more interesting."

"A lot of people are named John, particularly when you add men named Sean, which is an Irish version—"

I held up a hand. "I know all of the derivatives of my name, Jacob."

"But do you know what 'John' means?"

"No."

"It is derived from the biblical name, Yochanan, which means 'Yahweh is gracious'. You know who Yahweh is?"

I'd been an altar boy. I'd studied the Bible a bit. "God?"

"That's right. So you're name means 'God is gracious.' Some people have come to change that to 'God's gift.' There isn't much truth to that."

"Depends on the John. I've referred to myself as God's gift once or twice in my life."

"I don't doubt that. Anyway, your guy here no doubt was at the scene of the crime. His name was mentioned in more than one email. They believe he is the next target, along with Anton Yigevny."

"He was at the crime scene as well?" I asked, barely able to make that statement.

"It doesn't say that."

"What do you think?"

"Well, it is obvious that someone doesn't like Anton. Doesn't mean he was there."

I didn't want to think that a guy could stand there witness to the rape and murder of his sister just to get into a mob. I operate on the belief that people are scum, but even scum wouldn't do that. I *hoped* humankind had a better future than that.

"It would be unthinkable," I said.

"You just thought of it, so it isn't unthinkable. It would be horrible, but not unthinkable."

"I'd say he didn't do it. I think he is the one offing the guys who did."

"That makes sense to me. He might be doing it out of guilt for not being able to prevent his new buddies from carrying out such a terrible act."

"Exactly what I am thinking. You know what they say about like minds."

Jacob gave me a sideways glance. "Let's not push it."

"True."

"The only other thing I can tell you is that the guy at Galbadon's precinct sending the emails works the late shift. Most of the emails go out after 1AM. Maybe that'll help."

"I'd like to nail that son of a bitch to the wall."

"As would everyone in this department. Maybe you'll get the chance."

"You never know," I said.

"That's the bitch of life."

20

I walked out of Jacob's office, ideas and concerns running through my mind, seemingly bent on a coordinated destruction of my existence. Okay, so maybe it wasn't that bad, but it felt that way right then. This usually happened when I had done something wrong and was aware of it. I'd done wrong by Lavin. I'd done wrong by so many people over the course of my life. Two of them were dead; I couldn't let my stubbornness, by reason to live sometimes, get in the way of another friendship. I couldn't count my true friends on one hand because I really didn't have any. People puzzled me and the way I see it, puzzlement doesn't translate into friendship. Trust did. I needed to trust.

Karl still sat at my desk, staring up at the ceiling. I felt my body tense again, readying itself for another battle. Settling my nerves would have been a good idea. The only two things capable of doing that—a cigarette or some form of sex—were unavailable to me at that moment. I had to rely on my own ability to control myself. This was doomed from the outset.

"You're back," Karl said.

"Yes."

"Relax, John. I'm not going to yell at you."

"Of course you're not," I said, sitting down in the chair again.

"You didn't trust me."

"I didn't—"

"It's okay. I thought about it. I know what you were looking for. You were looking for a mole. You had to eliminate all possibility."

I couldn't believe that Karl was figuring it out so easily. I always considered myself to be some sort of psychological enigma no one could break down and understand.

"Something like that."

"Have you found out anything?"

I briefed Karl on what Jacob had told me. I told him everything, word for word as I remembered it, in an effort to be more forthright with people. God only knew if it would work at all.

"Wow, a fucking mole in the Brooklyn precinct. I never trusted those sons of bitches."

"Can't trust anyone," I said, smiling.

"Rat bastard. Listen, if I am going to turn dirty, I am not going to feed information to the Russian mob. I am going to steal a couple of pounds of smack or grab some drug money. And it will be a large amount. For me to go dirty, I need to get paid. Got it?"

"Got it."

"Good. Piece of shit thinking I'd turn mole. I should shoot you in the dick for that."

"You don't need to be a good shot to pull that one off."

Karl laughed. "Yeah, lie to yourself."

"I wasn't thinking of hitting you, by the way," I said.

"I was thinking of hitting you. You have this way about you. Makes people want to hit you. That scar on your forehead is living proof."

I rubbed my forehead, where the scar was. "That guy was a homicidal maniac."

"Sometimes the crazies know the most truth."

"Would explain any knowledge you have."

"Right. Anyway, what's first on the list. I am tired of sitting in this precinct. It smells like shit."

He was right, it did. The department always had an odor similar to used underwear. Imagine it; you'll get it.

"I want to speak to McCrory, see if I can find out about this Latanoff guy."

"He might be dead."

"That would make him easier to find then, wouldn't it?"

"In this city? You never know."

"Is that a stab at the homicide cops in this city? I would say that you Vice guys aren't exactly on the ball. I see a hooker on almost every street corner."

"Let's leave your social life out of this. Besides, at least we know where our customers are. You guys could trip over a dead body before you actually find it."

"Let's go see Pauline," I said, "before I really feel like hitting you."

"Yeah. At least I'll have some tits to stare at." I knew he said this to test me, to see if I would react and give away something about Pauline and I. I wouldn't do it, as much as I wanted to. The idea of him staring at my pseudo-girlfriend's chest bothered me. I knew how his mind operated. I knew how my mind operated. Karl's wasn't much different.

"Nice to see you, too," Pauline said after I handed her a sheet of paper with Latanoff's name on it. I tried to remain professional and pretended like nothing was going on with us. She'd said that what she wanted. You can never trust a woman to remain consistent. Never happens.

"Hello," I said feebly. She just glared at me. I didn't want to sound overly friendly or overly cold. I couldn't tell if I had succeeded but I did try to show some sort of feeling in my eyes. Very tough to do if you don't have a mirror.

"Hey McCrory," Karl said in his usual oily voice.

Pauline looked at him, then me. "They have you two working together now? I thought I subscribed to the apocalypse warning newsletter."

"It's just temporary," I said. I realized why Pauline was being less than nice to me. I hadn't spoken to her since Rick's death. I wanted to but my mind was focused on other things. I didn't see that our relationship had moved into such territory. You never get clear signals about such things. You're either not moving fast enough or you're moving too fast. I think it is a hormonal difference between men and women. Our brain chemicals just work differently.

"For my sake, I hope it is," Karl shot back.

"What do you want to know about this guy?"

"I'd like to know where he lives first and foremost, then some more detailed background later on," I said, and then with sympathy in my voice, "I don't want to cause too much trouble. Just get me what you can when you can."

"What, you getting all polite with me, Keegan?"

"I am always polite."

"And always a bad liar."

"You two want to continue this at another time so we can get to work?" Karl asked. "I really don't give a damn who is polite and who isn't right now."

"Obviously," Pauline said. "I can get you his address right now, along with some other quick stuff. That good?"

"That'd be great."

Pauline walked into the back of her office. I really needed work with the whole relationship thing. I normally operate on my own schedule without consideration for others because others rarely came into my life. My last serious relationship hadn't been that serious and had only lasted for 6 months. The first few months we acted as though it wasn't a serious relationship, so this thinking of others wasn't something that came to me naturally. I mean, was I supposed to call Pauline that night and explain why I wasn't so friendly? The idea seemed preposterous to me. I thought my actions and motivations were clear. This was one of the many mistakes I made when it came to dealing with people, particularly females.

"You're real smooth," Karl said.

"Thanks."

"No, seriously. Have you ever been laid before, ever?"

"Your girlfriend never told you?"

"This woman is all over you, I can see it just by the way she looks at you. Why haven't you done anything about it?"

"I don't want to talk about it."

"Hey man, if you're gay, you can come out to me. I'd be honored, actually. Never had a fag confess to me," Karl said.

I know I promised Pauline I wouldn't say anything to anybody. I couldn't remember if my manhood coming into question voided such a promise. It didn't matter.

"I already have, okay? And no, I don't want to talk about it."

"What do you mean?"

"Are you deaf? I just said I have done something about it. Now shut up before she gets back and overhears us. I promised her I wouldn't tell anyone from the department." I remembered this wasn't entirely true. She had sort of assumed Karl and Rick would know. That reminded me of Rick again. I shook the memory as best I could, which wasn't so well.

"Good going Keegan. You still have something in your balls besides dust. I'm impressed. How is she in the sack?"

"Stop it."

"No, really, how is she? She looks like the sort that would be an animal. A sexual dynamo. I've dreamt about her a few times, if I remember correctly."

"Shut up," I said in a loud, angry whisper.

"This bothers you?"

"Yes."

'Whoa, you have feelings for this broad? I didn't know you were capable of such things. Damn, Johnny Keegan in love. I'd have laid big money in Vegas against that."

"I didn't say anything like that," I said. I didn't want to get into this with Karl. I thought I was incapable of romance. Karl put me to shame.

"You didn't have to. I can hear it in your voice. It's why you twitched when I stared at her chest. I'll do my best to stop, but I can't promise you anything."

"Thanks, pal." I stared up at the ceiling. It seemed the only ceiling in the building that the janitors actually cleaned. I'd been working in the precinct for years and had seen one janitor. He later got fired for rifling through desks. I don't know if he took anything. Just shows how stupid people are. How dumb do you have to be to steal from police officers?

"Just being honest."

"Yeah, I know, it's one of your better qualities," I said. "Now shut the Hell up before she gets back."

"She's got you on that tight of a leash already, huh?" I didn't say anything. I just glared at him. "Okay, okay, I'll shut the Hell up."

Pauline came back with a few pieces of paper. I tried to get a reading on her. She didn't appear to be upset with me. Now, I was great at getting a reading on a suspect, or someone I was interviewing for a case. People have told me what I've done in such situations boggled their mind. When it came to emotional situations directly related to me, I could wear a blindfold and do better. Still, I felt certain Pauline wasn't angry with me.

"I don't think you had the right spelling," she said. Looking at her right then, she seemed beautiful; I don't know why. She just carried herself so well, so ladylike. I guess that's the best way to describe it. Along with this perception came again the fear of being tied down. I needed to get rid of that because I really wanted to be tied down. I was just afraid of letting my old self go. The idea that I wouldn't be able to answer to no one again frightened me. I almost craved the loneliness that nearly destroyed me. This is a dynamic about myself I've never fully understood. I don't think I ever will.

"What do you mean?" Karl asked.

"You spelled it with two 'f's. I found a man with the same phonetic pronunciation, but his ends with a 'v'. It has to be the same guy."

"What've you got?"

"He lives in Brooklyn." She handed me the piece of paper with the address. I wasn't too familiar with Brooklyn, but I noticed right away Latanov lived in Galbadon's jurisdiction. I didn't like that one bit. Coincidences never bode well for murder investigations.

"Brooklyn, huh?" Karl said.

"That's right in Galbadon territory." I looked further down and noticed that Latanov had listed Medina's work address for his job. What Pauline had gotten me wasn't much different than the information you could get on someone's credit report, minus the credit information, of course. "Interesting."

"Fantastic. I guess we know where we are heading first."

"I think we should pay Latanov a visit."

"That's what I like about you, Keegan. You think like I do."

"Don't horrify me."

Karl drove to the address we had listed for Latanov. I kept quiet on the way there because I wanted some time to settle my thoughts. I realized my mind had been overloaded the few days prior and I hadn't taken the rime to sort things out. Some of what was on my mind never could be sorted out. Death has a way of affecting everyone, including a homicide cop who dealt with death on a regular basis. Relationships also had a way of confusing. Not being an expert in that field didn't help me any. I couldn't see the path Pauline and I would take. Maybe we'd stay together for a short time and then I'd get antsy again and run away like I had in the past. Or, more frighteningly, we would stay together for the rest of one of our lives. Right then the thought came that she might have been the last woman I would get together with. It was the finality of it that jolted me.

I forced my mind to think about the case. My strongest argument involved Anton Yigevny killing Volkyv and Rick.

Volkyv's murder obviously didn't require much to believe in. If someone had done to my sister what Volkyv did to Ilana Yigevny I would want to shred him. I certainly could allow for that sort of murder in my moral scope. Believing it almost made me want to let Anton off the hook. Sympathy has a way of making one forget their job and their responsibilities.

I think what made me more certain of Anton's guilt in Rick's death stemmed from the moral difference in the murders. Rick didn't deserve to die, definitely not that way, and I knew him personally. This made me want to find his killer and it would negate the sympathy I felt for Anton. Thinking about it right then suggested maybe a flaw existed in my thinking. I needed some other link, some piece of evidence to point out the murderer more clearly. I wanted to know for sure someone was guilty. Right then I wanted that someone to be Anton, if for no other reason than simplicity. I didn't want to have to start believing in some other explanation at that stage of the game.

Karl drove fairly calmly. Most times when I had driven with him he sped more frantically than I did. Most people labeled me a psychotic driver, so this said a lot about Mr. Lavin's driving. I stared out the window, watching the water as we crossed the Verrazano Bridge. When I was a kid I was afraid of going over bridges. I think I'd seen a movie or television show where a bridge collapsed and the image stuck with me. I won't even get into what a TV movie about a nuclear holocaust did to me. I still shudder at the thought.

I watched cars next to us and coming toward us while we drove the Belt Parkway. I wondered what each person thought, what their life consisted of, what their goals focused on. How many of them found happiness? How many of them experienced it? I didn't think many. I could have been completely mistaken, of course. In imagining all of this I searched for my own place in the world. Would I be a father? The odds against that remained slim for years. I thought maybe Pauline threw some weight on the other side of that scale. In retrospect, I believe the death of my father and the loss of Rick sped that thought process along. I didn't know it then, but my overall view of life was changing, perhaps not rapidly but changing nonetheless. In most cases, realization comes after the fact. I think it is imminently difficult to make a realization in real time, so to speak. Realization requires reflection. A realization was formulating while I was in the car with Karl. Perhaps he smelled something.

"You're deep in thought. What you got on that broken down thing you refer to as a brain?" he asked as he lit a cigarette. I saw right then how ugly of a habit it was and how Rick must have felt sitting in the passenger seat while I spewed carbon monoxide at him. No, this didn't make me want to quit.

"Too many things," I said through an exhale. I saw a sign which said we were near Coney Island, not far from where Latanov supposedly lived.

"You'll bust it that way." I think Karl knew I had a lot to think about. He stayed away from talking about the volatile ones, which I was thankful for. It's always nice when someone bothers to use their sense of perception. Doesn't happen very often.

"Sometimes I wish it would bust. Certainly would make my life easier."

"We'd never be that lucky." Karl paused for a moment, flicking his cigarette in the car's ashtray. I was shocked cars still came with them. With the crusade against tobacco hitting all time highs, you would think you'd have to pay extra for an ashtray. "What angle you want to play with this Latanov guy? You want to be upfront with him, or do you want to see what he is willing to tell first?"

"Tough call. I don't want to scare him but I also don't want to give him a chance to play with us. I don't have the patience for it right now."

"You never have the patience for such things," Karl said.

"You sound like my mother."

"First time anyone's said something like that to me."

"It's a sideways compliment."

"Thank you," Karl said, extinguishing the cigarette. "So, which way do we go with this thing?"

"I say we play it by ear."

"Real professional. You read that in the homicide detective manual? Is that like homicide 101?"

"Homicide 101 teaches how you should never get partnered with a guy from Vice."

"So, now I am your partner. I guess, when the shit really gets think and pasty, you'll swear I was lead on this."

"You're learning."

"It doesn't take much. You guys are pretty transparent."

"That's a big word for you, transparent," I said. "Be careful you don't sprain your tongue saying it."

"My tongue gets plenty of exercise. Don't you worry about it."

"I don't want to know."

We arrived at Latanov's residence in the late afternoon. I could feel a dampness in the air, like it was going to rain. I never liked that feeling, the humidity, perhaps because I grew up near the shore and could always smell the salt water when it got humid. Basically, it stunk. This sense was a bit different but it still reminded me of my childhood. Unfortunately it didn't bring forth any happy memories. It just brought back the smell of fish.

I got out of the car and looked at the building. Karl finished his cigarette and looked as well, like we both waited for someone to come to us. No sense of what would happen came to me, no premonition about the future of the case. I expected one to. Fate rarely worked on my side. In emergencies, yes, She helped me through. I shouldn't complain.

Latanov lived in a two-story which looked to be about 80

or 90 years old judging by the architecture. I never truly studied architecture, I only remembered a few things from a trip to a museum when I was in grade school. The designs near the roof of Latanov's building looked a lot like the ones I'd seen in that museum. On top of that, I knew that most buildings in Brooklyn were about that old. Detective work, that's what it was.

"What do you think?" I asked Karl.

"I don't think much," he answered. "He's probably not here."

"Pauline is pretty good at her work. She'd know if it were a bogus address. I've seen her eliminate bad information before."

"I'm sure that's not all you've seen her do."

"Can we not get into this now?"

"It's all I think about. You know that. I could be watching the lottery drawing, noting that I have the first five numbers, and I'd turn off the television for a blow job," Karl said. I am not making that up.

"The world of depravity you live in."

"You'd do the same thing and you know it."

I thought about that for a second. "Depends on who's giving."

"Exactly."

We walked up the front stoop and I noticed that the name 'Latanoff' was printed underneath the top doorbell. He did try to Americanize his name. For what reason, I have no idea. The f's didn't offer anything that the 'v' didn't as far as I could see. Of course, there is always a reason for things. Just because I didn't see it didn't disprove its existence.

"Looks like our guy," Karl said. He rang the buzzer. I looked at him, only because he was the only thing to look at. He must have thought I didn't like what he did. "What? Is there some sort of homicide procedure about ringing a doorbell?"

"Not that I am aware of. We push the button, just like everyone else. We try not to complicate the uncomplicated."

"Shocker."

A man's voice came over the intercom. "Who's there?" There was a slight accent in the voice, almost undetectable.

"Strippergram," Karl said, in a high-pitched voice. I assume he was trying to sound like a woman. Instead, he sounded like a man trying to sound like a woman.

"What? Get the Hell out of here." The man sounded strained, sort of like he had just woken up but not exactly like that. I couldn't place the sound. It just didn't seem right.

"Mr. Latanov? NYPD here. We just need to speak to you for a moment."

There was no answer. I don't know if this meant the guy wasn't Latanov or if he didn't want to speak to us. I'd gotten used to people not wanting to speak to me once I told them I was a cop. Cops rarely bring good news and we never remember to bring along the coffee and donuts. We consume them very well, however.

"He doesn't want to speak to us?" Karl asked.

"Guess so."

"Was it something I said?"

I just glared at Karl, wondering if we should even bother busting the door in. Sure, it was totally against procedure but Geiger had given me plenty of latitude when it came to procedure with this case. His chances of making that promotion dwindled to near nothing when Rick was killed. If he couldn't at least settle the case Rick was working on, he'd be doomed. Not like I gave a shit, I didn't. I just liked having the freedom to do what I wanted.

We heard a gunshot. It sounded like a large caliber gun, though if fired in close quarters, anything could sound larger than it really was. My worries about whether or not to break the door in shattered with the wooden jamb as Karl thrust his foot into the white front door.

I drew my gun, instantly reminded of how long it had been since I'd needed to do so. Homicide cops were rarely put in this sort of danger. Karl had drawn his gun before he kicked the door in. He was already moving inside the building, a two-way radio in his right hand. He told dispatch about the shots fired, giving them the address and telling them we were moving in to investigate. Technically, we shouldn't have done that because it wasn't our jurisdiction but we couldn't stand there on the front porch and wait for the local cops to arrive.

Karl was at the base of a long staircase when I entered the door. He signaled that he wanted me to cover him as he ascended them. I shrugged, my way of telling him that I would but I really didn't know exactly what to do. I hadn't gone over such a procedure since the academy.

Before he made it to the third step, four shots came from upstairs. I could hear the bullets fly through the air and hit the wall behind me. Karl had ducked and fell backward down the steps. Judging from the bullet holes in the walls, one of them would have caught him in the head. If I were standing two feet to my left, I'd have caught one or two in the chest. I couldn't move for a moment. Instead I just stared down at the dark-stained wood steps.

Karl got up and fired back three shots. I didn't think this was a good idea because he had no idea who he was firing at. Still, I realized this was what I was supposed to do. That's what covering was all about.

Karl looked at me. "You okay?"

"It's been a while since I've been in a firefight," I said, noticing my voice tremble a bit.

"Alright, relax. Just keep your gun drawn and follow me."

I tried to calm my nerves, settle the uneasy feeling in the pit of my stomach, but every time I tried it only made things worse. I kept thinking I could have been killed. It felt similar to when you've just narrowly avoided a car accident and the realization hits you. Just multiply that a few times.

"I'm okay, really. Just a little shocked, that's all."

"I got you." He moved up the stairs again, staying close to the wall on our right. His gun pointed straight up the stairs as he took each one slowly. I followed, wondering right then if my job was really worth this sort of risk. Sure, being a cop was great but I wasn't sold on the idea that it was worth dying for. Not many things are.

Karl made it a bit more than halfway, far enough to be able to see the floor at the top. "Jesus," he said.

"What?"

"We got a dead one up here."

"Great. My assumption would be it is our good friend Latanov," I said, catching up to him on the stairs. "Shooter's probably gone."

Out of reflex, I turned and ran toward the door. Just as I made it, I saw a red Mercedes sedan swing onto the street from my right. The guy was moving fast. Luckily, because I have done this before, I was able to catch the first three letters of the license plate. I repeated them to myself as I walked back into the house.

"HKG," I said as I met Karl on the stairs again, "HKG."

"What the hell are you talking about?"

"Mercedes just whipped around the corner. First three of the license plate were HKG."

"HKG," Karl said in order to commit it to his memory as well. "That's all you could get?"

"The guy was moving."

"Might be our shooter."

"I'd guarantee it."

"Real justice in this world. These dirtbags are driving around in Mercedes' and I can't even afford a nice Jap car."

"Jap's a bad word these days. You should say Japanese."

"We won the war. I'll call them what I want."

"If you say so."

"My Great Uncle says so. He fought there."

"Okay," I said, holding up my hands. I realized the gun was still in my right hand, safety off and pointing not so far from Karl's head.

I realized this because he said, "Get that fucking gun out of my face, Keegan." He got touchy about things like that.

"Sorry," I said.

We moved up the stairs more quickly, figuring the shooter had already left and we were in no danger. This didn't sit so easy with me. Who knew how many came to take care of Latanov? Regardless, we made it to the top, Latanov's final resting place, without incident. I like when things happen without incident.

Latanov lay on the floor in a light blue velour jumpsuit. The logo on it looked like FUBU, but it was tough to tell because there was a bullet hold right there, with red blood staining the velour. I'd say it was a waste of a good jumpsuit but I never liked jumpsuits. I always thought they were a bit tacky.

"Waste of a good jumpsuit," Karl said. See what I mean.

"He looks like your size. Maybe you can salvage it."

"This guy's about six-three, two-fifty. I don't think it'll fit me."

"Eat a few more of those Twinkies you are so fond of. It'll fit."

"Thanks." Karl leaned down next to the body and did the obligatory check of the jugular. "Dead."

"Thought so. Lack of breathing gave it away." I noticed something coming out of Latanov's right shoulder. "What's that?"

Karl reached over and pulled out a syringe. "My guess? Heroin."

"Same way Volkyv bought it. Though that time the killer didn't leave anything behind."

"We rushed him. People forget things when they are rushed."

The killer had made a huge mistake. No doubt there would be a fingerprint on the syringe, unless he was smart enough to wear gloves. Still, he hadn't had the time to clean up the crime scene. Plus, we had a car to work with. That reminded me. I took out my Treo cell phone and called Geiger.

"Geiger, Homicide," he said when he answered the phone. He never answered it any different.

"It's Keegan, boss."

"What've you got?"

"Looks like we have another dead Russian mobster. His name was Latanov."

"Russian mobsters die a lot. What else?"

"I think he was working on the same thing Volkyv was. We interrupted the killer—"

"Obviously you didn't interrupt him enough, if this guy is dead." Geiger had a point. "You catch him?"

"No. But I have the make and color of the car and the first three of the license plate," I said, trying to sound hopeful.

"Well, that is something. Give it to me."

I gave Geiger the info and he told me he'd run the plate number to see if anything came up on a Mercedes. The problem was a lot of criminals steal plates from one car and put them on the other to foil cops like me. I know, it is against the law to do such a thing. That's why I called them criminals.

Karl reached into Latanov's pockets. The big guy sure wasn't going to be able to stop him. I looked at Latanov, seeing that he looked very similar to Volkyv. The major difference was the hair, which Latanov wore fairly long, in a ponytail. His hair was very light blonde. He actually had an attractive face, quite a contrast from Volkyv's menacing masher look. If he weren't so big, I would have said he was a pretty boy.

"Cell phone, wallet. That's all he had on him." Karl opened the wallet and positively ID'd Latanov. There were four $100 bills which he took out to look at then stuffed back into the wallet.

"Good boy."

"We Vice guys only take the crack man, only the crack."

"That's nice of you. Maybe you can finish off what's left in that needle," I said.

Karl looked at the syringe again. "Finished. Plus, my guess would be this stuff is crap."

"Good guess. The horse they filled Volkyv with before he died certainly would have killed him according to Coltrain."

"Horse?"

"Yeah, horse. You know, the street name for heroin," I said.

"*Horse*?"

"Yes. What, that's not the right term any more?"

"I don't know if it ever was. Maybe you've been watching some old 70's porns again."

"Is 'H' better?"

"Are you playing horse?"

"The basketball game? No," I said, starting to feel like a dumb kid. I felt that way a lot.

"Then, no.

"Brown lady?"

"God, what did you learn all of your lingo from cheesy cop novels? No one uses those words."

"So, what do they call heroin on the street?" I asked.

"Usually, they call it heroin. Some guys might refer to it as smack—"

"Smack, that's it. That's the one I was trying to think of."

"Don't strain yourself next time. Please. Now, you said Volkyv was shot up full of some bad *heroin?*" Karl asked.

"Yes. Coltrain said it certainly would have killed him."

"Well, does that tell you what it tells me?"

"I don't know, what does it tell you?" I asked. I walked closer to Karl and took the cell phone from his hand and started scrolling through it. I wanted to see who the last person Latanov called was. Luckily for me the phone was old and just like one I'd had a few years before.

"You're the Homicide expert. It tells me that you have the same killer here. Another serial case," Karl said, as if he were trying to sound official or something. I'd dealt with a serial case, or one that appeared to be the work of a serial killer. It's wasn't much fun. I had expected such a case to be thrilling.

"Most likely, which points to my suspect." I found the last call Latanov had made. It was perfect. "Bam!"

"What've you got there, John Madden?"

"Latanov's last call was made to a guy he had stored as 'Anton'," I said, doing my best to keep my cool. I didn't want to get overly excited about something but the evidence was starting to pile up. Unfortunately, I had this voice in the back of my head telling me to double-check everything. I knew I was just being cautious.

"Well, that certainly points in the right direction," Karl said. "You think it was Anton that shot this guy up?"

"Think so." Karl moved around the body. As he got near the pool of blood coming from Latanov's side, I said, "Whoa, don't go trampling through there. I know you guys at Vice treat murder scenes as is they were fingerpainting opportunities but we do things a bit differently."

Karl stopped. "Relax, I saw the puddle. And we only do that to make your jobs more interesting."

"I think we should wait for the local guys to show up."

"They should be here already."

"Agreed. But until then, let's not snoop around any more. We found what we were looking for."

"You think you're gonna get a hard time about using this as evidence for your case?" Karl asked.

"Of course I will. Doesn't matter, though. My case takes precedent, especially because of Rick. They can fight all they want but it won't do a damn thing. Shit, I might even request to take lead on Latanov's murder too." I thought about that for a second. "Screw that, let these Brooklyn bums deal with the paperwork."

Just as I finished that sentence, two uniforms came charging up the stairs.

"NYPD, freeze!" one of them said. I think he watched a little too much television.

"Frozen," Karl said.

One of the uniforms, a middle-aged guy with salt and pepper hair and a nose with some large bumps in it looked at me. "You're Keegan, aren't you?"

"That's me."

"And I am his sidekick. We're going to be in moving picture shows some day," Karl said.

"I recognized you from the precinct. You worked with Galbadon," the guy said in a scratchy voice. Fellow smoker, I figured.

"That's right."

"What have you got here?"

"We came to interview this guy," I said, pointing down at the carcass that once housed Latanov's spirit. I figured it was all downhill for his spirit after that.

"Yeah, and he wouldn't talk, so, you know," Karl said, pointing his finger like a gun and pulling the trigger.

The uniform ignored him which seemed to be a terrific way to deal with Karl. "You see the shooter?"

"No. But you'll notice that there are four bullet holes in the wall at the base of the steps. Shooter killed this guy, then fired on us as we came up the stairs."

"You sure about that?" the uniform asked, more out of concern for me than anything else. It appeared he wanted to go along with whatever we said so we wouldn't get busted for killing someone that maybe we shouldn't have.

"Absolutely. I'm sure you'll see there won't be any GSR on this guy here. His name is John Latanov. Well, it's probably Ivan. He Americanized his last name so I have to figure he did the same with the first."

The uniform nodded, though he didn't appear impressed with my knowledge of first names and all that. "Just for our paperwork, you've got your ID's I presume."

I handed mine to him. Karl did the same. The other uniform, a bit younger and nearing a weight that should have been unacceptable for the job, saw Karl's ID and said, "Vice? How do they have Vice and Homicide working together?"

"Some people are just that unlucky," I said.

"I read about Rick Calhill," the middle-aged guy said. I read his nameplate. His last name was Fulkerson. "He was a good cop. I worked with him when he walked a beat over ten years ago. Really nice guy."

"Yes, he was."

"Sorry to hear what happened," Fulkerson said.

I didn't say anything to that because I was growing tired of saying things about Rick and thinking things about Rick. I wanted to put the memory to rest; it was too painful. Instead of saying anything I just nodded.

"Let Walker take statements from you guys. I am sure you have other things to do." Fulkerson knelt down by the body and started examining it. I looked at Walker and noticed the sweat on his forehead. His last name was more than appropriate. This guy wasn't running anywhere. Except, maybe, to an all-night buffet.

We told Walker just about everything we knew, leaving out the Mercedes and the license plate. I kept that to myself because I didn't want whoever was going to handle the Latanov investigation to get on the trail of who I believed to be the shooter. I wasn't trying to hamper their investigation; I was only trying to prevent them from doing that to me. It had happened far too many times in the past. In a perfect world, all precincts would work together in harmony. In case you haven't noticed—or if you've been in a drug-induced cloud—the world isn't perfect.

Just as we finished saying our tear-filled goodbyes, my cell phone buzzed. I'd say it rang but the noise the thing made was nowhere near a ring. I fumbled with the damn thing trying to remember how Jacob told me to answer it.

"What the fuck is that? Sounds like a duckbill platypus jerking off," Karl said eloquently.

"Watching Animal Planet again, huh?" I saw a big tab on the screen that said 'Answer Call' and tapped it with my finger, then put the phone to my ear. "Keegan."

"We've got a lock on that Mercedes," Geiger said at the other end of the line.

'Hit me."

"You still at the scene?"

"Getting into the car now."

"How did things go with the Brooklyn boys?"

"They were pleasant," I said.

"Good. The car's Yigevny's. Registered under Boris but the son is listed as the driver, according to their insurance company."

"Nice."

"That's what I thought. I've got a Manhasset address listed. I think you two should head over there now."

"I don't think that's a good idea," I said, thinking out loud more than speaking to Geiger. I had a bad habit of doing that.

"What?"

"Look at it this way. If we rush over there now, odds are the kid isn't home and we tip off whoever is there that we are looking for him. I'd rather let him think he got away at this point. Let him relax a little bit. Tomorrow, we go on the hunt and nail him."

Geiger didn't say anything for a moment. He just let me sit there, sinking into the cheap cloth seats in the station car. Finally, he said, "It would also give the lab time to find out whatever was at Latanov's." I hadn't thought of that. It was good.

"Exactly. You think they'll share?"

"I already lobbed a call into the precinct. They know they have to work with us on the case. I told them it was tied to Rick's death, which it is," Geiger said, with no emotion in his voice. I tried not to let it bother me.

"Okay. So Karl and I are going to call it a night. I'm tired and he looks like shit. Plus, I had a few bullets shot at me and it kind of makes me want to relax for a bit."

"You okay?" I hoped Geiger was concerned about my well-being and not my ability to perform for him. I settled for a balance between the two. It was the best I could expect.

"I'm fine. Lavin was cleaning his gun and it accidentally went off four times," I said.

"You sure you're okay?"

"Yes, I'm fine."

"Good. Then you have no excuse but to get here on time tomorrow morning. I already have the guys in Brooklyn putting a rush on the Latanov scene. They should get you some sort of forensic information by the morning."

"I'll be there," I said.

21

I dropped Karl off at his ramshackle apartment in Queens, after a suicide-inducing ride on the Brooklyn-Queens Expressway, and headed home. He had tried to engage me in all sorts of conversation but I just didn't want to talk to anyone. Thoughts and worries and theories and various other issues came in and out of my head. I wanted to be alone, spend some time just thinking. That way I figured I would be able to sort things out and come to some conclusions. Maybe it would work and maybe it wouldn't. All that mattered was that I needed time to myself.

When I got into moods like that I usually ended up angering people so that's why I knew it was best to be alone. Most times the people that knew me best—my family for instance—refused to let me alone, instead trying to get me to talk about whatever was bothering me. The only time I could talk was after I had come to terms with my issues, not while I was still sorting them out. Trying to get people to understand that was one of the greatest difficulties in my life.

My apartment had a musty odor combined with the smell of something dying a slow death in either the garbage or the refrigerator. Normally I would let that sit for a bit, let it fester until the smell was near unbearable. I couldn't do that this time. I opened the refrigerator and was hit with the smell of rotting meat. After about a full two minutes of searching, I found a steak I had bought from the supermarket behind the condiments I kept on the bottom shelf. The date stamped on the steak told me it was about to celebrate the fourth month of its expiration in a few days. This was bad but nowhere near my record.

I stuffed the steak into the garbage pail which exhaled back a few other scents that were less than savory. I quickly tied the bag and walked out of the apartment with hurried intentions. I opened the door to the building and headed toward the garbage area. I bumped into someone because I really wasn't looking.

"Watch it Keegan," Pauline said.

I looked at her. She was dressed in a black t-shirt and jeans—not much different from what she had worn the last time I saw her. Her hair was down this time and I had a hard time deciding which way I liked it better.

"Hey," I said, moving the garbage bag as far away from her as I could. She was standing right in the alleyway where we kept our dumpster.

"Hey? That's all you can say to me?"

"Well, I am kind of in the middle of something here," I said, pointing to the garbage bag. I could feel something dripping onto the back of my pant leg. Another piece of clothing that would have to be destroyed.

"My God, did something die in your apartment?"

"Well, I guess you could say that. Though I think something became undead."

"You need a lot of work."

"So I've been told. What brings you around here?"

"I wanted to talk to you. It's about seeing you today."

"Alright. Let me throw this out and we can go upstairs."

"Sure."

I tossed the bag into the already-filled dumpster and walked Pauline up to my apartment. I had wanted to be left alone and even flirted with the idea of telling her that. Certainly not a good idea, I figured, to turn away a woman that was probably already feeling a bit underappreciated. Hell hath no fury like an underappreciated woman, or so my Uncle Paulie once told me. He had drank a vat of scotch that night, though, so his opinion on this might have been a bit skewed.

We walked into the apartment. Luckily, it was clean. At least, that's what I thought.

"You are a slob. This place stinks."

"Thanks."

"I could lie to you, but I would hope that the shape of this place is obvious to you."

"Yeah, I was actually just starting my cleaning work. That's why I was taking out the garbage."

Pauline sat down on my beaten couch and ran her hand along the top of the table next to it. "Dusting would be phase two, I presume?" she asked.

"Of course. Dusting is always a high priority in the Keegan residence," I said.

"Really?"

"Yeah."

"Let me see your duster."

"My what?"

"Your duster," she repeated.

"I had a '74 Duster some time back, in high school. Sorry, that car died not long after my virginity."

"When was that, last week?"

"Good one."

"So, where is the duster you use to dust your apartment?"

I shrugged. "I usually use an old t-shirt."

"Of course you do. So, basically anything in your drawer doubles as a duster, right?"

"Not exactly." I sat down in the chair across from her. "So, what was it you wanted to talk about?"

Pauline crossed her left leg over her right leg. For all her posturing in the precinct, she was a complete lady and I really liked that. I could also get a faint hint of her perfume. It smelled clean, really nice.

"Nothing specifically. I noticed you seemed a bit uncomfortable today and I am sure that sleazeball Lavin said something to you. Before you go running off I just want you to know what really happened."

"What are you talking about?"

"I am sure he told you," Pauline said. She actually seemed embarrassed. It didn't take my mind long enough to make the connection. "No, not that," she added.

"Then what?"

"I kissed him once, sort of a peck on the lips. It was at some function two years ago. I was drunk. So was he."

I couldn't tell how disgusted I was at the image of Karl and Pauline kissing that came to me. There was certainly a feeling of repulsion but I think because it didn't really seem to fit, it didn't bother me.

"He didn't tell me about that," I said.

"What?"

"Like I said, he didn't say a word. As a matter of fact all he has ever done is ask about you, saying he is curious, like he wanted to do something but never did." I appreciated Karl for not saying anything to me. Based on his track record I would have expected him to mention it as soon as I said something had happened between Pauline and I. It was comforting to know some people actually have compassion, even people like Karl Lavin.

Pauline leaned back. "You know, we never talked about it. He was so wasted he probably doesn't even remember. God, that would be fantastic if he didn't. I've been so embarrassed every time I see him at the precinct."

"Has he made any sort of remarks to you?" I asked.

"Nothing. I thought he was embarrassed too."

"He never feels embarrassed. If he hasn't said anything to you, then he doesn't remember." I was almost disappointed. The idea that Karl had chosen to be quiet about what happened had given me a newfound respect for him.

"Wait, if he didn't say anything, why did you act so strange today?" Pauline asked.

"Well, we haven't really spoken about how we would act at work. You told me not to tell anyone and I figured that also meant to act professional at work."

Pauline smiled. "Professional, yes. Anti-social, no. You acted as though you'd never seen me before in your life."

"I just felt a little uncomfortable."

"About seeing me at work."

"That, yeah, Definitely that."

"What else?"

"Not much else," I said.

"What else, John?" My name sounded good coming from her.

I didn't want to get into it. Any time I tried to explain to someone how I felt, it never came out right. Sure, when I was thinking it and saying it I thought it would perfectly explain how I felt in a way that people would come to a greater understanding about me. After several miserable attempts I have learned it is best to say little and leave the interpretation up to the listener. With Pauline, the stakes were a bit higher and I really didn't know what to do. I must have sat there with a blank look on my face because she said, "You could try answering me instead of sitting there like some jackass."

"I just felt weird because I hadn't spoken to you in a bit."

"John, your father and your partner just passed away. Plus, you're involved in a major case. I didn't expect you to call to chat. You don't seem the type to do so in any situation."

She understood, or so it seemed. Of course, in the beginning of a relationship women act as though they are so easygoing and understand everything. This changes rapidly, usually after words of affection, i.e. 'I love you', are exchanged and sex has occurred more than twice. Then, all of a sudden they don't understand a thing and are as easygoing as a bull that has just been shoed in the nuts.

"Yeah, but seeing you reminded me of the fact I hadn't spoken to you and I felt bad," I said, doing my best to sound sincere. I figured I could parlay this into some quality points.

"I am not the sort of woman who needs constant reassurance. You've told me how you feel about me. There's not need to maintain that constantly."

Had I really found someone who looked at relationships and their often failure the same way I did? I didn't think it was possible. This was trickery. It was a sell. Once I put the initial payment down this would all change. I'd kick myself for believing what I thought right then.

"I didn't know that," I said.

"How could you? You also probably don't know that I am not the sort of woman you have to spend every waking moment with."

"I thought all women sucked every minute of your life away," I said, half-joking. Actually, I believed exactly that.

"Most do. Most women are pains in the ass. That's why I don't have too many female friends. They are just too much to deal with." She paused for a moment. "What?"

"Huh?" I asked.

"What are you smirking about?"

I hadn't realized I was. "Nothing."

"Don't lie," Pauline said, leaning in closer.

"I'm not lying."

"Stop it. I know you are. Just spill it."

"Okay. To be honest, what you're saying just seems too good to be true. It just seems too perfect."

"You don't believe me, do you?"

"I didn't say that," I insisted.

"But you implied it," Pauline said, and she was right. "I don't blame you. Most women drive men nuts because they don't know how to stress what is important and let go what isn't. They just stress over everything."

"That's about right."

"I had two brothers. I know what women can do. I also saw what my mother did to my father. I'd never do that to any man I cared about."

"What about men you don't care about?" I asked.

"They can go to Hell, for all I care," Pauline said. It didn't seem like a joke, so I didn't take it like one.

"Alright, so I will take you at your word, for now."

"Will you, now?"

"Yes."

"Very sweet of you. This, of course brings us to the next question. What are we? I mean, are we dating? Are we not dating? Is there anything that makes you uncomfortable in these early stages? Can I introduce you to people as my, dare I say it, boyfriend?"

I hadn't really thought about any of that. "Guess so."

"That's a real noncommittal answer."

"I am good at those," I said. I stood up and walked into the kitchen. "Want anything to drink?" I opened the refrigerator. The smell was still there. What wasn't there was anything to drink other than a near-empty two liter of Diet Coke which was undoubtedly flat. Well, there was a brand new bottle of seltzer. I couldn't remember where that came from.

"What have you got?"

"Uh, Diet Coke?"

"That's fine," Pauline said. "And I like how you walked out right when the topic got heavy."

"Just a coincidence."

"Sure it was. Get my drink and get back in here."

I grabbed a glass out of my battered kitchen cabinet and checked it. About 20% of the light coming from my ceiling fixture could make it through the glass. A few swipes with the semi-clean paper towel and the glass was as good as new, or at least as good as it was going to be.

The bottle made no sound when I opened it. Not even the

slightest hiss—no last gasp. Pouring it into the glass produced no sound effects either. The poor soda had long since died, leaving behind cola flavored Kool-Aid. I hated flat soda. It was one of the reasons why I liked diet soda. It had so much more fizz and the fizz lasted longer than regular soda. Of course, when it sits in your refrigerator for months at a time, no soda can withstand the progress of time.

Like a mad scientist locked away in my secret lab, I poured the seltzer into the glass in hopes of reviving the dead soft drink. I had to be careful to balance the soda and seltzer so that it would maintain a healthy balance of taste and carbonation. Too much seltzer and the stuff would look more like rum than soda. Not enough and the poor girl might gag.

I figured I had the right mix so I opened the freezer to get some ice. There weren't any cubes in the tray, but there was plenty of ice in the freezer. All I needed was a knife from the drawer to the left to scrape some from the inside. It was a little whiter than regular ice but I doubted she would notice.

I walked back into the living room with the glass in hand.

"None for yourself?" Pauline asked.

"Nah, not thirsty," I said. Like I would even dare drink the concoction I made her.

"You got up just to get me a drink?"

I handed her the drink "Of course. I am not sure if it's flat or not."

"You got up because you didn't like the topic of conversation. And don't worry. I love flat soda."

That figured. I went through all that trouble for nothing. Who likes flat soda, anyway? 'Something else I didn't know about you."

"You have a lot to learn. Now, tell me. What did you think about what I asked? Where are we at?"

I decided I could be frank with her. One of the biggest problems with relationships is a lack of honesty. "I think we are at the stage where I like you, probably more than I have liked someone in a long time. I don't like talking about it, to be honest, and I don't like thinking about it most times either. I am very attached to my single lifestyle. That's the bad part. The good part is that you are the first person I have met that makes me want to give up that lifestyle. It's not going to be easy because there will be a part of me that would prefer to be single, even knowing that I was generally miserable that way. It's tough to explain. That's just how it is."

"I think I understand. Part of you is going to mourn the death of your single self."

"Right," I said, dumbfounded that she hadn't stood ready to call me an asshole and walk away.

"That's normal. I think, if things work out between us, that desire will fade. On top of that, I don't want you to completely give up your single self. I think, for a relationship to work, people have to continue to live their individual lives."

This was a cornerstone of my relationship belief system. It shocked me to hear it coming out of someone else's mouth. Whenever I told my friends about this stuff, they just raised their eyebrows.

"I agree. I'm not sure exactly what the balance should be only because I have never dated anyone who wanted anything else but to be together all day every day."

"Ugh. I can't stand that. Did you really think I was that way?"

"I had no reason to think otherwise."

"Great, I am going to have to deal with all of your preconceived notions about women because the ones that came before me screwed up," Pauline said. She said it so matter-of-factly, like it was impossible that women really acted like women.

She got up and sat on my lap, a rather forward move for her. "Hello," I said.

"You are such a nerd."

"So I've been told."

Pauline leaned in and kissed me. Again, like the time before, it felt right. It made me not think about compatibility or relationship issues or anything else you worry about when you start dating. I got lost in the moment, thinking about nothing but her, a feat extremely hard to accomplish normally.

We didn't have sex that night. I think we both wanted to and we certainly could have. For me, it just didn't seem right. The timing just wasn't there. Shockingly, I wanted the moment to have some sort of purpose, as hard as I knew this was to do.

Instead of having sex, Pauline laid in my bed next to me and we just talked about all the things that were on our minds. I talked to her about the Volkyv case. We had a discussion about Rick and how I felt guilty for his death. If I had been with him, perhaps he wouldn't have died. She brought up my father, seemingly knowing how much his death was bothering me.

I think what shocked me most was the fact that talking to her almost felt as good as sorting out my thoughts myself. She had insightful answers and chose to be quiet when I just needed to vent. I felt a lot closer to her after that night and I knew I had made the right decision when I told her about my feelings. Pauline McCrory was the one for me, or so it seemed at that moment. Let me tell you, that moment felt good. Everyone should feel that way about another person at least once in their lifetime. It changes you.

Pauline left early in the morning. We didn't go over how we would deal with each other at work because I think it really didn't matter anymore. We'd deal with that situation as we saw fit. Neither of us was stupid enough to make a major mistake.

After she left the bed felt empty. Normally I couldn't wait for a woman to leave so I could go back to having my bed to myself. With her gone, the bed just felt cold. Perhaps I was adding more emphasis to this feeling then. I don't know what the real answer is. I just know I wanted her back. This was an entirely new feeling for me.

The floor was cold when I touched my feet to it. Seems it was always that way. If I had any sort of money sense I would have saved enough money to invest in some carpet, or at least a throw rug. I had some money. I think the problem stemmed from my not wanting to spend it on things like carpet. I could blow a few hundred on a good night out but God forbid I spend the same amount on something to improve my living space. I've often wondered about how my mind operates. I haven't come up with any conclusions, yet.

My grandfather's watch told me it was 8:30 when the cab dropped me off in front of the precinct. I paid the cabbie and exited, taking in the sight of the building for a moment. It was old and dirty like most of the buildings in that area of the city. No one has the money to pay someone to wash the outside of buildings that are just going to get dirty again. The dirt added character you could say. You shouldn't say it, but you could.

"You are Detective Keegan?" a man said from behind me in a soft voice. I turned and saw a tall, thin man dressed in a very expensive-looking blue suit. He wore a yellow tie against a white shirt. This guy had money, no doubt. His hair was slicked back, the grays mixing in with the brown. His face, though leathery, was tough to attach an age to. This is how I met Boris Yigevny.

He was standing just outside a Mercedes limousine, his hands clasped in front of him. Though he appeared wealthy he also seemed feeble, the sort of man who avoided confrontation at all costs. It looked like he was even uncomfortable talking to me.

"Yes, that's me," I said. I couldn't imagine at the time who he was. I had never seen a picture of him, despite how well known he was to most people in the city.

"I am Boris Yigevny." That was all he said.

"Hello, Mr. Yigevny."

"I don't want to waste much of your time. It is my understanding that you are investigating the death of the man who took my daughter from me," he said flatly.

I didn't want to give him too many details, but I felt bad for him. The poor guy had lost a daughter—and from the looks of it he was about to lose a son as well. "Yes, I am."

"Konstantin Volkyv?"

"I can't comment on that," I said.

"It's no matter. I know he is the one. Do you have a suspect in the case?"

"Mr. Yigevny, I cannot speak to you about this. I understand you are upset and I would love to give you all the information you need. Unfortunately, there is no way to do that."

"Detective Keegan, please understand I do not intend to hamper your investigation. Just do a father the pleasure of knowing that the killer of his little girl has paid the price."

"You know that already," I said.

Boris took a step to the left and looked down. "Yes, I suppose I do. There is more to it than that, isn't there?"

"I don't understand what you mean." I wanted to get inside before someone saw me talking to him.

"Mr. Volkyv was not alone. That is what your counterpart, Mr. Lay told me yesterday."

"It appears that way. That's not my case. If you want information on your daughter's killers, you should speak to Mr. Lay."

"He doesn't know enough. I tried to talk to him but he wouldn't listen to what I had to say," Boris said, now looking me straight in the eyes.

"I don't know what you want me to do, Mr. Yigevny."

"There are more. These men never operate alone. I have been dealing with them since I first came to this country." Boris now looked up at the sky for a moment, then he looked back at me. He seemed humbled. "I made a mistake when I came here. I escaped the Soviet Union right before the collapse. After the collapse anyone could come. I needed to get out sooner. So, I enlisted the assistance of someone who could do such a thing. I didn't have much money back then so I made a promise. I kept that promise." He said the last bit with conviction.

"I am sure you did," I found myself saying for lack of anything better.

"They don't ever give up and they aren't ever satisfied, these men. They take and take. If you don't give them what they want, they take something else. I've already lost too much. I don't want to lose any more."

"I can understand that, but I still don't know how I can help you."

"I would ask you to halt your investigation into the death of Konstantin Volkyv. Let his killer finish his work. It is the only bright spot I can see in this dark void since my daughter was murdered."

"There's no way—"

"There's always a way, Detective. You could drag your feet. You could screw a few things up."

For a moment, I gave this serious consideration. The man before me was a gentleman from what I could tell, a good man who had his daughter taken from him because he had made a mistake years before. If it weren't for Rick's death and Geiger breathing down my neck, I might just have delayed finding Volkyv's killer. I couldn't do that. The detective and friend in me would never allow it.

I think Boris saw this in my eyes because he exhaled and said, "I can only ask."

"I wish I could help."

"So do I."

I wanted to question Boris about his son. Perhaps he knew nothing about what his son was doing or perhaps he knew everything and this visit was a way to buy his son time. There was no way to know and I didn't expect Boris would tell me if he did know. I had to go on instinct. Unfortunately, the instinct wasn't really helping right then.

"You have a good day, Mr. Yigevny," I said as I turned and walked toward the precinct.

"Нос Любопытной Варвары был оторван," Boris said in very smooth Russian. "Curious Varvara's nose was torn off."

"What?" I asked.

"You will see, Detective Keegan. Have a pleasant day."

"What the fuck did he say to you?" Karl asked me when I stopped by his office to discuss my meeting with Yigevny. Karl was wearing a short-sleeved dress shirt. I believed only used car salesman were supposed to wear those. Well, perhaps it fit, I thought.

"Curious Varvara's nose was torn off," I repeated.

"Who the Hell is Varvara?"

"I have no idea. He said it in Russian first, I think."

"You think?"

"He said something in Russian first. I don't understand Russian and I am fairly certain he knows that. So, I can only assume that he said the same thing in Russian first."

"Okay, makes sense." Karl pulled out his keyboard drawer and started tapping away. "Let's see what we can find on the webski."

I walked around his desk to look along with him. He went to a search engine and typed 'Curious Varvara'. Hundreds of results came back.

"Watch Curious Varvara slide objects into her—"

"I can read, no need to repeat it," I said.

"Maybe I should bookmark that one," Karl replied.

"Sure. Good idea."

"Curious Varvara wants to come to the United States. Will you help her?" Karl clicked on that link and about a dozen other windows popped up.

"Now you really screwed the pooch," I said.

He kept clicking with his mouse. "They won't go away. It's like an attack."

"That's what you get for being curious about Curious Varvara."

"I was only trying to help."

"By checking out a Russian wives website?"

"I know a guy who did that. He's always happy."

"Of course. Anyway, this isn't helping us at all."

Karl was still clicking his mouse. "Every time I close one window, another opens. This is ridiculous." He hit the power switch, shutting down the computer.

"Let's go speak to Geiger. Then, I know of someone who might be able to help us with the meaning of what Yigevny said."

"Why didn't you tell me that earlier?"

"I just thought of it," I said.

I decided to give Geiger only a small slice of my meeting with Yigevny. Normally he would yell at me for making contact with someone so involved with the case. Surprisingly he took this in stride. Maybe they finally gave him that Zoloft prescription he desperately needed.

"I think this is a good thing," he said, standing up and looking at the wall behind him. "Yigevny coming to you indicates he knows nothing about what's going on. He's just a father concerned about the investigation of his daughter's murder."

I decided the best thing to do was agree. "Sure. It bugged me a bit because of the way he spoke to me."

Geiger turned around. "What do you mean, the way he spoke to you?"

I'd said too much. Someone needed to teach me how to keep my trap shut. "He was just curious. It sort of unnerved me."

"Is there anything else?"

I didn't tell Geiger about the Varvara comment only because I wanted to find out what it meant first. If I told him then, he would just question me to no end. "No."

"You're sure."

"Yes."

"What do you think?" Geiger asked Karl, who had sat quietly next to me. This would be a good test of how Karl was at keeping *his* mouth shut.

"I wasn't there, but I'd have to agree with you two. If that was my daughter, I would be turning the city upside down."

"Right," Geiger said, turning back to the wall. "You guys are close to solving this. I am starting to believe more and more that it is the son, this Anton, who killed Volkyv."

"Yes," I said.

"Well, you've got information from Latanov's now," he said.

"We do?"

Gegier turned around and sat down again. "Oh, yes, forgot to tell you. That phone number you gave me from Latanov's phone was definitely Anton Yigevny. The car, like I told you yesterday, has him listed as a driver. Fibers found at the scene match those from Mercedes upholstery. So, I would say that starts to add up, don't you think?"

"I do," I said. "Just a few things bothering me."

"Like what?"

"We haven't found a murder weapon, which makes prosecuting the case nearly impossible."

"I'll worry about the DA. You just get me one more link to this Anton Yigevny." Geiger stopped. "You're going to see him today, I presume."

"I am. I just don't know under what capacity."

"Capacity?"

"Well, am I going there for information, or am I going there to arrest him?" I asked. I knew the answer. Anton couldn't be arrested until we had sufficient evidence.

"Don't go in there with any intentions whatsoever. Hell, I was thinking about just going there and impounding the Mercedes. That won't work, of course. Plus, we have to move quickly. I don't know how long the Brooklyn precinct is going to give us leeway."

"Probably not for long, knowing our luck."

"We shouldn't need too much time," Karl said. Neither of us responded. He didn't know what we went through.

"Just move quickly. Go over the forensics at Volkyv's apartment. Speak to the eyewitnesses at the site of Calhill's death. Tie this son of a bitch to one of these murders and perhaps we'll get an admission to the other."

In a perfect world, yes, I thought. "Okay, Boss."

"I thought you said Geiger was easygoing," Karl said once we were out of the office.

"Compared to other guys in his position, he is. Plus, he's a little agitated right now, considering what's going on and all."

"Still, he seems like an edgy guy."

"You don't know Geiger."

"I don't think I want to."

My first stop was the forensics lab. Unlike what they show on TV, our lab didn't look so hi-tech and you'd have to pay real close attention to know that actual forensic work went on in there. Still, the guys were competent and their work usually paid off, so it didn't matter what their lab looked like, at least in my opinion.

Luckily, Dan Schmidt was on duty, someone I knew and got along with. Life moves along so much better when you deal with people you know, particularly nice people you know. I know plenty of not-so-nice people. Sometimes, I am included in that bunch.

"Hey John," Dan said as he came around the large gray desk at the front of the lab.

"Dan. This is Karl Lavin, a fugitive from Vice who is working with me on the Volkyv case."

Dan and Karl shook hands without a word. "Sorry about Rick. He was a good guy," Dan said.

"Yes."

"I have some information for you on the Volkyv scene."

"Anything I can work with?"

"Well, you know about the blood on the knife already."

"Yes, it is Ilana Yigevny's," I said.

"Right. Well, we found some blood in Volkyv's bathroom, on the floor. Remember those spots?"

I did. I remembered how impossible I thought it would be to get any information from them. "In between the tiles," I said.

"Yes. Well, it's a match for the same blood. We found some other minor traces of Ilana's blood on Volkyv himself. I think that settles his guilt with that."

"I don't think there is much doubt left," I said.

"There were two other types of blood on a pair of pants we found in Volkyv's apartment. We couldn't find enough to get a complete profile, but one is AB positive and the other is B negative. I would assume these pants would be the ones he wore when he killed Ilana Yigevny."

"I'd agree with that," Karl said, seeming like he wanted to contribute to the conversation.

"What I find interesting is the shoe prints on the floor. The guys who were first on the scene obviously didn't take caution. There are two separate types of prints that I can assume are from police officers. I already matched one to a guy who was on the scene. There are two other sets of prints that interest me."

"Which ones are those?"

Dan reached for a manila envelope and opened it. "I've

got a size 7 female shoe and what looks like a size 9 men's shoe. We can't get a correct determination because the two prints of this shoe are smudged a bit. Could really be anywhere between a size 9 or a size 10."

"Aren't those the most popular size shoe?" I asked.

Dan shrugged. "Yes."

"What do you find interesting about them?"

"It's the woman's shoe. Perhaps there were two shooters?" Dan asked.

Right then I wished I had Rick there with his trusty notebook. I wanted to know what the time of death Coltrain settled on for Volkyv. My memory was decent but I never relied on it for such particular matters like the one I was facing right then and paying bills. If it were something like remembering a girl's phone number, I had that nailed down.

"Overworking that brain of yours again?" Karl asked.

"Just wish I remembered when Coltrain said Volkyv died."

"He probably said that when you asked him."

I looked at Karl. "What?"

"What you meant to ask was what time did Coltrain say Volkyv died?" Karl said with a smirk on his face.

"Do you think I am in the mood?"

"Do you think I care?"

"You really bring nothing to the table, do you?"

"I could bring Volkyv's time of death, if you ask me nicely."

"How?" I asked.

"Because, unlike you, I haven't drank my brain into gray goo, that's how. You should lay off the Dewar's."

"What time did Volkyv die?" I asked through an exhale.

"Now, is that asking nicely?" Karl looked at Dan. "Was that nice?"

"It sounded okay to me," Dan said.

"Stick to blood samples." Karl looked back at me. "Now, let's try that again."

"Just tell me, because I am going to call Coltrain in a second and get the information that way. Your usefulness window is expiring."

"2:13AM," Karl said, smiling.

"Thank you. You are an incredible resource."

"How does that help you?" Dan asked.

"I have a couple of thoughts about what happened after Volkyv got shot. One of those pertains to when the 911 call was made."

"What are you thinking?" Karl asked.

"A few things. We'll talk about it later." I looked at Dan. "So, tell me about that man's shoe."

"It's from a shoe brand called Geox," he said. "Ever hear of it?"

I raised one of my shoes. "Sure."

"What size do you wear?"

"Eleven," I said, "my family is gifted that way."

Dan laughed. Karl just said, "Christ."

"So, we can be certain it is not mine."

"How do you like them?"

"They are shoes. Someone gave me a gift certificate to a department store and the advertisement said these shoes made your feet breathe better. Can't tell the difference."

"Anyway," Dan said, "The prints we found are definitely from Geox, and I am going to assume that they are from the shooter. I'd place the guy somewhere over six-foot, judging by the bullet holes on the kitchen wall. I came to the conclusion that Volkyv was on his knees when he was shot, so the angle where the bullet entered the wall indicates the shooter's height. This isn't exact, though. It's almost impossible."

"So, if I said I was looking at a guy at 6'1", I'd be on the right track?" I asked.

"For now. I'd look for someone with one of those blood types, too, particularly the B negative. That's a rare blood type."

"You think that a guy who contributed to the Yigevny murder also killed Volkyv?"

"Yes. There was a small amount of B negative in the kitchen." Dan flipped through some folders. "I'm sorry, I thought I said that before. Here it is, yes. B negative mixed in with Volkyv's blood, which is A positive."

"Why would the shooter's blood be at the crime scene?"

"Well, we found some of Ilana Yigevny's skin underneath Volkyv's fingernails, but we also found some other skin on top of that, meaning it was fresher. The blood type matches the B negative but we couldn't get much else than that."

"So, Volkyv scuffled with the shooter, you think?" Karl asked, saying exactly what I was thinking.

Dan nodded. "Evidence points that way."

"I didn't know that."

Dan started to say something, then stopped.

"What?"

"You were out of commission when we found that out. I told Rick," he said, obviously bothered by having to bring it up.

"I see," I said. "Thanks for the help."

"I'm compiling a full report. It should be ready by later today."

"Great," I said, and we left.

22

Ten minutes later, Karl and I were sitting with Jacob, listening to the 911 call which alerted the cops to Volkyv's shooting and death. I don't know why we didn't check it out earlier. Much evidence can be gleaned from listening to the tape, but we rarely go to it until we have run out off options.

"I heard shots," a woman's voice said.

"Ma'am, where are you?"

"87th Street," the lady said, sounding distressed. I looked at Jacob, who was listening with his headphones. He raised his eyebrows. Jacob stopped the tape, then played it again. "87th Street…he's dead." That second part was very low.

"You bump that up?"

Jacob nodded. "Notice anything else?"

"No," I said.

"It doesn't sound like she is on a street. Where did Volkyv live?"

"3rd, between 87th and 88th," I said.

"So, she is saying that she was down the block from the shooting?"

"That's right."

Jacob was still listening to the tape through his headphones. "She's not outside," he said nonchalantly.

"Sure?" I asked.

"Absolutely."

"And I think I recognize the voice," I said.

Jacob held up a hand. "She stumbled on something, I am sure of it," he said in a whisper.

"I think I know who our female size 7 is, and it certainly wasn't one of the shooters. Interestingly enough, it is most likely the same person whose translation skills I was considering."

"I like when things work out."

"Bite your tongue," both Jacob and I said at the same time.

Our next stop was to check Anton Yigevny out in the department's computer system. I wanted some preliminary information before we confronted him about anything specific. There was no guarantee things were going to work out. Most people, if they are lucky, avoid getting entered into police computers. If you've never been arrested, you're not in our system, most likely.

The computer room, often a place of games and general tomfoolery, was quiet ever since Geiger had instituted a rule of signing in and out of the computers. There were now records of who was there, for how long, and if the rumors running around the department were correct, what you did. Some guys believed the department had installed keystroke recorders and internet software that tracked where you went. A few years back, guys were gambling on computer golf in there, and there were others that were cyberchatting. This, of course, reminded me of Rick, but it also reminded me of a guy named Peters, who was the original scumbag. I preferred not to think of either of them at the moment.

The computers had been updated about a month before, so they were lightning fast. This was one thing the police department could do, spend money. At least this time it was done well. The computers were top notch and even though I never bought the idea that faster computers paid for themselves with an increase in productivity, I appreciated them. I hated waiting for slow computers.

It didn't take long to access the NYPD database. Recalling

my password and login took some time but I was able to do it. I entered both into the database and was searching in minutes. Not long after that, I realized Karl had put the kibosh on us with his talking about how things were going well. Anton Yigevny wasn't listed in our computer.

"Shit," I said.

"How long you been on the force?" Karl asked.

"Over ten years," I said.

"And that's the fucking search you do? New York City only?"

"Yes."

"You've got a lot to learn." Karl came over to the computer and tapped away at the keyboard. "Let's do an entire statewide. What exactly are you looking for?"

"Height, weight, whatever else we can find."

"Well, here you go. He was picked up last year in Merrick, Nassau County. That was easy enough." Karl clicked on the link which opened up the file the Nassau County Police had on Anton.

"That was impressive," I said. "They teach you that the same day you learned how to shake down pimps?"

"You don't shake down a…Never mind."

"Right."

"Anton Yigevny is six-one. He weighs 195 pounds. It doesn't say anything about his shoe size, though."

"A guy who is that tall should have bigger feet. I am shorter than him and I have elevens."

"Well, you're just a freak."

"Thanks. Still, he does fit the height requirement."

"You figured that, didn't you?" Karl asked as he logged off the computer.

"I did."

"I think it's time we go see Anton Yigevny."

"Not yet, we have someone else to see first."

"Someone fun?"

"Oh, you'll love her," I said.

"Is she hot?"

"You wouldn't believe it if I told you."

"Really?"

"I'm telling you, I can't get her off my mind."

Mrs. Federov certainly seemed less than happy to see me again. Oftentimes I find I am not the most perceptive person in the world but I was pretty sure about this. The lovely lady had a way of expressing herself that left little to the imagination.

"You come to bother me again? Why?" she asked, holding the front door open just a crack. She had her hair tied up in a green handkerchief. The look was stunning.

"You're right, real hot," Karl said from behind me in a whisper.

"Who is this, a new one you bring?" Federov asked.

I had wanted to remain calm. When investigating, there is always more than one way to go about things. There is the aggressive way and the relaxed way. The relaxed way always seemed more intelligent to me. Sometimes, however, people refused to allow me to operate that way.

"You could say I came her to arrest you. There's no doubt I could do that."

"Threats. I do not have to stand for them."

"Mrs. Federov, please understand that it is completely within my power to arrest you right now. It is not a threat but a fact. We could start with your lying to the police."

"I did not—"

"We could then go on to how you stole things from a crime scene." Mrs. Federov's expression changed to one of shock. "How much money did Kostya have on him the night he died?" I asked.

"I don't...are you going to arrest me?"

I'd only taken a calculated guess that she had taken money from Volkyv. I knew she had been in the apartment. It was nice to hit pay dirt. "Let us in, Mrs. Federov. For now, all I want to do is talk to you."

Mrs. Federov seemed to ponder that for a moment, then relented. "Only for a moment, I have work to do."

I could have threatened her by saying she'd be getting no work done in a prison cell, but I saw no need for that, so I just said, "Thanks."

Along with a newfound attitude, Mrs. Federov seemed to have discovered her sense of hospitality. She offered us coffee which I accepted, even though I was uncertain of the cleanliness of her coffee cups. I figured the gesture was worth accepting.

Mrs. Federov returned with the coffee in brown ceramic coffee cups. This was a blessing—I wouldn't be able to tell if the cups were dirty; they were already brown. I took my cup but waited for Karl to take the first sip. He did, letting out a small cough afterward.

"Is everything okay?" Mrs. Federov asked.

"Yes. I'm a smoker," Karl said. I could hear in his voice that he was holding back a laugh. It wouldn't have taken much for both of us to lose control and break into complete laughter. It had happened to us a few times when we worked a beat together. There is really no way to save yourself from a situation like that.

"You want a cigarette? You can smoke if you want."

"No, it's okay."

"He's trying to quit," I said.

"Bah, quit. There is no reason to do so if it is something you enjoy. Better to do what you enjoy. You cannot live forever."

I found it interesting that a woman who had lied to the police and robbed a dead body was giving advice on how to live. She did, however, have a point. Even an idiot makes sense every once in a while. Actually, I think idiots make more sense than geniuses.

Mrs. Federov opened a small wooden box on the table next to her and pulled out a cigarette. She lit it with one of those old table lighters. This one was all silver and looked like it weighed ten pounds. Smoking the cigarette, Mrs. Federov looked like she might have been a very attractive woman at one time. She had that Russian elegance in her smoking, something I had seen before with a Russian stripper I'd dated in my twenties. Everyone should date a stripper. Get it out of your system so you realize it's not so great.

Through a smoke-filled exhale, Mrs. Federov said, "You came to ask questions?"

I decided to dive right in. "What time did you enter Kostya's apartment?"

"Quarter past two," she said, flatly.

"Was he still alive?"

She shook her head. "I am not an animal, even though he was. I would have called for the hospital if he was still alive."

"Did you check his vitals?" Karl asked.

"Vitals?"

Karl put his hand on his neck. "Did you check for a pulse?"

"No. It was obvious he was dead, Detective. There was blood everywhere."

"You did check his body," I said. "What did you find?"

"Nothing much. For a man who had so much money, he didn't carry much around with him." Mrs. Federov put her cigarette in an ashtray on the table. "Detectives, he owed me for three months cleaning. I did not steal from Kostya. I only took part of what he owed me. If I wanted to steal from him, I would have gone into the secret compartment in his closet."

"Secret compartment?" I asked.

"Yes, in the back of his closet. He cut a hole in there. I found it one time when I was cleaning. I was putting his clothes in the closet and it was open. He must have forgotten to close it."

"Had you stolen from him before?" I asked.

"I never stole. I am not a thief, Detective. Kostya was a bad man, but God does not tell us to only obey his laws for good people."

She didn't strike me as a religious sort, Mrs. Federov, but one never knew when it came to such things. I knew several religious nuts who seemed completely normal on the outside. I'd been suckered into a religious cuckoo meeting one time under the guise of a housewarming party. And I'd known the guy for three years.

"Did you ever look in that compartment again?" Karl asked.

"Once or twice. He always had money in there, and other things."

The 'other things' comment got me thinking. "What do you mean?" I asked.

Mrs. Federov gave me an incredulous look. "I am sure you know what I mean, Detective."

"What exactly are you talking about?"

"Drugs, he kept drugs in there," she said, taking a drag from her cigarette as if this conversation was too much for her. "He also kept a gun. I remember seeing a gun once."

"A big gun?" I asked.

"I know guns. This was a pistol. A big pistol. I think he used it to try and scare people. That's the sort of pistol it looked like. Someone like him needed to keep people afraid."

"When was the last time you saw the pistol there?"

She thought about this. "Maybe a week ago. It's tough to tell. I couldn't always go looking in there."

"We'll have to take a look," I said to Karl. He nodded.

"We know you called 911, Mrs. Federov."

If she was going to lie to me, there was no way for me to know. Her face stayed the same. She didn't seem shocked that I knew about it. Luckily, she didn't deny it, either. "I thought you knew that already."

"We never heard the tape before today. Why did you not say you were here when you called."

"It is defense—" she stumbled on a word.

"A defense mechanism?" Karl asked.

"Yes, that is it. From being in the Soviet Union. It was never a good idea to give the police too much information. Before long, you are going to jail along with the person you call about."

"I understand," I said, but I wasn't buying her story. "You were in Kostya's apartment when you called."

Mrs. Federov didn't say anything.

"It's okay, I know you called from there. We have a shoeprint that I am sure will match something you own."

"I didn't—"

"It's okay Mrs. Federov," I said, holding up my hands in a gesture for her to calm down. "I know it was you and I know you had nothing to do with Kostya's murder. I am just trying to get all the facts straight so I can find the person responsible."

"Why?"

"Because it is my job."

"Sometimes your job shouldn't be so important. Kostya was a bad man who did bad things. The man who killed him should be rewarded, not put in jail."

"That is for the courts to decide. In this country, we let our peers decide our fate."

"God should decide your fate. We have no right to pass judgment." Maybe she had a point. I'd read the Bible, and all throughout it, there is mention of how justice is to be God's only.

"And what does the Bible say of vengeance? Is that not God's place as well? This man who killed Kostya broke that rule."

"Or maybe he was an agent of God."

"An angel?" I asked.

Mrs. Federov shook her head. "Not angel, agent."

"I heard what you said. Just thought you meant something else. Anyway, no matter what you see this man as, he killed someone and it's not like I can let him get away with it. What if Kostya were your son? Would you still think the same way about this?"

Mrs. Federov extinguished her cigarette and frowned. "My son would never be like Kostya. He would never do the things he did. And, if my son did turn out that way, then I would expect God to deal with him the way he dealt with Kostya. He would deal with me, too."

"Well, the NYPD needs to deal with the man responsible for this. I am sorry you do not agree but this is how we do things. Is there anything else you can tell me?"

"No."

"What did you see when you entered Kostya's apartment?" I asked.

"Kostya. Dead."

I thought of something. "I am assuming you heard a gunshot, like you said before. Is that true?"

"Yes."

"Why did you go into the apartment? Weren't you afraid you could get hurt?"

"No," Mrs. Federov said. It sounded like she was going to say something else but she stopped.

"What?"

"Nothing."

"Why did you not feel like you were in danger, going into an apartment from where you heard gunshots?" I asked.

"I just knew it was okay. I waited."

I knew the time of death was 2:13AM. Mrs. Federov said she went into the apartment at 2:15AM. That wasn't a lot of time. I figured there wasn't much time between when Kostya was shot and when he died. Coltrain was pretty good with that sort of thing. So, what happened in the, say, three minutes between the shooting and Mrs. Federov entering the apartment?

"You couldn't have waited long," Karl said. Normally I would have shot him a look for interrupting but his question was good. It was exactly what I would have asked.

"What do you mean?"

"Well, Mrs. Federov, according to your statement, you entered the apartment at 2:15. We have Kostya's time of death at 2:13. That's only two minutes."

Mrs. Federov was a rock. Not one hint of an expression change crossed her face. "Maybe it was twenty minutes after. I didn't look at my watch."

"What made you think it was quarter after?" I asked.

"I had looked at my clock when I heard the shots."

"Okay." I still didn't buy her story. "You said you've heard things coming from his apartment before. Why did you think it was safe to go in this time? What I mean is, what made you think Kostya wouldn't mind you going in?"

Mrs. Federov opened the box and lit another cigarette. She didn't answer me for a bit. Instead she just stared at me and smoked. There was no way to know what was going on in her head but if I had to guess, she was casing me. She was trying to get a read on me. From what I've been told, that isn't an easy thing to do.

"You know more than you are telling me," she finally said. "I can see it in your eyes. You think you know who did this and you want me to say one thing so you know for sure."

"I can't comment on that," I said, realizing how feebly it came out.

"It's okay, I know. I am not going to tell you that one thing, Detective. I do not want this man to go to jail. That is where you will send him. He doesn't deserve that."

I wondered what made her conviction so strong about this. Sure, I understood that she thought Kostya was a bad man. She had to live around him because she needed his rent to survive. As a religious woman I assumed this bothered her. Still, it didn't seem enough justification. There was something else and an idea was starting to formulate in the back of my head.

"You saw the shooter, didn't you?" She wasn't going to answer that question. I just wanted to see the reaction. There wasn't much of one, just a slight widening of her eyes which to me meant I was right.

""No," she said, clearly lying. She was good, like I said, but she had her limits and it seemed I had found them.

"Now you are the one not telling me everything. Remember, I have enough evidence to put you in jail for obstruction of justice and tampering with a crime scene. These are serious offenses I am willing to overlook if you cooperate. And, I know you don't want this man who killed Kostya going to jail. I am going to find him with or without your help, so the least you could do is help yourself."

Mrs. Federov hinted at defeat. Her body sagged just a little. "I did not see the man clearly in the hallway."

Karl sat up straight, seemingly surprised that Mrs. Federov admitted this. I expected it, though not so quickly. I was prepared for a battle.

"What did he look like?" I asked.

"Tall, skinny."

"Did he speak to you?"

Mrs. Federov didn't answer.

"What did he say?" I asked.

"I don't remember exactly. He said something about killing a cat."

"Killing a cat?" Karl asked.

"Yes, that is all I remember. I thought he was talking about how he killed Kostya."

"How old was he?" I asked.

"I couldn't tell," Mrs. Federov pleaded. "It was dark. Everything happened so fast."

"Does the name Anton Yigevny mean anything to you?"

Mrs. Federov's eyes widened again, this time more noticeably. "Yes. I know the name Yigevny."

"Okay."

Karl wrote something down on a notepad. Mrs. Federov watched him.

"No, it wasn't a Yigevny that killed Kostya. Not a Yigevny. I am sure of that."

This, of course, meant to me that it was a Yigevny. "How are you so sure?"

"I just am. I have seen pictures of them in the Russian newspapers. There is no way it is that man."

"What if I told you that Anton Yigevny had a reason to kill Kostya because Kostya had done something to his sister?" I asked.

"I read that in the papers too." She shook her head deliberately. "There is no way it was him."

"It sounds like it could be," I said.

"But it isn't."

I could feel it. We had our man. "You removed something else from the apartment, didn't you, Mrs. Federov."

"No. I took nothing but the money in Kostya's pocket. I can give that back if you want me to."

I smiled. "We'll let that stay as our little secret. I was talking about something else."

"I don't understand. I didn't take anything."

"Mrs. Federov, when a gun is fired, a brass shell casing falls out of the gun. We haven't been able to find on at Kostya's. Did you take that?"

Mrs. Federov exhaled. "You know more than you appear to know. Вы должны бояться тихой собаки ."

"What was that?" I asked.

"It is a Russian proverb. 'You should beware of the silent dog.'"

"Who?"

"I was talking about you. You appear to be innocent, not

knowing anything, but you figure out more than seems possible."

I smiled again. "You took the shell casing, didn't you?"

Mrs. Federov nodded. "I did not want this man caught. I saw on television how the police can use those things to catch the killer. So, I took it."

"What did you do with it?" I asked.

"I still have it."

"Could you give it to me?"

At first, it looked like Mrs. Federov was going to refuse. After a moment, she got up and walked toward what seemed to be her bedroom.

"That was amazing," Karl said.

"What?"

"You knew all of that about her? You never said anything to me."

"A lot of it was guesswork. Sort of like throwing crap up against the wall to see what'll stick."

"Well, a lot stuck. She has some balls, this woman."

"I still don't think she is telling us everything."

"Of course not."

"I think she saw the shooter clearly. I think she recognized Anton and she just doesn't want to tell us. She sees this as a justifiable revenge."

Karl huffed. "Well, technically, it is."

"I know."

"That's what's great about Vice. There aren't any justifiable drug deals. All of the people I deal with are pieces of shit."

"You must feel right at home."

Mrs. Federov returned with a small Ziploc bag. Inside, I could see the shell casing. She plopped it on my lap and sat back down in her chair. She had a way with her, let me tell you.

"I should not be doing this."

"I appreciate your cooperation, Mrs. Federov."

I looked at the shell casing. It was to a .357 Magnum. I stood up.

"You are leaving?"

"Yes, unless there is anything else you want to tell us," I said.

"No, that is all. I have said too much. I have helped you put a good person in jail."

"No good person kills people, Mrs. Federov."

"That's what you think."

Karl and I moved toward the door. As I opened it, I remembered that I wanted her translation on something. "One more thing, Mrs. Federov, if you don't mind."

"Go ahead."

"Someone told me, 'Curious Varvara's nose was torn off' What does that mean?"

"It is an old proverb. It means not to look into other people's business."

"Really? Like, 'Curiosity killed the cat?'" I asked.

"Yes. If someone said that to you, you have been warned to mind your own business before you get hurt."

I didn't like the sound of that one bit. "Thank you, Mrs. Federov."

Outside, Karl said, "This case keeps getting more and more interesting."

"That's what I always say."

"What are you thinking?"

"I'd rather not take a guess right now. I have a few things in my head. None of them are any good, however."

"What's next?"

"I'd like to pay a visit to Alex Antanov. Something tells me he knows more than what he told me too."

"Everyone seems to hold back on you."

"Not today, buddy, not today."

23

Technically, the first thing I should have done was take the shell casing back to the lab. Even before that, it might have been a good idea to find that hidden compartment in K-Drugs' apartment and see if there was a .357 Magnum in there, as I suspected. I don't know why I suspected it, I just did. I didn't think Mrs. Federov would go back into the apartment so I figured the gun, if it was there, was safe. I wanted answers above all else and Alex probably had a few of them. I pegged him for being there at the Ilana Yigevny murder. Maybe we could get his blood type out of him. That would have been nice.

I didn't have a correct address of Alex but didn't need one. The Score was his home and I knew I would find him there again. Karl had first argued with me, saying that The Score would be the last place Alex would go. Always bet on humans being creatures of habit. It is amazing how many criminals are caught because they don't change their routine. We find it hard to do, break habits.

Unfortunately, I hadn't been completely right about Alex being at the bar. He had been there. When we arrived, that had changed.

"He left," the bartender said to us as we walked in. I assumed he recognized us from our last visit.

"How long ago?"

"Five minutes. Out back," the bartender said. He had a layer of shiny grease on his forehead. His hair was greasy too. I couldn't tell if that was hair product or body byproduct. I didn't care to know.

Before I could say anything else, we heard two gunshots. I drew my weapon, my body feeling slowed down from the fear I felt. We were getting into another gunfight.

Karl made it to the back door before I did. He swung it open and I heard him yell out to someone. He came back toward me.

"Alex is dead. Shot in the head twice. Get to the fucking car. It's the red Mercedes again," he said, running past me.

I holstered my gun and ran with him to the car. I had driven so I went to the driver's side and opened the door. As fast as my shaking hands could move, I started the car and backed out of the parking lot.

"Which way?"

"Left, left!"

"Alright."

I turned left out of the lot. Up ahead, I saw what looked like the red Mercedes. "That it?" I asked.

"That's it."

The squad car was equipped with a faster engine than most cars of the same model. Of course, nowadays, all cars are given the speed treatment because the average soccer mom needs 300 horsepower to take the kids around the block. Anyway, the car was fast and I closed in on the Mercedes, doing about 70. The guy driving caught this and accelerated even more. The car was a 500S, so he had a bit more firepower than we did.

"Don't lose him," Karl said. I noticed he still had his pistol in his right hand.

The Mercedes made a sharp right turn onto 7th Avenue. Luckily that street is fairly wide and I was able to make the turn myself. I'd been in a similar chase not so long before and it still wasn't as exciting as they make it seem on TV.

I punched the accelerator and got within about ten feet of the Mercedes. Karl lined up his gun in what seemed to be an attempt to shoot out the tires.

"Are you nuts?"

"Just keep close."

"If that car loses control, he could hit someone on the sidewalk. Use your head."

"Just drive!"

Before he could get the shot off, the Mercedes made a left turn. I tried to follow closely but we were moving too fast and I caught a car parked on the side of the road. I felt control slipping and tried to right the squad car. I'd done a pretty decent job and almost had complete control when a car shot out from a driveway on the right side and slammed into us. We crashed into a pole on the left side of 43rd Street. My head hit the steering wheel. Karl flew forward and I heard him hit something.

I think I lost about a second or two because the next thing I felt was Karl tapping me on the shoulder.

"You okay?" he asked. I looked at him. He had a small cut on his forehead, but other than that he seemed okay.

"Did you hit me over the head with a shovel?" I asked.

"No, but you've got a nice dent there," he said, pressing in on my forehead. I literally saw stars. "The good news is that it is in the same exact spot where the other scar is."

"Great." I felt the bump myself. Karl was right, it was in the same spot where I had gotten a scar a while back. I couldn't tell if it was serious or not, but I was bleeding. "Bad?"

"Could have caught you on the mug instead of the forehead. That would have been an improvement."

"Don't be a dick."

Karl didn't say anything to that. "We lost the son of a bitch."

"No question it was the same car," I said.

The engine had stopped running so I turned the ignition to the 'off' position then tried to start the car again. After a few cranks, she turned over and I was able to back the car up a bit. I didn't dare try and actually drive the thing. We'd destroyed yet another piece of city property—two if you count the pole. What the city didn't give me in salary and benefits I took in property. I felt it was my right.

After about seven cigarettes or 45 minutes for non-smokers, we had completed the necessary report at the scene. Someone had called the police from The Score and reported Alex Antanov dead. Any questions about whether he had anything to do with Ilana Yigevny's death seemed pointless. Whether he did or didn't, the vigilante had included him. Antanov certainly had something to do with it.

Standing on the street watching the tow truck take our squad car away, I thought of Medina. He was the only guy I couldn't place in all of this. He'd threatened me, told me to stay away, something I intended to disregard. From what Antanov told me, Medina had a vested interest in Boris Yigevny and could very well have ordered Ilana's rape/murder. That made him a prime target.

Anton Yigevny had to know about Medina and most likely wanted him dead. Medina, the way I saw it, must have expected Anton to come after him. A showdown was coming and I wanted to be there for it. It was very rare that such opportunities arise and I knew I needed to take advantage of this one.

"That brain of yours is working overtime again," Karl said, flicking his cigarette into the street.

"What's the matter with you? There are cops everywhere and you're littering?"

"Where are we headed? I know you've got something on your mind."

"We've done a pretty good job of predicting where Anton will go next. I know his next target."

"It's a shame we couldn't get to those spots *before* he killed those guys," Karl said.

"To be honest, I really wouldn't mind if Anton killed this guy before we got there. He'd be doing the world a favor, that much I can tell you."

"Another upstanding citizen?"

"Jaro Medina," I said.

Karl's eyes widened. "Oh, I know him. Been meaning to invite him over for dinner."

"That's the guy."

"We have a bit of a transportation problem," Karl said.

No more than a second later, a Ford Crown Victoria pulled up and Geiger stepped out. He wore a tan suit with a white shirt and I could see the sweat seeping through. He seemed stressed, even from a distance. On top of that, it wasn't common for him to go out into the field. Something was on his mind.

"Keegan, Lavin, please tell me you caught someone before you created this disaster," he said in dry voice. He definitely had been doing some yelling. It didn't seem that he was mad at us though that could change immediately.

Before Karl could say something to initiate that change, I said "No question it was the same red Mercedes."

"Yigevny?"

"Yes. He killed Alex Antanov. That's where we were, going to talk to Antanov at The Score when we heard gunshots from the back. We chased the car until someone crashed into us."

Both Geiger and I looked over at the poor slob who had smashed us. He was about twenty, I would say, wearing a worn out baseball cap, a torn pair of cargo shorts and a black t-shirt that said 'Don't Waste My Time.' He'd wasted ours and it is never a good thing to crash into cops. I told the uniforms to go easy on him but I didn't know how much that would help.

"Did you get the plate number?" Geiger asked, this time looking at Karl. Karl didn't flinch.

"No, we were too busy dodging traffic."

Geiger eyed him but didn't respond. Instead he looked at me and said, "Okay, what now?"

"He's going to hide for a bit I think."

"Any idea who the next target will be?"

"Jaro Medina," I said, not looking at Geiger.

"Don't you think you should head over to the Yigevny residence and arrest Anton before he is able to do more damage? I mean, you've got two dead men in two days. This case is getting away from you."

I wanted to disagree but couldn't. The case was getting away from me. Still, I had formulated a theory and I needed some time for it to be put into motion. For a long time I spoke against hunches, believing them to be nothing but fictionalized fantasy. Real cops didn't get hunches, things happened way too fast for such a thing to exist. Right then, a thought entered my mind. Where it came from, I had no idea. I just know that the thought made sense. I didn't want to tell Geiger or Karl about it because though it made sense, it also seemed far-fetched. Only a bit of time would help me determine the truth.

"I don't think we can go there and arrest him."

"You have the ballistics at both scenes. You have evidence pointing toward him—"

"He is the son of an extremely wealthy man. You know the sort of lawyer he can afford and unless we have something substantial to hold him on, he'll walk and we'll never get another shot at him. Is that what you want?" I realized I'd not only cut Geiger off, but I was yelling at him. Normally I would apologize. The need to do so didn't arise right then.

Geiger stared at me for a moment and I thought for sure he was going to lash into me. He didn't. "That's true. Still, I don't want this guy running around the city exacting vengeance without us trying to stop him. The papers already are going to have a field day with this. Today's headline mentions the possibility of a vigilante. They are comparing him to Bernie Goetz." Geiger had told me years ago that he had been one of the cops who arrested Bernie Goetz, the man from the early 80's who was dubbed 'The Subway Vigilante'. I remembered delivering the Daily News and seeing Goetz on the front page a few times. The entire city had become enamored with him. People love vigilantes. From what I can tell, people love those who do the things we all wish we could do but know we shouldn't.

"Let the media spin this any way they want. I'm not going to change the way I investigate this in order to make them happy or not." I knew why Geiger cared what the media had to say. There were many factors involved with getting a promotion. Public perception of your department ranked pretty highly.

"Just tell me you're certain of what you are doing. I'll back whatever you think is best, John, but you need to tell me what is going on."

I decided it was time to keep Geiger in the loop. For all the years I had known him he'd always done as promised. I might not have agreed with him all the time but he was reliable, which was better than what most people were capable of.

"I think whatever is going to happen is going to happen at Jaro Medina's place in Queens. I am going to take a car and Lavin and we are headed over there now."

"You think Yigevny is headed there?"

"Something like that," I said.

"What do you mean, something like that?"

"It's tough to explain." I had a hunch but didn't want to let anyone in on it yet, it was far-fetched. "I just know that Medina is most likely the next one on the list and someone is going to pay him a visit."

"You have any intelligence pointing this way?" Geiger asked.

I shook my head.

"What do you think?" Geiger asked Karl.

"I say trust him. The guy has been on this Yigevny dude's tail all week. Why doubt him now?"

Geiger nodded. He handed me the keys to his Crown Vic. "Go. Just make this one ends in a collar, will you?"

"I'll do the best I can."

The trip to Medina's business didn't take long because I laid on the accelerator and didn't lay off until we made it there. The Ford drove well but I knew it wouldn't perform so well in a chase because the damn thing was so big and the handling just wasn't there.

I pulled the car into the parking lot and turned it off. For a moment I just sat there, staring out of the window at the building. Several thoughts came in and out of my mind. Maybe I was becoming psychic. Perhaps my father's and Rick's spirits were guiding me. Whatever the reason, I knew the case, and a big part of my life would end in that building. I can't say I was afraid of dying. Bravery had nothing to do with it. My life wasn't in danger. I just knew everything would change from that day forward.

"What are you thinking?" Karl asked, doing his best girlfriend impression. I found he was pretty good at that.

"This is it," I said, "if you want to wait here, I don't have a problem with that."

"Cut the crap you overly dramatic bitch. Plus, nothing is happening here. I don't see the red Mercedes."

Karl was right, the Mercedes wasn't there. I did see a tan Chevy Suburban. I picked up the radio and called in the license plate number.

"Registered to Anton Yigevny," the woman said over the radio.

"Bingo," Karl said. "We calling for backup, or are we going in there solo, like Tango and Cash?"

"Solo." I pulled the lever for the trunk. "See if Geiger's got a shotgun back there."

Karl exited the car and I sat there, doing whatever possible to focus my mind for the work that lay ahead. I had been in a shootout the day before. I didn't doubt there would be another.

Freezing up wouldn't be an option this time. I really don't know what the right way to prepare for a gunfight is. All I can say is that nothing I did in that car really worked. The only thing that helped was thinking about Rick and my father, believing they were watching over me. That calmed my nerves just a bit.

I heard the pump of a shotgun. "Let's go," Karl said.

I got out of the car and took a deep breath. "No sense in delaying the inevitable."

"That's what I'm saying."

We walked toward the building and heard a loud scream. The voice definitely belonged to a man, and that man was in considerable pain. I thought it had to be Medina and I wanted to hesitate before going into the building. If anyone in the world deserved to suffer, Medina ranked high in the list. Fortunately, my cop instincts overcame my sense of justice. Sometimes the two do not work together.

"Someone sounds fucked," Karl said.

"Hopefully, by the time we get to Medina, Yigevny will have worked him over good," I said.

"You really believe it is Yigevny doing that?"

"Ask me later."

The front door was locked. Carlos had to be around somewhere, I thought. I wanted to do my best to avoid him. On a perfect day, Carlos was getting laid somewhere instead of standing guard for Jaro Medina.

Karl bashed the window with the butt of the shotgun. The glass spidered but did not fall. Karl gave me an empty look.

"Safety glass," I said.

"Fucking safety regulations. They only come into play when you don't need them."

"There's a way around it," I said. I took the shotgun from Karl and rapped the glass hard and quick four times. The glass in that one area fell into the building and we were able to turn the deadbolt and gain access to Medina's place.

"Nice," Karl said, "I see you majored in Breaking and Entering."

"I only minored in it. Too many night classes," I said.

On a normal day it would be safe to assume Medina's building would be full of people. That day it wasn't. Other than the scream we heard, the place was silent. In keeping with the proverbs I'd been hearing, I knew of one that warned to be afraid of the silent dog, not the barking one. Medina's building was a silent dog.

The corridor was dark. It led straight to the other end of the building, so I drew my gun and walked slowly down it, Karl behind me, no doubt pointing the shotgun at the darkness. All I could do was pray he didn't shoot me in the ass with it.

"Speak!" we heard someone yell from the right side of the corridor. There was only one door on the right side so it didn't take long to guess which way we had to go.

We walked over to the door and stopped. Opening it and rendering us vulnerable didn't seem like a smart idea. Instead, I pressed my ear to the door to try and hear what was going on behind it.

"Hear anything?" Karl whispered.

"Tough to do that when I am listening to you."

Turns out I didn't have to press my ear to the door. "It didn't have to be this way," I heard a voice say. It was Medina, this much I could easily tell. I took my ear away from the door. "Medina," I whispered to Karl. He nodded.

"I did everything you told me to do," another man pleaded. "What more can I do?"

"This is a mess, a complete mess. I had everything arranged. No one was supposed to get this close. No one was supposed to know."

"Maybe the cop screwed up," the other guy said.

"I had that arranged. You're the only one who could have screwed up." Medina sounded angry. I wondered right then if he were the one killing everyone. Thinking about it, there was sense to be made with that theory. Of course, to make that theory work, I had to know who was in the room with him right then. "I've lost two good men in K-Drugs and Latanov."

"How do you know it wasn't one of them who slipped up?"

"They are dead, that's how I know. A simple job, and it got screwed up," Medina said. "I wanted her frightened, she ends up dead. Now, two of my best men are dead as well."

"What about Alex?" The guy sitting in that chair must not have known Alex was dead. I knew who was in that chair, and my theory had not gained the credibility it needed. Anton Yigevny was not running around New York City acting as a vigilante to avenge his dead sister. The way I saw it, he had been hiding out, most likely somewhere under Medina's watchful eye. Whoever killed K-Drugs, Latanov and Alex, it wasn't Anton.

"Alex is the most loyal man I know," Medina said. "I had him leading those cops around by their noses. He always did exactly as told. There's no way it was him."

"And it wasn't me. I killed that cop, just like you asked," Anton said.

"You nearly compromised Galbadon."

"He wasn't supposed to be there. That other cop, the one with the big mouth, he was supposed to be there."

I wanted to punch Anton Yigevny for saying that. God must have been listening to my wishes because I heard Medina slap him across the face, hard. "It was because you didn't pay attention. We knew his father had died and he wasn't going with the other one. You should have contacted me instead of acting on your own. That's what happened with your sister too, right? You acted on your own."

"No," Anton said.

"You can tell me now. Lying isn't going to save you."

"You know K-Drugs. He always got out of hand. He did then, too."

The blood gathered in my hands. I could feel them getting hot. This kid was sitting there talking about the rape and murder of his sister matter-of-factly, like it was nothing to get upset about. Putting it together in my mind it became clear that Anton had been the one who made the whole thing go wrong. Ilana Yigevny was supposed to be scared not murdered.

"He never got that far out of hand."

"He raped her. He wasn't supposed to do that."

"Yes, he was. Killing her, now that wasn't part of the plan. Who caused that?"

"He did."

Maybe Anton was telling the truth. After all, we did find the knife in Volkyv's apartment. Still, he was there and he let it happen. If someone had done that to my sister, they would never have made it home. He would have been dead.

"I don't believe you. I think what happened was you panicked and she recognized something about you. Then, she had to die."

"K-Drugs was the one who killed her. Ask Alex, he'll tell you that."

"It doesn't matter who did the actual killing. What matters is now I don't have the leverage I need to get what I want from your father. It never should have gotten this far. We had the same problem with your mother."

"My mother?"

Luckily, the years I had spent listening to 80's hair metal didn't destroy my eardrums. Even though I was concentrating on listening to Medina and Anton, I was still able to hear the sound of a gun being cocked.

Karl heard it too and swung the shotgun around. Beyond him I saw Carlos pointing what looked like a 9mm at us. He and Karl fired at exactly the same time. The blasts were deafening. My ears immediately starting ringing. I saw was Carlos fly backward, blood gushing from a stomach wound.

Karl lay at my feet, screaming in pain.

"Where'd he get you?"

"Kill me," Karl said through grunts.

"What?" I asked. I bent down closer to him. Medina had to have heard the gunshots and would be on his way out. I had to get Karl out of there.

"He shot me in the dick. There's no use living." Karl grabbed me by the shirt. "Do it. Shoot me right in the head."

Karl was bleeding from the hip area, about four inches to the right of where he thought he was shot. "He didn't hit you in the dick. He wasn't that good of a shot."

"Yes, he did. Kill me, for Christ's sake."

I took Karl's hand and put it on his groin. "Look, no blood. You got shot in the hip, not in the dick. He would have needed some scope to pull that shot off."

Karl exhaled. "Asshole." He tried to lift his head up to see Carlos but couldn't. "Did I get him?"

"I don't think he's going to be shooting anyone soon."

"Did I get him in the dick?"

"I don't think so." Karl was bleeding pretty badly but it seemed he was going to be alright. "Listen, stay here. I am going after Medina. Call 911 and get an ambulance down here."

"Take the shotgun," Karl insisted.

"No. I am better off with the pistol," I said.

"You'll need the firepower."

"You keep it. We don't know if there is anyone else running through this building."

Karl thought about that for a moment. "Good point." He held the shotgun a bit closer to him.

"You just stay here and bleed. Daddy's gotta go take care of business," I said.

"Don't ever say that to me again."

It was time to open that door. I was surprised Medina hadn't come bursting through already. I could only figure he wasn't armed and the shots scared him off.

I kicked the door open and stepped to the side. No one fired at me, which was a major plus. Gun pointing into the door, I leaned in, and saw Anton Yigevny tied to a chair in the middle of a room which looked like a janitorial storage room. He was alive, and stared at me.

"Help me," he pleaded. He seemed tall, even sitting in the chair, and skinny, just like his father. His nose was a bit pointier and his hair was short. Other than that, he seemed like a youthful version of his father.

"Why should I?"

"He's going to kill me."

"A fate you most definitely deserve."

"But, you're a cop," Anton said in a whine.

"Yes, one with a big mouth. I've heard. Still, that doesn't cloud my idea of justice. For what you did to your sister, or let someone else do, you should fry. I am not going to help you."

"It's your job."

"And it was your job as a brother and son to protect your sister. Seems you failed at that."

"I had no choice. You don't understand."

"And I never will."

In keeping with the theme of things, someone fired from a back door. I hit the ground. Poor Anton couldn't move. When I was able to get up, I saw that he had taken a shot right in the head. There was a God. With all the death I had been experiencing I expected to be bothered by witnessing Anton's death. The only thing that would have made me happier was watching Medina die, slowly.

"You kill anyone?" Karl screamed from outside.

"No."

"You lying?"

"Shut up," I said. I got back down on the floor and crawled toward that back door. My hands were trembling. I tried to calm down but that is incredibly difficult to do when you know that someone is trying to kill you and you can't see them.

An overwhelming sensation came to me. It felt like an adrenaline rush but it also had a sort of calming effect as well. Whatever it was, it made me feel like everything would be okay, that I wasn't going to die in that room. My mind fought this, throwing me into survival mode. If I would have listened to that urge, I would have been lying right next to Karl and his shotgun, waiting for the cavalry to arrive.

No bullets came flying at me as I made it to the door. The floor was cold and dirty but this didn't bother me much because I knew it was better being down there than being dead. Not having ever been dead, I thought this hypothetically but I am pretty certain I was right.

My heartbeat didn't speed up like I would have expected. I could feel it beating harder, though. The sensation focused on my neck. This distracted me, making me more nervous. Knowing a man behind the door wanted me dead and was equipped to do so certainly was enough. I didn't need the fact that I was aware of my own heartbeat to help.

The fear had finally gotten to be too much. I am sure many guys would lie about how scared they were in a situation like this. The manly thing to do would be to say I wasn't scared at all, that my testosterone had taken control and calmed me, made me able to do superhuman things with nary an emotion. This wouldn't be the truth. What did happen was that I realized the fear of something happening to me became stronger than the fear of sitting there waiting. I decided to just do something.

I brought myself to my feet and grabbed the silver doorknob. It felt cold in my hand. Initially, I couldn't turn it. I couldn't build up the courage to twist it. No doubt this is related to the human survival instinct, the same one which prevents the sane among us from self-inflicted injury. Someone behind that door wanted to hurt me, so opening the door would bring injury to me by my own action. It took quite a bit of focus to get myself to open that door.

Actually, I never got the chance to open that door. I did start to twist the knob, a major achievement in its own right, but I wasn't the one who opened the door. Medina accomplished that feat. He stood there in the doorway, a 9mm pointing at me and a grin on his face.

"I believe I warned you, Detective," he said.

"I thought you were kidding," I replied, feeling the fear tremble through me, ending right at my fingertips. Unfortunately, this also made me aware of the fact that my gun was at my side, and not pointing at Medina in Mexican Standoff fashion. Remember, I wasn't very well versed in gunfight tactics.

"This isn't the time to make wisecracks. You could have minded your own business and avoided what is now about to come to you."

Arguably, this wasn't the first time I had faced Death. Death had come to me in a public restroom as some maniac bashed my head into a toilet. I'd been fired at a few times in front of a medical building. One time, while walking a beat, I'd even had a crackhead point a .22 at me. None of those compared to this one. The difference was I had a moment or so to contemplate my own demise. Over the span of what maybe was 10 seconds, I thought about all that I had wanted to do that I hadn't accomplished. Stupid mistakes flashed into my mind—particularly the time Suzie Montelbano wanted me to go into her laundry room with her in 10th grade and I was scared and said no. Thoughts of my father came to me as did thoughts of Rick.

Amazingly, fear did not come. Instead, anger took its place. Experiencing anger right then almost didn't make sense. I remember thinking I was just going crazy, that my mind created the anger just to deal with the fear. Research into such a phenomenon in emergency situations has yielded no theory. I only have my own experience. Trust me, I was pissed.

Before I had a chance to do anything with that anger—like I could have done something—the gun blast rang in my ears. Even at such close range, I didn't expect a 9mm to offer such a vibration. It rumbled through my entire body and I awaited a pain that didn't come. Shit, I thought, Death is easier than I imagined. To think I had been so afraid of it all my life.

The pain didn't come because I hadn't been shot. Instead, I saw Medina fall in front of me. He'd been shot in the back. I couldn't see anyone because it was too dark. I only heard a voice.

"You should have heeded Mr. Medina's warning, as well as my own," the voice said. It was Boris Yigevny.

"It took me a long time to figure out the meaning of what you said," I yelled back. My sense of hearing was severely impaired. I slowly raised my gun to point in the general direction of the voice.

"I sincerely wanted to give you ample opportunity to walk away from this. Even now, when you had the chance to leave, you stayed. I don't understand."

"It's my job, Mr. Yigevny. I can't just walk away."

Boris stepped forward, and I could see what looked like a .357 Magnum pointed in my direction. Again my body stiffened. I was going to die of a heart attack if I kept this up. "You knew it was me, didn't you?"

"I wasn't certain. The one thing I knew was that it wasn't your son. He was incapable."

Boris raised his eyebrows. "I left no clues."

"But you did. Most of all, it was the vengeance with which you dispatched with your daughter's killers. At one point I finally realized such anger could only come from a father, not a brother."

Boris exhaled. "I thought I could finish the job without getting caught. You wouldn't give up. I thought no one would investigate the murder of such scum."

"Even scum have rights, unfortunately," I said, "Justice, as they say, is blind."

Boris didn't say anything for a moment. "We cannot both walk out of here, Detective," he finally said, the look on his face as blank as could be on a living person.

"Sure we can. You can give up now. You've gotten your revenge."

"I won't live like I did in Russia again. I won't be a prisoner. There is no way I can deal with that."

"It's not like you have much of a choice. Even if you kill me, there are plenty of other officers on the way."

"And I can make it through all of that. No one would believe that someone of my stature would murder anyone. If I kill you, the only witness to all of this, I won't have a problem. Don't think I haven't thought this completely through." Boris had a look in his eyes. I'd say it was sinister, but it was more than that. It was calculated, totally devoid of any emotion.

"I just heard all that, and I have a shotgun, so there goes that idea," Karl yelled out from the hallway. It is one of the few times I was actually happy to hear his voice.

The look on Boris' face changed. I suspected he hadn't counted on Karl being there, or being alive for that matter. Judging from that look, however, I couldn't say he was dissuaded. Boris looked at me like he hadn't even heard Karl, as if all that mattered was me. Most times such complete attention would flatter me. This time, it didn't. Behind those eyes, I believe I saw resignation. His whole body seemed to slump just a little.

"They took my wife from me. They took Ilana from me."

"I am sorry for that, Mr. Yigevny."

Boris looked away. I couldn't tell what he was looking at, but it didn't matter. The glance afforded me the opportunity to bring my gun up to point at him. We had a real Mexican Standoff right there in Queens.

He turned back to me, saw the gun and smirked. "Now, they've taken Anton, my only son, the only member of my family that was alive." I must have had an incredulous look on my face because he said, "I know all about what he'd done. My son had been lost to this country, lost to the aspirations that do nothing but keep people down. It didn't matter, he was still my son. They have taken everything from me but my pride. That, I will not allow."

I wanted to say something about the fact that Medina was lying dead at his feet and thus unable to take anything else, but I didn't think it would matter. Fear rushed all throughout me. I felt weak with fear, nearly incapable of breathing. Ultimately, it had come down to him or I. Something in the back of my mind told me how he wanted it to end.

"We can both leave here," I said, "I can let you walk out of here." Surprisingly, I meant what I had said to him. I'd lost my father and I knew what that felt like. I could only imagine what Boris was going through.

"It cannot work that way, Detective. We both know this." Boris straightened his arm to point the gun more directly at me. "This is the test you have waited for all your life, Mr. Keegan. Every man looks for it, a chance to prove himself in the most dire of circumstances. How will you measure up?"

Words wouldn't come to me. Several of them flashed in and out of my mind, but none of them could make it to my mouth. Again, I knew this was fear and I felt like less of a man for it.

"Say something," Boris said, "do not deny me your last words. Do not make mine a plea for them."

It was his finger that made all of this happen. Many times I have wondered if his trigger finger was readying to pull or if he had just twitched. Either way, it happened. I didn't fire that bullet into Boris' skull. My own survival instinct did that. The will to live overcame compassion and understanding and hope. In the end, none of us really want to die, except, maybe, those like Boris Yigevny. He didn't just give in easily. He somehow managed to get a shot off as well.

I felt a strong blow to my left shoulder, which threw me back a bit, though I was still able to look straight ahead and witness my work. I didn't feel pain right away but instead intense heat. The pain would come, not more than a second or two later, though surprisingly it wasn't nearly as bad as I thought it would be.

My bullet entered Boris' head just below the hairline, a stunningly accurate shot considering my nervousness. Lead tore through what many people considered to be one of the greatest minds of our generation. Boris' head flew back then jolted forward. I saw the hole for a brief second and watched him fall lifelessly to the ground as if someone had yanked his skeleton right out of him.

I thought I heard something but it was tough to decipher from the ringing in my ears. I couldn't take my eyes of Boris, a man whom I had just killed. There was no sense of justification or even the knowledge that I had done the right thing. No matter how I thought of it, I had just killed. I'd taken someone's life. I looked at the gun in my hand. I'd carried a gun for years, never fully realizing that its sole purpose was to end lives. Like most cops I thought of that as a tool of my trade, even a form of security and protection. Through that gun I kept the world just a bit safer, I thought. If this was true then why was a good man and father lying on the ground next to a true criminal like Jaro Medina, the good suffering the same fate as the evil?

Logic would have told me there was no way to make sense

of it. The better part of my judgment would later kick in and help me understand. Religion might have been able to help me, show me that God has a plan for everyone and sometimes that plan includes exacting his vengeance. I think too much to fully believe in religion and there are times, particularly those few weeks after I killed Boris Yigevny, when I wish I didn't. Standing there, watching over two dead bodies, I made a decision. Obviously, decisions made under such stressful situations are never a good idea, but this was one I knew I would stand by.

I heard something again and could tell it was a voice. It hadn't been the ringing in my ears that had prevented my hearing it, it was the beating of my heart and my mental focus on things so far away. The voice was Karl's, and he had been screaming.

"John, are you alive?" His words brought me back and made me feel the pain in my shoulder more acutely.

"I'm here," was all I could manage to say.

"He's dead?"

"Yes."

Karl didn't reply right away. Perhaps the gravity of the situation weighed on him as well. "You okay?"

"Think so," I said, "Got a slug in my shoulder."

"Get over here. I hear the cars coming."

The walk to where I'd left Karl seemed like it took a lifetime. In many ways, it did. It took my lifetime and put it into perspective. From that point forward I knew what I could do and what I couldn't. I knew what fit into my life and what was important. At least I convinced myself of this.

I could feel the blood trickling down my arm, over my wrist and off my fingertips. I didn't look at it. An attempt to close my left hand was met with a considerable amount of pain. It reminded me of when I had thrown my arm out during a high school baseball game, though this pain seemed less natural, if that makes any sense.

Karl lay where I left him, the shotgun propped up on his

knee in what seemed to be a vain attempt to defend himself. If he would have tried to fire that gun it would have flown backward, most likely bashing him in the jaw. Still, his effort deserved recognition.

"That's a nice shot you took there," he said.

"Thanks."

"Sure you're okay? Looks like you are losing a lot of blood."

"I'll be fine," I said, noticing I felt light-headed. I sat down next to Karl, trying but failing to keep my mind from focusing on Boris.

"Who fired first?" Karl asked.

"I don't know."

"Sounded like a Magnum went first. He have a Magnum?"

I remember thinking that Karl said that to make me feel better, that he thought my knowing that Boris fired before me would calm my emotions. It really didn't but I appreciated the concern. "Who knows? Who cares?"

"It's the sort of thing you're going to think about for the rest of your life. Trust me on that."

I didn't believe him right then. I didn't want to believe anything. Karl Lavin was right, however. There aren't many days that I don't think about how it all happened. I haven't yet come to any sort of concrete conclusion.

Epilogue

Winds of change, while you're in the midst of them, rarely seem any different than a normal, everyday breeze. All you know is that the gusts are pushing you this way and that. It is reflection that makes you realize the wind had brought with it alterations to your life. Only then do you realize the importance of the wind and the changes it has made. Remember, any breeze could be the one that dramatically changes things and how you look at them. Unfortunately, it is impossible to tell until the proverbial dust has cleared.

I thought I'd been through it, that I had made it through the storm relatively intact. Certainly I had been through enough over those few days. To expect anything more would be to expect the impossible, or so I thought. By now I should know that the impossible usually is quite possible. I never learn.

Despite the wound to my shoulder, I only stayed in the hospital overnight. A few visitors came—namely my mother, Pauline, and the usual suspects from the precinct—and none of them brought flowers because they know I can't stand them. Of course, I might have appreciated them. Everyone chose to err on the side of caution, which is always a good idea when dealing with me.

Three days later, I found myself at the precinct, rummaging through my desk looking for a pen to fill out the last of the 50 odd forms they required me to submit. My left arm was in a sling, something the doctor said would stay that way for six more weeks. Just as I put my fingers on a pen, the catalyst for the next set of sweeping changes approached me. I caught him from the corner of my eye.

It was a lawyer that initiated the final phase. Lawyers have a certain gait to them and I could tell by this guy's approach that he had been at the game for some time. He moved through a police precinct with too much confidence to be anything but a successful, longtime lawyer. He stopped at my desk. I didn't want to look up. Lawyers in a police precinct rarely bring good news.

"Detective Keegan?" he asked in a gravelly voice that spoke of cigarettes. I wondered right then if that was how my voice sounded to others. To me, my voice sounded the same as it did when I was twelve.

"That depends," I said. I finally looked up and saw a slightly balding, generally attractive middle-aged man with glasses. He was dressed in a blue suit with a barely noticeable pinstripe. I immediately thought that I wouldn't mind having him on my side.

"Well, judging from the now trademark shoulder injury and the fact that you are at Keegan's desk, I assume I am correct."

"You are. How can I be of disservice to you today?"

The man laughed. It was genuine. "Nothing to fear from me today. I have been trying to contact you for over a week."

"I've been busy."

"So I've read in the papers." The man, Alan Cartwright I would later find out, plopped a manila folder on my desk. "You are the executor of one Richard Calhill's will, were you aware of this?"

Of course I wasn't. It stunned me to hear it. "No," I said, barely audibly.

Mr. Cartwright took a seat. I followed suit. "Mr. Calhill, about a week before he was killed, named you as executor of his will. You and his two children are his only heirs.

Considering they are not of age, I would need to inform their legal guardian of their inheritance."

"That seems to make sense."

"I figure I could kill two birds with one stone," Cartwright said. He put his briefcase on my desk and opened it. "On the same day, Mr. Calhill named you as the legal guardian of his children. This means, if you approve, that you will have custody of his kids. Do you agree to this?"

I needed air, a lot of it. "This comes as a surprise," I said.

"I am sure it does. Judging from how quickly he did this, I would assume he didn't inform you. You have the right to turn this down."

I thought about that for a moment. Sure, I liked kids and I felt bad for Rick's, knowing what they had been through. Still, I can't say that the idea of kids seemed appealing to me right then. I was a career single guy.

"What happens if I do?"

"Well, normally an effort would be made to place the children with their closest family members. I am sure you know that Rick was an orphan—"

"I didn't know that."

Cartwright's eyes widened. "I see. Well, we have had no luck locating anyone related to him. It is my understanding that he never was able to contact any family."

This took me back. Rick had never once mentioned this to me. Sure, I never heard him talk about his parents but I didn't even consider that he was an orphan. Upon investigation, I would find out that Rick's mother got pregnant at 15 and left him on the steps of a church. He stayed at an orphanage until he was fourteen, then lived with a foster family for a few years. It made me realize why he was so eager to make friends.

"Andrea?" I asked.

Cartwright shook his head. "Both parents are dead. She

was an only child. All we know of is an aunt that lives in North Carolina, but her health is failing."

"So, what happens if I refuse?" I asked, realizing how bad that sounded.

"The children would become wards of the state. The state will find foster homes for them."

"Homes?"

"It is not always easy to place two children in the same household."

"I see." I knew of what happened to kids in foster care. Most times, families willing to take such children are good people. Of course, there are other times when this isn't the case.

"So you know, Rick seemed to be aware that you might not be ready now. He has a neighbor who has agreed to take care of the children for up to a year until you are ready. Even if you just need time to decide."

"He did that?"

Cartwright nodded.

"Then I'd like to take that time."

"A good choice, if you ask me."

Cartwright had a few other surprises. Rick had left me, because he intended me to have custody of his children, a stock portfolio worth over $150,000. He in no uncertain terms stated that the money should be used toward the purchase of a house. He left the children trust funds that would be worth a substantial sum when they turned 21. Their college would be paid for. He had done everything necessary to ensure a good life for them. The last surprise was that he had left a small fund for me, to be paid for by his life insurance policy. This was the only thing he made contingent on my taking the kids. It was worth $250,000. Oh, and his apartment was mine.

I couldn't grasp all of this. Cartwright told me this was unusual but not ridiculously so. He left me his card and offered his services to me in handling the finances and all that. Technically, I didn't need to work, he said, because with the proper investments, I could make a decent living just off of what Rick left me. This was the final push I needed to act on the decision I had made when I had looked at Boris' dead body.

"Keegan, can you come in here for a second?" I heard Geiger call to me just after Cartwright left.

I walked into his office. I could tell something was going on. "What's up?"

Geiger smiled. "Good news," he said.

"Okay," I replied, thinking that good was a subjective term.

"First off, the mayor wants to give you an accommodation for acting so bravely with the Yigevny thing."

"He wants to give me an award for killing a brilliant scientist?"

"No, he wants to acknowledge that you did your job, and nearly paid for it with your life. No ceremony. Just an award. I have it here." Geiger pointed to a box on his desk. He extended his hand. "Good job."

I shook the hand weakly. "Yeah, thanks."

"Now, there's something else. You can take what is in this box and you can bring it to your desk."

"I could," I said, not knowing where this was going.

"Or, you could leave it right here."

"What?"

"How do you like the idea of having it in this office?" Geiger asked, smiling.

"What are you talking about? You can burn that thing, for all I care."

"I know this whole thing has been rough on you, but good things have come of it." Geiger paused, as if to add emphasis. "I got the promotion. They made me Captain."

I wanted to feel happy for him, really. He deserved the promotion. "Congratulations," I said.

"My first act will be to assign a new head of Homicide. That someone is you, Keegan. I can't think of anyone better for the job."

I heard the words. They rang in my ears not unlike the blast from a gun. I'd never been the sort to think about promotions and all that but I must admit that I always thought I would do well in Geiger's position. Right then, however, something else went through my head. Maybe it was spur of the moment but I think it was something I had been planning on since I had decided to change my life. I didn't want to be around death anymore.

"I am resigning," I said.

"What?"

"I'm sorry Boss. I am real happy for you, believe that. But this isn't for me any more. I can't do it."

"What happened with Yigevny, it'll fade. Plus, in this position, you'll never have to fire a gun. You'll do well here. They are going to give you enough leeway to make the changes you see fit. It's the opportunity of a lifetime."

"For someone else, perhaps. Not me." I took my badge and ID out of my breast pocket and placed them on Geiger's desk. My gun I put next to them. "This is it. I know this is right."

"You can't do this," Geiger said, I think because he didn't know what else to say.

"I just did. I'm sorry."

I walked out of his office. I stopped at my desk only to take the papers Cartwright left me. I remember not realizing it would essentially be the last time I would set foot in that department. All I knew was that I had to get out of there. The feeling was the most liberating one I had ever experienced.

The next few months would find me out in Southampton, resting, healing, and thinking at my Uncle Paulie's summer home. He had just retired from the FBI and was getting stir crazy. Karl Lavin, reduced to walking on crutches for two months, ended up joining us. A motley crew, we were.

The time was supposed to be spent thinking about my future. I needed to decide whether or not I would take the kids. Of course, I would, eventually. Also, I needed to think about Pauline, and where she fit in my life. She did, that was all that mattered. Also, I wanted to truly mourn the death of my father, who came to me almost every night in my dreams. Putting to rest Rick Calhill would also take a bit of time.

I'd walked away from the force before my time, most people told me. The pension I would get wasn't as much as it could have been, but it was sufficient in my mind. My father had also left me a small bit of money, so financially, I was well off. Mentally, I was a mess. The time at my uncle's house would cure that, I figured. Once again, I was horribly wrong.